The Farm

Ryan Stark

This is a work of fiction. Names, characters, corporations, institutions, organizations, events or locales in this novel are either the product of the author's imagination or, if real, used fictitiously. Any resemblance to actual persons (living or dead) is entirely coincidental.

Also by the Author:

Killing by the Book

ISBN: 1977597947

ISBN-13: 978-1977597946

For those forced into desperate measures by those who conspire to take away their basic human freedoms.

ACKNOWLEDGMENTS

Although writing is often a lonely furrow to plough, there are still a few others who contributed to the completion of this venture.

I owe a debt of thanks to Adrian Grogan, Sean Burke and Simon Peace, my former band mates in Fishheads. It was a tough decision to give up Rhythm & Blues to concentrate on writing and I thank them for giving me the space.

I'd also like to thank my employers who have provided me with an unused meeting room before and after working hours so that I can have a little peace and quiet. Now they know.

The biggest thanks must go to Google. Without their search engine and maps, I would have been unable to explore parts of the world that are currently off limits, nor would I be able to strip down a semi-automatic weapon blindfold.

Finally, once again, my huge thanks to my wife, Val. I have spent many early mornings, late evenings and long weekends locked away writing. Hopefully for a while, I will be able to spend some time with her. I know, for her, that is a mixed blessing.

Chapter 1

Greenford, West London, 23:30pm, Monday

As the chance presented itself, Connor Smith turned and fled, scrabbling down the muddy bank, splashing into the boggy rill. The chill water oozed through his trainers and his legs turned leaden. Stemming the rising panic, he scoured the hedge for an area where the hawthorn had died back. Ignoring the needles in his palms he stumbled through, tumbling headlong into the mire on the other side. He stifled a yelp as his knees impacted the ground in a smack of pain. His chest heaving, he scrambled to his feet and set out across the blackness of the field, slipping in the greasy mud, his eyes fixed on the distant lights of the estate. He had to stop, hinged in two as his lungs struggled to pump air. An image of the face flashed through his mind, the staring eyes, the half open jaw. He felt the need to retch but was dismayed that he had only made three hundred yards from the roaring traffic. Only once he was lost amongst the warren of streets could he consider himself truly away.

Behind him, back at the road, as the blood pounded in his ears, a dull thud broke the subliminal buzz of the traffic. An angry orange flame leapt above the hedge, even at this distance warming his face as he stared in disbelief. Maybe fire would be his saviour, cleansing and purging? And then he recoiled as headlights cast white fingers towards him, sweeping through the field of mist. It would only be a matter of time before they followed. Gripped with terror, he turned and ran until he reached the estate.

Should he have waited, helped out? Once the boxes had spilled, there was no way he was going to touch them. He was in enough trouble if they found his prints, let alone anything in the back.

Perhaps he should still go back? Show backbone in a crisis? He could say he had gone for help. For help? Seriously? Who would believe that?

He had never been a risk taker but then again, was tonight not proof he had the right idea? Then he recalled the staring eyes, the torn flesh, the blood and had to stifle the urge to vomit once more. What the Hell had he gotten himself into?

Anyway, how was he to know that idiot in the Vectra would start weaving all over the road? Surely a collision would have meant questions, insurance companies, police. Even now there would be police. He had to run to save himself. He was not going to take the rap for it, none of it. Behind, the plume of orange flickered across the field. Fire was cleansing. Any evidence would be destroyed.

With any luck.

Hitting the pavements, hearing his footfalls echo from the walls around him, Connor slowed to a brisk walk, regulated his breathing. Even this late, the less attention he drew the better. Gaining his bearings, he started on the two miles home and relative safety.

Chapter 2

Çanakkale Province, Turkey, 23:30pm, Monday

Satya Meheb sat on the tattered plastic sack that contained her worldly belongings and shivered. Winter was drawing in and the temperature at night was falling. Here on the coast, a biting wind added to the chill. Two hours earlier, she had choked on the clouds of dust thrown up from the departing truck; its human cargo, people she had known for nearly three days melting into the scrub grass and rolling dunes. With only the whistling wind for company, she felt totally alone for the first time since her Uncle Akram had dragged her from her home.

To the West, the distant sounds of industry echoed from the steelworks and a bright white crowned the horizon but here in the dunes it was as dark as the grave. To the North, the land disappeared into the inky void of the Sea of Marmara and the distant braid of twinkling lights on the other side.

With time to kill, she had explored the abandoned buildings. Tonight, Allah had been merciful. She had found running water, a shower. Jamming the door with a shard of rock, she had washed and changed, an opportunity not to be missed given the dusty trek from Aleppo, even if she risked the attentions of male refugees. Such was her age and such were their appetites. To the others, she was Ibrahim, grubby faced, boy's clothes, hair cropped short. Naked under the shower there was no disguise. Outside she heard the raucous, carefree laughs of men approaching, turning off the tap, holding her breath until they passed. Having pushed her luck, she quickly dried and dressed, abandoning her rags to the shower and changing into clothes purloined from a trader. She had felt the ground shake as he had peppered the road behind her with buckshot, but he was slow and she was quick. She needed to be quick these days. The clothes felt like silk compared to the ones she had worn to rags. The winter coat she had taken from the soldier was hard wearing and warm. Tomorrow, if the boat did not come she would steal shoes.

Less than two weeks ago, the attacks had started. Her father had been a member of *The Brotherhood of the Truth Faith*, a group of vigilantes on the streets of the war-torn city, known simply as '*akhuww - The Brotherhood*, making a stand against those who sought to destroy them and their Faith, their true Islamic values. As the attacks intensified, he had negotiated passage for Satya and her brother on a route to the West. One day, Alaam had been spirited away to the mosque, an act which the Imam had told her had sealed her parents' fate. She thought back to their house in Al Jalloum, the wood stove sending flecks of orange across the faces of her parents as they watched TV. The masks at the door, cracks and muzzle flashes. As they fell dead, she fell beside them, feigning death and praying to the prophet. Three days, a lifetime ago, found amongst the corpses, *the Brotherhood* had taken her to the mosque where even the rebels would not strike. By morning she was watching Aleppo smoulder through the slats of a packed Renault cattle truck.

She had brought few possessions; in her hand, she held the most precious, a small postcard album. Too dark to read now, she had to imagine the pictures. Blackpool, the Tower of London, Buckingham Palace, Stonehenge, the Arc de Triomphe, the Eiffel Tower; postcards sent by relatives who had travelled. Fantastic images against the dereliction and destruction of Aleppo and the hardships of the road. The Imam had told her *The Brotherhood* would take her to England; she would join Alaam, maybe even see those places for real. She needed to believe the Imam, that one day life would get better. That one day she and Alaam would be reunited with no need to fear the loneliness, the bombs and the bullets.

As the tears threatened she forced them back. She was stronger than that, stronger than the rebels, stronger that the naïve, impressionable girl they had left for dead. After three days, she had closed the door on her family, on Aleppo, retreating into herself, her eyes a window onto a less forgiving world. A passenger inside a tougher shell. Road hardened, impervious, unemotional.

Her migrant beast.

Before the attacks, she had rarely considered the West, images on the TV, in her album. Through school, she had been set on Damascus and Cairo, on the bustling, dusty cities teeming with life. Teeming with jobs that a female Muslim could do.

She had four hours yet. Hunkering down, she thought of Alaam. She had seen his sign on the truck from Aleppo, scratched into the weather-worn boarding. The abjadi character for 'A' superimposed onto the same western character:

Alaam had always yearned for Europe, away from the violence and the fear. The symbol reflected his Syrian heritage and his yearning to be European. An arrow symbolising progression. Had he passed this way too? She reached down and grabbed the rough tufts of grass between her fingers. Had Alaam huddled like her in these dunes? Or had he perished on a different, more dangerous route?

She scratched her arm through her sleeve, the tattoo still itching from three days ago when her uncle handed over everything he owned, putting trust in the traffickers. A mark of a different kind. Her right of passage.

A disturbance at the shore warned Satya she had been dozing. At first, she thought the men were fighting again. They were always fighting. Then she saw the dim strip of light skipping across the water and behind, the vague black outline of a boat pulling in to the nearest jetty. Instantly, she was alert, thrusting the album into the plastic wallet containing her papers, and that in turn into the inside pocket of her greatcoat. She grabbed the plastic sack and headed towards the jetty. From all around her, like termites from a mound, tens of men, women and children emerged, converging on the source of the light. There was safety in numbers so she quickened her pace and soon she was heaving through a squalid mass of humanity pleading for a place on the boat.

Chapter 3

Greenford, West London

So, what *had* he gotten himself into? The van, the frequent unscheduled trips, always at night. naïvely striking a deal with the devil. A quick backhander. An hour tops, drop off, then an hour back. Definitely too good to be true.

Soon, Connor reached his front door. Hopefully, the heavy rain of the last hour would wash the pavements clean. Latching the door behind him, he retrieved his mobile. He clicked the number, cursing as the voicemail picked up.

"It's Connor. Jesus Christ! Jesus, Jesus, Jesus! If I had known what was in the back, I would never have agreed." Again, he felt his diaphragm pump, spattering the hall carpet. He wiped a hand across his mouth, spitting foul remnants. "Look, this is madness. From now on I'm out. Just pretend I was never there, right?"

Yes, and of course it was that simple. The fire would destroy any evidence. Nothing would be traced back to him. Things would carry on as they always had. As if nothing happened. Just who was he kidding? His heart was racing, roaring in his ears as the panic took hold. Every night he would see her face, her staring eyes. The image could never be erased.

Jamming the phone into his shoulder, he walked to the kitchen and swilled the acid from his mouth.

"OK, I screwed up. That bloke was driving like a maniac. Lucky I wasn't killed. Bloody idiot! Anyhow, I don't want anything to do with this from now on. Just leave me out, OK?"

Connor closed the call and slung the phone onto the hall table. Who was he trying to convince? They would never forget. They had made her disappear; they could do the same to him. He checked his watch. 01:30am. Jesus. He had lost forty-five minutes already. It was only an hour to the drop-off, maybe fifteen minutes to unload and an hour and a half at most back to Southall. He couldn't hang around waiting for that knock at the door.

Why did he feel he needed to be involved anyway? He had a

good job, good prospects, nice house. Now all that was gone because of one impetuous decision.

But there were more immediate concerns. He had to separate himself from the events of the night. Fortunately, his profession had taught him about cleanliness, sterility. Removing his shoes and socks, Connor headed for the bathroom. Grabbing a couple of plastic bin bags from the cupboard under the bathroom sink, he stripped off every item of clothing, emptying his keys, his watch and loose change into the sink and turning on the tap. He threw his clothes and shoes into one of the bin bags, sealed it and then placed it in another bag.

Then he showered, scrupulously lathering every inch of his body, wincing as the stringent soap dug at his wounds, bruised knees and a gash on his shin. There was a wield the size of a small country on his forehead. Only when he was sure every trace of the night had been removed, did he stop scrubbing and allow the warm water to cover his face.

But he would never purge the far more terrible images that filled his mind.

Chapter 4

Çanakkale Province, North Western Turkey

Elbowing through the crowd, Satya soon felt the wood of the gangplank beneath her boots. Inside her pockets she had papers, false identities which would see her through the borders and into Calais, where she was to meet the man, catch the ferry.

On the horizon, the lights of Şarköy winked. Europe was so close but a lifetime away. Her schooling would mean something there, perhaps more than in Cairo. Her gender would mean something, or more importantly mean nothing. Europe would afford her opportunities that Syria never could.

Forcing forward, smelling the desperation of the crowd, she felt the flimsy plank bowing under the weight of bodies. Clinging to the rope handrails, she hauled herself forwards until she was facing a mountainous man with a grizzled salt browned face. He snarled something at her in Turkish which she didn't understand.

"Senin dövme nerede? Sadece dövmeler olan insanlar için."

She shook her head as the hand pressed her back, the mob crushing her against it.

"Dövme! Dövme!" The man grabbed her arm and dragged it from her sleeve. He pointed to the tattoo. "Dövme." Her arm thrown, she surged forwards with the crowd, and saw the deck opening up before her. But the relief was short-lived as the man reached back and pulled her to one side.

"I have passage, see." She bared her forearm again and showed the tattoo. She glanced up at the man, confused as his face broke into a broad grin. She felt a club of a hand delve beneath her coat. Rough fingers rasped her skin, between her shirt buttons and around her breast.

"Bizim delikanlı. Ben gizlemek için bir şey olduğunu düşünüyor." *I think that our young man has something to hide.*

Terrified, Satya prayed to Allah that he would investigate no further. His hand came from beneath her shirt and he caressed her cheek with the back of a calloused forefinger. His eyes bore a hunger she had seen before.

"Bu bizim gizli, küçük adam olacak. Gece bitmeden seni tekrar göreceğim." *This will be our secret, little man. I shall see you again before the night is over.*

Then he placed his large paw on her shoulder and with a cackle of laughter, heaved her across the deck to the relative sanctuary of the boat.

A bargain had been struck and she knew she would need to make good on it later.

Chapter 5

Southall, West London, 3:00am, Tuesday

An hour later, Connor Smith had bleached the bathroom clean and scrubbed the vomit from the hall carpet, and for good measure, he went over it all again before showering. Wearily, he pulled a bottle of water from the fridge and collapsed on the sofa utterly drained. It was 3:00am. He could afford an hour before the inevitable knock at the door.

But only an hour.

The phone call was a mistake. He could have blagged his way out, said he had no idea what the van was carrying. Impetuous and rash? Then there was the trail across the field but once into the houses, they would need a bloodhound to follow him and then a good one as the rain had been falling in sheets. Hopefully, unless someone had seen him, they would assume he had abandoned the van and left in the other car.

With a jolt, Connor awoke, cursing himself for closing his eyes even for a minute. The room was black, a faint amber glow through the curtain. 3:20am. Still early. Then, his heart jumped as he remembered the plastic refuse bag in the bathroom. Leaping up, he scaled the stairs, found a waterproof coat and some gloves before circling back and grabbing the bag. Making a cursory check that it hadn't leaked he descended the stairs. From the kitchen cupboard, he retrieved a lighter and some fluid and stuffed them into the coat pocket. Then he stepped out into the cold damp air once more.

Fortunately, the rain had abated, leaving an orange sheen across the silent pavements. Here and there, windows glowed as early shifters ate their breakfast, babies squawked fitfully or insomniacs tossed and turned. Notwithstanding, he stuck close to the walls, making his way towards a row of houses undergoing renovation. He passed them each morning on his way in. There was always a half-filled skip behind the flimsy fence. Easing his way through a gap between two panels, he lobbed the bag into the closest skip and squirted a jet of fluid before tossing in the can and igniting the pyre. Even through the dampness of the rain, the small blaze took hold, so Connor scooted back through the fence and jogged around the corner to watch it grow. Once he was satisfied that the skip was well alight, he turned for home, safe in the knowledge that not even Sherlock Holmes could track him down now.

Chapter 6

Çanakkale Province, Turkey

The diesel engine started with a throaty cough below decks, shaking Satya from her doze. The small deck teemed with bodies, sitting, lying, shivering from the cold, cradling small children, jealously guarding their meagre belongings. Everyone aboard had paupered themselves to take this elite route out of Asia. The man to her right smelt of garlic and chewing tobacco, and the woman to her left of sweat and urine, but at least she was aboard. A myriad different stories, a myriad hopes for a brighter dawn.

But first they had to negotiate the Sea of Marmara and the perils of the night.

The iron gunwale shuddered as the engines throttled up and the anchor chain rattled against the hawse beneath. A clunk of gears meshing and a smack of the wash against the hull, and the dark stone of the jetty began to slide by in a breeze of salt and diesel. She pulled the rough woollen lapels of her coat about her as the cold scoured the deck.

Fortunately this was a short sea journey, unlike Lesbos and Kos. She had heard of the drownings and the arrests but such was the desperation, people were willing to risk everything. The rebels had left many to rot along the roads. Other had died to traffickers who reneged on their bargains. Many that made it to Dikili or Akyarlar, avoiding the complacent gaze of the Turkish authorities, then perished in the Aegean or languished in a Greek holding camp awaiting repatriation. But Satya had been fortunate. *The Brotherhood* had contacts. Still, she and Alaam had cost their family two million Syrian Pounds. In her mind, she pictured a small English house, fields so green she could scarcely believe there could be such a place. She pictured her uncles and cousins, the open arms of her brother. Now she let the tears come, if only briefly. Every hour was another hour away from Hell and another nearer to them.

Above her, the night had turned blustery and inky clouds scudded by as the small boat, buffeted by waves, cut a furrow northwards towards Şarköy. Another truck, another day and she would be in Bulgaria catching the train. As the waves smacked the hull and the chatter of the passengers lulled to a murmur, she felt her eyelids grow heavier and allowed herself the briefest of catnaps.

A boot kicked at her foot and instantly she was awake.

"Ah, küçük adam. Ben bazı bitmemiş bir iş olduğunu düşünüyorum." *Ah, my little man. I think we have some unfinished business.*

The eyes of the deckhand were lascivious and hungry as he yanked at her coat, but Satya was having none of it.

"Fuck off, cocksucker," she spat. Three days in a cattle truck and a whole new vocabulary. She had grown beyond her years and beyond intimidation from men like him. She hunkered further into the corner, looping her arm through the pierced framework. The dark salt-weathered face in front of her erupted in a hearty belly laugh.

"Ben küçük bir ruhu ile bir kadın gibi. Şimdi hadi biz bir anlaşma vardı!" *I like a woman with a little spirit. Now come on, we had a deal!* Again, the tar yanked at her coat, but again she pulled away. The tar huffed, irritated by her non-compliance. The old man next to her roused.

"Ne oluyor? Çocuğu rahat bırak." *What's going on? Leave the boy alone.*

"Yaşlı adam Kapa çeneni. Kendi işine bak." *Shut up, old man. Mind your own business.* A calloused paw swung and the old man was bowled over. The deckhand grabbed, this time a better purchase, and he hauled Satya across the boards, laughing at her ineffectual punching and gouging. Soon she faced the gaping void which led to the lower decks and instinctively she braced against the frame, feeling her elbows and shoulders tear as the brute pushed harder from behind. She swung her leg and caught his shins but the man was as strong as an ox and twice as stupid. As the pressure became unbearable, she tumbled headlong down the steps and into the dank sweaty cabin below. Hitting a table, red and blue sparks filled her vision, as the breath was forced from her chest, and a clatter of cutlery and crockery filled the air.

Instantly he was upon her, his weight bearing down as his hands grappled with her waistband and his own with equal hunger. She could feel him hard against her leg now. For a moment, Satya felt herself yield to the inevitable, self-preservation over self-respect but the migrant beast within her began to anger. Out to her side, her hand touched something metallic and she instinctively grabbed, swinging and with a growl, hit the man's neck. His eyes boggled, the prongs of the fork embedded deep into the flesh. Confused, he rolled onto his back, a hideous gurgle sliding through his clenched teeth. Satya pushed him off and stood transfixed for a moment by the small pulsing stream of red oozing through his fingers. Then she snapped back. As the man writhed on the floor, she could see his filthy worm of a manhood flopping ineffectually from his open trousers. The rage overwhelmed her and she stamped on it with all her might, hearing the wind leave the man's lungs as her heel dug into his pelvis. And then she was off up the steps and around to the back to the boat.

Alarmed by the uproar, other deckhands were scanning the decks and, seeing her, they made off after her. The game was up. Maybe the man was dying? They were within two metres of her now and closing. With a grunt, she ducked their flailing arms and sprinted towards the front bulkhead. Grabbing her bag, she climbed onto the gunwale edge and, as the crew's shouts grew ever nearer, she cast herself off into the black foaming sea.

Disappearing below the surface in a plume of bubbles, the oily brine burned Satya's throat. She flailed around disoriented, searching for the surface. Her senses dulled by the murk and the cold, she picked up the vague throb of the boats engines pulsing through the dark. Then an intense chill leaked through her clothes, dragging her down, and it was all she could do to stop herself exhaling. Suspended in slow motion, she searched for a point of reference. Then she saw a light from somewhere below her, or was it above? Her lungs ached and her eyes prickled red as she dragged herself towards it, the thick coat, for which she had been so grateful, drawing her back. She saw her father, his lips forming her name and his hand stretching for hers and an immense sorrow filled her as she once more relented to the inevitable. Alaam was running through the fields shouting for her, willing her on. A numbness, calm, deceptive and seductive, crawled through her body until the light seemed unimportant and the cosseting safety of the water was all she needed to make her troubles disappear into the night.

Chapter 7

Alperton, London, 4:00am, Tuesday

The roar was growing louder now. The ground vibrated through his soul, shaking bones loose inside his flesh. The man on the tracks was sneering, an apathetic, mocking grin, his skin was sun-bleached leather and white hair cascaded down his shoulders. Disjointed laughter echoed in the air and wormed into his brain. He was gripped with the need to escape, to flee the behemoth bearing down on him. He tugged at the man with all his waning strength but the roar became thunder and the thunder became howls and the air was filled with viscera and gore. Before him, his arms were ragged stumps, oozing streams of scarlet and he could see his hands, rising up like startled mantises. But the train would not stop, the bloodied stumps could not grab them through the spinning, scything wheels, and the screech turned into an unremitting scream.

As the last wail left his mind, Detective Inspector Scott Daley jolted, eyes wide and disorientated. For a long moment, he was lost, as one is in a hotel room, or waking on a train, or the first night on holiday. Dawn had yet to make an appearance and the surroundings were grey, alien and deathly silent.

It had been six months since he had been hit by a train, not that he recalled the first week, swimming in the molasses of an induced coma, but since then he had rarely been alone. Trapped inside the iron maiden of unconsciousness he had suffered the incessant beep of the machinery and the fleeting voices, unable to communicate, unable to tell them all to bugger off and leave him to his vegetative state. When finally, they had woken him to the agony of his injuries, the vice-like grip on his head and the miasma of the morphine trips, he had begged for them to remain, to take his mind off the horrors that visited when he was left space to think.

He had underestimated the effects of the accident, the irresistible force that had broken his shoulder, cracked his skull and let loose the monsters which ripped at the fabric of his sanity. The anxieties and the rages and the violent nightmares.

After his release, Daley had spent a while in his old house - Lynne's house now since the divorce - as he had recuperated physically. He had hoped it would be like old times, away from the office, away from the Met. Lynne had helped him through physical recovery but it was clear that only time and the Met's Psych team could fix his mind. The long convalescence had allowed the gremlins of paranoia and self-doubt to scamper freely about his subconscious. Six months to dwell on things too deeply. The quack had warned of the psychological trauma but Daley had dismissed it with the same complacent bravado that he had afforded to his marriage, and to a Class 90 Diesel locomotive.

And look how those ended up.

More significantly, for their first time in his life he had been brutally warned of his own mortality.

Back in his own house, Lynne had stayed over briefly and together they transformed his spartan hermitage into a place worth coming home to, until the day she no longer came home to it. Three days ago, Lynne had decided she was going to leave. Three nights for the monsters to roam unfettered and the nightmares had already returned.

So much for being cured.

The quack had signed him off until today under strict instructions he should assume light duties, avoid stress. Some hope. Daley would avoid the physical heavy lifting but the mental strain, that wasn't so easy.

Switching on the lamp, Daley found a couple of Tramadol and swilled them down with an inch of stale water. It had been six months. The headaches had subsided, but were always worse in the mornings. He mentally checked there were enough tablets to see him through the day, where the other packets were in the house, drawing a mental map just in case.

And that was another problem for him to address sooner or later.

The clock beamed 4:00am and was rewarded with a curse. He sighed, wincing as he hoisted himself upright using his bad arm, and made his way through to the bathroom.

First day back.

With a dispensation from *Bilko* Bob Allenby to take it easy for a day or two he would turn in after the rush hour. Afford himself a lie-in. He could hear Dave now. *What time do you call this? Here we are up at the crack of dawn - lovely girl.* Same joke every day. But his mind had different ideas. 4:00am. Taking a pee, swilling his face under the cold tap, he returned to bed, willing sleep to return but knowing it wouldn't, instead enduring that fitful doze that knew the alarm was just around the corner.

Six months out of the saddle. How different would it be since May? How many faces had changed? A deep gnawing doubt clawed at his soul. Could he do this anymore? Did he want to?

Deborah Whetstone, his sergeant had been acting up in his stead and had kept him abreast of goings on, but without actually being there it had gone in one ear and out of the other. Kicking around the flat was driving him crazier than any head injury and he needed something to take his mind off his own troubles and back onto someone else's.

Roll on 9:30am.

Chapter 8

Satya's time on the truck had taught her four rules to live by.

Rule one - trust no-one. There was not a soul on the planet she could rely on. She needed to keep up her guard at all times.

Rule two - keep your belly full and your bladder empty. The truck would grind for hours across the endless roads. The men could relieve themselves through the slats, sending plumes of spray across the tarmac, boasting of their prowess if they hit a passing car. Obviously, as *Ibrahim*, they had cajoled her into joining in but without the requisite equipment, she had tried to ignore the men's puerile fascination with urination. The other women on the truck were seemingly unfazed by this behaviour, keeping their heads covered and their liquid intake to a minimum until there was a discreet place to empty themselves. What was it with men and their phalluses?

Rule three - kill or be killed.

Since leaving the Al Amanzel mosque in Aleppo, she had curled up, foetal and small, hoping to remain unnoticed for the entirety of the journey, taking only brief peeks through the slats as the truck trundled through the grey snowy hills towards the plains of the border. But in less than two hours, the truck had parked and they were ordered off. The driver and his mate waved AK-74 semi-automatic rifles, forcing them into lines. Was this all to end in a ditch? How far had they travelled in two hours? Were they near the border or had they travelled further into the lawless heartlands where the corpses of the naïve lined the verges? She waited eyes tight closed, her heart pounding. Then a voice whispered close to her ear.

"When I say, run to the gate and crawl under. Follow the stream for two kilometres. Go through the culvert under the road and keep quiet. There may be patrols. Keep going until you see a white house and a truck. You have two hours then the truck leaves. Miss it and you are on your own. I see you again, I shoot you. Asalam o alikum."

Satya opened her eyes and watched the rifle as the man

passed down the line. She imagined the bullets inside the magazine. Was one meant for her? Would she feel the point tearing through her skull or her heart? The driver's mate stood ten yards away, his own rifle on his hip. Then, at intervals, each of them set off on different courses, a strategy, she thought, to avoid them all being taken if one was discovered. Before her, a man and wife headed for the gate and disappeared under it.

Then it was her turn. The voice rasped *Adhhb* and, clasping her plastic bag to her chest, she ran as fast as her legs would carry her, scrabbling under the gate, icy slush against her arms and legs. Staying on all fours, she searched for the dark scar of the stream. With her head low, she ran to the bank and slid down into the water. Suddenly, though less than four inches deep, her legs turn to wood and she could barely drag them through the freezing stream. There was no way she would make it in the water. Ascending the opposite bank, she heaved herself out and crouched down. She was immediately engulfed in a thick silence. Behind she heard the lorry engine start and listened as the wail of the gearbox faded away, then nothing but the song of the stream and the atonal howl of the wind. They were all, like her, utterly alone.

She ran along the far bank cutting corners as the stream snaked its way through fields of walnut trees, dipping down the bank to avoid hedges and fences. Without heed for the time or for anyone following, she ran until her legs ached and then, through the tears and the pain, she ran some more. She ran for her father and mother but most of all she ran for Alaam, sure he too had come this way. The lorry would not leave without her, would it? Cut adrift from her family, from her life and from the rest of the world, all she could do was run.

Seeing two dark shapes ahead, she slowed her pace, regulated her breathing. It was the man and his wife. With youth on her side, Satya had easily caught them. She slowed as she reached them but the man urged her on:

"Go! Don't stop for us. Just go!"

So, she redoubled her pace leaving the two shapes to the grey night behind.

She seemed to have been running forever. How far was it to the white house? All around, there were endless plains, the grey carpet of snow and the skeletal carcasses of walnut trees reaching for the heavens. Still the stream snaked, turning this way and that. Was she to run all the way to Europe?

Then she fell to her knees and listened. Above the trickle of the stream, she could hear footsteps, hard rapping boot heels lazily walking on tarmac. She must have reached the road over the culvert. Stealthily, she re-entered the stream, now unaware of the cold. She measured her steps, barely disturbing the water, until she could see the culvert piped beneath the road. At one and a half metres, she could easily walk through at a crouch. Above, the border guard stood legs apart, talking into a mobile, oblivious, an orange glow from his cigarette. Slung over his shoulder, pointing skywards, a rifle bided its time. Inching forwards, she stepped gingerly inside the culvert. The echoing flow of water masked the splashes from her boots and for a moment she listened to the soldier. He was speaking in Arabic to his girlfriend, his attentions elsewhere. Satya crept through until at last, she felt the cold breeze hit her face. Looking back the soldier had closed his phone and was urgently peering into the dark in the direction she had come.

"You. Stop. Stop or I will fire!" The soldier had spotted the man and his wife. As she watched, he unslung his rifle and shouldered it. "Stop or I will fire!" There was a flash which briefly lit the soldier's face, then a crack, short and dead in the winter air. Satya stood rooted to the spot. What should she do? Torn between self-preservation and the need to do what was right, she considered the soldier, then the black of the stream. Grappling her way up the bank to the road, she watched as the alarmed soldier spun on his heels and, with a gasp, raised his rifle once more. Another flash and a crack rang out. She heard the bee buzz past her head. Now she was committed to act or die.

Dropping her bag, she launched herself at the soldier growling like a possessed demon, impacting his midriff. As another shot bit the night, she felt herself falling over edge of the culvert and into the icy rill, the soldier beneath her wheezing as the air was driven from his body. In a fit of panic and blind rage, she thought about her mother's staring eyes, of the blood pooling around her father, of the complacent laughs of the gunmen and she grabbed the soldier's hair and pushed the face under the water, leaning all her weight over her shoulders.

Behind her, arms and legs thrashed at the water and a froth of bubbles spat at her face. Then a shadow loomed over her, between her hands a boot slammed down on the head and through the cheeks she felt the cracking of bones and the body fell limp.

Releasing the head like a searing coal, she rose and looked down at the body. He was a boy, no more than Satya's own age. She imagined his family, around the fire, pictures on the mantelpiece, so proud. She thought of the girlfriend awaiting his return, cradling her phone and dreaming of the night. To take a life so cheaply, was she any better than the rest?

"We owe you everything, boy. It was him or us. Now quickly, grab a leg. We must get him into the pipe. It will buy us some time."

In a daze, Satya complied. Soon the soldier and his rifle lay out of sight of the road and the burbling of the stream was the only sound that cut through the winter wind.

"There will be time to think later, once we are on that truck." She felt her bag thrust into her arms and, following the man and his wife, she set off away from the bridge, her feet placing themselves one in front of one another, automatic movements from a mind overloaded by the things it had seen, overcome with grief for her family, overwhelmed by the tableau of death she had witnessed.

Time blurred, she felt arms haul her from the stream, voices shouting, urging her on, she felt her sleeve pulled up, she heard the truck start and finally she allowed herself time to cry.

Now as the fleeting memories drifted through her mind and chill of the sea turned to a warm blanket around her, Satya remembered the fourth rule her time on the road had taught her.

Rule four - Survive at all costs.

She hadn't felt the arm reach for her, nor the roughness of the wooden hull against her side but, as Satya fell onto the bottom boards, her face exploded in a torrent of sea water and then instinctively gasped aching lungfuls as she coughed and spluttered. A hand clamped across her mouth and a voice rasped a whisper:

"Keep quiet. You have to keep quiet."

Chapter 9

Southall, West London, 4:00am

Keep quiet. I have to keep quiet!

Connor flattened himself against a wall and peered down the Close, hoping he hadn't been seen. The blinding headlights lit the sleeping street as bright as day. Jesus, he was here already. How had he made the round trip this quickly? In the bowl of the cul-de-sac, a shadow passed across the beams, briefly checking Connor's car before heading for the front door. Ducking behind a dwarf wall, Connor crossed a parking space and crouched into an unruly shrub which had usurped the corner of the street. It smelled of dog crap and stale urine. Each day as he left, he cursed this bush for impeding his view of the traffic. Now he prayed that its matted foliage would cover him until the car had gone. The shadow moved from his door, pressing a face to the dark windows before glancing up at the top storey. For Christ's sake, I am not in. Get the message and bugger off...please!

So now it was certain. He wouldn't be allowed to simply walk away. His indiscretions would not be forgiven.

They knew where he lived. Well, of course they did. But for the sudden realisation that he had not disposed of the bag, he would have been in the house, dozing on the couch, perhaps asleep in his bed. Would he have gone the same way as she had? An immense terror gripped him as he huddled deeper into the bush, closing his eyes tight against the glare of the headlights. What the Hell was he mixed up in? He would have to disappear for a while and let the dust settle.

Eventually, the engine gave a subdued roar and headed towards Connor. Shrinking down, closing his eyes tighter, he listened as the throaty gargle of the exhaust rounded the corner, becoming ever more distant. The Close became still but for the sound of waking birds and the thud of his own heart. Racing back to his house, shutting the door behind him, Connor paused on the light switch. The less attention he brought to himself the better, at least until he could talk his way out of the trouble he had spent the last three weeks talking himself into. In a few days, it would all be yesterday's news.

Now wide awake and alert, Connor bounded up the stairs, rifling cupboards and wardrobes for as much as he could carry and stuffing them into bags and cases. Downstairs, he collected his keys, his wallet and cards for his bank accounts, as well as his passport and driving licence. There was no saying how long it would take for the situation to calm down.

Retracing his way through to the living room, he tidied away his breakfast things, less clues for them to follow. Then he flattened himself against the wall and froze. Pressed against the glass of the bay window, silhouetted by the sodium orange, the face examined the gloom of the living room before once more disappearing into the still of early morning.

Chapter 10

Sea of Marmara, 1km South West of Şarköy, Turkey

"Keep quiet. You have to keep quiet."

The words were English, urgent, the accent strange. Above Satya, white beams scoured the sky. There were gunshots. Grabbing the hand, she pulled it from her mouth, steadying her breathing, peering up at the silhouette above her. He was young, maybe her own age, but even in the starkness of the torch beams she could see he was light skinned.

"Who are you? What's happening?" She shrunk down into the bow, the memories of the tar still fresh.

"The Coastguard patrol has found your boat. It's lucky you jumped when you did. Stupid but lucky." His tone was mocking. "All the others fled when they saw the patrol. If it wasn't for Vasil catching a crab with his oars, we too would have gone back. You have the tattoo?" Satya rolled up her sleeve and Pietr grabbed her wrist and angled it in the faintness of the lights. "Good. We have to stay quiet. I think you're the only one who escaped."

Dragging her eyes over the edge of the gunwale, Satya was assailed by the noise of the loud hailer, blinded by the whiteness of the searchlight trained on the clumsy fishing boat, rendered minuscule by the huge white *Sahil Güvenlik* vessel. Engines roared as it throttled back to take the boat in tow. She saw the sailor, her attacker, on the deck, holding a cloth to his neck as he raised a pistol at the men in white. She saw him fall to his knees then heard the crack. She hoped the shot had hit his balls. Then she felt the skin of the soldier in her hands and her gorge rose, a stream of salt and bile into the frothing waters.

"We must go. I can hear a helicopter." The other man's voice was urgent and sounded as if he was chewing gravel.

Above, the air pulsed with the beat of blades. A pillar of white scanned the water. The second man, a shadow against the night, readied the oars and, with the merest ripples on the ink black water, they were heading away from the pandemonium.

As they ran the boat ashore, light was beginning to creep over the distant horizon and Satya could see the boatmen more clearly. Pietr had an angular face, aquiline. His eyes were sharp and searching, his hair jet black and close cropped. The other man - *Vasil* - was a few years older, with a face like a crumpled dishcloth, salt-lined and sun-parched. Perhaps they were brothers, father and son maybe. Beside her, sodden and ripped, lay her plastic bag. She had been shivering for an hour on the water. Her throat was dry and she needed to pee. Then, in a sudden fit of anxiety, she searched her pockets for her papers, hoping the plastic wallet had survived the inundation. Bringing it out, she sighed audibly. The papers were safe, postcard album, the photographs of her family were dry. The zip seal had done its job.

"Where are we going?" Her voice trembled from the cold, from the fear that had held her captive since Aleppo. Did it matter? She was across the sea and away from the patrol.

"Change of plans. The police found the truck. They called the Coastguard. It seems the Turkish government have a conscience on migrants all of a sudden." A wry smile broke across Pietr's face. "Vasil and I also have a conscience but it is measured in dollars. We will get you to your rendezvous in Sofia. What's your name?"

"Ibrahim." she lied.

"Do I look stupid?" Beneath her coat, the damp tunic had stuck to her skin, her shape now obvious even in the greyness of dawn. Coyly, she closed the coat around her.

"I am Satya Meheb."

Pietr stared for a moment, as if processing the information. Then he smiled. "And tomorrow you will be someone else," he replied glibly. "Come on, we have to go."

He reached for her arm as she stepped off the boat, but she insolently shook him away. Together, they hauled the tiny boat until they breached the high tide line, upturning it and stowing the oars beneath. Vasil swept the grooved sand with his boot, trusting the waves to finish the job before it was noticed. Holding tight to her worldly belongings, weighed down by the sodden coat, she followed the pair through the dunes, a small copse of cypress trees and through a grove of olives to an old stone cottage, unlit and derelict. The fear now overwhelming, she stopped. *Rule one - trust no-one.*

Pietr turned and sighed impatiently.

"Quickly, we must get inside before dawn."

"Who are you? Why should I trust you...?" She began to back away towards the trees.

Pietr sighed once more and raised his eyes to the Gods. He reached out and grabbed her arm, pushing up the sleeve, revealing the mark. "The tattoo! You have the tattoo, otherwise we would have thrown you back. We don't get paid for anyone unless they have the tattoo. Those are our orders. There were six people on that boat. Only you made it. Look, you want to get to England and we want to get paid. Now, come on!"

Satya stood firm, her arm outstretched as Pietr tugged at it. "Where are we going?"

"We have a car. We are taking you to Sofia so you can catch your train. So we can get paid. Hurry."

"Pietr, we have to get a move on. The patrol will be along the beach soon." Vasil barked, his voice urgent. "Bring her or leave her. I don't care. She is trouble."

Pietr glanced at Vasil, then at Satya. and huffed. He brought out a dark object from his pocket and thrust it into Satya's hand. It was solid and cold against her flesh. "Does that make you any happier? Now come on, otherwise they will catch us."

She stared down at the Makarov 9mm, then up at Pietr. Her father had a gun. It was bigger than the small semi-automatic in her hand. She saw him use it to kill a lame horse, watched the muzzle flash and a small black hole appear. She had seen the eyes swivel and the legs twitch. Then she saw the black masks behind the splintering door and the rapid darts of fire as her mother and father fell. She saw the terrified eyes of the soldier on the bridge as he raised his rifle. The gun felt heavy in her palm.

"Look, girl, either shoot us or trust us," snapped Vasil. "We are not going to be arrested, even if *you* want to be. Come on Pietr." Then, turning back, he added, "Oh, by the way, the safety is on."

***

As the two men strode away, Satya stood conflicted. On the shore of a strange sea in a strange land, she had to decide whom to trust, or whom she feared least. Was it within their interest to harm her? She was their paycheque, yet still that brute of a sailor had chanced his arm? There was no going back. She had to trust in Allah, that he would be more benevolent to her than he had been to her family. She thrust the weapon into her trouser pocket and started after the two men. Reaching the cottage, Vasil dug out some keys and opened the door. Following the two men through a derelict living area, through a door beyond, Satya was assaulted by the warmth; a log fire cracking in the stone ingle lit up the room with dancing yellow flecks.

"What took you so long?" The voice was sharp and scolding...and female. A head appeared from the wings of an armchair by the fire. "The patrol has intercepted the boat."

"Yeah, Mama, we saw it but they have to be faster to catch us, eh Papa?" Pietr's face was smug and grinning, adolescent bravado. Satya smiled to herself, remembering how her brother used to cheek her mother. Was Pietr to feel the back of a hand too?

"Shut up, Pietr. Go make a warm drink while I get this girl out of her wet clothes." The woman rose from the chair. She was older, perhaps in her fifties with jet black coils of hair and round pebble eyes which darted between Satya and the men. Away from the heat, she pulled a shawl about her shoulders. Then she barked at the older man: "Vasil, get the bookcase."

Vasil strode over to a tall narrow bookcase and dragged it aside, revealing a hidden doorway. The woman picked up a lamp and ushered Satya towards the void. "Come girl. No time to stand on ceremony." Then to Vasil: "Close it behind us. Clear this room up in case the patrol comes calling, and take off your coats and boots. We must look like we were sleeping."

Again, the hairs on Satya's neck stood as she sensed another trap. Pulling out the Makarov, she thrust it forward, pointing it at each in turn, unable to decide which to trust least. Vasil cracked a broad grin and took a step towards her, his arm outstretched. She aimed the pistol at his chest, her hands quivering, the muzzle bobbing like a fly in a jar. As he took a second step, she squeezed the trigger but it did not yield. Vasil grasped the gun and tore it from her hands.

"Like I said, safety is on." He pointed to the small oval catch on the side of the gun. "Look, girl. No more games. Time is short. If we wanted you dead, you would be dead. The water would have seen to that. Now, follow Maria through and get changed before you catch a cold. But first, I show you..." Vasil flicked the oval catch. "Safety off. Aim along barrel, both notches in line. Relax and squeeze trigger slowly." He aimed at a picture above the inglenook. Then he flicked the catch back and handed the gun back to Satya. "Safety on. Now go!"

The woman disappeared into the hidden room. Satya stood a moment longer. Out of options, her heart in her mouth, she followed through the hole, behind the fireplace and into a windowless room around four metres square. As the bookcase slid back, Satya took in the sparse room. It smelt of must and wood smoke. There were no windows or pictures. In an alcove, beside a crackling fire, an open wardrobe was filled with clothes on hangers. A rickety chair with a bowl of water and a towel stood beside a bed with a bare mattress. On the far wall, a rough glory hole toilet reminded her how full her bladder was.

Maria took Satya's wet greatcoat and draped it over a fireguard, clouds of steam billowing from the saturated fabric. Then she turned and held Satya's shoulders, her expression softened. "Child, you have to trust us. You are not the first and you won't be the last. *The Brotherhood* pays us well to transfer you to Sofia. Already we have lost thousands of lire because the boat was intercepted. If the patrol thinks they stopped the boat before anyone could get off, your disappearance may not have been noticed. Now find some clothes that fit you; at least two sets. Here you can use this bag." The woman pulled a canvas rucksack from under the bed, small but large enough for Satya's needs. "Stay here and keep quiet. We will go to bed now, in case the police come calling. You should also try to sleep. You leave at 10:00am." And with that, she hugged Satya briefly and disappeared. The bookshelf slid back into place. Immediately she was alone, Satya rushed over, pulled her trousers down and squatted over the toilet, feeling the intense relief but she kept the Makarov pointed at the hole in the wall.

Washing away the sea salt, she luxuriated in the warmth of the water and the heady fragrance of the soap, her skin soft and, for the first time in days, free from dust. She had already enraged the prophet by disguising herself as a boy, showing her face in public, cutting her hair to a short bob to escape Aleppo. The Imam had assured her the end justified the means and Allah would be merciful. She thought back to school, to the magazines that were smuggled into class, the women in Paris or Milan, fashionable and elegant. She thought of her own breath moist on the inside of the burkha she was forced to wear. The clothes were European in style, more colourful than the ones she was forced to wear. She would need to blend in, to become invisible in the West, as she had in Syria and through Turkey.

She chose a pair of black woollen tights, a knee length skirt, a blouse and a round necked jumper. The clothes were strange, the smoothness of the fabric, how slender her legs looked in the tights. She found some sturdy boots that fitted. Finishing the outfit with a stylised combat jacket and a dark blue woollen hat, she imagined herself, textbooks under her arm, cresting the steps of the Sorbonne, or along Regent Street, arms laden with shopping. Taking up her postcard album, she flipped to Trafalgar Square and pictured herself striking a pose as the fountains played behind her.

Little was salvageable from her tattered plastic sack, except some underwear, which she hung next to her coat. The rest she would abandon. She picked up the plastic wallet and her purse from the bed, along with the beaded necklace taken from her mother's corpse, and stuffed them into the bag. She picked a few more articles from the wardrobe; a warm jumper, two pairs of trousers and a couple of blouses. Then she curled foetal on the bed and waited, occasionally sipping a cup of sweet black tea, chewing on some honeyed bread and fingering the barrel of the Makarov. As her mind replayed the soldier's face, the grasping paws of the sailor and the silence of the sea that nearly became her tomb, Satya Meheb drifted into an anxious sleep, alone and filled with foreboding for the day ahead.

Chapter 11

North London Homicide Unit, Lambourne Road

On any normal morning, the journey from Alperton to Lambourne Road crawled its way around Hangar Lane. Twenty minutes of frustration for Daley to study, in intimate detail, the tailgate of the car ahead, but today as if commanded by some invisible god, the traffic parted. 10:00am. What a difference a couple of hours could make. Yet still he spent an agonising half an hour in the car park, examining every square millimetre of the steering wheel, every dark corner of his soul, deciding whether the deafening silence of his flat was any better than the roaring chaos of the team room. Around him, the underground space echoed to tyres screeching, doors slamming and footsteps on concrete. The blue door to the stairs enticed him to enter, to join the fun inside, to stop being such a wimp.

He leapt in his seat as the passenger door opened and Detective Sergeant Deborah Whetstone thrust a take-out coffee at him. Plonking herself in the passenger seat, she threw him a stern look which, to be fair, looked no different from the miserable, hang-dog expression she usually wore.

"Well, are you going to sit here all day?"

"You've dyed your hair. Blonde. I like it."

"Stop changing the subject, sir." Daley took the coffee and smiled.

At thirty-three, Whetstone was about five years younger. She was small in stature but her rugged determination and a brown belt in judo more than compensated. Both had served them well on a number of occasions. She had large brown eyes which always betrayed her innate compassion towards others, even when the trials of the job had torn the smile from her round face. But now, her features were serious and challenging.

Daley sighed. The tipping point. Up to now, he could have bailed, phoned in, feigned a grating throaty drawl to emphasise the true enormity of his contagiousness but Whetstone had rumbled him.

"Deb, I don't know whether I am ready. I don't know..."

"What? You want Occy Health to sign you off for another six months? Speak to your union rep, and they could be promoting me to DI." She smiled. "Must admit the extra pay came in handy even if I did have to suffer the weekly hairdryer treatment from *Bilko*."

"Sorry Sergeant." Daley threw her a smile. It had been a while since he had heard D/Supt Allenby's derogatory epithet but it suited the slim, balding man with a penchant for barking ineffectual orders when he thought he could get away with it. Fortunately, experience always triumphed over rank as did a deaf ear conveniently turned. "Looks like you'll have to wait for the next train to get a promotion."

Deb wasn't so sure. Whilst *Detective Inspector Whetstone* had a ring to it and the extra pay was always welcome, she was relieved to see Scott Daley turn up that morning. She would be even more relieved if he shifted his arse up the stairs and into the office.

"Bollocks! Allenby made my life a misery. I never knew who was the Inspector - me acting up or him acting down."

"Welcome to my world, Deb."

"Also, Harrison's running a book on you wussing out and I need my winnings to pay for that coffee. You go first and I'll hang about here. Once you are in the thick of it, it'll be fine. Anyway, Allenby is waiting for you in his office. Says he may have something for you to get your teeth into. Break you back in gently."

Daley shrugged. "Break me back in gently? Still broken from the last time."

Before the gremlins could rally and persuade him otherwise, he was out of the door and striding up the steps to the team room with Whetstone as rear-guard in case he had second thoughts.

Chapter 12

Bath Road Commercial Vehicles, Bath Road, Reading

Leo Hastings wiped his greasy hands on his overalls and reached for the mug perched on the ramp. As with every job on a car of this age, the hardest part would be removing the years of crap from the underside and freeing up the bolts. These Korean cars were great when they were new but this one was well past its sell-buy date. The replacement gearbox would last long enough for him to sell it on. A thicker grade of oil would also hide any minor rattles. It would sound like new.

But you know what? Today he could not be bothered. It was time for a late breakfast. The works.

"Daz. Look after the shop. I am off for an hour or so." Above the dissonant squawk of the radio, a voice hollered indistinctly back.

Stripping off the latex gloves, removing his overalls and sloshing the remnants of tea down the oil stained sink, Leo felt lucky today. He may even stick some of the money on a nag and hope for the best. There was plenty of it and most of it would be off the books. OK, it was strange for a walk-in with a handful of cash but not unheard of. The Transit Connect had arrived the previous week and was only sitting in the yard awaiting prep. He had not even started swapping registration documents. The new owner would appreciate one less name on the logbook anyway, and what the VAT man didn't see would not hurt him. The money all looked legit. He'd put the notes up to the light, used the UV scanner. All pukka. Ask no questions, get no lies.

***

Higher Analyst Trish Steadman studied the entry in the log. There were around three hundred vehicles on her list and she knew that most would be in a garage or off the road by now. She commanded a radius of fifty miles around Slough and all the Automatic Number Plate Recognition cameras within it. Rather than the ones carried by mobile units, these were fixed to the roadside on the off-chance that a listed vehicle would pass. It was then her job to report to the inquiring force and allow them to follow up the sightings.

"Sir, could you come and take a look at this?" Behind her the supervisor turned and leaned over her shoulder. "This vehicle has just pinged on the M4 East bound but according the log, Teeside pinged it on the A1(M) just outside Newton Aycliffe fifteen minutes ago."

The supervisor scratched his head. "Well, one of them is bogus. Send it as a priority to the Inquirer. Let them sort it out."

Trish clipped the relevant images and data logs, zipped them up and attached them to an email to a Sergeant Dave Monaghan in the Met. Then the screen pinged once more - an Audi Sports car Southbound on the A432 in Windsor. Ten minutes later, the email system had filed the unsent email under *Drafts*.

Chapter 13

Through the tiny panes in the swing door, Daley surveyed the team room. They were all still there, as if cryogenically preserved on the day he had left and conveniently defrosted this morning. The whiteboard in the corner was decorated with photos and names, arrows and sketches, from a crime he had not investigated, and screens showed reports he would not need to read. The world had moved on in his absence. Gingerly, he eased the doors open and walked through. Heads turned and the room fell silent.

"I see you finally got fed up of Jeremy Kyle, you skiving bastard." Sergeant Dave Monaghan's Irish brogue cut across the air, as the man turned, beamed broadly and strode over to Daley, his hand outstretched. "Good to have you back, sir."

"Only so much shit telly a man can take, Dave, and I got bored playing with trains." Daley took the hand and held it firmly, as the months of nothing began to dissolve. The room once again resumed its prickling hubbub. He realised he missed the Murder Investigation Team and the camaraderie of the North London Homicide Unit, a forgotten corner of the Met's Homicide and Serious Crime Department, languishing in Ealing. *The Dispossessed* as the team had christened themselves were supposedly temporary tenants at Lambourne Road, awaiting rehousing, redeployment or redundancy, whichever the Commissioner decided. But as that decision had been outstanding for four years, those who had been holding their breaths had long since turned blue.

Behind him there was the click of a door catch on the glass panelled office they all called *the Goldfish Bowl* because D/Supt *Bilko* Bob Allenby spent most of his time staring out at them through the louvre blinds with his mouth open and no idea what was going on.

"Inspector Daley, welcome back! Come through. You too, Sergeant." Allenby circled around to the safer side of his desk and waited for Daley and Whetstone to make themselves comfortable. Chief Constable Summerhill had given him a hard time following the incident when he had defended the maverick actions of his junior officer. After all, Daley had only been on that rail track because of own inability to stand up to his superiors and accept the Inspector's judgement above his own. His hair was thinner and greyer and his waistband wider. Policing had moved on. More than once he had considered closing his blinds and thinking about the golf club.

"How you feeling, Scott?" Allenby smiled warmly, wrinkling the patchwork of thread veins across his cheeks.

Daley glanced across at Whetstone, who raised her eyebrows. "Never better, sir. A coiled spring," he said wryly.

"Hmm. Well, coil yourself around this." Small talk over, Allenby cast a manila slip folder across the desk. Daley scanned the four sheets inside distractedly.

"Josh Turner, twenty years old, disappeared a month ago in Chatham Woods Nature Reserve, just North of Ruislip."

"Missing persons enquiry, sir. Really? This is a Homicide Unit." Daley's shoulders dropped. He had been expecting an easy reintroduction but a *misper* was taking the piss. Allenby held up a hand.

"Hang on, hang on! The local force thought it was a *misper* too until the dog was found."

Daley quickly skim read the report again. "Dog?"

"The lad was walking the family dog, as usual. They both failed to return. Apparently, he was very reliable, responsible, doing well at college, even visiting his sick grandmother every evening. No evidence of depression or other psychological indicators. His parents became alarmed when he didn't return, phoned it in. Next morning, the body of the dog was found by another dog walker, barely covered with leaves just off the main path. His phone placed him in the vicinity of Chatham Woods at around 8:23pm on the night he went missing at which point it was switched off. Since then, nothing had been heard of him."

"So, no evidence of a body, or a struggle?"

Allenby shook his head, solemnly. "The local force made a search but they found nothing. Toxicology on the dog found huge levels of barbiturates, leading the Investigating Officer to conclude that the dog may have been killed to keep it quiet."

"Suggesting that this was probably an abduction?"

"Quite. Take a look, see what you think. I've spoke to the Investigating Officer, a DCI Somerville over at Harrow. She's expecting your call."

Daley flipped through the four sheets of scant information, the photograph of the dog. "OK, I can see the parents may be worried, but what elevates this to something Homicide may be interested in?"

Allenby leaned forwards and picked up three more files, handing them over to Daley.

"Karen Sherwood, 29 years old from Eastcote, a mile from the Turner's house. Missing since August. Diane Fletcher, 27, also from Ruislip, didn't return from a night out with the girls. Andrew Bryson, 26, from Moor Park. Went along to Craven Cottage for a football match and never returned."

People didn't simply disappear; they either left or were taken. Whilst most of them returned, there was still a small, stubborn percentage who did not. Despite virtually every inch of the UK under the constant scrutiny of CCTV, it was all too easy to fall between the cracks and vanish, living in an off-grid world of hostels and casual employment, false names or changed identities. If, Daley mused, a person did not want to be found then they would not be.

"So, what make you think these are connected? There must be fifty or sixty cases like this on Command and Control or Missing Persons systems across the patch. What makes these four people so special?"

"Apart from their proximity to each other, not much. They all seemed to lead perfectly normal lives. The local police looked at indicators for crime, drug use, inappropriate friendships or relationships, bank and phone records were examined, but the trails all went cold, as if these people had disappeared off the planet."

Which, of course was impossible. Nothing Daley had heard so far pointed to anything more than a series of separate missing persons enquiries. A series of wild goose chases into fruitless cul-de-sacs. He sensed a *but*.

"But?"

"But nothing. Just like you, the local forces considered these to be separate, unlinked cases. Until Josh Turner went missing.

Then the presence of the dog got the Investigating Officer to suspect something more. She discovered the van. White Transit, the smaller type - *Transit Connect?* Josh kept a diary. Growing pains, trouble with girls, that sort of thing. Buried in amongst that he made passing references to a white van parked in the car park on the outskirts of the woods. Seems he likes to make up stories about the people and things he saw. The white van was apparently owned by gun-runners, doggers, even secret agents monitoring espionage activity in the park."

"Or a delivery driver who lived locally and didn't want to leave the van outside his house," commented Daley, somewhat less than rapt.

"Maybe, but the IOs curiosity was piqued. She contacted the family and friends of the others. Karen Sherwood's partner recalled she had mentioned being followed by a white van. Andrew Bryson, still living with his parents; they remembered a couple of occasions where a white van had been parked opposite their house. Diane Fletcher, similar. Her flatmates recall her telling them of a white van slowing down beside her on her walk home from work."

"A white van. That's pretty tenuous. Almost everyone in London thinks they are being followed at some time or another."

Allenby sighed and reached for a different folder, this time passing it to Whetstone.

"Last night a small, white Transit van went off the A40 Western Avenue, Greenford, hit a lamppost and into the bushes on the other side of the footpath. The vehicle caught fire but not before the load was cleared from the back. Fire Service managed to extinguish the vehicle before it was totally destroyed. Traffic put it down as an unfortunate accident - until they found the hand."

"Sir?" Like Daley before, Whetstone hastily reread the report. "Blimey. You don't see that every day." The traffic officer taping up the scene had been drawn to an object lying in the grass. Upon closer examination, it had turned out to be a severed human right hand. "Are we sure it came from the van, and not just been left there by some other passer-by, or a dog or a fox?"

"Not a clue. Patrick Gascoigne is in attendance. Ask him. There is blood evidence in the rear of the van and as yet, we don't know whether it is of human or animal origin."

Daley shuffled in his seat. He couldn't remember the last time the blood had been animal in origin. "We'll get straight on it, Sir." So much for light duties.

"Scott, I want you to concentrate on the missing persons case. Deb, you follow up the van crash."

"Sir, surely..." Daley started to protest, a teenager denied TV in his room. Allenby held up a hand.

"Before you start, that's the way it is. I want you, Deb, to assist Inspector Daley to check out these mispers, to identify that van. And...I want you, Scott, to assist *Acting Inspector* Whetstone to look into the crashed van, find out if that hand belongs to any of our missing persons. Alright?"

"There are millions of white Transits around, sir. How can you say that this is the same van?" Whetstone was aware of the frustration building inside Daley. Far from making his first day back easier, this was creating complications that neither of them needed.

"That's for you two to find out. If the two vans are separate, then we can re-evaluate. DC Taylor spent some time yesterday looking on Vantage for similar reports of a white van acting suspiciously."

Vantage was the web based incident recording system. It was used by many forces to record and store details of incidents. In the hands of an experienced and inquisitive office like Steve Taylor, many threads from seemingly disparate incidents could be pulled together.

As they rose, Allenby called after Daley, closing the door behind Whetstone.

"Scott. It's good to see you back. How's the shoulder?"

Daley flexed his arm in a circular motion, demonstrating he was fully fit, refusing to wince as it caught. "Yeah. It's fine. Aches in the cold, that's all. Come on, sir. A misper case, surely?"

"You have been out of the game for some time, Scott. I need to know you are ready. Apart from that, Deb's done a great job in your absence. She is going for Inspector, you know that?"

"No." Daley huffed, disgruntled. "No-one tells me anything."

Allenby smiled. "Look, get yourself back into the swing and we will see how it goes. Apart from that, I think that the crashed van could turn into something bigger. She will need your experience."

"Sir." Daley sighed and reached for the door handle. Allenby half-opened his mouth, as if to say something but seemed to change his mind. Daley waited a long moment for the thought to crystallise. During the wild disembodied dreams of his induced coma, Allenby had been a frequent voice in the ether, sorrowful and guilt-ridden, asking forgiveness for putting Daley in that situation. And in the dreams, he had forgiven him. Real life was different. That would require some visible show of contrition. "Was there anything else?"

"No, you get off now and let Sergeant Whetstone do the heavy lifting for a day or two..." Allenby nodded at Daley's shoulder, "...so to speak."

***

Twenty minutes later, Whetstone manoeuvred her Golf onto the verge beside Professor Gascoigne's black Jaguar S-Type. A large blue tent glowed eerily in the winter gloom from the portable lights blazing within. A small Honda generator buzzed, barely audible above the roar of the traffic. A uniformed cop, who was lazily reclining against the door of his gaudy yellow and blue traffic car, examining his fingernails, raised his eyes and smiled at her.

Keith *The Uniform* Parrish and Deborah Whetstone had been an item for over six months now. Maintaining a relationship in the Force was never an easy thing. There was talk of a flat together, although this was still only canteen gossip.

Donning latex gloves and shoe protectors, Whetstone entered the tent and was hit by a smell of damp bonfires and burnt diesel. The tent surrounded the van completely, two carefully aimed spotlights giving the scene a surreal, staged look. Gascoigne and a forensic robot were busying themselves in the blackened interior. There was an underlying metallic taste in the air.

Blood.

"Ah! Deborah, my dear. Interesting, this one." Gascoigne

was a portly man, almost twice Whetstone's age. Christened *The Dark Lord*, he had turned down early retirement for the macabre delights of forensic pathology but, as the man himself had asked ruefully, what had he got to retire to?

Other than forensic gear, the van was empty. In the front, the seats were skeletal and charred. The windscreen was smoke-blackened but not broken. At the rear, the plywood panelling on the sides and floor were scorched and warped. The bulkhead had protected the load space from the main ravages of the flames.

Gascoigne jumped down from the rear of the van and stood, hands on his hips. "Looks like the fire started in the engine bay soon after impact and was fortunately extinguished before it could completely eradicate all the evidence. Simon is processing the cabin. Not a lot there, but the plywood lining of the load space effectively insulated the metal sides, roof and floor from serious damage. There is a little water ingress but even that is minimal."

"And the hand?" Whetstone prompted.

Gascoigne opened a cool box, retrieving a transparent plastic Ziploc bag. He held it to the light. "Judging by the nails, a female right hand, no rings or tattoos. Ageing is difficult without tests but not young and not old, say between twenty and forty years old. The skin has evidence of pigmentation, so maybe IC4 or IC5 in origin, and a cursory examination suggests that it was severed pre-mortem. The removal is clean but there is no injury or damage, so we can rule out surgical amputation. I suggest the hand was separated from the arm around a week ago. There is some desiccation which indicates it has been frozen."

"Dismemberment?" Whetstone frowned. "So, the rest of the jigsaw puzzle is somewhere else?"

"Potentially, *puzzles*. Take a look at this..." Gascoigne lifted the wooden floor panel. At the left edge was a significant pool of dried blood, fanning out and running along the pressed ridges which stiffened the metal. The white painted surface was criss-crossed with rivulets of brown tracking toward a drain hole near the rear door latch, giving it the appearance of an abattoir floor.

Perhaps, considered Whetstone, the van had been used to carry meat, possibly being cleaned each time but, just like the dust behind her sofa at home, this would be out of sight and out of mind. "That's careless, Prof. Is it human?"

"Simon carried out a Phenolphthalein test." Gascoigne reached for a series of cotton buds, each with pink tips. "As you can see, definitely blood. We repeated the exercise with Hematrace cards." Gascoigne held up a bag containing a number of small plastic cards. Each had two purple stripes; a control indicated that haemoglobin had been detected in the blood, a second that it was human in origin. "Again, as you can see all positive."

"But would this quantity be fatal?"

Gascoigne pondered sombrely. "My guess would be yes. However, my preliminary finding, based on colour and under these lights, suggests that the blood was spilled post mortem. Oxygenated blood is usually darker and this is relatively light in hue. I will need to test it in the lab, though."

"Could this be more than one person's blood?" asked Whetstone scanning the scene, grimacing with the smell.

"Potentially, Deborah, but I can't be sure. However, can you get that switch?" Whetstone followed the pointed finger, clicked a glowing red switch and the space was plunged into semi-darkness before Gascoigne illuminated a *Maglite* torch. Fine sprays of mist were cast about and the load space fluoresced purple beyond the blood pool.

"So here is our main pool. Around it, beyond the margins..." another fine mist uncovered a brighter purple stain, "...is a second pool, and here..." another fine mist, "...a third. Altogether we estimate four separate blood samples, although when we analyse the samples we will know for certain whether they are different people or multiple instances of the same person."

Whetstone gazed around at the glowing bed of purple. Was it a coincidence that a white Transit Connect had turned up carrying four different blood samples at the same time as four people had reported a white van following them before going missing? Of course, lots of white Transits crashed, rather less co-incidences happened.

"And these stains here? It looks like someone has been daubing the walls in some kind of ritual." Vast swathes of the plywood lining, metal walls and floor were a solid mass of purple.

"Not so, I'm afraid, the dark Satanic mass. Luminol also fluoresces with bleach. Those are outside the margins of our samples and indicate some over-zealous cleaning. Lights please."

"So, what's your guess Professor?"

"The front offside tyre is deflated and there is quite a chunk out of the curb a few yards back. Either the vehicle veered off the road, puncturing the tyre, or it suffered a catastrophic deflation pitching it into the kerb. Either way, the impact with the post has fractured a fuel line or something similar resulting in the fire. I would guess only one occupant, the driver. The passenger door is pressed against the hedge, yet the driver's door was ajar when we arrived."

"So, did the hand come from the van?"

"Well, the grass here was trampled and muddied when we arrived. There are deep tyre tracks in the verge under that chequer plate and several boot prints in the mud."

Whetstone carefully lifted the chequer plate and surveyed the rut with her torch. "So, a second vehicle was following the first or arrived soon afterwards and the hand was accidentally dropped whilst the load was being transferred?"

"Possibly."

"They weren't expecting a crash and, with the fire, they were in a rush."

Gascoigne waved an arm at the scene. "All just conjecture until we have the test results. I would say you are looking for the remains of at least two bodies, probably more, one of which was very recently dismembered. And somewhere out there you are looking for a dumpsite."

"Can we ID the van?" Whetstone had noticed the rear number plate had been removed.

"Presence of mind in a crisis, Deborah. Front plate was melted by the fire and the rear was already missing when the police arrived, as was the VIN plate by the windscreen. The one in the engine bay is burned but intact. PC Parrish has a transcript."

Scanning the corners of the load space with the bright beam of a torch, Whetstone frowned. She recalled the horrors she had seen, those yet to be seen, each stripping another layer from her soul. The more crimes she investigated, the more she saw man's inhumanity to man, the reasons why people were driven to extremes. What extremes had the driver of this van been driven to and what were still to come? On a damp, cold Tuesday, did she really want to know?

"So, can we identify *anyone* involved, Prof?"

"Well, the boot prints, I estimate, are size eleven work boots. Simon and I will collect any available DNA evidence but I think your enquiries lie elsewhere."

Chapter 14

1km South West of Şarköy, Turkey

The grating of the bookcase across the stone floor started Satya awake. As the old woman's head appeared, she drew the Makarov from under the pillow, flicked the safety and levelled it at her with both hands. As the muzzle bobbed and quivered, the old woman raised a tray of bread, cured meats and some coffee, and smiled.

"Murder on an empty stomach? No, get this inside you first. Then come through and slaughter us all once you are fed! Vasil has chosen a passport which you can use across the border. The picture is a little fatter than you but it will do. The border guards are more interested in money. You have to be going soon, so eat, drink, collect your things and hurry."

Satya cautiously watched the old woman place the tray before returning through the hole. This time the bookshelf was not pushed back. She could hear the men talking. Vasil, the older man, was scolding Pietr and the latter was defending himself in that tone of complacent arrogance she had often used herself, but the language was foreign to her, neither Arabic nor English. Avidly she tore at the meat and bread, devouring it as if it were to be her last meal. The men sometimes returned with stolen food but the rations had been meagre and the men argued, so Satya had relied on her own initiative. She had scavenged whatever and whenever she could; figs and dates from the fields, stale bread from the bins behind bakeries, once resorting to shoplifting, even if that had nearly resulted in a backside peppered with buckshot.

Finally, Satya decided that having survived the night she had to trust someone sometime. She pocketed the Makarov, collected her newly acquired possessions and turned into the hole beside the fireplace.

Chapter 15

Emerging from the blue cocoon into the dull November morning, Whetstone peeled off the latex gloves and threw them into the Forensic bin.

An unidentified hand, some unidentified tyre tracks and buckets full of anonymous blood. Three, maybe four samples.

The freezing wind blew chill splinters down the carriageway and she pulled her coat about her. Keith *The Uniform* was still loitering by his car but someone had conjured up a brew with which he was warming his hands.

"Keith."

"Deb." It was the first time they had spoken in three days, shift patterns being what they were.

"So, what do we know about the van?"

"Registration is VH07 YMK. Last known keeper, Abbey Commercials in Wealdstone. Dave Monaghan is checking traffic cameras but I don't hold out much hope." He lifted a finger in the general direction of the limp, lifeless camera hanging from the post that the van had collided with. "Come and look at this."

Keith lifted his backside from the wing of the traffic car and headed towards the ditch separating the verge from the hedge. The two stood peering intently at the muddied grass on the opposite side.

"Looks like someone ran."

"Where's it go to?

"Across Marnham Fields then onto the estate, I think."

"Can you take a look when you're finished here. See if you can find out where the trail leads." The oppressive mist which cloaked the field through the hawthorn was keeping it damp and boggy well into the morning. "Mind you, from here, if they had a car on the estate, they could be anywhere."

"They hadn't planned on crashing, Deb. Why would the van driver scarper across the field, rather than leave in the other vehicle?"

Whetstone stole a sip of Parrish's tea. "Doesn't have to be the driver going that way. Could have been a dog walker some other time. Maybe the other car picked him up further along the road. I'll get Gascoigne to check the ditch before he leaves. He'll like that!"

Before putting in the call to Lambourne Road, Whetstone dallied.

"So, you free later?"

Parrish turned his eyes towards her. He was the archetypal traffic cop. Tall and thickset with a square jaw. The black stab vest, adorned with all manner of modern policing equipment gave him a formidable solidity.

"I have the right to remain silent, Ma'am." Parrish raised his eyebrows and stared forlornly into his empty tea cup. "I'm on earlies. I get off at 3:30pm then I need a kip. Give you a call later?"

Whetstone nodded wearily, worried that later may mean never.

Chapter 16

Bloody mispers! Jeez.

Already feeling a spare part, Daley had adopted an air of insouciance, sauntered over to his desk and slumped into the familiar chair which today seemed hard and uncomfortable. Someone had been playing with the levers and buttons. Switching on his PC, he scratched his head at the password prompt. Had it really been that long? Around him the room hummed with a quiet industry. Everybody was busy except him. There were new faces, new names to learn. With Allenby at the helm, who knows what bad habits they had picked up...or what good habits he would have to knock out of them again. It felt like starting a new job and it unnerved him, separate, out of place. Idly, he opened the desk drawers; the contents untouched in months yet still familiar as if it were yesterday. Daley shuddered as he held a sheet containing a Venn diagram, reading the names, seeing the huge buffer beam coming towards him and feeling the impact.

With nothing else to occupy him, he clicked the forgotten password link.

So why the misper case in preference to the *Hand in the Van*? A severed hand screamed homicide, his forte. Whetstone dealt with people, he dealt with death. Six months convalescence had given him time to think. Maybe Allenby favoured Whetstone's approach over his? The thoughtful, stepwise gathering of information, the rational decision making over his impetuous, slightly reckless approach. Whetstone had been his partner for over two years now. She was well qualified to lead a murder investigation but, with twice her experience, so was Daley. There was definitely something going on. Some subtle change in the pecking order. Was this the beginning of a move sideways? He resolved to play Bilko's little games. Prove himself fit to resume his old duties. And he would deal with Whetstone as and when the time came.

Having reset the password, the Met PC cranked itself into life and slowly stuttered towards a home screen, the blue ring of death going round and round... Daley huffed and grabbed his coffee cup. Somewhere in the world, people were racing sports cars, diving on coral reefs, even lying on loungers with beautiful women and sipping cocktails. Did they ever sit and watch a tiny blue ring spin round and round...?

Once the PC loaded, it was no less frustrating. He had pushed the mouse around his desk for an hour before declaring enough was enough. Six months had left his inbox so full that it couldn't take any more. Today, he knew how it felt.

Daley located the files for Sherwood, Bryson, Fletcher and Turner. The Investigating Officer, one DI Theresa Somerville, had been thorough but found little to link the disappearances except their similar locations, the mysterious white van and the time they were thought to have gone missing. Around 8:00pm on a Monday evening. Cycling through to Turner's file, according to his mother, he left with the dog at 7:30pm on Monday 9th October. The connections were flimsier than a stripper's G-string.

Daley found a laminated map behind one of the filing cabinets, unrolling it onto his desk. With a marker, he drew a line from the Turner's semi following the route given by his parents to the entrance to the Nature Reserve.

Karen Sherwood lived in Eastcote, near Ruislip. On 26th August she, her partner Rhys and two-year-old son Cameron had travelled to Notting Hill for the Carnival. Towards the end of the day, they had returned to Notting Hill Gate to take the Tube home. Rhys Sherwood told Harrow Police that the pair had become separated by the crowd. He had continued on with the child, agreeing by text to meet Karen at home. CCTV had followed her as she caught the Tube at Notting Hill Gate travelling to Earl's Court on the District. Cameras saw her change to the Piccadilly line for the trip to Eastcote. The last sighting was of her leaving Eastcote Tube station and walking North towards home. The partner had been ruled out of the enquiries; he had stopped off at his parents on the way home. The grainy staccato images from the CCTV camera over the station's entrance were the last anyone had seen of her.

Diane Fletcher's parents' house was in Ruislip, less than a mile from Karen's. She had travelled to Earl's Court on 10th September for a hen night. Afterwards, she and a few friends had taken the Tube home. They had been tracked as they had entered the Tube at Earls Court, separating at Notting Hill Gate, where Diane took the Central line up to West Ruislip. Again, some monochrome footage from the station's CCTV were the last images of her.

Andrew Bryson also lived with his parents in Moor Park, a few miles North of the other two. A passionate Fulham fan, he had made a familiar pilgrimage to Craven Cottage by Tube on 29th September. After the game, Andrew had joined his mates in the pub until around 8:30pm when he too had embarked on the Tube ride home. As with the others, the last sighting was of him leaving Moor Park station and heading North to his parents' house.

Less than two weeks after the disappearances of Fletcher and Sherwood, the tabloids had solved the case, dubbing their abductor *The Zone 6 Snatcher*, a moniker that gave the case an added cachet, as well as terrifying every Tube passenger venturing beyond Zone 5. With Andrew Bryson and Josh Turner, the stories were edging towards the front pages, probably explaining why they had winged Allenby's way and been dumped on Daley.

Surveying the drawn lines on the map, Daley could see nothing noteworthy about the locations except that they were all within the space of a few square miles. Phoning Harrow Central, Daley arranged to meet the SIO at Chatham Woods Nature Reserve, Turner's last known location. There had to be some significance in the proximity these people had to each other, either by virtue of their disappearances or because of where they lived.

Unless there was none.

So, what of the white van? Somerville had made an addendum to each of her files. Sherwood had mentioned to a couple of workmates that a white van had been following her, matching her pace. When she had turned, it had driven away. A similar story from Fletcher's colleagues at the insurance company in Wealdstone.

So why did no-one take a registration number?

Fearing a potential stalker, it seemed the most obvious thing. It marked the drivers card. Let him or her know he or she had been clocked.

Had Josh Turner had been more astute? Nowhere did he mention a registration number.

Behind his eyes Daley felt a familiar pain, a butcher's skewer being pushed from one temple through to the other. Taking the blister pack from his pocket, he popped out a single tablet then checking about the office, agonised over the second. He popped out the second and lined up the two tablets in front of him. Picking up his coffee, he swilled down one of the pills and stared at the second, the smooth, white pebble resting on the lines of his pad. Pulling the carton from his pocket he reread the pharmacy instructions, the list of side-effects and the recommended dosage and in his mind, he counted the hours. Resignedly, he scooped up the small white thing and dropped it back into his pocket.

Chapter 17

Suddenly, I am aware.

Blackness. No sound. No colour. No sensation. In free-fall but not dropping.

Am I dead? Is this death?

Oh my God, oh my God, oh my God. Is this death? An endless, shapeless void? No up, no down, just an infinite mass of nothing? Maybe this is limbo? A state between states. Maybe this is where I learn the truth about God and the Devil, about Heaven and Hell, about the black, endless eternity? I should be at peace now so why am I so terrified? I sense a long, slow wail echo across the black and I know it is me as the howl fades away unanswered.

I am thinking back. Back to what happened and the memories are not coming. Like a dream at the moment of waking, it slips away. A vague moment of panic, a flash of silver, then nothing. It is as if I have just begun to exist in this black. No memories, no history. It was another world where I used to be and where I can no longer return. A world of...of what? I know it existed, so there must be memories but I don't know where they are. They are somewhere here suspended in this gaping nothing, for me to collect. But I have no limbs to swim. The black is not a viscous fluid like water. It undulates and flows like fine sand, oozing around me while I stay still, unmoved. How can I navigate through the darkness when the darkness itself navigates around me?

Is this what death is? I expected an end. Defined and final, absolute but this blackness confuses me. It is a paradox; emptiness devoid of shape or colour but seemingly deep and endless, like floating through a starless universe.

Cogito ergo sum.

With no form and no memory, still I think, still I am.

So, what then of life? What then of the years of experience, of honesty and truth, of honour and friendship and love? What of hate and spite and envy, of treachery and war? What sense does it make that it should all distil down into this soulless nothing? No rewards, no punishment, no consequences. Just nothing.

Nothing but that.

It lies there in the void, hiding between the shifting molecules of sand. It senses me and I sense it. The predator and the prey. And it knows the path between the molecules. It can squirm and writhe between them, unseen and unheard, circling the space where I am floundering in this wilderness of nothing. It feels the vibrations like a spider on a web, sensing the panic, the desperation. It is approaching but I cannot see or hear anything. I just know it is there. It is waiting for me to complete my journey, patient, prowling and with a hunger forsaken souls.

Chapter 18

Edirne, Edirne Province, North Western Turkey

"My name is Nadia Lazaro. I am travelling with my cousin Pietr and uncle Vasil to our factory in Haskovo. We make clothing for customers in Germany. I was borne in Damascus, Syria, where my parents worked at the Damascus University in the Faculty of Mechanical & Electrical Engineering. I am an Economics student at the same University. My Uncle and Aunt have taken me in after an air raid killed my parents and destroyed my family home in Al Mezzah. Currently, this is my gap year so I am learning about the business."

Pietr nodded appreciatively across the rear seat of the Skoda. "Two hours and finally you have it. And your date of birth?"

"*Alqurfa, alqarf. Kunt alhimar albaeir!*" shouted Satya in frustration. However much she concentrated, there was always one fact she forgot.

Pietr guffawed loudly. "Remember, cousin Nadia, if you have to swear, do it in Bulgarian - *mamka mu, mamka mu. Ako ste zadnika na kamila.* Now, come on cousin, again." There was an impish glint in his eye. She threw a fist across the car and scowled, turning to stare at the featureless highway. Then she began her recitation once more.

"My name is Nadia Lazaro. I was borne in Damascus, Syria on 25th July 1992. I am twenty - *and a half,*" she thrust out her tongue, "years old...and I need the toilet." Ten minutes later, as they pulled into the truck stop north of Edirne, she was word perfect and had earned her comfort break.

Still in the North of Turkey, the roads were a procession of featureless horizons and dusty trucks. It had been slow going since Şarköy. Having discovered that Satya, maybe others, had escaped from the boat, there were blocks on most of the roads. *The Brotherhood* had guided Vasil through the scattered industrial parks to the north of the town, zigging this way and that, through barns and warehouses and factory units. Once clear, he had put his foot down. In the back, the two youngsters had squabbled most of the way, mocking him when he rebuked them. They all needed to be on their mettle and these two were getting far too familiar. Studying the car park carefully, Vasil stepped out into the chill November air.

"Stay close to the car. Take Pietr with you to the bathroom, at least to the door. There are police and spies from the trafficking gangs so don't draw attention to yourself. I get coffee." Vasil left the Skoda and walked off towards the main building.

Satya stretched in the cold morning air. The breeze carried a fine wispy snow and aside from the garish red of the service station, everywhere was a depressing utilitarian grey, which seemed to have rubbed off on Vasil. Pietr lit a cigarette and she watched the wind take the smoke. "Vasil needs to lighten up a little, don't you think? He can be a real *kopele* at times." He smiled at her. They had agreed that all their communications would be in English but apparently not the curse-words. "Before we left, he lectured me about girls, *foreign* girls. Like I am a schoolboy?"

"Like I am interested in you, anyway." She folded her arms indifferently.

"Even so, he says not to mix business with pleasure. He thinks I will take a fancy to you, that you will not make the rendezvous and we will not get paid. That is all he ever thinks about. Money."

"And will you? Take a fancy to me?" she toyed.

"Who knows? Maybe you will take a fancy to me? Swear undying love because I saved you from drowning. And of course, I am very good-looking." It was true. He was tall and slim and, she supposed, quite good looking. His brown eyes had a sparkle, a raffish charm in his smile.

"Saved me? Who said I needed saving? I grabbed for your arm, that's all, to save me the swim. You were just...convenient! And good-looking is a matter of perspective. After that long drive, coffee is better looking than you." She smiled and stared down at the tarmac. There was no doubt he was handsome.

Pietr's shoulders dropped and he feigned an expression of hurt, before dragging at the cigarette. "Huh, you are just like my father. He thinks I am lazy, always looking for the easiest way to get things done."

"Maybe he is right. He is still your father. One day, he won't be there." She recalled sitting, her head in the crook of her father's shoulder as he asked her about her day. She wanted to tell him about the truck, the boat to Şarköy, of her flight across the barren borderlands, of the young soldier. A tear grew in the corner of her eye and she looked away, wiping it with her sleeve, hiding the weakness.

"I do! I do respect him but he still needs to lighten up. He gives me so much grief. No-one says this trip needs to be a trial."

"This is a trial? You should be in a cattle truck with ten smelly farmers from Homs who have not washed in days and enjoy pissing through the sides. That is a trial. Even in this breeze you get a shower."

"Oh, yes? Well, I am driving the rest of the way. Vasil will almost certainly buy *Sujuk*. Then you will know the meaning of smelly when he sits in the back and chews sausage all the way to Sofia. That stuff reeks to the heavens."

Satya laughed. She liked Pietr. He was easy company. He was smoking, fingers crooked around the glowing tip, like James Dean, leather jacket and jeans and she wondered about his life. Back in Aleppo, her strict Muslim household would prevent her speaking to him without a *mahram*, a chaperone, her face beneath the hijab. Now, she felt comfortable in her Western clothes. Blessed with light skin and western features, unremarkable, anonymous, right here, right now, she blended perfectly. Despite Vasil's warning, she felt she could stroll across the forecourt, walk into the gas station and buy cigarettes, unheard of in Aleppo. Outside Syria, Islam favoured its followers more kindly.

Setting off for the toilets, she counted the cars around the lot. A couple were large Mercedes but most were small like their Skoda, dusty and travel scarred. How many other migrants were travelling this same route? How many were State Police?

"Pietr? How many do you take on this trip?"

He turned and eyed her curiously. "This time, just you. *The Brotherhood* pays us for two but this time we only have one. Usually when the boat gets through, there are dozens of drivers willing to do the journey. This place would be filled with cars and vans, all pretending to be commercial drivers or tourists. We have to fight for the business. This time I was lucky. I found you before anyone else. But there are other routes, so there could be others like you here now. We should take Vasil's advice, cousin Nadia."

"Did you transport someone called Alaam, a man, a little older than me?"

Pietr's face hardened and he looked away towards a coach disgorging passengers. "I don't remember names. Everyone changes their names. There are too many. And the police always ask for names."

"He is my brother. He had a tattoo."

"You all have the tattoo."

"No, he had a special one." Stopping at the entrance to the toilet block, with her finger she traced the symbol on the wall.

"Maybe, look, I don't remember everyone."

Pietr's tone was evasive. Had Alaam had followed the same route, ridden in the same dusty Skoda? Maybe slept in the same bed she had last night?

"So, the police are here?"

"Police are everywhere. Vasil is not just buying coffee and *Sujuk*. He knows most of them. They are easily bribed and will turn their heads the opposite way for a few lire.

Satya was suddenly aware how vulnerable they were. On the road with the soldier, she had been rash. She had let down her guard. And again, on the boat. That must not happen again. Having relieved herself, she quickly returned to the car.

Pietr followed like a wounded puppy, afraid he had overstepped the mark. "I was only kidding, Nadia...but you do look good in your new clothes. They make me think of a girl I knew in Budapest. She had short hair like yours but she wasn't nearly as pretty." Pietr smirked and drew self-consciously on the cigarette.

Satya glared. Quickly she jumped into the car and wound down the window to let in the breeze. "You can't get around me that easily. Just because I am young and Muslim, doesn't mean that I don't understand men, their deviousness." This type of attention she could handle. "How long is it to Sofia?"

"Three hours. We have plenty of time."

Once over the border to Bulgaria and Europe, they would drive as far as Sofia Central Station on the A1. In Europe, she would assume another identity, which Vasil kept behind the glovebox. Then the train would take her across Europe to Paris. There, another driver would take her to the rendezvous point outside Calais. Pietr assured her it was a route that had been used many times.

A hundred yards away, the dull sunlight flashed off a glass door and Vasil emerged with some takeaway cups. Plumes of smoke surrounded his face from the foul tobacco he rolled. Handing the cups out he opened the driver's door. There was a strong odour of garlic and spices.

Pietr's shoulders dropped. "Hey, Vasil. I thought I was driving."

"Just get in the car, boy. We are being watched." Pietr made to speak but Vasil held up a hand. "They are looking for the girl. She killed a border guard. That is why the boat was intercepted. We need to leave now, before they see our passenger."

Satya's stomach knotted and the coffee began to shake in her hand. She looked behind but they had left the truck stop alone. How many eyes were lurking behind the glass of the cafe, watching the girl and the boy flirt? She could deny it, that it must be another girl. In her homeland, the penalty for murder was hanging, though many disappeared for less. Would Europe treat her more leniently? Would she even make the border? In front of her, the two heads were fixed and forwards, each of her companions keeping their counsel.

Once more she was merchandise, cargo to be moved. She wanted to explain, to tell them it was either the old couple or the soldier. How could she have left them to the mercy of the guard? How could she trade their lives for hers? Much had changed in the few days since she had entered the mosque, since she had stepped out of her burka. And now she was branded a murderer.

Chapter 19

Chatham Woods Nature Reserve, near Ruislip

Daley had driven past the gates to the car park at Chatham Woods Nature Reserve any number of times but never turned in. Policing didn't lend itself to cosy strolls or walks in the woods with a dog. The car park was shielded from the main road by around ten feet of dense, unruly hedging, muffling the sound of the traffic to little more than a swish as each car passed. With space for around twenty vehicles it was all but empty. Sodden autumn leaves matted and brown across the fading white lines and kerbs attested to little patronage.

He pulled up across from the only other car, a silver Insignia. As he opened his door, a woman left the Insignia, slung the strap of her handbag across her shoulders strolled over, her face consumed by plumes of vapour.

"DI Scott Daley. Thanks for meeting me so quickly." He stretched out a hand.

"DI Theresa Somerville. No problem." Taking his hand, her grip was firm and held for a long moment, a switch between pleasantries and business. She was a slight woman, early thirties, even wrapped in a voluminous chocolate brown coat, slim and unassuming. Of course, they had already spoken on the phone but his mental image did not fit the reality of the person. Her voice described a larger woman, hair swept back, more severe, more masculine. Though, he had to admit that his preconceptions were coloured by Lambourne Road where he suspected they laced the tea with steroids. Her hair was tied up, as deep an auburn brown as her coat, and surrounded a round, business-like face with high cheeks, subtle dimples and a permanent happy smile.

Below the hemline of the coat he couldn't help noticing calf-length boots in preparation for their walk. His wellingtons languished in his hallway. This was one of those acts of foresight that women regularly perform whilst men's minds were elsewhere, yet if a woman ever reminded them, it would be considered nagging.

"Let's walk, shall we?" Her voice, soft with a sing-songy lilt, made him think of Western Scotland, Fife, Midlothian, maybe Edinburgh and was refreshing against the brash, vowelly South-eastern accent which surrounded him every day. It was a voice he wanted to listen to.

A footpath led from the road, across the centre and into the woods. Following Somerville, Daley imagined a boisterous red setter bounding this way and that after a smorgasbord of smells and sounds. He imagined Josh Turner, headphones in, slouching along the footpath, lost in his own world, irked at having to walk the dog despite the fact that the dog was effectively walking itself.

"So, Inspector. What deems my missing persons enquiry so important that a homicide detective has been assigned?"

"Funnily enough, that's exactly what I asked when my *Super* dumped it on me." He wanted to tell her that shit always sinks downwards, that he had stopped to draw breath and his Sergeant had jumped into his shoes, but she turned her head and glared.

"Dumped?"

Daley winced. "Sorry, inappropriate. Poor choice of words. I've just returned from prolonged sick leave and he wanted to ease me back in gently."

"Nothing serious I hope?"

"I was hit by a train."

"Ah, that Inspector Daley! You're quite a celebrity. Young PCs stand on street corners hoping you will walk past and they can put your badge number in their wee books."

"Uh?"

"Sorry, inappropriate. Train-spotting joke." She flashed a vengeful smile.

Daley frowned. Perhaps this unassuming woman was more of an adversary than she looked. "Anyway, I found connections with another enquiry that we are running which made me think differently. I must say, it's a long time since I was asked to trace a missing person."

"Unfortunately, they take up fifty percent of my time. In the UK, over 300,000 people are reported missing each year, and whilst some are serial offenders, that still leaves around 190,000 individuals. That's equivalent to three quarters of the population of Harrow. Fortunately, most are found or come back home of their own volition but there is still a stubborn few who choose never to be found, or are deceased. That's over 300 people found dead or as identifiable body parts, and the vast majority in the Metropolitan Police area."

"Yes, my team are working on one now. The *Hand in the Van.* A crash on the A40 last Monday?"

"I read the bulletin after you called. Is it one of my *Zone 6* victims?"

Daley shrugged. "Yet to be identified."

Turning left, Somerville indicated a gap in the hedge, where twenty feet further on the path opened onto a wide expanse of green land. "So, we think Josh walked this way." She pointed to an intersection in the path to Daley's right. "There's a loop around the Eastern side of the woods that comes back out there, around a mile and a half. It's a popular route for dog walkers during the day but at 8:30 in the evening, the place seems to have been empty. No witnesses."

"And the van?"

"In the car park. His parents said he often mentioned it after returning from walking the dog. A white Transit Connect. Josh had a vivid imagination. He gave nicknames to the people he met. There was the superstar, a woman he described as made up like a clown and always wearing heels, even in the mud. There was the army vet, who wore a khaki camouflage coat, and the lovebirds, an elderly couple who always held hands. There were many people; all of them had colourful lives in the mind of Josh Turner. He believed the van belonged to a team of international terrorists and drug smugglers who were holed up in an underground bunker awaiting the fall of Western democracy."

"He sounds quite lonely."

"Yes, Inspector. According to his lecturers, he is not a great mixer. His parents said he kept himself to himself."

Around the curve of the path, a West Highland terrier careered past. An equally small man, with a pronounced cough walked smartly after it, jets of vapour issuing each time he hacked. He smiled at DI Somerville.

"Hello, Inspector. Any news?"

Somerville shook her head and the man disappeared off towards the estate.

"Colin Wilks - Cardiac Colin. Josh is popular with the other dog walkers. For many, it is the only time they speak to another human being."

"Maybe I ought to buy a dog myself."

"Thought the same." Somerville smiled at Daley and for a brief moment he was surprised to see himself reflected.

"Sad though. Since Josh went missing, many of them have stopped coming here."

"And they all checked out - the walkers?"

"Yes. Mostly middle-aged or pensioners, a few joggers. We had a patrol here for a week or so, questioned everyone. We managed to identify most of Josh's characters."

Having crossed a hundred or so yards of open field, the path forged a corridor through a dense copse.

"Through there is where we found the dog." Somerville's arm, perpendicular to the track, pointed into a thick wooded area. Beyond a few feet, it was just a confusion of bushes. The pair delved through the spindled branches across a spongy carpet of rotted leaves to a tree flapping with torn blue and white tape.

"The dog was lying by the tree. Placed there, according to Forensics, rather than dragged, say, by a fox."

Daley looked back towards the path, even in the nakedness of winter, invisible through the trees. The small clearing was silent but for a blustering wind which moaned though the sticks throwing phantasms of detritus about his feet.

"What about that way?" Daley indicated deeper into the woods.

"Possibly but unlikely. This whole area used to be part of a farm."

"A farm?"

"Yes. There is a derelict smallholding over there and a path around thirty yards that way." She reached out and pointed through the trees. "We checked it out and there were a few footprints in the yard, a few indistinct tyre tracks but no evidence of the property being otherwise disturbed. We figured that if the abductor had taken him that way, then it would be to a waiting car. We searched the smallholding but it yielded nothing significant."

Daley stopped. "The white van?"

"Well, there were multiple sets, suggesting someone had been parking there regularly. Common tyre makes, so unless we could track down the vehicle... Could be doggers, or ramblers or kids. The patrol kept an eye on the farm gates but saw nothing."

Returning to the path, the two resumed their circular route.

"So, the others, Sherwood, Fletcher and Bryson. They all reported seeing a white van too."

"Yes. Without a registration number, though..."

Reaching the car park, Daley felt he had learned very little. There was simply nothing to go on. He proffered a card and watched as DI Somerville started her car and drove away.

A search of vehicle records had returned 2,500 white Transit Connects of around the right age that were still on the road. So, seeing one pass, slowing down to ask directions, stopping to take a phone call, even parked up as a boiler was fixed, was not necessarily suspicious.

Unless these were unfortunate coincidences, there had to be something more.

Chapter 20

Loughton Street Forensic Laboratory, Ealing

There are some unwritten rules regarding the siting and composition of public buildings, devised by town and city planners since time immemorial.

Firstly, make them anonymous, as difficult as possible to find. The use of public money being under such scrutiny, none should be wasted on signage. Avoid even the smallest plaque and if possible, leave existing signs in situ. After all, they will only be misleading on the first visit. The savvy visitor will be wiser on their next.

Secondly, the smaller the plot the better, adding to the illusion that public servants endure endless hardships in their mission to serve us. Public parking should be kept to a minimum and used for siting portakabins; why waste tax-payers' money on empty tarmac? After all parking is abundant in the lucrative council run pay-and-display six streets away.

Thirdly, if there is an ornate, arched entrance boasting stout Edwardian oak swing doors, brass polished handles and stained-glass lights, atop sweeping granite steps, keep it locked. Members of the public might scuff the brass. Add a sign saying *Please use public entrance* and direct it toward a foreboding, grey-painted side entrance and a corridor more akin to the toilets in an East European Employment exchange.

And fourthly, there should be absolutely, unquestionably, definitely, unequivocally, no possibility for the public to enter the offices where our stalwart servants of the *great unwashed* toil tirelessly to make their pensions as quickly and effortlessly as possible. The public should be confined to pale, depressing, waiting rooms, given numbers or tickets and allowed plenty of time to watch their lives ebb away to public information films. That way, they won't come again.

Primarily, supposed Daley, these rules were aimed at avoiding questions as to how, where and by whom their tax dollars are spent, safe behind the opaque veil of Health and Safety legislation and Risk Assessments, the proliferation of which has enabled civil service empires to flourish with impunity behind the faceless facades of public buildings.

And so it was with Loughton Street Forensic Laboratory. Overlooked by the Luftwaffe, successive Lord Mayors and even the Royal College, to which there was a rumour the laboratory was affiliated, it hid in a narrow Dickensian side street. The cobbles rattled the fillings from one's jaw (Health and Safety only applied within the building). Any sane person would have parked in the pay-and-display in Pitman Street and walked around the corner. However, Allenby kept a tight rein on expenses and, as Lambourne Road was a mere half mile away, *Shanks's Pony* was the order of the day. Of course, Professor Patrick Gascoigne had his own marked space, off the road in Pitman Street, along with a key to the overbearing front entrance, so he had already returned by the time Daley and Whetstone arrived. The pair were forced to negotiate a route past the ubiquitous industrial wheelie bins and enter via a *tradesman's entrance.*

"What do you know, Prof?"

"Now there's a sight for sore eyes. Welcome back, Inspector Daley. It's been very quiet without you. Back you are and now this! Oh. By the way, thanks for the mummy. A page in the memoirs." Daley nodded, the reference back to his last case...not quite his last, fortunately.

The examination room was wood-panelled, around half the size of a tennis court, resembling a 1940s drawing room put to a more grisly use. Along three walls were harsh white counter tops subsumed under sinks, microscopes, centrifuges and other scientific paraphernalia unidentifiable to Daley. Below, were dozens of drawers and cupboards. Set into the last wall, a large viewing window looked in from Gascoigne's small office. Fortunately for Daley, all but one of three stainless steel examination tables were empty. The professor, wearing greens, stood at the middle of the three. He crooked a figure for the pair to follow him to his office.

"So, let's start with the van. There are four distinct blood samples from the load space. The fire ingress and some fastidious cleaning have destroyed any others. The good news is that, subject to further analysis, one of the samples matches the hand. A full screen will take a day or two but DNA and ethnicity analysis should provide more of an insight into the others.

"There were three sets of fingerprints, aside from those of the hand. There is no evidence that the owner of the hand rode in the van. I have the sent the details across to Sergeant Monaghan. With regard to other trace evidence, there is nothing concrete at this stage. We will undertake a more thorough examination later today. However, I wouldn't hold out much hope."

Whetstone scratched her head. "What about the driver or any potential passenger?"

"Nothing, Deborah. There was a keyring on the key, a souvenir of La Musée d'Orsay in Paris. Nothing else was left in the cabin." Gascoigne hunched his shoulders. "We will have to see what Simon finds."

"What about the hand?" asked Daley.

Gascoigne clicked his computer keyboard and swung his monitor around. "Let's start at the sticky end. It's a clean, almost surgical cut. The skin has been pared away before the radius and ulna have been transected with a saw. Look at the cut." The Professor clicked and a new image made them start. "It is clean, like a joint from the butcher. There is minimal trauma to the flesh but, judging by the wound, significant bleeding, so my guess would be amputation pre- or peri-mortem."

"So, she was alive when it was amputated?" Whetstone grimaced, unable to comprehend how someone could endure the pain.

"Or near to death, yes."

Another click and another image, focussing on the bone ends. "The fine striations suggest a power saw. Looking at the actual hand, the skin pigment suggests, as I suspected, IC4 or 5. Age-wise, it's difficult, anywhere between late teens and early thirties. There are no tattoos, ring marks or significant scars. No nail varnish, nor signs of any left in the cuticle. The shape of the nails and of the overall hand suggests female, although we can never be sure these days. Also, nothing significant under the nails. She didn't fight her attacker with *this* hand, if indeed she was attacked."

"Pity it couldn't have been the left hand. That might have had a wedding ring, or at least a tan mark."

"Pity it had to be either hand, Deborah." The Professor cast her a rueful look over his specs." Anyway, judging by the fingertips and palms, the owner does no significant manual labour, although she has a slight allergy to soap or washing up liquid. Most significantly, the hand has been frozen and subsequently thawed out."

"So in summary, it's a female hand, amputated peri-mortem, stored in a freezer and then either lost or mislaid. Apart from the fingerprints, we know no more."

Daley had hoped for more. IC4 or IC5 meant that it didn't belong to his *mispers*. Could there be another missing person yet to be reported?

"A *healthy* female hand. I can see no reason why this hand needed to be removed and without the rest of her, that's as far as I can get."

"Well, Prof. Let's see what the fingerprints tell us. Oh, and let me know as soon as the bloods come through. I am sending some other DNA profiles across. Please could you match those too?"

"I will, Scott..." but it was in vain, as impetuousness got the better of the Inspector and he raced out, leaving Whetstone shrugging to a bemused Gascoigne. "First day back...kid...new toy."

***

Returning to Lambourne Road, Daley crested the top step, puffing and cursing the weeks of idleness. Monaghan and Taylor were deep in conversation at their island of desks. No doubt they had been seconded to Whetstone and would have little time for misplaced dog-walkers.

DS Monaghan was the senior member of the team, in terms of age if not rank; that dubious distinction sat with Allenby. Hailing from Ireland, he was soft spoken, had a relaxed avuncular style and warm, if not always genuine, smile. A true backroom boy, he was precise and punctilious, preferring the certainty of fact to the vagaries of witnesses or suspects. DC Taylor was cut from similar cloth, albeit of a darker hue woven originally in Africa, and the two worked well together. Taylor was, in appearance, very different to Monaghan. Tall and slender, with a defined stoop from too much computer work, he had a more genuine smile, deeply hidden behind a facade of shyness.

"Gov, we have a name for our hand!"

Noting the self-satisfied grin across Monaghan's face, Daley hoped for a breakthrough, one that would crystallise before Allenby returned. Missing persons was a rookie's task. He needed murder. To his chagrin, Whetstone edged past and made for Monaghan's desk. With a flourish, Monaghan gestured towards a rather stern-faced head and shoulders filling his screen. "Meet Varsa Ruparelia. Twenty-seven years old from Wembley."

"What do we know about her?" Whetstone leaned over Monaghan. Behind her, Daley scanned the colour image, taken in a custody suite somewhere in England. It showed a woman of Indian or Pakistani descent with round full cheeks and a fiery, dogmatic look in her deep brown eyes. *Hello Varsa.* Daley studied the face. His first impression was of a woman who wouldn't be messed with, who would always rise to a challenge.

A woman who took one step too far.

"Well, gov," added Taylor. "She was born in Lambeth of Ugandan Asian parents. Graduated from City University with an Honours degree in Nursing and is NMC registered. Nothing after the arrest. Also says, at that point, she was single."

"Have you cross-referenced against *Missing Persons*?" Daley asked the obvious, knowing that Monaghan and Taylor were too thorough not to have made it their first port of call.

"No-one of that name. Also working through local hospital morgues but no luck yet."

"Keep trying. Anywhere with an accident and emergency department in the Greater London area."

"...And there's no matching deaths at the Register Office," added Monaghan.

"Do we have an address?" asked Whetstone.

"She renewed her passport last year. Last known address is 15a Clarence Road, Wembley. Cross-checking with HMRC, up until recently she was an Office Administrator for the Medway Klein clinic in Northwick Park. They lodged a P45 lodged on

October 31st."

"Why would a trained nurse be working as an Office Administrator?" In Daley's experience, most people find a career and move within it. Some change tack favouring lifestyle over career. A trained nurse becoming an office administrator hinted at a story to tell.

"Dunno, Sir. Maybe she found that Nursing and Midwifery wasn't all it was cracked up to be."

Daley shrugged. "Is she still on the register?"

"Appears so. I can check with them directly."

"She intends to go back to it one day."

"Maybe she's just resting. Taking a career break." suggested Taylor.

"Or she has been dismissed and had to take any job she could get in the interim."

"We need to take a look at her flat."

Chapter 21

Then I am aware again.

The thing hovers just beyond where I could see it, if my eyes could see. I feel it uncoil, sending tendrils through the void, examining corners, searching for me. Now, it cowers and skulks, biding its time until I fade away, to drag me away. Around me, the darkness slithers and the prickling lights fold and shift.

This world has to be limbo...or purgatory. The transient state from the world that was to the world to come, or perhaps to nothing. Who knows? Perhaps the reckoning, the Day of Judgement, is still to come?

I float here in this limitless void, a victim to the vagaries of this space, biding my time in a world where time is an illusion and I wonder, is it the realm of ghosts? Haunted souls floating on the current of this paranormal morass, occasionally breaking through to the world that was, occasionally pleading to return to life before being pulled back, subsumed again by the dark. Am I a ghost? Do I return to the world as a spectral memory? Is that what happens when I am not aware in this world?

Then I sense the chirping of the crickets, the regular rubbing of the wings, cutting through the void and making the dancing lights sing to the rhythm. I look for the grass where they hide but all I sense is the black and the lights. The gentle sighs and beeps from the machines are comforting, soft and regular and insistent. There are voices, ebbing and flowing in the radio static, like an old recording, words indistinct and distant. These noises are the protectors, who guard our lost souls from the monster until it is time for us to return, or for us to move on.

They protect me from the monster.

Whilst they are there, the monster cannot drag me away to the darkness. I know this to be true but how? Where does that memory come from? Where do I come from?

And inside, deep inside, the deep, wrenching pain of separation builds until it is almost too much to bear. Everything I am, everything I have ever been is now lost.

There are memories, like the parallel world of a dream, remembered but not recalled. Why cannot I not remember?

Chapter 22

Wembley, West London

Varsa Ruparelia's apartment was on the third floor of a smart gated block on Clarence Road. Whetstone flashed her warrant card at the elderly concierge and persuaded him to let them in. As they entered, they were hit by a wall of warm, stale air. Something was very wrong. The curtains were shut and the lights on. In the living room, the TV prattled to itself. There was a strong odour of bleach. Daley looked anxiously at Whetstone before turning, dismissing the concierge and promising to return the key.

"Miss Ruparelia?" Whetstone called from the door. "It's the police. Are you in here, love?" The pair waited as motes of dust swarmed around the stuffy hall. She tried again. "Miss Ruparelia?"

"Right," said Daley donning some latex gloves. "You take the living room and kitchen. I suppose I better brave the bedroom." Whetstone nodded, happy to defer.

Down the hall, the bedroom door was ajar, a slit of darkness behind the frame. Daley's heart began to hammer and he reproached himself. If she were lying dead, it wouldn't be the first body he had seen. He licked his dry lips and grasped the handle, easing the door open. He found the light switch and flicked it on before allowing himself the luxury of a breath. The room was empty and stale, curtains drawn, the bed made. He sighed as Whetstone entered behind him, regaining his composure.

"Nothing, Sir. There's a plate of half-eaten food on the table, place set for one. TV and electric fire on. Handbag on the sofa. It's as if she's come home, made dinner, then just decided to put her coat on and leave again."

"Well, if her handbags still here," noted Daley, "she wouldn't be going far. You women are surgically attached to your handbags."

Whetstone grimaced. "Bit insensitive, Sir. If she's right

handed, and we have her right hand, how would she carry it?"

"Ah. Good point, well made. Anyway, coats still over the chair too."

"Judging by the state of the food, she left some time ago. Her leccy bill must be huge." Whetstone switch off the TV and, reaching down, clicked off the fire, watching the bars dim and crack as they finally took a break.

"Not sure that would be her main concern, right now. Let's see if Forensics can tell us how long it's been there."

"Strange she should leave without her handbag, though. I mean, crap jokes aside..."

Daley cast an eye over the mantelpiece and leafed through some mail on the table. There was nothing spectacular. Under the letterbox, a small mountain of free newspapers had piled up, pushed back as they had opened the door. The TV licence needed renewing. The Residents Association were holding a meeting. Someone had taken a summer holiday in Fuerteventura.

Whetstone was scratching her forehead. "This place has been searched."

"Oh, yeah. What makes you say that?"

"Look, the sofa has been moved. You can see the indentations where the legs used to be...and the table."

Whetstone looked into the kitchen. Again, everything had been placed back carelessly, revealing rings of grime.

Daley checked the bedroom. "I think you're right. There are holes in the dust around the bedside lamp and the cosmetics on the dressing table."

The bedroom was spartan, utilitarian. There were no ornaments, no pictures on the wall, nothing warm. Opening the bedside tables, Daley ran a hand through each draw but there was nothing unusual. Perhaps whoever searched had been successful? The wardrobe yielded no clues. As he closed the door, something caught his eye. The plinth board below the door was askew. More out of curiosity than anything else, Daley lightly kicked it and felt it yield. Crouching on all fours, he gently prised out the loose piece of boarding.

"In here, Deb."

Drawing out the small book, Daley quickly confirmed there was nothing else in the cache. Whetstone peered over his shoulder as he flicked through around a hundred pages packed full of jottings and trivia which Varsa Ruparelia had thought noteworthy or even useful. Many of the entries were dated, many underlined or with names next to them. She used initials throughout; a scant disguise for her victims, which would easily be resolved.

"Ah." Whetstone raised her eyebrows. "Looks like Varsa was one for keeping secrets."

Daley flicked towards the end of the book, towards the last notes Varsa took.

"Hang on, look at this."

Daley flattened the book with a latex finger at a page containing a hand-written table. "This is our van."

Date	Reg	Devices	Units	+/- units	Procs	Farm?
Apr 12	VH07 YMK	5	7	+2	7	7
May 12	VH07 YMK	5	7	+2	7	7
Jun 12	VH07 YMK	3	5	+2	5	5
Jul 12	VH07 YMK	5	7	+2	7	7
Aug 12	VH07 YMK	3	6	+3	6	6
Sep 12	VH07 YMK	5	7	+2	7	7
Oct 12						

"She's keeping track of it. Its comings and goings maybe?"

"For devices, read stock, I suppose. Something high value and easy to sell on."

"Units? Procs? Farm?" Daley shrugged and pulled a plastic evidence bag from his overcoat. He needed time to disseminate, to correlate, to contextualise.

"Do we have her phone?" Whetstone checked the handbag, as Daley frisked the pockets of the overcoat, eventually locating a mobile but the battery had run down.

"Same as mine. We can swap the battery." Whetstone rooted around in her own handbag, removed her own phone and handed the battery to Daley.

Daley played the voicemails.

"Erm, this is dated 28th September."

'Varsa. It's me, Connor - Connor Smith. What you're saying is stupid. We're all on to a good thing here. Haven't I told you to keep your head

down? If you rock the boat, it won't be just you who who'll fall out. We'll talk tonight, OK?'

"Sounds like she's ruffled some feathers. That was the last voicemail she picked up."

The next few were from Varsa's mother. At first the tone was indignant. *Why hadn't she called? Out of sight, out of mind, inconsiderate girl.* Soon though, they became increasingly concerned and angry at the lack of response. By the fifth message, desperation had set in and a distinct chill had descended. The sixth message, turned the room sub-zero.

'Bloody Hell, Varsa. I thought we'd agreed to keep quiet. Now we're all being asked questions. I'm going to have a word, see if I can sort something out. I'll say you don't know anything, that you were mistaken, but you have to stop lighting fires. It's not our business and you should stop asking stupid questions. The best thing you can do is plead ignorance, or God knows what's going to happen to you. You'll be on your own. Just let it drop. Look. You might have gone but we all still have to work here. Anyway, call me, Connor, OK?'

"So, she listened to his first voicemail and chose to ignore the rest."

Soon, following a few more anxious messages from her mother and sister, Whetstone had reached the final unplayed message.

"This is dated 12th November, Monday, at 18:30."

'It's me, Connor. Jesus, Varsa. Don't you ever phone back? Where the Hell are you? Look, call me, please. Everything's cool here now. Looks like we got away with it. I have even been asked to do some more work for them, you know, outside the project. If I am lucky it will mean more money, who knows? But for now, Varsa, keep a low profile and I'll try and get you back in. Call me, please."

Dropping the phone into a second plastic bag, Whetstone cast down the coat and sighed. "Let's get this back to Lambourne Road. And get a uniform over here until Forensics have been over it. I don't want that concierge getting nosy."

Chapter 23

Road works, Northolt

Whetstone had set the Team Brief for 09:30am the next morning. Conscious of the resources, media interest and perhaps just the awkward questions that would entail, Allenby had yet to sanction a full-scale murder enquiry. At least until the rest of Varsa Ruparelia's body turned up or he could be convinced that an unlawful killing had taken place. Notwithstanding, he had sanctioned the team to investigate further, which left Daley, in his temporary support role, at a loose end whilst other officers were despatched hither and thither. So, he had spent the afternoon on his missing persons files.

He had driven to Eastcote, Ruislip and Moor Park and visited the families of Fletcher, Sherwood, Bryson and Turner, obtaining preliminary DNA samples from each and fending off difficult questions when he introduced himself as a Homicide detective. Perhaps that tactic needed a rethink. The Fletchers, Sherwoods and Turners were deep in denial, fully expecting their loved ones to appear at any moment, that he was wasting his time. Why wasn't he out looking? The Brysons however were defeated. A month or so ago, Andrew had left for Moor Park Station, as he had done every other Saturday for four seasons and was not coming back. There was something stoic and resigned about his parents, so certain that there was no hope.

Daley twisted his neck and squinted along the row of cars. Through the smog of exhaust, he could vaguely see a yellow hard hat and a checked shirt holding a stop/go board which seemed fixed on stop.

The voicemails on Varsa's phone troubled Daley. Again, he saw the challenging eyes from the mugshot. They were the eyes of a woman who would not back down from an argument. *If you rock the boat, it won't be just you who who'll fall out.* Did he see the *agent provocateur,* the stick poised below the hornet's nest? Had she poked inside, rooted around and been stung? *Bloody Hell, Varsa. I thought we'd agreed to keep quiet.* Did others fear the sting? At work, on her project? Who would be scared enough that they needed to silence her? Hopefully, Connor Smith, the person who had left the voicemails, would enlighten them when Whetstone caught up with him. Daley felt distinctly separate, watching from the side-lines as the team, his team, looked unlikely to call on the sub.

A fitful rain had beaded the windscreen, adding to his claustrophobia. After weeks of boredom, he had hoped work would return substance to his days but he felt isolated and overwhelmed. Times, dates, names, locations. Fortunately, Whetstone would run the team brief. Whilst a relief, it was still an annoyance. After so long away, would he have embarrassed himself, or would it come flooding back as if barely a day had passed? Deb Whetstone already had her feet under his desk. Maybe now he had to consider her competition? Maybe the competition was already over?

A horn sounded. Raising a hand, he eased his car along to fill the agonisingly small void. The check shirt ahead was now close enough to have a head which seemed to spend most of its time jabbering to a colleague in a hole behind the barriers. He glanced at the dash clock, reflexively checking his watch. The samples would need to be at Loughton Street today. If the traffic was bad now, it would be worse later. He pressed the Bluetooth button and scrolled through to Gascoigne's number.

Chapter 24

Sofia Central Station, Sofia, Bulgaria

Vasil had driven a circuitous route from Edirne to the border. He had claimed he was avoiding the tolls but Satya knew he was avoiding the police. From the truck stop it had taken an hour to the Bulgarian border and its gateway into Europe. Vasil had ignored Pietr's adolescent pleading and continued to drive, ordering the boy into the rear. He had told him play cards, look out of the window, pretend to be cousins. For his trouble, he had endured the infantile banter between the girl and his son, the disquiet growing. These two were far too familiar. But at least she looked less like a murderess fleeing Turkey.

The border to the North East of Edirne enjoyed a massive, if complacent, presence of border police. If word of the guard's death had reached this far, either they were disinterested or keeping it quiet. The E80 fanned out into a number of lanes which slowly snarled their way under the gates. Vasil had pulled into what he believed would be the shortest, marked for Bulgarian nationals and EU citizens.

Satya had spent half an hour watching an image of an anthropomorphised melon on the back of the van in front, as the windscreen wipers scudded angrily across the glass. Even with music from the radio and several hands of cards, the time had dawdled, and Pietr's consistent wins had become tiresome. Twenty-one was a game she had played frequently with Alaam, yet still she seemed to draw high. Between rounds Pietr had quickly cleared the cards and re-dealt, leading her to suspect they were marked.

When, finally, the melon disappeared, she saw the austere gatehouse, formal and square, a strip of window eyes surveying the lines. Inside black shadows took papers from reaching hands through tiny hatches. A young guard was stationed outside. Like the soldier on the bridge, he cradled a rifle, pristine and shining, probably never fired. As they drew level, a gnarled, middle-aged agent mumbled to Vasil through the hatch. She imagined Alaam sitting in the back of this Skoda, anxiously thumbing cards as the guard peered in. How closely did the image in her passport match her face? Briefly she raised her head as his eyes flicked from her picture to her face, checked the visa. In her pocket, against her thigh, she felt the shape of the Makarov. How quickly could she remove it and put a bullet in that pock-marked face? Then, the papers were returned and a hand waved them forward. A car carrying three Bulgarian nationals drew little attention, especially when it reeked so unpleasantly of spiced sausage and sweat.

Vasil turned briefly. "We travel regularly to Haskovo to work. These guards are used to me and my nieces and nephews crossing the border. And tonight, someone else comes back in your place, so he will be happy."

Others were not so lucky. Further along the border plaza, trucks were being dismantled, their human cargo lined dejectedly against a wall, metres from Europe. For Satya, they emphasised the uncertainty of her future. When the car reached Sofia, she would be on her own. The Skoda would turn around and Vasil and Pietr would be gone forever.

Shortly after, Pietr had been allowed to drive, leaving Satya alone in the back seat to her thoughts. Outside, the terrain had subtly changed, the brown had given way to lush greenery, the dust to dirt, the faces in the cars, more light-skinned. In a road atlas from the seat pocket, she had attempted to trace the route, to make sense of the Cyrillic letters but soon car sickness had urged her to take a nap. When she awoke, it was to the chaotic wide, grey boulevards of Sofia.

Now, Sofia Central was draped in a mattress of grey cloud. It was a 1970s concrete monstrosity, a great theatre to locomotion renovated with an ideal of post-communist modernity which had fallen short. As the navy blue Skoda pulled up at the end of the taxi rank, parking perpendicular to the main building, Satya realised that she had made it to Europe. The claustrophobic feeder road, between the station and the garish canopies of the Central Station monument, hung with humidity and people blustered about with raincoats and umbrellas. Everywhere Satya looked, there were uniformed men with sharp eyes and side arms. She gazed up at the immense flat canopy roof, held aloft by x-shaped pillars, draining every scintilla of light from the drab sky. The pillars reminded her of weight lifters, legs apart holding the canopy over their heads, sweating and straining under the weight, ensuring everyone could see the name. Above the door a great skeletal clock ensured everyone could see the time. There was no excuse for lateness or getting lost. A far cry from the turn-of-the-century faded grandeur of Aleppo Grand, this was a brash nod to European values, and modernism after the demise of Zhivkov and communism.

Opening the glovebox, delving behind the lining, Vasil retrieved an envelope, exchanging it with the papers in Satya's hand.

"From now on, you travel under your own name. Many people travel this route so you will blend in. But be on your guard. Migrants are in the station. They will fill the halls and they will empty your pockets. You have tickets so you will not be seen as a migrant. Don't behave like one! There will be State Police and border checks so you must know your story. You are a student returning to Paris to spend Christmas there. It's all in the envelope. Read it thoroughly while you wait for your train."

Outside the car, a chaos of taxis and people, of rumbling luggage and perpetual roadworks, added to the disquiet she felt. Thus far there had always been a safety net. The men on the truck, Vasil and Pietr, even the old man and his wife in the damp culvert. Now, she would be on her own. Despite the horrors of Aleppo, her life had been one of sheltered innocence. She knew little of the world beyond the sanitised, filtered images from CNN and Al Jazeera. Until three days ago she had never known hunger or loneliness or fear. Now she could hardly recall anything else. "What happens when I reach Paris?"

"It's all in the envelope. Now you must go." Vasil glanced about anxiously.

Satya scanned the contents, a passport, maroon and gold, opening from the right unlike her Syrian passport, and tickets along with some notes, maybe fifty euros and a few Bulgarian *lev*. It was the first money she had seen in a month. She unfolded an A4 page, text made granular by numerous passes through a copier, Western names, times, dates swimming before her eyes, synapses straining to leap between cultures. She looked at Vasil, stern and business-like, head craned around the front seat, then at Pietr beside her. She felt she had known them forever. Was it really only 12 hours since they pulled her from the Sea of

Marmaris?

"You OK?" Pietr's expression was dour but behind, Satya saw concern. She had seen it in her mother's eyes at the school gates, her Uncle's eyes at Al Amanzel as her hair was shaved. As then, she nodded, bravado borne of fear masking her unease. It would be simple. She would find the platform and wait for the train. She would read the details in the envelope and recite them to herself. The time would pass quickly. She had made the leap from Asia to Europe, from chaos and bloodshed to culture and equality. Having come this far; the rest would be easy, wouldn't it? Gathering her things, she opened the door and stepped out into a chill wind that would herald another chapter in her life.

Chapter 25

Medway Klein Cosmetic Clinic, Northwick Park

Whetstone climbed from the driver's seat, slightly confused by what she had found as she had entered the anonymous gates across an eminently missable driveway. In fact, she had missed it once and had to double back.

Someone values their privacy.

Less than fifty yards from the road, a grand Baroque country house arrogantly looked down as she drove across the courtyard, past a few sleeping limousines and ranks of garages and through a tired archway, into what must once have been a busy stable yard, now the car park for the clinic. Medway Klein, Varsa Ruparelia's last known employer, occupied a motley arrangement of mews buildings, converted stables and other utilitarian red brick constructions clustered around the yard. It was pristine clean and packed with upmarket cars. The hall itself towered imperiously above the low buildings, overseeing things from beyond the arch. There was a general air of new money about the place. Faded gentility plastered with a thick rendering of ostentation. To her left, a smart UPVC frontage proclaimed itself the visitor's reception and she zigged and zagged through the rows of expensive horsepower to reach it.

Monaghan's speculative call to Medway Klein had secured Deborah Whetstone an appointment with Jean Challoner, the Head of HR. However, apart from confirming that Varsa had been dismissed, putting names to the initials in the diary and, after a good deal of arm twisting, providing a few addresses and phone numbers, she immediately pleaded the fifth and clammed up tighter than a pawnbroker's wallet, citing Data Protection and client confidentiality. Nothing a warrant would not fix later. Knowing when she was beaten, if only temporarily, Whetstone made her way back to reception, introduced herself to a smartly dressed woman and waited.

After a few minutes, a woman dressed in nurse's scrubs turned the corner, her gait just a little too fast for her legs, giving her a staccato rolling walk akin to controlled falling. Marion

Edmonds had been Varsa Ruparelia's supervisor. She was a slim woman, around six feet tall with unruly auburn hair which defied every attempt to tame it. Her skin was the colour of milk chocolate, perhaps a throwback to distant Eurasian origins or more likely, thought Whetstone, a slow roasting on a sun-bed somewhere in the Med. Her superficial compassionate smile flashed on and off like a Belisha beacon. She had a hurried, frantic way about her, attempting to do several things at once. It reminded Whetstone of her mother since her father's death. Her eyes were round and sympathetic as she scanned the warrant card and smiled nervously.

"Busy Day?" Whetstone broke the ice.

"Frantic, you know." Marion Edmonds looked briefly down at her hands, her face a tapestry of fleeting emotions, then she flicked on the smile. They took seats in a small, modern breakout area by a vending machine off the reception. Behind them a stream of other employees chattered and sighed as they left the building for home or a ciggie.

"Oh, you must think me rude. Would you like a cup of tea or coffee?" Whetstone waved a hand. It was a little early for distraction techniques.

"So, what do you do at the clinic?"

"I am a senior scrub nurse. I work theatre-side, assisting the surgeon. Anyway, how can I help?" Brief and to the point, non-committal and basically uninformative. Marion Edmonds Belisha smile flashed on as she sat at the counter and gave an edited version of her full attention to Whetstone.

"We're looking into the disappearance of Varsa Ruparelia. I believe you worked with her here at Medway Klein?"

"That's right. She was an administrator in OR. Part of my team. She kept the paperwork straight."

"Was?"

"Oh, yes. She left at the end of October. Have they not told you that?"

Whetstone was bemused by the response. The date precise. No hint of concern or sympathy. Eager to separate herself.

"And have you heard from her since?"

Edmonds glanced around the small space. She picked at the

quicks of her nails, anything, Whetstone surmised, to avoid eye contact. "She phoned once shortly after she left but no, I haven't seen her."

"Do you know if there was anything troubling Miss Ruparelia before she left?"

"No. I tried not to have too much to do with her." Marion leaned over the table and lowered her voice. "She wasn't particularly liked."

"In what respect?"

"To put it bluntly, she was a bit of a nosey parker. She liked to stick her nose into other people's business, listening in on conversations, you know, nothing was private with her around."

With Medway Klein being such a very private place, Whetstone doubted that Varsa's colleagues would welcome such close attention.

"And you think that got her into trouble?"

"Rumour was it got her sacked."

"How so?"

"Well, she saw things and jumped to conclusions. We were a close-knit team before she arrived but she wormed her way in, sort of divide and rule, I suppose. It got that we were afraid to say anything until we had checked she was nowhere about. At the end, most of us just avoided her."

At the end? Before she was sacked? Before she was killed?

"And this - nosiness - did it ever escalate to anything else? Threats? Blackmail?"

"Oh, yes, frequently. In her eyes, we were all jumping into bed with each other, or pilfering or fiddling expenses. Most of us just told her to bugger off and grow up. It was all very petty. Except for the nurse. That was nasty."

Whetstone looked up at Edmonds quizzically.

"Lorraine Lucas. She was a junior nurse on the wards. She was sacked back in August for stealing drugs. That was all down to Varsa. We all knew that Lorraine was supplementing her income, so to speak, but myself and my manager had taken her aside and threatened her with disciplinary action. We suggested it would not look good on her file and she stopped. Then Varsa started telling tales. A stock check showed discrepancies. When we spoke to Lorraine, she was adamant that she had not taken anything else, even happy to be supervised. But still items went missing and eventually Varsa made enough noise that it unsettled everyone and Lorraine was let go."

Marion shuffled in her seat. "The problem is that after Varsa left, most of the missing stock turned up in a cupboard. We wondered if Varsa had set Lorraine up."

"Blackmail?"

"Maybe, but I didn't hear about it."

"Varsa kept a diary. Did you know that?"

Marion's eyes dropped to her hands "Only indirectly, Sergeant. I never saw it, but it makes sense. Either that or she had a brilliant memory. A diary makes sense."

"She referred to people by initials. I wonder if you recognise any of them? For example, NS, SF, CA, LL, CS, er, ME, which I assume is you?"

Edmonds smiled and craned her head to peer at Whetstone's notebook. "NS is Nick Snowdon. Nick is a Consultant Surgeon but he also owns Medway Klein. SF probably refers to Steven Franks. I can't think of another one. He works for Chronotech and Medway Klein as a driver. The two companies share the same site. CA is Caz Albin. She is MD of Chronotech. Oh, and LL would be Lorraine Lucas, the nurse."

"And CS. Is that Connor Smith? What can you tell me about him?"

"Connor? Oh, he is a Junior Surgeon on my team. He hasn't turned in today. We have phoned his home a couple of times but he hasn't picked up."

"So, tell me more about Varsa, about the circumstances of her departure?"

"I think basically everyone got fed up of her. Too many complaints. She even went straight to the MD, Nick Snowdon. That really got everyone's back up. She thought she knew everybody's secrets and that made us all uncomfortable but it made us more uncomfortable that she was spreading them about."

"There were entries about you and Steven Franks." In for a penny, Whetstone drew an inference from the initials on her list and tossed it in like a steaming turd. According to Varsa, Edmonds had been cosying up to several of her male colleagues, including *SF* - Steven Franks. Edmonds visibly flinched, her eyes widened to the size of marbles and she looked about her, alarmed. Behind her, a TV looped BBC news to no-one. They were not being overheard. Now she was self-consciously twisting her wedding ring and manufacturing her most authentic wounded expression.

"How many times!" she rasped in an anxious half-whisper. "There is nothing going on between me and Steven. We are just work colleagues. We car-share, that's all." Her tone was subdued yet insistent, maybe an eagerness to protest too much.

Whetstone studied the terrified expression on Marion's face, inclined to believe her. She thought back to the Spring when she and Keith *the Uniform* had met. He had been dating a WPC in Traffic, or Road Management as they now called it. Their relationship had soon become public and Whetstone had become a pariah for a month or two. She searched her own soul as to whether the pain to which she had subjected WPC Morris had been worth the happiness she had stolen from her. But in her case, the storm had passed. Now, barely a squall blew up when she ventured onto the first floor.

"Is that what you told Varsa?"

"Well, yes. She started spouting about no smoke without fire and I told her to do one. Apparently, she had seen me and Steven embrace once. Well you do, don't you when you've known someone a while? It doesn't mean you want to jump into bed. It's just a casual friendship." Marion picked up some flyers from the counter top and distractedly scanned each one. "Varsa made it dirty, you know, sordid, like we were shagging each other's brains out. It's not like that, honestly. She had a vivid imagination."

Maybe no fire but a faint whiff of burning. "So what happened?"

"I don't know. I mentioned it to Steven, who laughed it off. He said he would deal with it."

One gains from a casual friendship; one loses from an affair, thought Whetstone. "And did he? Deal with it?"

"I don't know. Varsa left and it blew over. When push comes

to shove, though, you can't go around threatening people."

Whetstone raised he eyebrows, From salacious gossip to threats in a single unchoreographed leap. "Was she threatening you?" She watched Marion's face, the eyes. Construction or memory? When asked about her job, Marion had recalled memories, eyes flicking right. Now they very definitely flicked left. Construction.

"Not threatening as such. Just being obnoxious."

"What sort of a man is Steven? When he said he would deal with it, do you think he would take matters into his own hands?"

"He may have spoken to her, warned her off, or had a word with Snowdon. As well as being MD, he's the Consultant surgeon on our project, Delta, so ultimately, if Nick sacked her, Steven may have been partly responsible. Either way she left so the problem resolved itself."

"Delta?" Whetstone recalled the word from the diary.

"Oh, It's one of Medway Klein's research projects. It's what my team are working on. It's quite important and Nick stands no messing."

"Who else is in the team, Marion?"

Well, as I say, Nick is the surgeon, I am the scrub nurse, Connor Smith is the Junior Surgeon and we draft in a couple of other OR staff when required.

"So, do you and Steven Franks share a lift home every night?"

Marion again scanned the room, her voice low and conspiratorial. "Not anymore. Varsa saw to that. Steven's wife came to the clinic and warned me off. I don't need that kind of trouble with a teenage daughter and all."

"What can you tell me about Steven and Connor Smith, Marion?"

Marion looked up into middle distance and smiled to herself. "Those two are as thick as thieves. I think secretly Connor has a bit of a man crush on Steven. Seems to follow him everywhere. Steven just plays along. To him Connor is just an irritating puppy."

"And Varsa? We've heard she might have been causing trouble for Connor Smith too?"

"Varsa tried it on with everybody. Steven is in and out a lot. She had been taking a keen interest in his comings and goings and Connor told her to leave off. It's just not right to be telling tales on your colleagues. We've all got to work here, after all."

"And Steven Franks? Was he up to something, do you think?"

"Of course not! Like I said, Varsa read more into a situation that was actually there. Steven used to say she needed a good seeing-to but that he wouldn't touch her with someone else's." Marion allowed herself a short, disingenuous titter, very much, Whetstone thought, for her benefit.

"She wrote a lot about Steven in her diary. Tracking his movements, recording details of procedures and devices."

"Like I said, she read more into a situation that was actually there." There was a hint of nervousness in Marion Edmonds voice now, her feet were fidgeting below the table, a bounce in her heel. Important projects, tables of figures. Whetstone was still hearing edited highlights.

"But if Steven and Connor both thought she needed warning off..."

Marion shrugged. "I suppose. Steven just wanted Varsa to stay out of his business. With Connor in the OR where she worked, he got him to tell her as much."

"And did she stay out of his business?"

"I doubt it. That wasn't like Varsa. You asked me what sort of a man Steven is? Well, yes, he definitely would take matters into his own hands, and I know he did."

Whetstone paused her pen and looked at Marion.

"A few days before she left, I was going home. Steven usually picked me up in the supermarket car park, so I have to walk through the Hall grounds and out through the back gate. Strictly speaking it's not allowed but...well. Anyway, I heard raised voices. Usually the Hall courtyard is empty, but it was Steven and Varsa standing by his car. They were arguing about something. Steven sounded like he was reading the riot act to her and she was having none of it. He can be quite overwhelming when wants to be so I thought I would step in but they saw me and stopped. Varsa hurried off and Steven told me to mind my own business and go and wait by the car. He was quite abrupt, which is unusual but I put it down to Varsa being nosey again."

"Do you think Steven hit her?"

"Well, she had been crying. Steven had his hands on her arms, you know, grasping her." Marion raised her hands and gripped imaginary biceps. "He does have a quick temper. I don't know if he would hit a lady, but then, Varsa was no lady, if you know what I mean. He's never hit me." Marion flicked a nervous smile and Whetstone could not help thinking that now the car shares were over, Steven Franks character was being dragged through the dirt rather too enthusiastically.

"And Connor? Could he be violent?"

"Doubtful. He is all noise, a jack-the-lad. He may have tried it on with Varsa, give her one to keep her quiet, if you'll pardon my crudeness. He even tried to chat me up once. I just gave him a withering look and he ran off with his tail between his legs. He's just a boy, really."

Marion paused for a moment, casting an eye over the counter top, rearranging condiments in a straw carrier. There was something she needed to say but was afraid to do so. Eventually she continued. "I think Steven and Connor fell out too, though. Last Friday evening, I took the shortcut to the supermarket again. This time Steven and Connor were having a set-to."

"Could you hear what they were saying?"

Marion puffed and shook her head. "No fear! This time I left them to it." She smoothed out her tunic top across her knees and looked out at the rain-glossed car park. "So what do you think happened to Varsa, Sergeant?"

"We are keeping an open mind. We are concerned she may have come to some harm."

Marion raised a hand to her mouth. She thought about speaking but decided against it.

Whetstone pressed. "If you have information which we should know about then tell me now. It will save a lot of time later. You may not have liked her, Marion, but don't you think you owe her the truth?"

"I don't know. It was nothing." Marion paused and bit the quick on her thumb."

"It's never nothing when a colleague disappears, is it Marion?"

"When Steven said he would sort it with Varsa, there was more to it. He told me to leave well alone."

"What do you think he meant by that?"

"I don't know."

"Was it about the units? About the farm?" Whetstone recalled the table in Varsa's diary. She baited a hook and cast it, allowing the ripples to settle as Marion sized it up and swam away.

"I have no idea what it was about, honestly." But the eyes had flicked right. Memory. There was another layer of truth beneath this superficial veneer.

Ten minutes later, Whetstone had said her goodbyes and reassured Marion Edmonds that their chat would remain confidential as long enquiries allowed. She needed to speak to Nick Snowdon but that could wait. Smith would also need to be found. However, now Franks' name was floating to the top of a short list of suspects.

Chapter 26

DC Mike Corby dialled Whetstone's number, blowing out his cheeks wearily. Arthur Street in Wembley was an endless line of run-down terraces, just outside the Olympic park regeneration zone. Lorraine Lucas had been dressed in her pyjamas and dressing gown despite the hour. Short, plump and blotchy, around forty-five, her roots needed the attention of a good hairdresser, her cleavage needed a couple of acres of fabric. Inside, the TV was on and the air hung with tobacco smoke and weed. There was a disconcerting film of grubbiness which clung to everything including the inside of his nostrils. She offered him tea which he politely refused for fear of catching something.

Once the television was off, and she had lit up another smoke, Corby had asked Lucas about Varsa Ruparelia. She returned the verbal equivalent of projectile diarrhoea. Lucas held a grudge the size of the stadium visible above the houses outside. Sorting the facts from the rhetoric and discarding the copious expletives, Corby found that she had been out of work since August and clearly blamed Varsa for her dismissal and reduced circumstances.

"So, were her allegations false?" Immediately Corby regretted the question.

"You're bloody naïve for a copper. Act your age! Nursing is a hard job and pays bugger all. Even this shit-tip is expensive. Of course I was on the take - at first. I mean a few tablets here and there, packs of towels and toilet rolls. They didn't miss 'em. I never took anything dangerous, mind. Anyway, I cornered her in the toilets. I didn't fall with the last rain shower. I gave the vicious cow a slap and told her to piss off! The way she went snivelling off, I thought that would be the end of it. Then, what does she do? She goes squealing to management and I am called in to Challoner's office and Marion Edmonds was there with her pretty-perfect northern charm telling me that I have been thieving. There was no point denying it so I held my hands up. I got a warning and I stopped."

"And did you actually stop?"

She cast a hand about the room. "I mean it might not be much, love, but at the end of the day... Yes, I stopped. Just wasn't worth the risk of losing my job and, now my card had been marked, they would be watching me even when I went for a dump. Anyway, it all goes quiet, Varsa starts avoiding me, taking a different corridor when she sees me, picking on someone else for a while. Then suddenly I am back in the office and given my P45."

Lucas paused and dragged a lungful from her cigarette. "It wouldn't be so bad but I hadn't taken so much as a paperclip since they gave me that warning. I told that stuck-up cow in HR but they weren't listening. Bloody Varsa again, poisonous bitch!"

Corby paused. His eyes flicked to the ashtray, a mountain of sodden filter tips and grey ash and mused that this was probably the extent of Lucas' life. After a dismissal for theft, references would be sparse.

"So why do you think Miss Ruparelia picked on you?"

"Easy target, love. Predators always go for the stragglers. She knew I needed the job, liked a little toke now and again."

"Did she ever try to blackmail you?"

"Oh, you are sweet and innocent, aren't you, son. Does mommy still cut your crusts off your soldiers?" Then her voice hardened. "Of course she did. Why else do you think I was back in that office? Because I wouldn't pay her. She caught me in the staff room skinning up, making some for my tin and must have though all her birthdays had come at once. Next thing I know she's after a pony a week, which of course I didn't pay. There was only thirty or forty in it for me. Bastard deserves everything she gets."

Back outside, Corby swallowed lungfuls of the stiff chill afternoon. The thick atmosphere of the house had stuck to his skin, clogging his pores and binding the grease on his fingers into a grimy film. The odour of sweat and smoke and cheap perfume clung to his sleeve as he pulled his phone to his ear.

What would he tell Whetstone? Was Lucas capable of killing a blackmailer? One paycheque away from the gutter and now without that cheque. He had seen people kill for a lot less. Killing was easy and a habit just made it easier.

Chapter 27

Sofia Central Station, Sofia, Bulgaria, 4:00pm, Tuesday

As her eyes became accustomed, Satya's senses were assaulted by the noise and bustle inside the massive hall. The space echoed to the sounds of tannoys and the subliminal roar of air conditioning motors and passing conversation. Momentarily disoriented, she began to realise how *foreign* everything about her was. White, European faces, hair auburn, reds and blondes, long and flowing, Cyrillic text, distant and alien. Yet, paradoxically, she blended perfectly thanks to Maria and the clothes from the secret room. A frieze ran the full length of the hall, maybe two hundred feet, locomotive wheels and tracks and points, wheels turning, drawing her nearer to the UK.

She imagined Alaam entering this place. He would have adopted a swagger, observed the people around him, mimicking their posture. Alaam had no fear. Nor would she have! She threw back her shoulders and strode purposefully, wishing she had a mobile clamped to her ear like everyone else. The boards flashed and she realised she didn't know the word for departures. She shrugged as she had seen so many Europeans do and found an empty seat, glancing up each time the illuminated letters ran down the board like orange raindrops down a window. At least she could read the clock. 16:00.

She checked the time of her train. 23:00. There were hours to kill. She peered at the faces about her. In Aleppo, people kept to themselves, outsiders were to be avoided, explosive vests too easy to conceal. Now she was the outsider. Suddenly, she felt totally alone and self-conscious. She imagined Vasil and Pietr, laughing and counting their cash as they returned to Şarköy, job done.

Searching the overhead signs, spotting the universal symbols of a man and a woman, she sought out the toilets and an empty cubicle. Gingerly lowering the filthy lid over the bowl, she took out the envelope Vasil had given her. The passport photograph, taken by the Imam, showed a wide-eyed girl, hair cropped and uncomfortable. She thrust the book into her pocket. She scanned the array of tickets and the computer printed itinerary. Almost three days on trains, changing at Vidin, Budapest, Zurich, Basel and Strasbourg. Her head swam with times and dates, strange names. Then she found the small book of postcards and photos, familiar, grounding her. Soon she would have a new picture for her book. She and Alaam beside the bronze lions in Trafalgar Square waving to the camera. All this would soon be a memory. Just a few more days.

And then there was Paris. Would she even see the streets, the Eiffel Tower, the Champs-Elysées, fleeting glimpses from the windows of the train?

Overwhelmed, she longed to stay in the cubicle forever. Her entire universe in this tiny space, the melamine walls, the grubby porcelain bowl and broken seat. Tangible, solid. She leaned against the partition and closed her eyes.

Allah, I am lost. I am lost to my family. I am lost to my home and I am lost to you. I know I have been a wicked girl, that I have stolen, that I have taken a life. I know I must be punished for my crimes, but is not this banishment enough? Please help me. Please show me the way.

But in the flickering neon, it was not Allah but her father who came to her, benevolent and smiling, so real she could almost touch him, mouthing words he had used many times when she was younger and struggling with the incomprehensible teachings of the Quran or fathomless complexities of her homework.

Satya, life is not a single long journey but many short ones. Do not hope for where you will be at the end, for then it is over. Instead look towards the next trip and the experiences it will bring. The journey will be over before you know and your memories will be the treasures you gathered along the way.

For now, the person that was Satya Meheb would retreat behind the migrant beast who was travelling West. An anonymous tourist, the faceless traveller. She opened the folded paper and read the details of her trip to Vidin. R7626 leaving at 23:00. That was all she needed. She would find the information desk and they would point her to the platform. She would use money to buy food and she would sit on the platform and wait for her train.

There would be no going back.

Chapter 28

Northolt, West London

Steven Franks testily twisted the heater knob completely into the red. The fan was about as strong as a nun's fart and his feet were leaden. As usual the Target Roundabout was rammed back along Western Avenue with the sheer weight of traffic, as *Capital FM* put it. He was going nowhere for a while. Scrabbling around in the dashboard cubby, he checked his phone. Now it carried a small white 5. They knew this pile of shit didn't have Bluetooth. Why did they keep texting him? Checking for police cars, he clicked the icon with his thumb.

He had joined Chronotech as a driver because it was a piss-easy job for a good salary. Moving stuff from here to there, managing his work, managing his time. As long as he kept people sweet - *job done.* Same old, same old but completely in control. Franks loved that he could do things his way and in his own time, with no-one breathing down his neck.

So why were there five texts now?

A horn sounded behind and he edged up to the car in front before peeking at the messages.

Connor Smith? What did that knobhead want? And what was so damn important it needed all these texts anyway?

Smith had always been a pain in the arse. Most of the people at Chronotech were anally retentive geeks, brash opinionated dickheads or just weird oddballs. He could handle them, same old same old. The surgeons were definitely the weirdest. They never smiled or made eye contact, even when speaking directly to him. They were all bloody psychopaths; how else could they hack and slice at people and enjoy it?

Then there were the nurses. Such was the turnover he couldn't keep up. Christ, some of them were fit, and up for it too. There was always a side room and an eager nymphet who needed bringing on. It was the only perk worth having and he had had a few. Lately, however, he had allowed his promiscuity to become somewhat messy, breaking the cardinal rule of infidelity - crapping on one's own doorstep. He had allowed his working relationship with Caz Albin to stray over the line. An affair with one's, admittedly stunning, boss was never a good thing but it would always spell trouble in the long run. Their affair had started after a works party the previous year. It had taken very little for him and Caz to become lovers. She liked a bit of rough and he liked to provide it. Soon, he was working extra travelling time into his schedule to be with her, more elaborate lies to tell Jill, his wife. Even now, he could see her willowy silhouette profiled in the doorway of the ensuite as he lay in her bed, looking forward to the energetic night ahead.

The horn beeped again. Keeping an eye on the rear of the car in front, annoyed that his reverie had been disturbed, Franks opened the first text.

There's been an accident, Steve. Don't worry. It's sorted. Connor.

Accident? What type of accident? Franks applied the brakes rather too sharply, sensing the crawling car in front slow down. Briefly looking up he tutted and gesticulated. Then his eyes dropped back to the texts.

Steve. There has been a crash. Varsa Ruparelia. Please call.

Edging up the slip road, Steve grunted. Speaking of knobheads, Varsa Ruparelia was a prime example. Nosey and spiteful, she had soon latched onto his proclivity for big breasts in tight scrubs. The shrivelled-up spinster was simply jealous. One good session would have sorted her out, but not from him. She was strictly minor league. Some other schmuck could have that dubious pleasure. Still she had found out about him and Caz, and that had needed sorting.

Steve. Help me. They are coming after me. I am going to hide out. You got me into this. You had better get me out.

Little prick. Just who did he think he was talking to? Gotten him into what? The clinic was a cushy number as long as everyone towed the company line. Whatever trouble that dickhead thought he was in, he would have to sort it out himself. Since the first time they had met, that moron had been toadying up to him. *Hey Steve, how's it going. Hey Steve, love the car. When I become a consultant...* The tosser couldn't manage a piss without spraying his fingers. Franks clicked open the final text.

Help me Steve

But now that did sound alarming. Furrowing his brow, Franks reached for a water bottle and took a slug. Bemused, he closed the text conversation and surreptitiously glanced at the other number. His phone had not recognised it, nor had he, but he knew who it would be. The TV was full of dramas where unregistered pay-as-you-go mobiles - *burner phones* - were used but this was one of the few times they had resorted to using them. Then only for texts, never calls or voicemails.

It was the same message as before: *Keep a low profile. Police.*

What, with Varsa coming between him and Caz, Jill being her usual spiteful self, with Connor Smith being unable to look after himself, *and* dealing with the farm, this was all starting to get out of hand.

Chapter 29

Moor Park, 5:00pm, Tuesday

It would be difficult to determine whether the Moor Park estate was an outlying district of Rickmansworth or even Watford, or whether it was a small residential town in its own right. It lay astride the rail route which the Great Western had driven through the countryside in the nineteenth century, and that the Metropolitan line had followed early in the twentieth. However, it was not until 1910 that the line was graced with a station, a halt called Sandy Lodge after the inland links golf course to the East of the line. By the Twenties, the popularity of a good walk spoiled had spawned another larger course in the grounds of the ancient Manor of More, or Moor Park, soon after usurping the name of the station, much to the annoyance of its neighbour. Along with Rickmansworth Golf Club in the Forties, the triumvirate enclosed an area around the rail track which soon became prime commuter belt but little else. The town itself, formal lines of Twenties and Thirties semi-detached houses, tree-lined and gentile, kept a somnolent watch on the line, over a copy of the Sunday Times and an aromatic Earl Grey.

The Bryson's house, one of those original semis, immaculately kept and eye-wateringly expensive, sat on the corner of Baldwin Avenue, a brisk walk from the Underground. Daley pulled up outside, marvelling as always over how moderate salaries can finance astronomical mortgages. On the drive, an aged Mondeo and even more aged Fiesta, perhaps alluded to how. Robbing Peter to pay Paul. Malcolm Bryson was a gas fitter, Irene Bryson a supervisor in a nearby call centre.

The front room was for best; a TV played through the wall from the living room but there wasn't one in this room, just highly polished deep oak furniture and battalions of neatly arranged ornaments. A glass cabinet held a shelf of gleaming cups and trophies as well as a number of sporting medals on brightly coloured ribbons. Behind them sat photos of a fit youth beaming from beneath a mop of brown hair.

"Are all these Andy's?" Daley had seen the photos on his last visit and needed an ice breaker.

"Andrew, yes," corrected Malcom Bryson. "He was keen on football when he was younger. There was talk of him being signed for the Watford Player Development programme." The man in the doorway was around 50 years old, slim, his hair was grey and receding, his skin almost as grey with drawn cheeks and heavy eyes. A cigarette quivered between two fingers.

"What happened, if you don't mind me asking?"

Bryson shrugged. "Motorbikes, Inspector, or rather falling off one. Just before his nineteenth birthday. Pelvis and right leg. Anyway, what can I do for you?" Malcolm cast Daley a business-like smile and waved towards one of the chairs.

"As I said on the phone, there are some details about his case that I am looking more deeply into. You are aware there have been other disappearances.

"Karen Sherwood and Diane Fletcher." Bryson nodded, drew on the cigarette, and tapped off a slug into an ashtray. "Yes, the other policewoman mentioned them. Then there was that boy in the woods a few weeks back." Bryson looked down at Daley's card. He raised his eyebrows. "Homicide? So, you are treating the disappearances as murder?"

"Not at present, sir. Keeping an open mind at this stage. I am following up DI Somerville's investigations. A fresh pair of eyes, that's all."

"Ah. Fair enough."

There was no evidence that the boy was dead. Still, after almost two months, it could be only one of three things. Either he did not want to be found, they had not looked in the right place or he was dead. The door opened. and Irene Bryson entered with a tray of tea and biscuits. Daley smiled appreciatively and watched as she placed the tray very deliberately onto a lace table cloth on the occasional table. There was a pause and Daley got the feeling she was about to speak, but held her tongue. She sat herself in a second easy chair beside her husband.

"I must stress that at this stage we are not connecting Andrew's disappearance with that of anyone else. I just want to build up a more complete picture of your son if I may. By understanding more about him, we may be able to find out what was in his mind at the time of his disappearance, maybe even where he has gone. So, tell me about Andrew."

Mr Bryson sat back, allowing his wife to speak. Mrs Bryson shuffled in her chair. "Well, Inspector, he was still very much a single lad. He liked to go out with his mates. Liked his football."

"Was there anything troubling him? His job, maybe?"

"Obviously, it's not the job he wanted but he never complained." Andrew Bryson worked in a local supermarket. He had worked his way up to Assistant Manager. Light years from league football but a longer, if less lucrative, career path with little potential for injury.

"What about his life generally?"

"Not especially. He had his moments, like anyone. It's not easy going to University, being independent and then coming home and trying to fit back in. People change when they go away."

"Which University was that, Mrs Bryson?"

"Keele," interjected Mr Bryson. "He attended Keele." Mrs Bryson looked at her husband before turning her eyes to her lap. A pecking order, thought Daley.

"And when did he graduate?" Daley nodded towards another of the photos in the cabinet.

"Around five years ago. Politics and Sociology. Not the most employable degree. I did warn him..."

"He doesn't seem to have done too badly. Assistant Manager at 26."

"Shop-work, Inspector. We always hoped for more, but he seemed to be happy nevertheless. He was saving for a deposit. He wanted his own place by the time he was thirty. Of course, it was different in our day. House prices today are stupid."

Daley had no idea what an Assistant Manager of a supermarket would earn but he guessed that with an overtime allowance it would top £25,000. Not the largest of salaries but living at home was probably a shrewd move if he needed a deposit in the next four years.

"Is he popular? Does he have many friends?"

"Yes, Inspector." Irene Bryson felt comfortable enough to

contribute. "He was a very popular lad. He spent a lot of time out on the bike with his mates. He enjoyed going into town and, of course, there was the football. He was a Fulham fan. He went to all their home games. I suppose he still wanted to be involved in some way."

During his divorce, Daley had been cajoled by a colleague from Hendon into buying a season ticket for Fulham FC and, together they had learned the truth of the phrase *the other man's grass may be greener, but he still has the headache of cutting it.* The average Premiership season was an allegory for life in general, with massive highs and crashing lows and an awful lot of humdrum. There was unfulfilled promise and incredible frustrations and the feeling that all of the hard work and money put in had amounted to nothing.

Craven Cottage had seen the direst performance in living memory, he had learned a whole thesaurus of Anglo-Saxon adjectives but the terrace camaraderie had given him something worse to focus on than his own life. Maybe it was the same for Andrew Bryson? Fulham had hovered around the middle of the Premiership table, doing just enough to keep from dropping but not quite enough to hit the big time. Just enough talent to succeed. That summarised how Daley felt right now. Perhaps Andrew felt the same?

"What about girlfriends? Is there anyone serious?"

"No! Andrew was too busy playing the field!" Malcolm Bryson threw Daley his best jack-the-lad smile. "Sometimes it was difficult remembering the name of the current one, eh, Irene?"

Irene Bryson tutted at her husband's impropriety. "Ignore Malcolm. He's just jealous. We married young, Inspector."

Daley smiled obligingly. "Would it be possible to take a look at his room?"

Irene Bryson fidgeted and rose from the chair, taking Daley's cup despite it still being half full. "Malcolm will take you up. I have things to do." She cleared up the things and shuffled distractedly out to the kitchen. Daley followed Malcolm Bryson up the stairs, where he paused and indicated a plain white door, like all the rest, closed, clean and tidy, orderly and neat. "That is Andrew's room."

Pushing open the door, Daley smelt fresh paint, new carpets. Bedrooms smelt of trainers and sweat, colognes and scents but this room was empty, devoid of life. The walls were magnolia, posters and pictures gone, the carpet a neutral beige. The light from the window created the only decoration in the otherwise bare room, cold and soulless. Puzzled, he turned to Bryson.

"Was this how he left it?"

"No, we have redecorated. It upset Irene. Andrew's things are in the wardrobe."

Daley was confused. The maternal bond was often so strong that a child's room would remain untouched for years; even an adult child who had left would have a place to return to. Yet this room had been sanitised, even made ready for taking in house-guests.

Idly, Daley opened the wardrobe and thumbed through the racks.

"So, did Andrew often stay out late?"

"Most Fridays. Those men at the supermarket. They were the wrong crowd. He could do so much better."

"Ah, but he's a lad, surely. Plenty of time for growing up."

"He was 26, Inspector. By his age, Irene and I were married and he was on the way." As he watched Daley rifle through the few remaining possessions of his missing son, Bryson's eyes darted about. Daley felt as if he were intruding, that moving a single item was an act of vandalism.

"At least he kept his room tidy."

"Andrew? No. He was forever leaving stuff about the house. I don't know how many times we told him."

"Tidy now though."

Bryson nodded, leaning past Daley to tuck a shirt sleeve into the wardrobe, pressing the door shut.

Opening a drawer on the dressing table, Daley looked through a few old match tickets and programmes, noted the times and dates. He recalled a few games he himself had endured.

"Still, he loved *The Whites*."

"Football was all he ever thought of. He needed to move on with his life, settle down, get a proper job."

Before closing the door, Daley took one last look around and felt a chill. For Karen Sherwood's husband, Diane Fletcher's flatmates, so certain were they that the missing would return, everyday life had continued around them, as if they were not dead but taking a nap. Yet the grief was still tangible.

Here there was nothing.

Descending the stairs, Bryson stopped. "Let me show you something, Inspector." Opening a door in the hallway, he switched on a light. Daley immediately recognised the Honda CBR900RR standing in the middle of the garage. In his teens, he had dreamt of owning one but his father had pushed him instead towards cars. More difficult to fall off four wheels.

"He kept it well." The bike was immaculate, neon-flecked and dust-free.

"Andrew, no! He was too busy to look after the bike. I had to fix it after the accident. Forks were a mess. After that, he never maintained it. That was all down to me. I have stripped and rebuilt it. New exhausts. Top end rebuilt. A couple of new tyres. It has new discs and pads. Running better now than when it was new."

Daley studied the garage. Whitewashed walls and the floor sealed with maroon paint. Along the back wall, an empty bench and above it, tools inside forensic outlines were pinned to a sheet of perforated hardboard. Spanners hung in order. There were no oil stains, no rags or spare parts. This was not a garage. This was a shrine.

On his trip home, Daley thought about the Brysons. They disturbed him. Their grim acceptance that, after only two months, their son would not return. The swiftness with which he had been erased from the house. He though back to his own parents' house in East Ham. Eventually his father had been consigned to the glass cabinet in the wall unit; a few photos, a pocket watch on a stand, yet he was talked about every day. His mother said hello to her dead husband each morning and goodnight each evening. Did the Brysons talk to their son this way?

Chapter 30

Southall, London

Fuchsia Close, where Connor Smith lived, was a tired *cul de sac* not a million miles away from the site of the crash. At 6:00pm the road heaved with parked cars, so Whetstone and Corby approached on foot. Number 9 was in a row of five town houses. Red brick and relatively modern with a small utilitarian fence surrounding an uncared-for thatch of lawn and an empty block paved drive. Whetstone gripped her fingers around her warrant card, as Corby pressed a finger to the bell and listened as a weak chirrup sounded on the other side. After a few seconds, he pressed it a second time. Whetstone tutted and crossed to the front window. Peering through the nets, she could see no sign of life. DC Corby shrugged and crouched to the letterbox.

"Hello! Mr...Oh shit!" reeling backwards, Corby felt his eyes prickle and brought the back of his hand up to his nose. "Sniff that gov. Remind you of anything?"

Whetstone dropped down and lifted the flap. She was immediately hit by the acrid stench of bleach and peroxide. "Get onto base. Get a forensic team out here. I want this place examined now."

Corby puffed his cheeks and found his mobile. Here we go again!

Chapter 31

The armchair faced the television, not Daley's preferred place. That was the sofa next to the occasional table and the battery of remotes but today had not been about what he preferred. On his lap, his mobile hopped like a cricket, Whetstone's number lit large. He let it ring. They knew where to find him. Barely 6:00pm, the street outside was black and the streetlights cast amber rectangles across the chimney breast, empty, skewed and incomplete, like his inglorious return to Lambourne Road.

Was it naïve to assume he could simply place his backside into his chair and everything would be the same? Hell, even his chair had been fiddled with. Still, as senior officer in the team room, he had expected better than a folder full of missing persons, a pat on the head and *go play nice*. Aside from two words with Allenby, he had been left to his own devices all day. A new dynamic had developed. Corby had changed from the slightly effete newbie to a confident detective, Monaghan had assumed more of a lead role within the team room and Whetstone had become the Inspector, if not in rank. Daley had even noticed changes in Steve Taylor although these were subtler.

And he could take credit for none of it.

Of course, the more he delved, the stranger the mispers case became. Seemingly random but subtly similar. Late night Tube rides, mysterious white vans, all within a five-mile radius. Or was his atrophied mind seeking a link? How did the dog fit in? Drugged and killed. Why leave potentially damning forensic evidence?

Then there was the *Hand in the Van*. Varsa Ruparelia. A severed hand, probably whilst she was alive. A killer on the loose and he was watching flies on the wallpaper, excluded. Was Allenby in on this? Had this morning's meeting been simply a platitude? Would he ever find a way back into the team, a way back onto the case?

Would he ever find himself again?

In his dark living room, he could hear the slow steady pulse, a distant rap behind the white noise of the space, lurking in the swamp of the night; the monster prowled and waited for sleep. He could feel the air washing into his lungs and sighing back out. The job was slipping away. His life was slipping away.

As he stared, the pattern on the wall blurred, sparking red and blue, pulsing and exploding in the blackness. The thudding came closer, gaining in momentum, ever deeper, the beat increasing. He could feel the colossal weight of iron and steel bearing down on him from behind. The air rushed into his lungs and cascaded back out as the thump of his heart turned into the mechanical pounding of the pistons and he screwed up his eyes as the colours exploded and a howl echoed across the emptiness between the walls.

Then it was quiet.

He was hyperventilating, cold and clammy. A familiar pain behind his eyes, his shoulder began to ache. With shaking hands, he reached for a pack of Tramadol, washing two down with the warm, stale water that had been there since morning. Across the wall, rectangles of white pulsed large then shrunk to nothing as a car disappeared unseen into the night. Gradually, his breath slowed and the room embraced him, cosseted him, kept him safe from the monster.

This was stupid. He knew it was. A grown man afraid of the dark? He had to get a grip and stop his imagination running amok. He flicked on the TV. Colours burning bright. He needed to dispel the image etched onto his mind, the twin orange eyes of the monster, the explosion of red and the blackness. The deep, lurking comatose blackness where a monster of an entirely different kind skulked and cowered and cajoled and waited for its opportunity to rent him limb from limb.

Changing channels, he found a rerun of Saturday's game between Fulham and Arsenal away at The Emirates. It was half-time, it was two apiece and some twat from the eighties who once had a curly perm and a crap record as a goalkeeper was eulogising about what it was like in his day. So, he switched over. He needed to speak to Lynne. Her line was busy. He flicked on a game show. Staring at the screen, not seeing, not caring, not thinking as the pain started to pour from his body like sand through his grasping fingers.

Chapter 32

Arthur Street, Wembley, 6:00pm, Tuesday

As the knock came at the door, Lorraine Lucas jumped from her chair, tipping an ashtray across the carpet.

It was the tally-man. Tuesday night and she didn't have the cash. He knew that. Sign on Tuesday, giro Thursday. Frantically, she switched off the light, hoping he hadn't noticed it leaching through the closed curtains. Virtually everything in the tiny terraced house was on tick, including the bloody house. Creeping across the living room, she peered along the hallway at the indistinct shape silhouetted against the frosted panes in the door. It was that weaselly man they always sent. This would be a cinch. Hancocks by name, Hancocks by nature. If she pulled down the zip on her tracksuit top a little, showed some cleavage, he would be too busy trying to get his face down those to press too hard for the money. Yet she was four weeks in arrears.

Maybe she needed to step it up a gear. Slipping out of her tracksuit bottoms, stripping off the tights, she pulled a minuscule denim skirt from behind the settee and slipped into it, wriggling her *man-crusher* hips through the waistband. Then she retrieved a small bottle of scent and spritzed her thighs and her pubis. Exhaling into her hand, she checked her breath. It would be one end or the other.

Outside an arm moved up and another knock.

Or maybe it was that policeman? The tall one with the wide smile and the boyish blush to his cheeks? The silhouette did seem taller than the tally-man. Still, showing a little flesh never hurt when dealing with men. Checking her hair in the hall mirror, taking the zip down just one extra notch, she walked to the front door and twisted the latch.

The face that greeted her was the last she would have expected, given the trouble with Varsa, with Marion and the rest.

"Oh, hello." What on Earth could it be at this time of night?

Suddenly feeling self-conscious, Lorraine drew up the zip and smoothed down the denim skirt. She smiled and stood aside, beckoning her visitor to enter. She knew his sort of women and it definitely was not her, however it was her experience that breasts and asses and thighs were all the same. Sex just as satisfying, especially in the dark, especially when it was illicit, especially when it was delivered on a plate.

The visitor eased past and she felt her nipples stiffen as a taut crotch touched her hand. This would be a doddle. A hand may be all that was necessary.

She barely saw the arm rise but she felt the scratch on her naked chest, glimpsed the white of the plunger as the liquid disappeared. Then suddenly she was floating to the ceiling, cramped against the artex and looking down as her body collapsed to the floor. The visitor closed the front door and she saw her arms being held and her body being straightened onto the carpet. Then a green fringe circled her vision, getting ever tighter and it grew like grass, obscuring her view and the second syringe hit her and the grass grew black across her eyes.

Chapter 33

Fuchsia Close, Southall

The scene inside Connor Smith's town house was strikingly similar to Varsa Ruparelia's apartment. A life interrupted. Breakfast things lay washed on the drainer, the curtains were open. Upstairs the bed was made and the bathroom immaculate. If not for the overwhelming reek of cleaning fluids, this could have been any other house where the occupants were out working.

Except now it was evening.

Around forty minutes after Corby had put in the call, Gascoigne arrived, none too happy about being pulled away from his dinner engagement, and confirmed that the similarities were even greater.

"The hall carpet has been scrubbed using bleach and hydrogen peroxide. It's still saturated, so I am guessing that an incident took place just here, inside the door, in the last twenty-four hours or so. It's localised to this area of the downstairs. The stairs are clean. However, upstairs..." Whetstone followed Gascoigne as he climbed the stairs to a pristine bathroom. "Again, using Luminol, it appears that much of the action was concentrated in the bathroom, particularly the bath but again, it has been scrupulously cleaned."

"Same as Clarence Road?" Whetstone's stomach tightened. Was there to be another van, another severed hand?

"However, I have yet to find any blood. And of course, no stray extremities. Could just be an obsessive cleaning compulsion, Deborah."

Whetstone gave a nervous half-smile. However, prosaic that may sound, Gascoigne had a habit of being right in these matters. OCD was yet to be classified illegal, yet a full forensic sweep on a clean house would make her a laughing stock.

But there was something more subliminal and it took Whetstone a few minutes of wandering around the tidy, organised upstairs rooms to discover it. No toothbrushes by the sink, no soap in the dishes and no towels on the rail. In the bedroom, a dozen or so empty hangers in the wardrobe. Varsa's apartment was the sort of lived-in untidiness that she would promise herself she would one day tidy, whereas this was a show home.

So why not the same here?

The scrubbed carpet and walls in the hallway, the pristine bathroom, the complete lack of any other evidence confused Whetstone. "Maybe Varsa was the exception rather than the rule?"

"Sorry?" Corby stopped rifling through paperwork.

"Maybe we have two kill sites, weeks apart. Varsa's killing two weeks ago, the killing here last night."

Whetstone pondered Allenby's hunch that this case and Daley's mispers were linked. Had Karen Sherwood stood in this kitchen, sharing small talk with Smith? Had Andrew Bryson enjoyed a can of Carlsberg following the match? Had Diane Fletcher's limbs been separated from her torso in the bathroom? There were a million theories for every situation.

"Perhaps Smith gets his kicks from chatting up girls and bringing them back to his bachelor pad, where he murders them. Perhaps Varsa wouldn't play ball so Mohammed went to the mountain. Maybe someone else died here and we just stumbled on it?"

"What, so Connor Smith is our killer?"

"Maybe, Mike. Two separate houses, both reeking of bleach? I'm just saying, there has to be a connection. This could be the place where he was murdered or his kill site. If Varsa was murdered a couple of weeks ago, who's blood is here?"

"If there *is* any blood, Deborah." It was Gascoigne, descending the stair with his kit bag. "Haven't found any yet."

Whetstone huffed. "Have we found a phone?" She was feeling increasingly uncomfortable with the unnatural state of orderliness. Growing up, her parents had an entirely different view of tidiness, which meant rearranging piles of junk to give the appearance of order. Since her father's death even that had stopped.

"No, nor a laptop or a tablet."

"Empty hangers, no toothbrush. Car's missing from the drive. He's not been killed. He's done a runner."

"Certainly looks that way." Maybe, having abducted and killed with impunity, the van crash changed everything. The game was up and Smith had decided to run.

"Gov? I've found a phone statement. The number matches the voicemails on Varsa's mobile...and here are the records of the calls."

"At last, something certain!" Whetstone ran her hands through her hair and puffed her cheeks. At that moment, Keith *The Uniform* would be clocking off and she was stuck in this place.

"So, we have the right Connor Smith and now it looks as though he has gone missing too."

Whetstone moved across to the small modern mantelpiece and picked her way through four or five smiling photos. A small sallow face, blond haired and blue-eyed, beamed out from several of them. At the top of a mountain he had climbed, arms around the crew on a night out, posed and formal with the family. Whetstone chose the climbing one. She handed the frame to Corby.

Digging out her mobile, she hovered over the redial key. However much she looked at a crime scene, she always worried she had missed something crucial. Something that Scott Daley would see as plain as the nose on his face. How could two places be so similar yet so different. Could a single killer be responsible for both disappearances, maybe both deaths, yet leave such different wakes behind him?

And why was there no blood?

Corby sighed. It was getting late. "I'll have a word with the neighbours. See if they saw anything unusual. See if they saw a white van."

"No, Mike. Nothing's happening here now. Get Uniform out. They can keep an eye on the place. If Smith is our killer we need to find him now."

But, as she cancelled redial and pocketed her phone, Whetstone wondered if she ever would.

Chapter 34

Chatham Woods Nature Reserve, 8:30pm, Tuesday

Sometimes, colleagues could be a real pain in the arse. Tom Phillips watched the call fade, wishing to Hell that they would all just eat shit and die. He was annoyed at himself for not being more insistent, furious for not leaving the phone at home but with Megan the way she was... The bloody Trade Fair always coincided with the only two weeks of the year that he could have Jessica all to himself. How long had he been promising to take her to Florida? Soon she would be too old and the magic would have vaporised into spots and teenage angst.

You need to be more flexible, Tom, a team player. You know how important this fortnight is to the business. We've got to be able to count on you.

Raising his wrist, he checked his *Fitbit.* Around a third of the distance covered but his time was down. That's what comes of taking calls in the evening. All work and no play...

"Baxter!" Behind him, the rescue greyhound was doing its best to expend minimal effort in keeping up. These days, 5 kilometres was a stretch and there were plenty more enticing scents than a sweating human to divert him. "Baxter, for God's sake!"

Ahead, the gate to the car park was still open, which was a bonus. The task of snaking around the post wasted valuable seconds and the alternative, an athletic leap over it, had ended in disaster before. Even more of a bonus for the owners of the white van parked there, white beams tracking through the bushes to the road. He checked the time. If they didn't get a wiggle on, the old parkie would turn up and lock the gate, marooning the vehicle until 8:00am the next morning.

"Baxter!"

No, he didn't need telling that his sales figures were down on the previous year. Following on from a bad summer, he was way off target. Everyone was suffering, so why pick on him? Why was he always in the stocks at the weekly wash-up? The global slowdown wasn't limited to sales of outdoor swimming pools. Everyone was pulling in their belts and, when the money got tight, the first ones to padlock their wallets were the rich. *That's how they sodding-well stayed rich!*

In his arm holster, his phone buzzed again. Checking the screen, he clicked the small inline buttons on his headphone cord.

"Megs, hi. What's the matter?"

When he and Suzanne had split, Tom had resigned himself to life as an absentee father. The break-up had been inevitable. He was always away and Suzanne had an eye for the men, which apparently landed on Brian, an estate agent from Ruislip. He had taken an office job in Harrow but that had been too little too late and he had moved out, taken his debts and his overwhelming guilt with him, setting up home less than three miles away. Brian had negotiated a decent price on his new house. *The bastard!*

Jessica had been eight and, for her, the break-up had been devastating. Suffering a string of illnesses, real and imaginary, she fell back at school and for a while there was talk of a court order to prevent his visits because they were too traumatic. But *Boring Brian* had stepped in there too. Now there was no reason for a court order as he rarely saw her.

"Hi, *Hon.* Call at the garage and get some pickled onions on your way back."

He had met Megan the hard way. She had reversed her Mazda into his Mercedes in a Waitrose car park. There was no serious damage but he had seized the opportunity. Getting her number, inviting her out and all that followed, had been surprisingly simple. How could a woman so absolutely gorgeous, so utterly amazing, have been missed by the entire male population of the world? Even more mystifying was that she had settled on him.

When the new baby arrived, things would be different. If he could get the Commercial Development Manager role, then the money would be less but it would be a salary, not just OTE. He could rely on his income, on his holidays. Jess would get that holiday before it was too late. He would be able to patch things up with her.

Staggering to a halt, resting his hands in his knees, Tom could feel the cramp starting to bind his thigh muscles. He needed to keep going otherwise it would be pointless, the lactic acid would pool and he would be hurting in the morning. Taking a slug of water and a deep breath, he set off again across the car park and up the path in to the woods.

"Got no money, Megs, but don't fret. I'll walk back to the garage when I'm finished."

"Awww. You are *sooo* sweet."

He knew she was teasing but, hey, he loved it when she teased. "Anyway, back in half an hour. I'll sort it then. Bye. Bye-bye-bye-bye."

Closing the call, focusing on the dark path ahead, Tom could just make out Baxter foraging in the undergrowth. He hoped to God the damn dog had not found another hedgehog. Last time the vet's bills were astronomical and with a baby on the way... Stepping up his pace, he swatted the dog on the rump.

"Come on pooch! Only another 2k and you can curl up in front of the TV."

The pains in his legs subsided. Tom found a second wind as he regulated his breath - two paces in, two paces out, two paces in... Even Baxter was keeping up a steady canter at his side. He imagined Megs lying on the sofa, 'bump' creating a hill the size of Ben Nevis atop which a brown cairn of *Maltesers* would slowly be consumed. She had a small table packed with essentials. Getting up, even for the ever more frequent wee breaks, was akin to manoeuvring an oil tanker out of port. All she could wear these days was a tracksuit. Always odd colours as the trousers were size 12 and the top size 16. She bemoaned feeling frumpy and maybe, just now she was a little, but he wasn't going to tell her. After the birth, her inner *gym-bunny* would shine through again.

Only another couple of weeks.

Two paces in, two paces out, two paces in. His legs were loosening up and the cramps had gone. A quick check of the *Fitbit.* 143bps. He must be over half way by now.

Up ahead he glimpsed a shape against the darkness. The woman seemed to be looking for something or someone. There were rarely dog walkers about at this time. Tom yanked out his 'phones and let them hang.

"Rusty! For God's sake! You are the absolute..." The woman was peering into the dense wood. "Come on now! Enough is enough!"

Slowing to a halt, Tom caught his breath as Baxter ran up and greeted the woman with that superfluous, bounding enthusiasm that only dogs had. "Problem? Tom Phillips. Can I help?"

The woman was slight, with long dark hair and a coat that was far too short for the weather. There was a look of concern in her eyes. Dark path, late night, he understood and resented it. Not every man was a pervert.

"Jill Franks. Look, my dog has run off after something and he won't come back." She scanned the sheet of black once more but apart from a patter of light rain and the wind-borne creaking of branches, there was nothing.

"It's the hedgehogs. My Baxter just can't leave them alone. Bloody nuisance at times. Or maybe a fox. If he has found a pile of their poo, he'll need a good hosing down, I'm afraid."

The woman smiled. She held up her watch but it was too dark. "Do you have the time? To be fair, I'm glad you came along. I hate being out in these woods so late, especially after what happened to that boy. Rusty!"

Tom had almost forgotten the missing boy. Though the police had not said as much, he assumed that the boy had tied the dog to a tree and pissed off, leaving it to die. Humans had a cruel streak. He twisted his wrist. "09:15. Look, he can't have gone far. Baxter, find the other dog! Go on, boy!" The greyhound looked up and cocked his head. The sounds were unfamiliar and didn't suggest a reward of food, so he sat down by the humans, assuming that was what was required.

"I'm starting to get worried. Do you think we should call the police? I don't like it out here on my own."

Tom raised his eyebrows. *So now I'm a rapist or something?* Still, she was very attractive. As she bent forward, her skirt rose. Her legs were long and shapely. Maybe that's how it started? A quiet path, no-one around. Maybe that was her game? "What for a dog? You have to be joking. Leave him. You get back home. He will turn up as soon as he sees the other dogs being walked. Is he micro-chipped?" Then he added, "Would you like me to walk you back?"

The woman turned. In the dim light from the lamps along the path, he could see her face for the first time. She was smiling. Her lips were full, slightly parted.

"That would be kind. I only live a short way away. I could make some coffee?" He imagined his hand running up those long thighs, the feel of her skin. He wondered, was there even a dog? Instantly he was ashamed.

Was she a tart? This was an odd place to pick up a trick. Maybe she was just lonely? What harm would it do to walk her home? "Look, I have to get on. Where do you live?"

"Just back across the road... Hang on. Is that him? Out there. I thought I saw something. Look."

Tom felt both annoyed and relieved in equal measure. He sighed and crouched beside the woman staring at the blanket of trees. White and green prickles filled his vision. "I can't see anything. Where?"

She stretched out her arm, pointing, and his nostrils were filled with a flowery scent. "Over there by that big tree. Look."

Still he stared. Was that a movement or just a trick of the darkness, his mind seeing what it wanted to? Baxter had edged between them and was sitting, staring obligingly in the same direction but for no reason.

There was a shuffle behind Tom that caught him off guard and briefly he was confused. The sharp stab hit his neck and a coldness spread up to his head and across his shoulder. Then he remembered the newspaper reports of the boy and his dog and his last thoughts were filled with panic.

Chapter 35

Sofia Central Station, Sofia, Bulgaria

Drawing her coat about her, Satya shivered in the razor winds that raced along the platform. Beyond the facade of the station, Sofia Central was tired and deserted, a sea of dirt, graffiti and flattened discs of dried gum. Glancing up at the clock, as she had done for three hours, she watched the numeral change. In that time, she had learned that the fall of communism had done little to improve the punctuality of Bulgarian trains.

And now the clock showed 23:00 and she had the platform to herself. From a door, a portly station employee once more made his patrol, a compassionate, avuncular smile as he passed. Her Bulgarian non-existent, his English poor, he shrugged his shoulders, the best apology he could offer for the tardiness of the service.

To her left, Satya noticed the pinpoint of light and heard the rails sing. Above her, the robotic voice of the Tannoy echoed and the porter turned on his heels and pointed at the light, nodding. Finally, this was her train and it couldn't come a moment too soon.

Earlier, leaving the toilets, seeking out the familiar double arched sign, she had devoured a Big Mac and Fries, a life-long vegetarian, sacrilege taking second place to hunger. Then, as she headed for the small store along the hall to stock up with bottled water, she had been stopped by the man.

She had noticed him before, in the burger bar, eying her from four tables away. He was slim, around her own age, wearing a heavy blue bomber jacket, black polo necked jumper and jeans. His hair was short and his wrist sported an enormous watch. He was very handsome, yet sinister, like a character from a French *film noire*. Or maybe it was that she was very naïve. The next time she had looked, he had gone.

Now he had returned.

"Zdraveĭte. Kazvam se Gregor. Kakvo e tvoeto?" *Hello. My name is Gregor. What's yours?*

He was blocking the doorway, his words incomprehensible. In any language, it was a chat-up line. She had smiled and looked away, trying to edge past, embarrassed that her face was so exposed, keeping her eyes to the ground.

"Pŭtuvate li sami? Sofiya mozhe da bŭde opasna. Mozhe bi tryabva da pŭtuvame zaedno?" *Are you travelling alone? Sofia can be a dangerous. Maybe we can travel together?*

Sighing heavily, she raised her eyes to look at him. He was smirking, lascivious and leering. Behind in the main hall, security guards were lolling about. Should she make a run for them, make them notice? Or would they just would notice her? She sighed again, replying in English:

"Sorry, I do not speak Bulgarian. My family are waiting on the platform."

The man raised his eyebrows. "You don't look English?" He chuckled to himself. "Let the family wait. We should have a drink together?"

She felt the hand rest on her arm, the fingers flexing, a tarantula crawling. Rotating her elbow, she pushed it away, feeling the imprint lingering.

"Sorry no. I have to go - my family are waiting." She lowered her head and ducked under his arm but he was too quick.

"Please. Stay and talk. Five minutes. Surely they can wait?"

"No. I have to go." She tried to sound insistent, rather than annoyed, though now it was a struggle.

"Hey, please...", he mewled. "Just for a few minutes."

"I said I have to go," she hissed. The migrant beast flexed its muscles and stared at the man angrily. The muzzle of the Makarov beneath her coat pressed into the man's ribs. Briefly, they stood deadlocked.

"Vie dvamata! Izlez ot vratata." *You two! Get out of the doorway.*

The small rotund woman barged her way through, pushing the man backwards, the Makarov digging deeper. Satya had seized her opportunity and smartly walked off, diving into the crowd. Briefly glancing behind her, she could see the man, his eyes scanning this way and that as he scoured the bobbing heads for her. She headed towards the end of the hall, where a wide stairway led to the mezzanine restaurant. Ascending quickly, she crouched down behind a low parapet wall. For a quarter of an hour, she watched him prowl the concourse, dipping in and out of doorways before finally he left through the glass entrance doors. Sinking down behind the wall, she sighed. *One short trip at a time.* How could she have been so stupid? Would she really put a bullet in his belly in the middle of the busy concourse? So much for a low profile. She had to keep a check on her migrant beast. And anyway, that accursed safety catch was on!

For the next two hours, she had feigned sleep below the parapet wall, all the time on her guard for the man's return. Cautiously, she had made her way back down the steps and followed the route that the Information desk had given her. She had showed her ticket to the corpulent porter and been the only other person on that desolate platform until the lights of the approaching train scoured the dark and wheezed open its doors.

Then, as the train pulled away towards Vidin, she had walked its length just to be sure she had not been followed.

Chapter 36

The ketamine I gave the woman was sufficient to floor a shire-horse. Lorraine Lucas' breathing had slowed. A quick pant in and rasp out every fifteen seconds. Her lungs must be like the sump of a tractor. Perhaps it would be better if they simply stopped trying.

Better for her but not for us.

There are no lights in the yard now the van headlights have been extinguished. So close to the open doors, not even the moonlight helps. We have to fumble to find the right body. The male is hard and muscular whilst Lorraine's flesh is fat and doughy as we pull her off the van and drag her to the table.

It was a risk driving to Wembley with the police so interested in the van, especially with the runner in the back, sleeping like a baby. His time will come sooner than he would wish. Taking her was easy. Taking them is always easy but Lorraine practically invited it. She was never on the list, incidental, but she had spoken to the police, encouraged their unwelcome attention. She had to go. Knocking on her door, inviting myself in, I mused how similar to the other one it had been. The only difference, the smell. Varsa's flat smelt of Eastern seasonings, of washing powder, of coffee and a lilac perfume. Lorraine's house smelt of marihuana, tobacco and body odour, thinly disguised by a cheap flowery scent. Still the revulsion I felt, we both felt, as we carried her through the back to the van, will be more than made up for by the satisfaction of the next few minutes.

With effort, we haul the obese frame onto the table and, once the doors are shut, I switch on the light. The eyes are open and I watch the pupils react as they see themselves in the mirror on the ceiling. The eyeballs start to dodge this way and that as the brain, trapped within, paces its cage. At least, someone is in there to enjoy the fun - for now.

I pinch the fat of the leg, a hard pinch, orange-peel reddening but there is no reaction. Used correctly, ketamine can incapacitate without unconsciousness. She will see but not feel; a spectator.

In his 1943 paper *A Theory of Human Motivation* and subsequently in his book *Motivation and Personality*, published in 1954, Abraham Maslow outlined a hierarchy of needs which every human being strives for to achieve completeness, or as he later proposed, to reach the sixth level of self-transcendence. The essence of a person is their whole. It is their mind, their body, their soul and their being. Each level is the foundation upon the which the next must be built. The art of torture is to take away each in turn. The essence of the person is diminished until finally, it is gone.

The art of redemption is to recover each in turn after it has been taken away.

She unzips Lorraine's tracksuit top, and cuts through the ash stained vest, watching as the plump breasts slide down onto the arms, her finger runs across the nipples, feeling them harden. The denim and the underwear are removed. The body is now naked, grotesque and mottled. The eyes, blinking, fill with tears, self-respect pouring with them as they track down the reddened cheeks.

She is the expert in the mind, so I give her the first few minutes. I know this is her thing, not mine. The removal of self, the removal of security, of emotional safety, reducing the essence of the soul. There is a pleasure in the exploration of the physical form in all its intricacies. In all its shapes. The slow and deliberate invasion of all that is held private until nothing personal remains. I watch as her fingers touch the skin, her tongue tastes the fear, probing and caressing, as they have so many others on this table. Scientific application of acts of defilement, stripping away the layers of self-respect, removing the last vestiges of self-worth. Intimate and animal; a mental souvenir.

Then she is done, wiping saliva from her face, lost to a rapture that only I can provide. Now it is my turn.

I take to my task like an expert, not one learned in books but by practice; the gradual separation of the body from the mind, then the mind from the soul. The ancients were experts, prolonging the process for hours even days. Of course, they did not have ketamine, or power tools. For us, time is short. As the knife pares, the saw cuts, the mouth is unable to move, yet the bowels and the bladder vent, basic physiological needs now impossible to maintain.

When at last the mutilation is complete, when the whole has become diminished in stages, I watch the eyes. They blink uncontrollably as they stare at the mirror, all humanity now gone. The animal in the slaughterhouse at the point of death, alone, helpless, beyond hope. I wanted Varsa, want Lorraine, to see her lungs intumescent and pumping. I want her to see her heart bloat and falter before she finally dies. I want her to see her dead self before her brain finally yields.

Varsa saw.

She smiles at me as she licks blood from her hands and then moves to Lorraine's ear and quietly, seductively, whispers into it.

"We always get what we want. Never ever try to stop us. Never try to come between us."

Chapter 37

Vidin, North West Bulgaria, 5:05am, Wednesday

The trip from Sofia to Vidin had passed without incident. Apart from the driver, there were four other travellers; a pair of teenagers whose attention was entirely devoted to each other and a man curled up on the seat, asleep with his coat over his head. Satya had sat in the corner of the last seat of the last carriage. The fourth person, the dour, life-worn conductor had punched her ticket and idly walked forward. For the next six and a half hours, she was alone with the passing lights and the hum of the air conditioning and the somnolent click of the tracks as the train had meandered its way through the darkness of the mountains and across the fertile plains toward Vidin.

She awoke as a hand touched her shoulder and saw the round, thread-veined face of the conductor.

"Vidin, miss. Tova e nashata spirka. Tryabva da si trŭgnete ottuk.

"Sorry? I don't speak..."

"Vidin, Miss. Train terminates here."

Collecting her bag and coat, she thanked him and alighted.

At 5:00am, the backwater that was Vidin was as still as the grave with as much charisma. Dawn was an hour away and there was something post-apocalyptic about the booking hall, tiny by Sofia standards. A surly-looking man in a leather jacket was busily unbinding newspapers to display on his stall, chuntering to himself under his breath. A wiry, hunched individual in overalls was burnishing the floor with an industrial polisher and two cleaners were gossiping busily as they cleaned tables in a small cafeteria. Too early for commuters, the hall was otherwise empty. In the cafe, Satya indicated three ready-made sandwiches, shrugging at the assistant as she gave the price, handing over another precious ten euro note when the finger pointed to the display on the cash register. She still had days to go and her cash reserves were dwindling.

She sat and checked her itinerary. She had forty minutes until her train so she decided to find the rest rooms. The trip to Budapest was long - around thirteen hours. She could but hope it would be as quiet as the last.

When she reached the platform, her train was already standing, still slumbering, awaiting a gentle prod from its driver. At this time, Aleppo would be alive to the sounds of mopeds and taxis and the call to prayer for Salat al-fajr bouncing from the rooftops and defying even the deepest of sleepers. By 9:00 the sounds of drones overhead and gunfire would send people back to their houses until Salat al-zuhr.

The carriage doors were open and, checking her seat reservation, compulsory on this train, Satya found herself following one of the railway employees along the aisle as she placed tickets into the tops of the seats.

Eventually, the carriage doors closed, the train began its laborious crawl out of Vidin station and Satya stole a few hours rest. Despite having the whole carriage to herself, her sleep had been fitful at best, the man from Sofia on her mind. Now in a coach with around a hundred seats, at least thirty already full, she could relax. Safety in numbers. Her hand still clasped the Makarov in her pocket, though. Now and again she flicked the safety off and on.

As the ever more verdant scenery had passed by, she realised she had no idea where the train was taking her. Of course, she knew of Sofia, of Bulgaria and she knew the names - Budapest, Zurich, Basel, Strasbourg, Paris, but given a map of Europe, could she accurately place a pin on any one of them? Until now, her faith had been in the Imam and her Uncle Akram, in the *The Brotherhood,* in Vasil and Pietr. She had trusted Allah to help her through, her father's words to give her courage. Was it right to have blind faith? It was true that the other man's grass was greener, greener with every passing kilometre, but was it right to believe that she could live in the West, to grow and prosper? If Sofia and Vidin seemed alien, then why not London? How long would it take to adapt? Would she ever?

She pulled out her postcard album and ran her fingers over the flowing manes of the Trafalgar Square lions and wondered how the bronze would feel under her hand. She closed her eyes and pictured Alaam sitting opposite, his face etched with tiredness racked with anxiety as they travelled northwards together separated only by time. Alaam would not allow himself to succumb and she would draw strength from him. He will be there in Tower Hamlets when she pays the black cab driver and walks into her uncle's store.

Soon, overcome by boredom and tiredness, Satya became oblivious to the passing kilometres, oblivious to the changing passengers. She was even oblivious to the man in the fifth carriage, two hundred seats behind, who had hunkered down for the journey. He had walked the length of each carriage until he found her. He made a mental note of her seat number and studied her as she slept before returning once more to his seat. Placing his coat over his face, he thought back to Sofia, to an opportunity missed and one yet to be taken.

Chapter 38

Lambourne Road, Ealing, 9:30am, Wednesday

Inside the team room, the hubbub stilled as Daley entered. To his right, Whetstone had positioned herself by the Incident Board. Then he remembered this was not his show and sidled awkwardly past propping himself uncomfortably on the corner of a desk. Allenby had taken up prime real estate next to Monaghan, and was exchanging whispered words. Soon, all eyes were focussed on the board and Deb Whetstone.

"Right guys, Varsa Ruparelia, single, 27 years old, living in Wembley. Sometime in the last fortnight, she arrived home, made herself some supper and disappeared. No sightings of her since Wednesday 7th of November. She left the lights, TV and fire on and vanished without taking her coat, mobile, keys or handbag. Then, Monday night, her right hand turns up at an RTA off the A40 at Greenford. Blood in the cargo area of the van, samples found at Miss Ruparelia's apartment *and* on the rear exit door of the block into the private car park, they all match that of the hand.

"Our *starter for ten* is that she came home expecting a quiet night in. She had a visitor or visitors, whom she probably knew, and invited them in. So guys, we need to know what happened on that night and where she went. What was going on in her life that could get her killed? Mike, what do we know about her?"

Deb Whetstone turned to the Incident Board, adding photos, names and interconnecting lines, a spider's web of data which would twist and writhe into patterns and associations over the coming days.

"Miss Ruparelia lived alone. According to her mum, she rings home around twice a week and they usually only see her a couple of times a month. Two weeks ago, the phone calls stopped. I asked if they thought there was anything troubling her. Her father said that he had a feeling there was something but he didn't know what. Her mum was just angry. *Sooner or later all daughters forget their mothers.* They were naturally curious but not overly worried. Her father called her headstrong and independently minded.

"I also went door-to-door in the apartment block. Except for her own floor, no-one knew her. Those on the same landing were blind or deaf or both. No-one recalls hearing or seeing anything out of the ordinary. No-one remembers the last time they saw her."

Whetstone reflected as she wrote. So many people in the world yet so many individuals, even in a building of sixty or so residents. A person could disappear for weeks before anyone realised they were missing. Some disappeared forever.

"So, work. Steve?" continued Whetstone. Taylor, a son of the digital generation, turned to his monitor.

"Miss Ruparelia is a qualified surgical scrub nurse. She worked for Medway Klein, a private cosmetic clinic in Northwick Park, as an Office Administrator between April and October. She was dismissed on 31st October. Before that, she worked as a nurse at Charing Cross before being dismissed for misconduct last January. Insubordination."

"This is why she is working as an administrator," added Daley. "She was dismissed from the hospital trust and then lost her job again in October."

"Nobody we spoke to had a good word to say about her," added Whetstone.

Daley mischievously raised his eyebrows. "Sacked twice, now she's lost a hand. She's not having a great year, all in all." There was a hint of rebellion in his voice which forced Whetstone to grit her teeth. A murmur of amusement spread across the team room before being stifled by a commanding cough from Allenby. Team briefs were so much more fun when the boss had a board meeting, mused Daley.

"Ok, let's concentrate, please." The room stilled as Whetstone threw daggers at Daley and stole back her authority. "Right, Varsa's apartment. Forensics suggest she was attacked shortly after opening the door. There was a struggle which resulted in slight blood loss in the hallway. Then she was dragged across the hall and into the bathroom and probably dismembered in the bath. The hand suggests removal pre-mortem. The murderer has come fully prepared for the task and to clean up afterwards. Despite that, there were blood traces under the legs of the hall table, on the bathroom door jamb and on the rear doors of the building leading to the car park."

Propped on the corner of the desk, Daley's back ached. He had woken that morning, still in the armchair from the previous evening. Hopefully, the pills would quell the pain before anyone noticed. He needed to be on top of his game, especially with Allenby not ten feet away. He dutifully listened but today it felt voyeuristic. Six months ago, Gascoigne would have phoned him. Today it was Whetstone's gig and he was having trouble mustering enough interest to care. DNA would identify the perpetrator and the investigation would be over within a couple of days. Still it irked him that he was on a wild goose chase searching for strays, yet this case screamed murder.

Whetstone continued. "Also, the apartment was searched before we arrived but they missed this..." She held aloft the evidence bag containing the notebook. "I'll get the pages scanned but the gist is that Miss Ruparelia kept notes on the comings and goings of her colleagues and we suspect, for some reason, it got her into trouble. She mentions a few people by initials and we have already put names to most of them. Details on the handout.

"Marion Edmonds is Miss Ruparelia's team leader. She told us Varsa was a nosey parker who enjoyed riling her co-workers, even threatening them. She was not above reporting them to management. I sensed a lot of bad blood there.

"Lorraine Lucas was a ward nurse until she was sacked for pilfering. Mike went to see her yesterday. Mike?"

Corby leafed through to the correct page of his notebook. "Yes, gov. Claims she was bang to rights for the stealing, received a warning from Marion Edmonds and HR and stopped. Then she was sacked for a similar offence she claims she didn't commit."

"Which would agree with what Marion Edmonds told me," added Whetstone. "She claims Ruparelia started telling tales on Lucas. Stock was found missing and Lucas was sacked."

"She was adamant that she stopped thieving after the first warning."

"Edmonds told me that after Ruparelia had been sacked, they found cupboards full of the stuff Lucas was supposed to have stolen. Lucas claimed Varsa had tried to blackmail her.

"Then there is Connor Smith, a Junior Surgeon at the clinic. He seems to be the closest Varsa had to an ally. He was asked to tell Varsa to wind her neck in, something he obviously wasn't wholly successful at. Play the voicemails, Steve."

Taylor clicked a small portable recorder and the team listened to a digest of the voicemails from Varsa's phone.

"Steve, did you have any joy getting through to Mr Smith?" Whetstone asked.

"No, gov. His phone is switched off. He switched on and listened to my message this afternoon but then he switched it off again."

"OK." continued Whetstone. "So, whatever Smith is involved with, I am guessing it's illegal and he's asking her to keep her head down. Varsa decides not to listen and is silenced...which means it must be worth killing for. Mike and I went around to Smith's gaff last night. Evidence of an incident but Smith had already skipped. We cannot rule out the possibility that Smith is our killer and has only been found out because of the crash.

"Finally, there is *SF* - Steven Franks. He's a driver for the sister company, Chronotech, based on the same site. Ruparelia thinks he is having an affair with Caz Albin, his boss, and possibly with Marion Edmonds."

"Sounds like this Franks has been helping himself to Viagra and vitamins from the clinic pharmacy." added Daley, desperate to add some levity to the otherwise tedious proceedings. "I wouldn't have the stamina these days. Maybe Lucas was his dealer?" Once more a murmur of amusement coursed through the room.

"OK, OK, settle down." Whetstone struggled not to show her annoyance. She held up a photocopy. "This is a table of deliveries and collections from the diary. We don't fully understand the figures yet but that's the same van. So, Franks makes deliveries and collections of sensitive equipment to and from the clinic and Ruparelia has picked up on it. Could be he was using the crashed van to skim a little off for himself. Marion Edmonds tells us that Ruparelia and Franks argued outside the garage where the van is parked, just before she went missing.

Fast forward to last Friday night. Edmonds, who has a knack of right place, wrong time, sees Franks outside the garage again, this time arguing with Smith."

"And do you trust Marion Edmonds, Deb?" This was Monaghan.

"Yeah, Dave. She couldn't iron tramlines onto a shirt sleeve without feeling guilty."

"Just remember, if we think there's no smoke without fire, maybe Miss Ruparelia did too. Whetstone picked up a sheaf of papers and asked Corby to distribute them. "Miss Ruparelia seemed to have an angle on everyone in her diary. There are countless petty squabbles and a couple of dangerous liaisons. Lucas is robbing the place blind. Franks is screwing his boss *and* possibly Edmonds, too.

"So, Lucas was dropped at Snowdon's feet like a dead bird and now she is sizing up Albin and Franks. Then she stumbles on something juicier than theft or adultery. Look at the sheets.

"Franks and Smith are up to something. Ruparelia starts sniffing round and Smith tries to shut her up. Maybe he succeeded. Now, Ruparelia's hand turns up in the van and Smith has done a runner." Whetstone pointed to a photograph of a burned-out carcass in a ditch at Greenford. "What about the van, Dave?"

"Well, Deb. Early 2007 Transit Connect long wheelbase bought by Abbey Commercials in 2011 and sold on for cash about six months ago. Buyer is untraceable. No fines or tickets outstanding and nothing salvageable in the van. None of the fingerprints match their employees."

"Anything on the other tracks in the grass?"

"Continental 255/55 R19 tyre which is fitted to a number of high-end cars. The presence of the tyre marks could be coincidental. No witnesses."

"Guys, let's find out what happened to Miss Ruparelia, the evening she went missing. I guess that makes Smith and Franks our prime leads. Sergeant Monaghan, DC Taylor. See what you can dig up on them, phones, bank statements. DC Corby, let's see if we can trace the van's movements over the last few weeks. Also, we need to build up a picture of Miss Ruparelia's life, her friends, her associates, her enemies. Meanwhile Inspector Daley and I will check out Franks."

"So, are we treating this as a missing persons enquiry or a murder, Inspector?" It was Allenby, a low monotone voice which cut through the atmosphere of the team room. Daley started, presuming the comment was aimed at him, relaxing slightly as Whetstone turned to respond. He had almost forgotten *Bilko*, lurking in the shadows, assimilating, waiting to pounce with the $64,000 question. It was clear that Whetstone had too. She glanced at Daley, who shrugged. *This primed petard is all yours.*

"No body, sir, just forensics. The hand," she unnecessarily pointed to a gruesome photograph, "indicates removal pre-mortem. The notebook suggests she was far too nosey, escalating to blackmail. Then her life stopped a week or so ago. The phone calls ceased and her flat was deserted as if she had just walked out. Based on all this, my call would be murder."

"Of course, sir, she could have surgically removed her own hand and wandered off to start a new life with Smith. That's an option?" Daley elicited a small rebellious murmur from the room. Whetstone puffed.

It was too early for quips, as Allenby's scowl attested. "OK, I can't sanction a full-blown murder enquiry until we have a body. In the meantime, we have to consider she has suffered grievous harm, so investigate as a murder, as far as you can."

Daley, turned to Whetstone and whispered, "What he means is don't waste the budget and goodwill until you find a body. Typical Allenby. He doesn't want us scouring the county for a corpse, for Varsa to turn up in a nut house *sans* hand two weeks later, leaving him to explain to the Chief Super and half the Press why we spent the Christmas Fund chasing ghosts. Hey up, stand by your beds. Here he comes..."

Whetstone sighed as Allenby eased himself from his chair and sidled over to the Investigations Board.

"Nice work Acting-Inspector Whetstone. That's great progress for the first day into an investigation. Plenty of avenues to follow."

"Thank you, sir." There had been an uncomfortable emphasis on the word *Acting* which had not gone unnoticed by Scott Daley, if the smirk on his face was anything to go by. "Once we speak to Steven Franks, I feel we will narrow things down a little."

Allenby turned to Daley. "So, how's the missing persons case going?"

It was Whetstone's turn to smirk, this time the uncomfortable emphasis landing on *missing persons*, the weight of importance diminished. At least she was still *Acting* Inspector and not a social worker chasing ghosts and strays.

"So, so, sir. I've been out to the parents and workmates. I collected some initial DNA evidence and sent it to the lab. I have requested the CCTV footage for the cameras around the car park in Chatham Woods."

"Well done, Scott. I can see the rest has done you the world of good." With a grin, the Superintendent headed back to the sanctuary of the Goldfish Bowl.

"Thanks, sir...", and once he knew he was out of earshot, he added, "...not at all patronising."

Whetstone looked up and grinned callously. "I think he's relieved you're on the case. Means he can get on with the paperwork while I chase the bad guys and you hang leaflets on lampposts."

Behind Daley's eyes, the familiar ache had returned. He dug around in his pockets and fished out the pill he had saved earlier. He would swill it down when he was out of sight.

Chapter 39

They had found fingerprints. That was the only answer...

Pressing the button, squinting as the stark LED shone bright in the pitch black, Connor Smith checked the time. 9:45am. He would need to venture out soon, if only to find a toilet. He removed the duct tape from the small hole and put his eye to it. Outside was quiet. Not a soul.

Mr Smith. This is DC Taylor of the Metropolitan Police. We are worried for your safety, sir. When you get this message, please could you contact me on...

They had found his fingerprints in the van or on the fence or identified his footprints in the mud.

But how would they know that the fingerprints were his?

Covering the hole, he allowed his eyes to readjust to the darkness before running around, doing a recce, checking each spy hole in turn. A 360° view.

Should he reply to the voicemail? Turn himself in? Explain? Surely without any evidence, there was nothing they could pin on him. He would explain his part in the whole mess. He could return home and it would be all over.

But this was murder. This was Varsa. The eyes, the gaping mouth, rough, blackened flesh. He was used to blood but not in such quantities. It was like a butcher's storeroom in the back of that van. If they had his fingerprints, he would be guilty after the fact, or for aiding and abetting. If they couldn't pin it on anyone else, they would pin it on him. Why should he go to jail for someone else's crimes? No, the police would wait for a while.

In the silence, he felt like the only person on Earth. Apart from rats and pigeons, he had seen few other signs of life. The floor beneath his sleeping bag was hard and unforgiving but the alternative was even worse. He imagined his house on any other Tuesday night, warm from the central heating, curtains closed against the world. A take-out and Call of Duty on Xbox. Instead he had spent the night here. His face was freezing and he was all alone drowning in a sea of black when instead he could be safe inside his own house, drinking coffee in his own mug, phoning his parents, phoning his mates, phoning anyone.

But the face at his window had turned his stomach to jelly.

He clicked on the electric camping lamp, starting at the rat as it fixed its eyes on him, twitched whiskers and scampered away. Pouring water into a kettle, he fired up the small stove and prepared the last of his dehydrated soup. Leaving so quickly, he had been unprepared and there were only so many cans he could fit into the rucksack. Sooner or later he would need to venture out, find more food, take a dump.

Then there was the van. The slow rumble of the diesel engine had woken him in the early hours. Using the spy-holes he had followed the headlights until they became taillights around the back. He had watched as they had unloaded and driven off. He had seen the registration plate - VH07 YMK - the same as the van he had crashed on Monday. At one point, they looked up towards him, freezing, eye pressed tight against the hole. Had they seen him? Had something outside given away his presence?

Unable then to sleep, he had spent the night struggling to piece together the fragments, to explain the mess he was in. He had driven the van. He had jumped at the chance but they had known he would. Was he really that transparent?

But the van was just a vehicle. There was much more. Things had been wrong at that place for a long time but it wasn't until the arrival of Varsa Ruparelia that it had become a problem. Until then, it was just hearsay, conversations in the staff room. Sleeping dogs. Contained.

Varsa had joined with her propensity for gossip, for blackmail, and she had seen a situation to exploit. She had watched Marion, Steve and him and she had drawn her conclusions. Most of it was idle tittle-tattle; a game to feed her false information and watch her machine go into overdrive, chasing her tail. Rumours of relationships, of fallings out, of petty theft. It had been canteen amusement. She had latched onto Lorraine Lucas, a bigger bone to chew on, literally. Her spitefulness stepped up a gear and Lucas was sacked.

Then she started to ask about the farm.

They had asked, him, Connor, to warn her off. An impossible task and God knows he had tried, but her hunger for grist to feed her rumour mill had led her close to the truth and she too had been sacked. In his heart of hearts, he must have known that not even that would be the end. The staring eyes in the back of the van told him it was now over.

Now there was a new problem. The farm.

Connor crawled back to his sleeping bag and lay cocooned in this forgotten corner of the world and he began to sob as the loneliness and isolation consumed him.

Chapter 40

Medway Klein Cosmetic Clinic, Northwick Park

Whetstone was still bloody annoyed with Scott Daley. She didn't want him anywhere near Nick Snowdon, the truculent mood he was in, but Allenby had forced her arm. With his return, the team room had begun to feel claustrophobic. After six months of playing lead violin, she was no longer attuned to second fiddle and in the last twenty-four hours the music had subtly changed. She couldn't help wondering if another agenda was in play. That brief moment when Allenby had pulled Daley aside, had they exchanged more than pleasantries? Had some private instruction been given? Daley's behaviour today had been extreme, insubordinate, as if he was trying to provoke a reaction. Mind you, a good kick in the nuts may have put him back in his place.

Or maybe this was Daley's way of reclaiming his patch? In his absence, Whetstone had become aware of how much she had relied on him, how much more comfortable she was validating someone else's reasoning rather than trusting her own. She knew she was a good detective but as for deduction, that seemed a long way off yet.

Then again, there were the pills. Daley was popping them like *Smarties*. That can't be good. After her father's death, Whetstone's sister Louise had been prescribed anti-depressants for a while. They had made her worse rather than better, robbed her of her soul.

Daley climbed from the driver's seat.

"Can you smell that, Deb? "Is that ether or iodine or plain old bull...?"

Whetstone glanced around at the courtyard. She was slightly tired of the constant quips. "Maybe it's the smell of a smart-arse who thinks he's being clever."

Daley frowned. "That's what comes of hanging around with detectives." He started towards the reception. The receptionist recognised Whetstone and walked the pair through an adjoining corridor to a vast hallway, which Whetstone assumed must be Medway Hall proper.

"I hate these places." Whetstone lolled back in the comfortable chair, casting her eye around the vast entrance hall and up the sweeping balustraded stairway beyond. Though the decor was strictly nineteenth century, marbled floors, ornate panelled walls, pictures of bucolic serenity, there was an air of insincerity about the place. Beyond the faded gentility, lay new money, a veneer of pretence. "They prey on people's insecurities. If you're not insecure before you arrive, you are when you leave."

"Keeps them coming back for more, I suppose. Bet she's not insecure being here." Daley's eyes were fixed on the round bobbing backside of the receptionist as she walked away. "You ever thought of having any work done, Deb?"

"Cheeky bastard, sir. What makes you think I need anything done?" She suddenly felt very conscious of her boobs and pulled her coat across her chest.

"Well, you *do* know you what they call you around the nick, don't you?"

Whetstone turned her head to Daley and frowned. This was all wearing very thin. "And what might that be, *sir*?"

"Couldn't say, Sergeant."

"Better had though, Inspector, or you might need some work done."

Daley smiled. "They call you Sergeant Sour-dough. Can't think why. Everyone in that place is a miserable sod. You're no different."

"Well, anyone would be miserable with you on their case." She turned away and stared out into the courtyard.

"There's one silver lining though, eh? That nickname won't work if you're ever made up to Inspector. They'll have to come up with something else to wind you up."

"Harassment in the workplace. Met has rules." Whetstone slouched back into her seat. *Ever* made up to Inspector? Chance would be fine thing now that Scott Daley had returned. She wondered whether he knew what they called *him* back at Lambourne Road.

Daley steered the ship towards different rocks. "I can understand a little upholstery in the bra department. A lift here and there might be an improvement, but trout pouts and botox, they leave me cold."

"I can tell, sir. That last course was a mistake. No wonder you hid in your living room for months."

"Hmph." Daley cast his eye towards the front desk. "That receptionist. Do you think those are her own, or she's had some work done, you know, *perks* of the job?"

"What, breasts, sir? Definitely work, sir. Bet she's also got nipple rings and a stud in her..."

A relieved Daley was saved from himself, as a tall athletic man in a tailored three-piece suit rounded a corner and threw them an outstretched hand and a winning, if completely disingenuous, smile.

"Nick Snowdon. MD. Come through."

The three exchanged banal pleasantries as they crossed the lobby into a sumptuous inner sanctum. Around seventeen feet square, an overtly modern desk occupied the space in which a snooker table might once have stood. The walls had been brutally modernised and covered with modern framed prints by the Impressionists. The desk boasted a computer with multiple screens, two landline phones and, Daley observed, at least three mobiles dotted about. This was a man who liked to keep his finger on the pulse, to remain connected in a room for entertaining visitors, for schmoozing and romancing investors. Beneath the carpet, the floorboards, perhaps the only period feature, creaked and crunched as they moved across to a corral of easy chairs around a table in the bay window. Seated at one of the chairs, framed against panoramic views of a broad paved rear courtyard through the windows, a woman turned her head to appraise the pair before rising, kilometres of leg showing through the split in a knee-length business skirt. Behind her, ground staff tidied borders and the immense lawned garden stretched off into the greyness of November.

"Caz Albin. Director of Chronotech. I'm afraid you have caught us during our daily catch-up."

"I run the clinic," explained Snowdon. "Caz runs our research company, Chronotech. The two organisations share the clinic's medical facilities, and Medway Hall houses the research facilities and our respective offices. Offices are expensive. The only way we can afford the upkeep of such a grand place."

"So, what is it exactly that you do, Mr Snowdon?"

"Well, Inspector, Medway Klein is a private cosmetic clinic - nips and tucks. We pander to the vanities of the rich and famous. We also perform a good deal of work at cost for the NHS, burns victims, cancer patients, and so forth. In addition, we undertake projects on behalf of commercial clients, helping to perfect new surgical procedures."

"Chronotech is one of those clients," intervened Caz. "The company was formed five years ago to develop prosthetics and biomedical solutions." She rose, straightening her jacket. "I will leave you to your discussions."

Whetstone watched as Caz Albin swayed across the floor, slightly slower that was necessary, a quick glance cast at the pair as she eased around the door. Snowdon proffered a coffee pot, which the two declined. Hopefully this would not take too long.

"Now, how can I help? The Constable who telephoned earlier mentioned Miss Ruparelia and Mr Smith?"

"Well, sir, we are trying to trace them both." Whetstone huffed under her breath as Daley took up the reins.

Snowdon pondered through a mask of professional concern then brusquely passed across a file "This is Miss Ruparelia's personnel file. I'm sorry, Inspector, it's a little thin. For legal reasons, we keep very few records aside from the statutory ones. There are contact details if you need them. However, as far as Medway Klein is concerned, Miss Ruparelia left on the 31st of October."

The files were lean bordering on anorexic, only a few time-sheets and a log of dates which confirmed what they already knew. The covers were well worn, the spines stretched and creased, attesting that they had been sanitised. Snowdon obviously thought he had heard the last of Varsa Ruparelia. Daley passed the files to Whetstone who glanced fleetingly at them before continuing:

"So, what was Miss Ruparelia's role here up to that point?"

"She was an Administrative Assistant." Delivered flat, no context.

"Do you have any forwarding details?" asked Daley, bemused by the brevity of the response.

Snowdon shook his head. "I'm afraid not, Inspector. Just the home address in the file."

"And Mr Smith?"

"Mr Smith is a Junior Surgeon. However," Snowdon shifted his position, "he hasn't turned up this morning... unless he has arrived whilst we have been speaking." Snowdon nodded at the table. "His address is in his file."

Daley smiled his gratitude. Snowdon could have written his responses on a post-it note and still had room for a couple of *smileys*. "So why did Miss Ruparelia leave?"

Snowdon scratched his chin, his eyes were sharp, guarded and cautious. "I am afraid her behaviour became unacceptable. As she was still under six months' probation, as was our right, we decided not to retain her services."

"And how did she take that?"

"Predictably, Inspector. She kicked up a small fuss and we escorted her from the premises. She rang me a couple of times directly but after the first call, I resolved not to pick up."

"And have you had any contact with her since?"

Snowdon shook his head indifferently.

"We have heard that there was some trouble between Miss Ruparelia and other members of staff, namely Lorraine Lucas?"

Snowdon's face flashed annoyance. If Whetstone were to trust her intuition, she would believe that he didn't give a damn about either Ruparelia or Lucas but was angered by tales out of school. Maybe that was how he coped. A professional detachment, concentrating on the tasks to be performed, the decisions to be made.

"Miss Lucas was a little, er, light fingered... Miss Ruparelia brought it to my attention. I am afraid she had to go. It was petty theft. The damage was small, so I left my managers to deal with it. They warned her off and that was that until Miss Ruparelia came banging my door down and I had no choice. We estimate the theft cost us around a thousand pounds, but replacing Miss Lucas cost us five times that amount. After that, Miss Ruparelia became increasingly unpopular with her colleagues. Nobody appreciates a tell-tale."

Whetstone cast Snowdon a cold smile. The irony was not lost on her that now she jotted down notes about Medway Klein employees, as Varsa Ruparelia had done, even though the motive was different. "What can you tell us about Miss Ruparelia's time here, who else she came into contact with? It would help to build a little background on her."

"I'm not sure I should divulge that information. Our work here is quite sensitive and I need to respect the safety and privacy of our staff and clients. I am sure you understand, Sergeant, Inspector?" Snowdon's expression was cold, without emotion.

Daley did understand. He understood the delaying tactics downstairs whilst the paperwork hits the shredder upstairs, the cosy chat at the front door while the villain legs it out of the back. The amiable bonhomie as the assistant plunges the knife into the shoulder blades.

"Yes, Mr Snowdon. I can understand your business is sensitive but our focus is on Miss Ruparelia and her well-being. We believe some harm has come to her and we are very keen to trace her whereabouts and those of Mr Smith. It's very likely that the others might be able to help us, too." He beamed his own cold, professional smile.

Snowdon grunted. He leaned forward, his eyes hardening. "Maybe the employment agency can help? The details are in the..."

Daley sighed, the frustration now rather too obvious. "Let's stop dancing round our handbags, shall we? Either you can take my word for it that we will exercise the appropriate degree of confidentiality and tact...or I could get a warrant and send a load of sizes nines in to tear this place apart, whichever suits."

Snowdon shifted in his seat, clearly annoyed. "I am sure you could, Inspector. Look, I have explained that our relationship with Miss Ruparelia ended some time ago. I have explained that Mr Smith is not at work. I don't think there is any more to add."

Whetstone bit her tongue as she stifled a sharp intake of breath. Rather than softly, softly catchee monkey, Daley was laying land mines. She had sat quietly, biding her time as Snowdon and Daley enjoyed their fractious conversation, irked that she was again a passenger in her own investigation. The past few months had allowed her to stretch her wings without the pervasive presence of her senior officer to refashion every good idea she had. She had thought that acting up for a few months might have proved her more than just his sidekick.

The room descended into an uncomfortable silence. A hedge trimmer buzzed beyond the window. Snowdon settled back in his chair and sipped once more at his coffee. The world still turned, if subtly different. Snowdon puffed, collected his thoughts and took a sip from the bone china cup. He didn't need a stand-up row right now. What he needed was to get the two visitors out of his office.

"So, was Mr Smith trouble too?" Again, Daley waded in.

Snowdon huffed again. His eyes rolled, the switch thrown back. "Sorry, Inspector?"

"Oh, I was just filling in the blanks. Maybe the ship isn't as stable as it could be. You seem to have a few issues with staff conduct. I wondered if Mr Smith was also trouble."

Snowdon placed his cup on the table and linked hands across his lap. Despite the stone expression, his dander was rising again. "I am unaware of any problems with Mr Smith."

Not an unequivocal no, thought Daley. More plausible deniability. "Does he make a regular thing of skipping work?"

Snowdon fought to keep his patience. "We are not his keeper, Inspector. He and Miss Ruparelia were not that close, trust me. It's a fuss about nothing."

"From what we have heard, he was instructed to speak informally to Miss Ruparelia about her behaviour. That would imply a degree of closeness?"

Snowdon scratched his forehead, more tales told out of school. The annoyance was now all too plain. "Well, yes but we nipped that in the bud. Basically, he was informed that his relationship with Miss Ruparelia was not conducive to his continued employment. As far as I am aware he realised his error of judgement. Look, Inspector. I am not sure what you are inferring..." Once more the air in the room prickled.

"So, when was that?" Whetstone spotted her opportunity and jammed a metaphorical foot in the door. "When did you speak to Mr Smith?"

"Around the middle of September, Sergeant." Snowdon stood and moved to the window, gazing out over the shaded courtyard across the glistening dew mottled lawns, away from the challenging eyes of Daley. He turned back towards Whetstone, his expression once more serene, no sign of the annoyance with Daley, the switch rethrown. "You know, Sergeant. Something has just occurred to me. Maybe Smith was the agent provocateur and Varsa the patsy, as you might say?" Snowdon's tone was mocking and disingenuous. "Perhaps Connor was planting ideas into Varsa's impressionable mind. Look well if we have been casting aspersions in her direction when we should have been focussing on Mr Smith. I feel quite bad about how we behaved to her now."

Whetstone was unimpressed, a soliloquy for their benefit, an exercise in divide and rule. She was not to be diverted that easily, except by Daley.

"Sounds like bollocks to me. Do you honestly believe that or are you just yanking our chain?"

"Sorry, Inspector?"

"I mean, one minute Miss Ruparelia is public enemy number one and the next she is the victim of some unscrupulous co-worker. Which is it to be, Mr Snowdon?"

"I don't know," snapped Snowdon. "You're the bloody detective. You work it out!" He turned his head towards the less challenging view of the garden. "Look, all I said was that maybe we got it wrong." His irritation now too obvious, Snowdon walked to his desk, grabbed a business card and handed it to Whetstone. "Look, just talk to whoever you like. Alison will show you to Caz's office." The words were more of an order than a statement.

Snowdon re-buttoned his jacket. Whetstone collected her things. As they made for the door, Daley was bemused that all of the time they had been in the room, they had been scraping at the surface, inches from pay dirt. There was still nothing to tie Ruparelia to Medway Hall beyond the end of October. Except the phone calls. The time had come to cross that bridge. He delivered what had become known as a Columbo moment.

"There is one other thing that is concerning me."

"Oh, yes and what may that be, *Inspector*?" Snowdon spat

testily. "Look, if we could just get this over with?"

Daley was unimpressed. "It seems Mr Smith rang Miss Ruparelia several times outside work hours. There are calls prior to her dismissal and as many afterwards that she never picked up. He called her twice around the time she went missing and again on Monday night. He seems very keen to speak to her."

Snowdon gave an indifferent shrug. "Like I said, Inspector, I am not their keeper."

"Mr Smith seems to think she's in trouble, tells her to keep her head down, not to rock the boat. Sounds to me like they were a lot friendlier outside work than you were led to believe. So, what boat was she rocking? What trouble might that be?"

Snowdon huffed. "Like I said, Miss Ruparelia had a habit of getting herself into trouble. I think that was sage advice from Mr Smith, don't you? I mean, look where rocking the boat led her."

"And where, exactly, did it lead her, sir?"

Annoyance flicked across Snowdon's face as he let the question wither. Still this grilling was not over. He smoothed down his jacket. "Now, is that all?"

"There is another number, here at Medway Klein. Called for a week or so up to the point we believe she went missing. Do you know what that would be about?"

Daley held out his notebook and Snowdon peered at it impatiently before checking a typed list. "That's the desk phone in the OR Reception. Perhaps, as you suggest, she was ringing Mr Smith?"

"But she had Connor's mobile; she would call him on that. So, who else might she be ringing?"

"Oh, I don't know. I am not down there every day."

Daley smiled and flipped the notebook shut with a slap. "Sorry to have taken up so much of your time."

"Just one more thing, Sir." This time it was Whetstone. "Does the clinic own a van?"

Snowdon cocked his head sideways and feigned incredulity, his temper now completely frayed. "A van? How should I know if we have a bloody van? Do I look like site services? I really have to be getting on. Inspector? Sergeant?"

Chapter 41

Away in the furthest corners of this realm of ghosts and monsters, there is another world. It ebbs and flows like the bituminous blackness, closer still, then drifting further as I try to fix it. The voice of the angel breaking through the silence. A story, a child's story in the infinite black, comforting, drifting over the music of the machines. It tells of wizards and goblins, of spells and magic.

I am suddenly aware of things known and things forgotten. Of mythologies and stories, the Incubus and the Succubus:

> *The Lilû who wanders in the plain.*
> *They have come nigh unto a suffering man on the outside.*
> *They have produced evil.*
> *Evil being, evil face, evil mouth, evil tongue.*
> *Sorcery, venom, slaver, wicked machinations,*
> *Which are produced in the body of the sick man.*
> *O woe for the sick man whom thy cause to moan like a šąharrat.*

Then it occurs to me. What if the veneer between this world and that of life is gossamer thin. A single lamina of molecules, through which consciousness can pass? What if there is a way to see and be seen in that other world, the world of the living? What if there was a way to return?

Am I the Lilû and is this blackness, the plain I am forced to wander? Have I become evil? Would returning to the world render me the ghost, the phantom, the Incubus?

If this veneer to the other world is a one-way mirror, maybe there is a way for me to see through? Maybe there is a way for me to squeeze through the molecules, to re-enter the world of the living? A way to find my aggressor, a way to right the wrong. A way to haunt the living.

I can escape the eyes of the evil monster, the Alû-demon that covers my endless days, that waits to pounce.

What if I can become a ghost?

Chapter 42

The receptionist led Daley and Whetstone back through the entrance lobby of Medway Hall and up the grand sweeping stairway to the first floor, past austere patinated portraits which had almost certainly been painted in the Far East and bussed there during a previous renovation. Daley led, making small talk with the woman, as they crested the top where a corridor ran left and right, viciously capped just beyond the stairwell by utilitarian fire doors, magnolia walls and ranks of equally utilitarian teak faced doors, each bearing a number. The corridor was another example of the commercial vandalism which saved these places from demolition.

"Ah, Inspector, Sergeant. Alison, bring some tea, will you?" Daley smiled his thanks. Although directly above, the room could not be more different to Snowdon's ground floor office. Ultra-modern, impersonal and practically empty, it carried success temporarily. The whole room could be packed into a tea chest and carted away when the lease was up. Again, there were the familiar prints on the wall. Standing behind the plate glass desk, Caz Albin smiled, scrutinising Daley for a brief moment, before skirting the desk and taking a couple of strides toward him.

"I hear you have been upsetting Nick, Inspector. Not a good move. He can be quite prickly." The woman smiled and thrust out a delicate manicured hand, which was surprisingly firm when shook. Albin was around Daley's age, immaculately made-up, dressed in a lemon tailored jacket and a blouse which hugged her figure, and an expensive scent filled the space between them.

It was a look that depressed Whetstone; one she could never achieve, however much the mirror flattered her. Her legs were too short, her boobs too small and all the bumps were a couple of inches too low, too high or too large. She envied women who looked like Albin. It gave them the ability to open doors, to be noticed. A magnetic quality which tended to blur the room around them, whatever else was going on, transcending intellect and ability.

Right now, she was being noticed by Daley, who was aware that once more his attention had been captured. He mused that that was probably the aim; one he was happy to play along with for now. She smiled at him in a way that almost made his shirt buttons pop.

Daley gestured at the pictures. "Somebody likes their Impressionists. You have quite a collection here and in the office downstairs."

"Prints, alas. Please do take a seat." She returned to her desk as Whetstone sat alongside Daley, slightly irked but wise to a game they had to play where women in positions of power were concerned.

"I love all things French. Do you have a favourite, Inspector?"

"I am afraid I am a philistine, Ms Albin. When I see a piece of Impressionist art, I hope there is a box of biscuits underneath."

Caz Albin smiled graciously. "Now, how can I help?"

Daley decided he need to make her work a little first, define a few truths, watch the body language. When the bullshit came, he might avoid slipping in it. "Exactly what is it that you do here?"

"Well, Inspector. We are a biomedical research company. We design and develop bioelectric prosthetics for restoration of neurologically compromised motor function..."

"Sorry, and in English that is...?"

"Oh, yes, terribly sorry, Sales spiel." Albin flicked a business-like smile, her eyes never leaving his, deep, engaging, her fingers playing with a stray lock of hair. "OK, so we make a range of biomedical implants. Specifically, we manufacture cochlear implants which can be fitted to people with a number of serious hearing impairments, allowing them to perceive sounds and improving their quality of life. We also manufacture retinal implants which follow the same principle, although they are totally internal."

"And artificial limbs?" Daley indicated an image in an open sales folder on the desktop.

"We supply the skeleto-muscular implants which manufacturers use to provide autonomous motor function to the limbs. The false nerves and wiring, if you will." Albin leaned towards Daley and smiled. "The bionic man has a lot to answer for!" Alison entered with a tray and set it down. The conversation stalled until the PA left.

"Varsa Ruparelia, right?" enquired Albin, pot in hand, steering back to the purpose of the visit. "I recall the name, Inspector. I have probably seen her around. I am sure she deals with some of the administrative support on the Delta project. What makes you think Chronotech may be able to help?"

Whetstone seized her opportunity and slid some words in edgeways. "Probably nothing, Ms Albin..."

"Oh, Caz, please." Her smile was warm and generous, aimed solely at Daley and utterly synthetic.

"Caz," Whetstone obliged. "You mentioned Delta project?"

Albin raised her eyebrows, shifted in her seat and studied Whetstone for a moment. "Yes. It's one of a number of projects we are working on. Why do you ask?"

Whetstone chose the route of silence. Albin fell into the abyss she created.

"Delta is a bionics project. It deals with the interface between the human nervous system and the prosthetic, improving the feedback. For example, touching something hot with a prosthetic hand and feeling the sensation of heat, even the pain, without any physical damage. Perceiving objects seen by a camera that the human eye is not looking at. As it is extremely commercially sensitive, I would prefer to leave it there at this stage. Obviously, I would co-operate with a court order or warrant." She crooked a sympathetic smile, which did not wash.

"What makes the project so sensitive?"

"Well, it's the Holy Grail of biomechanics. We already have prosthetic limbs which can be controlled by the brain. Often these require an external control box or a huge exo-skeleton; the user *wears* the device. What we are working towards *is* the Bionic Man, prosthetics indistinguishable from the flesh of the human wearer. Cameras which look, feel and work like eyes. Better than eyes. Super senses.

"So, if your research was revealed to a competitor...?"

"Catastrophic, Inspector. Confidentiality is paramount and we pay our staff accordingly." Albin paused and looked to the window. The sky was grey and full. "What has this to do with

Miss, er, Ruparelia?

"Just background," he lied.

Now bored by the science, Whetstone seized an opportunity to divert the conversation. "Do you have an employee named Steven Franks?" She caught a glint in Albin's eyes as the name resonated. The pair indulged her mental thumbing through the staff roll.

"Indeed, we do. Steve is our driver. He does a lot of work for Delta." She raised an eyebrow, intrigued. "O-kay, so yes he would be connected to Miss Ruparelia."

"Where can we find Mr Franks now?"

"Well, on the A1 probably, if he has left Newcastle yet. We have a sub-contractor up there. Device electronics are flown into Newcastle Airport for assembly nearby."

"And when is he expected back?"

"Oh, later today, I assume. He left here on Monday afternoon, away Tuesday, returning on Wednesday. I can ask him to call you when he arrives?"

Whetstone smiled appreciatively. "So, is he based here, usually?"

"Yes. Steve also looks after the Project inventory. Without any patents, we need to keep careful track of our devices and make sure they are all accounted for at all times."

Daley recalled the table in Varsa's diary; the lists of deliveries, the quotas, the column showing differences. Was this Varsa tracking the devices or was she tracking Franks? Had she found a flaw in their systems? "Are they all accounted for?"

"As of last Thursday, when we ran an inventory, nothing was missing. Devices get damaged and need refurbishment. Hence Steve's trip to Newcastle. He was collecting components. He also transports devices to and from Cardiff for *refurb*."

"What about medical supplies, drugs, dressings?" Maybe Lucas was not the only one pilfering drugs.

"No, Sergeant. Drugs aren't required for the process and dressing are supplied by Medway Klein. We do not get involved."

"Do you have a record of Mr Franks' movements in the last month or two?"

"Insofar as we keep an Outlook diary of his trips, so we know where he is." They watched as Albin turned, detached a tablet PC from a dock and tapped at the screen. "His current trip is certainly in the diary."

On a hunch, Daley threw a grenade into the discussion: "So the van that Mr Franks is driving, a white Transit Connect. Does it belong to Chronotech?"

"I know nothing of cars but I have seen him with a white van. It would be part of the fleet."

"And he's driving that back from Newcastle now?"

"Presumably."

"And the registration?"

Albin shrugged her shoulders. "Who knows, Inspector. I can barely remember what colour my car is? I'll get a printout and, of course, a copy of the deliveries and collections he's made. It might take a day or two..." Her face gave a cold, professional smile. Now she understood Snowdon's irritation.

"Do you mind if I send one of my officers around?" Daley felt he would need to limit the sanitisation to the limp brown folders to those in Medway Klein.

Albin smiled. "Sure. Of course. Obviously, as regards Intellectual Property, we may have to withhold some detail until you have a warrant." She smiled directly at Daley and ran a finger through her hair, pushing it behind her left ear. "Anything else, just ask."

Already Daley sensed damage limitation. He leaned forward, reciprocating the smile, mildly flattered but wise to the game. "I would be most grateful." He handed her a business card.

Whetstone shuffled her feet under the uncomfortable chair and ho-hummed. *Get a room, you two.* "We are also linking a Connor Smith with Miss Ruparelia. I wonder if this name means anything to you?"

Albin shook her head indifferently. "No, I'm afraid not. Does he work at the clinic? Nick would know more than me."

"Miss Ruparelia also mentioned a farm. Would that ring any bells?"

"A farm? No, nothing springs to mind, Inspector." Again indifference. "Maybe this was some aspect of her private life?"

"Potentially." Daley doubted it. A table of dates and values, of devices and procedures, of discrepancies, this was very much work related. The question was how. He clapped his hands onto his knees and stood. "Well, I think I have taken up enough of your time. If you can let Mr Franks know we would like to see him as a matter of urgency. I will send someone round for those records."

"If they would ask for me, Inspector. Anything I can do to help."

***

Leaving the oppressive warmth of the clinic into the chill, damp morning, Daley instinctively turned and peered up at the Hall. Snowdon was at a window, studying them both, perhaps ensuring they left the premises.

"Well, that was an hour wasted!" Whetstone was searching her bag, trying to locate her phone, wondering if she should use it to beat Daley. His behaviour with Snowdon had bordered on truculence and with Caz Albin, obscene. "She was all over you."

"Yeah, I noticed." Daley smirked undiplomatically. "Oh, and I reckon no work. All her own."

Whetstone grunted.

"Just a game, Sergeant. Just a game."

"Not from where I sat. Anyway, we're no further forwards than we were last night."

Daley wasn't so sure. They had a much deeper insight into the life of Varsa Ruparelia. Spying on her colleagues, her dismissal, the universal animosity towards her. Caz Albin had set a context. The secretive environment, the stringent need for confidentiality; all feeding Varsa's meddlesome curiosity, feeding her diary. Had she blackmailed one person too many?

"What do you think they're hiding?" Daley felt that all the words they had heard had been selected carefully.

"Perhaps, they're just being economical? An unwritten rule of Medway Klein. Given what they do perhaps it pays to keep quiet about it."

A group in surgical scrubs disgorged through a side door, lighting cigarettes and eyeing the pair suspiciously. "I wonder how many of them are happy to discuss what they do for a living?"

Whetstone was definitely not impressed with what *she* did for a living. For six months, she had fought to manage Allenby's interference and now Scott Daley was making a difficult situation unbearable. "Let's just get out of here," she spat testily. "This place gives me the creeps."

Daley felt the phone buzz in his pocket and he took a surreptitious peek.

Hi. This is DCI Somerville. I am out at Chatham Woods Nature Reserve. You need to come out here now.

Briefly caught off balance, Daley performed a mental regroup. What had they found out at the nature reserve? Had one of the *mispers* turned up? He needed to finish here as quickly as possible. He flicked the key fob and leaned for a moment against the car door, oblivious to the storm brewing.

Steeling herself, Whetstone spoke. "Can I say something...without getting my head bitten off?"

"Probably not."

"I am not trying to pull rank but Allenby asked me to take a lead on this case."

Daley considered. "Yes you are, and he did, so you are."

"Didn't seem that way. I could barely get a word in edgeways, especially with Snowdon. How on Earth do you expect to find anything out if you just keep getting his back up? I thought at one point you two were going to come to blows, and the next minute you were fawning all over Caz Albin like a love-sick puppy."

"You know how it is. Whatever buttons you have to press."

"Maybe but they were my buttons to press, they were my interviews to lead. Look, I can handle this. Those comments about *dancing around handbags* and *threatening to take the place apart*, they weren't drastically helpful. You have to show a degree of sensitivity."

Daley felt his pulse quicken. "What, so six months as an *Acting* Inspector and you're telling me how to run an investigation? Is that it?"

"It's my bloody investigation, *Sir!*"

Daley turned his face forward and *harrumphed* under his breath. He jabbed an angry finger at the air in front of her. "Look, you might have had it all your own way for six months but now I'm back. We do things my way, and if that involves ruffling a few feathers then so be it. Someone around here is getting away with murder, quite literally, and I am not going to hide behind their sensitivities, or yours, and wait for another corpse to turn up."

Whetstone resisted the temptation to remind him there was no corpse yet. "He clammed up as soon as you ladled in with your size nines. This business doesn't enjoy a good PR at the best of times. Even how he takes his coffee is classified."

"He was being deliberately obstructive, Deb. This is a murder enquiry. He can't be allowed to withhold information, however sensitive his business."

"Is it a murder enquiry? For all you know, Smith could be holding Varsa somewhere. They could be in some *shag palace* blissfully unaware, boffing each other's brains out."

"Without her right hand? She's dead, Whetstone."

Whetstone flounced dramatically. There was no way to win when Daley was in one of these moods. She had hoped that a Class 90 locomotive might have knocked some sense into him. "All I am saying is less is more. What do we know coming out that we didn't already know going in?"

Daley grunted. He threw open the car door, slamming it behind him, yanked the ignition key and fired up the Audi.

Chapter 43

Elstree, 10:00am, Wednesday

Despite the warmth of the bed and the lingering memory of her body, the inevitability of morning was forcing Franks to evaluate his options. The sudden stream of texts, The pleas from Connor Smith for help. They alarmed him. That the police wanted to interview him with regard to Varsa Ruparelia simply puzzled him. Connor had mentioned Varsa but Franks had assumed some adolescent spat or petty squabble between them. Now, he knew that she was missing and he had been one of the last to see her.

He tried to recall the encounter outside the garage. More questions about his itinerary, claiming he was not where he was supposed to be, that his load was short or wrong, that he was fiddling his mileage. Veiled threats, never specific. Always some detail for him to fret over.

Throwing back the duvet, he crossed to the bathroom, admiring himself in a full-length mirror. The endless gym-work had sculpted his torso and, even in his Forties, he had staved off the sagging gut of middle age. A dragon tattoo prowled the length of his broad left biceps, flexing its flanks as the muscles tightened, the tail flicking playfully around the nape of his neck. The head, around the side of his elbow, surveyed the mirror, the eyes cautious and menacing. With a body like this why would he bother with Varsa Ruparelia?

The Police could wait until he was ready. Caz had phoned regarding the visit from a rather self-opinionated Inspector and his tame poodle Sergeant. By all accounts, he was a wimp and she was a dyke; no contest. He tried to recall what she had said but his mind had been elsewhere, thinking of the previous night. She took lovemaking to an entirely new level. Not that the clinic nurses weren't skilled in that department but there was Prosecco and Champagne.

And right now, he could enjoy both.

Of course, he knew she was using him. Caz Albin used

everybody but she was also incredibly beautiful. He was quite content to be used, at least for the time being. Maybe there would come a time when making love to her would become less interesting, more of a duty but for now it was a prize worthy of the envy of those who knew.

Caz had left and the house was empty, a huge eighties mausoleum echoing to the sound of nothing. She had told him to hold up there until the police lost interest, she would cover for him at Chronotech. Wednesday was a free day in his schedule, when his diary said Newcastle but his lust drew him here. A lost day but without her, it was a wasted day. Today though, he needed to be somewhere else.

He could not spend all day cooped up in her prison. He would head home for a change of clothes then find Smith for an explanation. With everything running so smoothly, with the farm under control, they didn't need a spanner in the works just yet. Searching for his phone, he tried to think where last he had seen it. The van. It would have to wait. The van was inviting too much attention. He would need to drive the BMW today.

Chapter 44

Chatham Woods Nature Reserve

I am out at Chatham Woods Nature Reserve. You need to come out here now.

Whatever was happening with the *Hand in the Van*, Whetstone would need to manage without him for a while. Dropping her off at Lambourne Road, Daley discreetly checked in at the Comms. room. There was nothing on the feed about Chatham Woods.

By the time he reached the Nature Reserve, there were several marked cars in the car park. Walking along the path, he was challenged by a tall, gangly PC, just out of nappies. He flourished the warrant card and was directed through the trees along a corridor of blue and white tape which brought an ominous lump to his throat.

"Ah! The celebrated Inspector Daley! Come and join the party! Seems like hours since I sent my text. I thought you were standing me up." DCI Theresa Somerville was dressed in a white jump suit, her round face consumed by a broad warm smile. At her feet, matted and wet, lay the corpse of a greyhound. A forensic officer was carefully processing the area. Momentarily Daley was confused, recalling a red setter from their previous meeting. Was it the same tree? She sensed his confusion and set about resolving it.

"Meet Baxter. Seven years old, a rescue greyhound belonging to Tom Phillips and his partner Megan Haslett. Last night we had a call from Miss Haslett telling us that Mr Phillips had not returned from his run. We advised that she should give it a little more time, but by early morning, he had still not returned home. Control sent a car out and, having spoken to Miss Haslett, the PC traced Mr Phillips's route, found Baxter and called it in."

Daley looked back. The gangly constable was visible pacing a square metre of the path. This dog had not been dumped so far into the woods as to be invisible. To his left, fifteen or so metres further in, the wind fluttered a tatter of blue and white tape. This was close to where Josh Turner's dog was found.

"Any sign of the owner?"

Somerville shook her head. "A few footprints in the mud by the path. I am getting those analysed. His phone is also missing. Last call made was at 5:30pm. Last call received was Miss Haslett's request for pickled onions, then it was switched off."

Daley canted his head. *Pickled onions?*

"Pregnant. Eight months."

Daley nodded. Eons ago, Lynne had been pregnant. Eons ago, the prospect of fatherhood scared him. She had craved Worcestershire Sauce flavoured crisps. The scan had shown an empty hole with a withered umbilical cord. Soon afterward, the cravings had been taken away and the empty hole had moved between them, unacknowledged, unspoken, unresolved.

"Barbiturates?" Daley recalled how the setter had been killed.

Somerville shrugged, "Most likely." She rounded the dog and walked over to him. He could smell her perfume. "So, I think we have to consider Tom Phillips is number 5?"

"He could be out here with a sprained ankle but yes, I suppose so. Can you copy me in on the details. I'm going to have a look around."

"Keep to the tape and give me a call if you find anything... and don't mess up my crime scene, Inspector Daley."

Daley smiled and retraced his steps back toward the gangly PC.

***

Deb Whetstone cast down her pad and took a deep breath. Ordeal by Team Brief was tough enough without Scott Daley seeking to derail it. Then there had been the debacle with Nick Snowdon which was bordering on the aggressive. At the moment, Daley provided more obstacles than solutions.

Allenby was in his office right now. Should she speak to him? Let the D/Supt have a word on the QT, ask him to ease up? Or would that prove her inadequacy, her inability to fight her own battles? Perhaps she should request he be removed altogether?

Then again, should she cut him some slack? Once his feet were properly back under the table, the kinks ironed out, perhaps he would be back to his normal self.

As Daley had left the briefing, she had watched him slap the pill into his mouth, glancing furtively about, hoping no-one had noticed. But someone had. Monaghan had already remarked on Daley's seeming reliance on the tablets. To his knowledge, the Inspector had taken five that morning alone, this latest making six - and it was still only 11:30. That couldn't be good.

He was obviously not fully fit. Right from the get-go she had known. She hadn't worked with the man for two years, seen him pitch into difficult situations head-first, even earning the epithet *Suicide Scott Daley*, not to know when something was wrong. The previous morning, meeting him in the car park, she had been unnerved to find him sitting in his car, clasping the steering wheel, breathing heavily, his eyes like pennies. And when she had returned with coffee, he was still there. Perhaps it was just a bedding-in process, re-orienting himself? Or maybe it was she that needed to re-orient, to return to their previous ways of working? She would speak to Allenby when she had the chance.

Turning back to her desk she pushed aside the indecision. These problems had a habit of working themselves out. Opening her notebook, she phoned Steven Franks' mobile. The phone went straight to voicemail, so she left a cryptic message. Across the office, Monaghan and Taylor had become rather animated. Over their shoulders, she could see a rap sheet on the monitor. It was Steven Franks'.

"Deb. Franks has form. ABH. He beat up a student in 1999."

An altercation outside a pub on match night, influenced by alcohol. It didn't sound particularly serious but it landed Franks six months suspended and the student some colourful bruises.

"Anything else? It *was* over twenty years ago."

Taylor flicked the mouse and the screen scrolled up. "A few speeding fines but other than the ABH, nothing."

"You'll need a damn sight more than that." She regretted the testiness in her voice. This was not Taylor's problem. "What about Connor Smith? Anything turned up on him?"

Taylor shook his head.

Returning to her desk and scooping up her mug, Whetstone wandered over to the kitchenette.

And where the bloody hell was Daley anyway?

Chapter 45

He had underestimated the distance around the perimeter to the point where Somerville had told him the gates to the old Chatham Woods farm buildings would be. After an hour, Daley began to regret not using the Audi; the walk back may be equally as long. Several times, the pavement petered out to muddied verges, at one point disappearing completely forcing him to dodge the speeding traffic.

He assumed it would be a circular route, through the farm and back along the path Somerville had indicated. On his phone, he had recorded the location of his car and of the dead greyhound. Beneath the overcoat, the sweat clung uncomfortably to his shirt and the clammy, sodden legs of his trousers stuck to his shins. His shoes were wrecked. Sighing, he could picture his wellingtons, picked up that morning and left in the boot of his car. At least the exercise had kept him warm.

Taking a breather, he called DC Taylor, asking him to cross reference all known phone numbers for Steven Franks and Connor Smith with those of Sherwood, Fletcher, Bryson and Turner. Also, had any of them had been patients at the clinic? Then he asked him to check on the game at Craven Cottage on 29th September, the state of the Tube on that afternoon, and lastly, could he trace a taxi driver that might have picked up Bryson from Moor Park.

Finally, the edge of the woods turned down a dim, tree-lined lane. Here, the verge fell into a deep ditch filled with vicious rusty brambles and dank brown water, forcing Daley to walk on the deserted road. Soon, a towering set of galvanised metal gates loomed over him, a peeling, painted board warning:

Chatham Woods Farm
No Entry. Trespasser's will be prosecuted

Gritting his teeth at the errant apostrophe, Daley rattled the mammoth padlock. Rusted and solid, the gates had not been opened in a long while. The tops were lined with barbed wire. It was unlikely anyone would climb them. There must be another way in. To his left, the road snaked on, dark through the canopy of trees. In for a penny, now thoroughly soaked and desperately uncomfortable, Daley decided he might as well venture further on up the road. In his pocket, his phone buzzed. It was Whetstone.

"Daley?"

"Where are you?" Her tone was interrogative, like his mother when asking if his homework was done. Daley chose to ignore it. A new leaf.

"Chatham Woods Nature Reserve. Where Josh Turner, the dog walker went missing. Another dog turned up dead. There's a runner who didn't return home last night."

"I need you back here, sir. We have to find Franks." He could tell that *need* meant *want*.

"I know. I should be back soon. Just tying up some loose ends."

The tiny speaker rattled as Whetstone exhaled deeply on the other end. Tough Shit. He was still her superior. He still had to manage the *Zone 6* case even if her priorities were different.

"So how are your investigations going, sir?" Did she really care? Maybe the point of the question was to ask why he was bothering with this pissy little misper case at all? But there was something niggling, like a crossword grid where all the answers are in plain sight, if only he could see the clues.

"Slowly, Deb. This new abduction is fresh. It might give me something to go on." As he strolled down the bleak country lane, Daley's spirits rose slightly as he realised that, however damp his trouser legs, however wet his hair, Whetstone seemed to be drowning. She had no idea what she was doing or where she was going. It could only be a matter of time before she asked Allenby for help. Rather than leave her to drown, should he throw her a lifebelt? Like Whetstone, he only had ideas with no cohesion. Like Whetstone, he needed a firm hold which he could use to pull the ideas together. Like Whetstone, he was fed up of playing a game of divide and rule.

At the outset of the investigation, there was always a phenomenal amount of pressure on the Investigating Officer. Seniors would be looking for a swift result, peers and subordinates would be looking for decisive leadership and family, friends and colleagues of the victims would want answers. Then there was the minefield that was the media. With the potential for slip-ups, for the slightest comment to be taken out of context, to instantly flip from hero to zero, the press had to courted carefully. Fortunately, Bob Allenby was the media's sweetheart and tended to protect his team. Conversely, that often made it harder because they never knew what he had said.

"Look, Deb. Give me half an hour. I promise..."

"I can't spend my time covering for you, sir. You know that."

Daley was irritated. She was present when Allenby had handed him this losers brief.

"Half an hour, right?"

"OK. I'm going after Franks. I need you here."

Daley pocketed his phone. Stopping, he realised he had been walking, engrossed in the call, without regard for where he was. The galvanised gates were around a quarter of a mile back. There had not been a vehicle along the road for five minutes and noise from the dual carriageway had faded. This was a fool's errand. With a huff he turned, not relishing the long trek back. Then he noticed something strange. The overgrown ditch had followed the edge of the road along its entire length, half full of dank brown sludge and evil-looking brambles, but here it had been bridged and culverted. Beyond, subsumed by the dense hedge, there sat a rusting gate and beyond that two hedges demarcated the route of an overgrown drive. Curious, he crossed the bridge and yanked at the gate which yielded immediately. It had been used recently, the overgrown brambles disguising the opening. There were fresh tyre tracks across the threshold and through the mud and weeds beyond.

This had to be another entrance to the farm.

Closing the gate and following the path, he soon found himself in a small yard, damp and overgrown, dead, brown weeds cracking the mould blackened concrete. Forlorn against the encroaching wood, stood an old turn-of-the-century redbrick farmhouse. Blinded by metal shutters, stained by graffiti, it had been battling the elements alone and losing. Through the roof, rafters like bony fingers clawed at the grey clouds. A few wooden sheds, rotted and collapsed, swarming with weeds and bracken, bordered the yard in front of him. Except for the tapping of rain on leaves, the yard was still and deadly silent. Something unnerved Daley, raising the hackles on his neck, that undefinable feeling of being watched. Examining the flattened grass, he found the tyre tracks in the sodden mud. They looked fresh. The tracks ran around the perimeter of the yard towards the wooden sheds.

Maybe that's where the van was parked, hidden between abductions?

Pulling out his phone, he dropped a text to Monaghan. *Find out as much as possible about a derelict farm in the grounds of Chatham Woods Nature Reserve.*

Suddenly feeling exposed, Daley made his way to the eaves of the first shed. Little more than a byre, the grey sky peered in through snapped and twisted laths that tumbled down to the puddled floor. Not even good for firewood, overgrown with nettles and bracken, the building had been empty for years.

Crossing the open front, Daley checked out the second shed. It was much healthier than its sickly neighbour. The doors were solid and padlocked, a stout lock chromed and shining. He tried to peer through the ill-fitting panels but inside was black.

The running footsteps were almost subliminal, some primitive instinct urging him to turn as the man threw himself headlong at Daley, hammering his back into the shed doors with a resounding crack which jarred through his shoulder and arm. Caught off guard, Daley fell to his knees briefly winded. His attacker hovered for a while before letting loose a vicious kick at his side. Parrying with his good arm, Daley dodged sideways as a boot impacted the wooden doors beside his head, sending echoes around the yard. Another kick followed, this time less powerful, but still it left him sprawling into the mud. The man seized his opportunity and turned and fled. Looking up, Daley saw him head for the rear of the house. Was there a way in? Rising to his feet, Daley brushed himself off and, his ribs straining for breath, set off after his assailant, wishing to God he had worn the old grey suit, rather than the new brown one to impress Somerville.

Rounding the rear of the house, Daley stopped dead, staccato footstep ricocheting off the walls. Beyond, a motley assortment of run-down buildings surrounded three sides of a concrete yard the size of a basketball court, now cracked and invaded by weeds and moss. Left, a garden to the rear of the house was untended, an overgrown jumble of weeds. Ancient, rusting equipment lay were it had been left. Aside from the persistent cooing of pigeons, there was no sign of life. Daley looked about for his assailant, his senses in overdrive, his breath rasping through unexercised lungs. Down at his feet, he saw the footprints in the mud tracking towards a large open hay barn. Slowly and deliberately, hearing his heart booming in his ears, he eased forwards. If his attacker had come this way, he would be cornered and all the more dangerous. The only way out was straight through Daley. A locomotive may have tried that and succeeded but this man was a different prospect. Younger and more agile than a Class 90, Daley had to keep his wits about him. A sound to his left and a flash of colour. Swivelling on his heels, Daley launched himself at the shape, grabbing wildly as he flew. Catching the man around the legs in a tackle that would have thrilled his rugby teacher, yet broken the heart of the surgeon who had fixed his shoulder, the two men tumbled to the ground, mud and grass flying around them. As the man scrabbled and scratched for a foothold, Daley delivered a monumental crashing fist to his stomach, driving the air from his body in flatulent rasps. Quickly, Daley dived on top, rolled the man on his face and yanked an arm up his back, forcing a squeal of pain. Then resting a knee onto his back, he pressed down.

"Look, son. I am hot, tired, wet and grubby. I am miles from my car and I am hungry. God alone knows how I am going to get this suit clean. So, if you know what's good for you, give it up." He yanked the arm higher. The man yelped briefly and then sunk down, defeated.

With his free hand, Daley found his phone and called Whetstone.

"It's Daley. Look, get a car out here, to Chatham Woods Farm. Not the main entrance, there's another one further along the lane. Oh, and a change of clothes if you can. I've just bumped into Connor Smith."

Chapter 46

Houndsfield Close, Pinner, 11:00am, Wednesday

This had all gone much too far.

He needed to speak to Caz. This was one of those occasions when anonymous pay-as-you-go phones would have worked a treat. Franks briefly considered buying one but the last time they had asked for a name and address. What part of anonymous did they not understand? Of course, he could collect his own phone from the van but where it was parked was best avoided, at least for the time being. And anyway, the phone would tell them where he was.

Franks parked up outside the Close and scanned the pristine lawns of the nine houses in the cul-de-sac, paying special attention to his own. Apart from a few second cars on drives, the Close was empty, deserted during the working day. He felt around in the rear foot well for the North Face waterproof, then cursed. That was in the sodding van too.

Bracing himself, Franks alighted and, ducking his head against the icy darts of rain, made a dash down the Close and through the door of Number 4, wheezing as the cold stole his breath. He almost broke his neck tripping over the suitcases in the hallway.

She appeared around the living room door, a fleece dressing gown pulled about her, a glass half full. Already the house smelt like a distillery. He steeled himself for the inevitable.

"The police have called. They need to see you. I did try to ring but it just went to voicemail."

"I left it in the van." He indicated the luggage. "What's all this? Going somewhere."

"No but you are. I've had enough."

He nodded at the glass. "I can see that."

"So, who was it last night? Barely in from three days away, I see you for five minutes and you're back out. Which tart were you warming yourself on this time?"

"You know where I was. Working."

"What? All night? Pull the other one." The words were spat, full of venom. There was never any pretence. Well accustomed to his immorality, his lack of loyalty, she knew exactly where he had been.

"Look, there are things I have to do. Things that can only be done at night when it's quiet." Franks didn't want to elaborate about the farm. He shouldn't need to. He had already had a similar conversation with Caz, arriving two hours later than expected and he explained the lost time in the usual way. When Caz asked, he was with his wife. When Jill asked, he evaded the question.

"You should be here with me! I barely see you these days and, when I do, you smell like a whore's cleavage."

"Oh, put another record on, will you?" Franks was in no mood to argue but he could be persuaded. He pushed past and headed upstairs for his gym bag and a coat. The less time he spent here the better. He would take out his frustrations on a cross trainer and, if he was lucky, one of the yummy mummies that hung around between school runs.

"What do the police want? You got some girl half your age into trouble, or maybe you were just too rough and left marks?"

"Oh, grow up. It's just some work thing. It's none of your business. You just keep your bloody nose out. I won't tell you again!"

The police again. Calling his work, calling his home. They really did want to see him. Thinking back over the last few days, about everything that had gone on. Assuming that they would know what had gone on. Was there anything that would interest the police?

The farm.

Always at the back of his mind there was the farm.

And the phone calls from Connor. He wasn't explicit but he had spoken of Varsa. Of an accident. Surely Varsa was history? Or maybe that was it. Varsa causing problems even after she had gone.

They had to talk about it, to get the facts straight before the police had a chance to speak to them separately. He had phoned Marion and she was solid but Connor was a loose cannon.

He leaned over the bannister. Already his anger was piquing, as it did the moment he and Jill clashed swords, as inevitably she pressed the buttons. But now it was exacerbated by Smith and his texts which would even now be on some detective's desk.

"If you bring your shit, your tarts into this house it *is* my business. We might be married but this is my house and don't you forget it. My mother left it to me and I can have you out any time I want."

"Your house? Your house?" Bag in hand he trotted down the stairs, now in full flow. "Who is it that puts food on the table? It certainly isn't you, you work-shy, barren cow. There is always some excuse or another with you while I am out earning a crust. It might be your house but you have never brought a penny into it. So, what if I need a little pleasure now and again? I get little enough from you. Maybe if you got out of this dump once in a while..."

"You reek of her, you cheating bastard. Who is she this time? Some nurse from that clinic, hitching her dress up like some bitch on heat. Jesus, if they knew you like I do."

"I am warning you. Don't push it. Not today." Last night, he had arrived home. There had been a meal, things were going great. Until he announced he had to go out again.

"Why? Too near the truth. Is that it? Telling everyone you are off on your deliveries when all the time you are thigh deep in some whore. I know what you're delivering and you don't need a truck for that." She mimicked a tiny manhood with her pinkie.

"That is bloody rich coming from you! At least I bring money into this house. What do you do but sit and watch that television? How do you think that makes me feel, eh?"

"I don't know because you're never here! Look at you now. Five minutes after you walk through that door, you are going back out again. Who is it this time? Some slapper from the gym? Is she sitting waiting in your car, warming herself up?"

Then she was reeling backwards and the palm of his hand stung. She fell hard against architrave, a crack resounding as her head impacted. He stared at her, sitting against the skirting, tears welling in her eyes, and turned away. Her hand reached for the back of her scalp. Empathy had deserted him years ago, when they had buried their son, buried their future. His ribs still ached from her fists the previous Sunday. They were as bad as each other. Maybe he should have stayed at the farm, or at her house, bided his time and waited for Caz to return, enjoyed the time away from the tension and the eggshells and the sharpness of tongues.

He reached for the front door handle and opened it as the woman, making for the doorbell, started and regained her composure.

"Steven Franks?"

His eyes darted from her face to the small wallet she mechanically opened and then back to the stern serious face. Reflexively, Franks slammed the door and dropped the latch.

Shit!

He turned back to Jill lying in the living room clutching her head. He heard the rapping on the door and panic overwhelmed him. What was this all about? The texts from Connor, Caz telling him to remain at Elstree and now the police hammering on his door.

That made it a whole lot more urgent. Now he knew he didn't want to speak to them.

"What have you been telling them, you bitch?" He turned and fled to the back of the house, as she shouted after him, hoping he got what he deserved. Escaping through the rear, he leapt straight into the arms of a tall, square traffic cop. With a swing, he brought the kit bag around and into the copper's neck, sending him sprawling. Without breaking stride, Franks dashed down the garden, out of the gate and onto the track that led back to the road.

***

The situation was changing quicker than Whetstone had anticipated. Calling Lambourne Road, dispatching Corby to assist Daley, she considered this new turn of events. Smith at Chatham Woods and Franks absconding.

Unable to contain her patience, Whetstone had decided that Franks needed bringing in. They could link him with Varsa Ruparelia, with Smith and now indirectly with Chatham Woods. He drove a white van and, although it was twenty years ago, Franks had proved himself handy with his fists.

Added to that, she was fed up with waiting for something to happen, whilst Daley's misper case was yielding all the fun.

She reread the email Daley had sent. *Another abduction at Chatham Woods. Going to check it out.* Now he had fallen over Smith at the same place. A farm. Could it be a coincidence? Did Smith's presence at Chatham Woods link the *Zone 6 Abductions* and the *Hand in the Van*? Daley would be insufferable if it did.

Beside her, Keith Parrish was leaning intently over the steering wheel as the radio chattered, searching ahead for Franks' BMW. There was a glamour to the uniform made all the more seductive by the short sleeved black shirt. He was incredibly sexy in civvies but there was something about men in uniform. The engine howled as he took each corner slightly faster than she would have liked.

It would only be a matter of time before Allenby handed over the case to Daley.

Up ahead, a dot on the horizon marked Franks car. As they had returned to the traffic car, Franks had disappeared in a fog of rubber smoke out towards the A404. If they didn't apprehend him, they would lose him in the maze of roads in North Harrow. Gunning the throttle, Parrish eased back into the seat and adjusted his grip on the wheel. The Met 530D Touring was basically the same model as Franks car, except this one had more horses, uprated suspension and better brakes, not to mention the blues and twos which were at full chat. Soon the distant dot became large and Parrish knew that he had the car. He hung off a safe distance and clicked the radio button.

"In pursuit of grey BMW, Tango-whisky-one-two-xray-victor-charlie, South on Moss Lane, Pinner toward Church Lane and Nower Hill."

Whetstone's finger nails dug into the squab of her seat as cars dodged out of the way. She knew Keith had days like this but she was thankful not to share too many. Franks car careered sharply out onto Church Lane, snaking through traffic at the junction, bewildered drivers stopping dead, forcing Parrish's 530D to skate to a halt.

"Come on, Doris! Can't you see the bloody lights?"

After light years, the driver eased the car back and Keith again floored the throttle. Franks was slowing, dodging the mid-morning mobile chicane along Nower Hill. Up ahead the T-Junction with Pinner Road was a solid line of traffic crossing their path in both direction. Franks car bobbed on its suspension as he hit the junction and his horn blared. A gap appeared in the traffic and he screeched through on the wrong side of the bollards, threading down between the lines of startled drivers, as Parrish followed him every inch.

"In pursuit, Pinner Road, junction of Capel Gardens and Melrose Road heading towards junction A404. Speed forty, four-oh, miles per hour."

As the cars closed rank behind the fleeing BMW, Keith flashed his light but Franks was making distance between them. Then suddenly there was a squeal from underneath the car and Whetstone lurched forwards as a huge swathe of red emerged from the fire station to her left.

"Shit, shit, shit!" Parrish hammered on the steering wheel, the adrenaline coursing through him as he scoured the road.

It was too late. Franks was gone.

***

Reinforcements would be another half an hour, so Daley cuffed Connor Smith to a stanchion on one of the outbuildings. Wet and quivering the two stood deadlocked, Smith refusing to speak a word, his sullen eyes flicking nervously around the yard. He tugged at the handcuff but, although rusty, the stanchion would not budge. Daley had found a corner out of the breeze. His head was pounding, made still worse by the impact with the unforgiving wood of the shed doors.

Three days back, he was beginning the understand the difference between working and idling away time on the panel. For one, his face was still raw and burning from his first regular shave in six months. For another, there was the hassle of selecting a clean shirt every morning, matching it with a tie and remembering to change into them each day. For the past six months, he had cultured a respectable growth of stubble and recycled the same hooded top and tracksuit bottoms until they could stand up and run a 5K on their own.

Then there was the alarm clock. An invention from the odious mind of a sadist. Benignly burning electricity for twenty-three hours, fifty nine minutes and fifty nine seconds, sharpening it's blade, waiting to pounce. Then, at the very deepest moment of unconsciousness, squawking its war cry, shattering the silence and raising heart-rates to vein busting levels before once more being sent into self-satisfied repose to await its next moment of torture. During his recuperation, it was switched off, allowing him to seek out his natural circadian rhythm which was somewhat at odds with the North London Homicide Unit's expectations.

Not that the alarm clock had been much of an issue for the last three mornings. Since returning, Daley had woken early and endured restless hours waiting for the alarm to hoot anti-climactically, as his mind turmoiled and agonised over the ignominy of the *Zone 6* case, the chaotic state of the *Hand in the Van* investigation and the plummeting nose-dive his career had taken.

And last night, the van had occupied his thoughts.

Until now, the white van was the only connection between the two cases. Anonymous, without a registration, it was no connection at all. Now, having run into Smith, the two cases had metaphorically collided. Why was Smith here? Was this the farm that Varsa Ruparelia had written of in her diary?

But the van itself was a paradox. How could Franks have travelled to Newcastle in the van yet it ended up on the A40? He stared across at the shed, at the padlock. Was there a second van behind those solid wooden doors? Was that where the stolen stock was kept?

Reaching into his pocket for a handkerchief, Daley's fingers felt the foil blister pack. Some of the blisters had been damaged by the ruckus, rough edges teasing his fingertips. Just a nail would open the foil. A short distance from pocket to hand, from hand to mouth, from mouth to stomach. Turning away from Smith, Daley rested his head against an upright. Surely one wouldn't hurt, one more day? Extreme situations call for extreme measures, after all. The pain in his temples redoubled and he could feel the top of his skull squeezing his brain. With Herculean strength, he dragged out his hand and stared down at his palm. It was empty.

Shit, shit, shit. How could he have allowed himself to become dependent? Was this really dependence? Was he really that weak, that pathetic? He could stop anytime he needed to, couldn't he? But he still had the headaches, he was not sleeping. It would be foolish simply to stop taking the pills, hope it would all go away. From behind, he heard the slow grinding rumble, the atonal bellowing of the horn, felt the ground shaking and the pressure of the monster as it sped towards him. Cowering from the impact, he heard the cry. He spun around.

"What the fuck's the matter with you?"

Smith was shivering on the cold concrete leaning against the stanchion, his arm above his head. Apart from the soft patter of rain and the bluster of a chill wind against the walls, the yard was dead. Not even birdsong cut the silence. As quiet as the grave.

Gathering his wits, Daley eyed Smith. "I'd be more worried about myself if I were you, son." What had happened in those brief seconds? If any of this got back, he would be more of a laughing stock than he was already. He pointed a commanding finger at Smith. "You - stay!"

"Piss off, you twat!" Smith glowered ineffectually and rubbed a bloodied hand across his cheek, rattling the cuffs against the stanchion. It was the bravado of a man who had yet to open the door to the baying crowd and the waiting gallows.

Behind Daley, the house stood forlorn and neglected, stoically watching the unfolding drama, the most excitement it had seen in over a decade...probably. He forged through the bracken which had subsumed the kitchen garden, trying shutters here and there. Daley figured Smith would have preferred a safer, drier, less visible hiding place than the barns, but the shutters were all bolted to the frames, solid and immoveable.

Except for one.

Glancing back at Smith and smiling, Daley ran a finger over one of the bolts. There were clean scrapes around the edges and it was loose. They were all loose. Each had been held with pliers and sawn through with a hacksaw, then stuck back into their hole with Blu-Tack. Behind, the window was dilapidated and peeling, the panes long gone. Daley reached into his pocket for his phone, lighting it like a torch, peering into the darkness. Checking Smith was still secured to the ironmongery, he climbed in.

The inside was as black as night and except for bullet tracks of light piercing the gloom, Daley could see nothing. There was a taste of damp and mould in the air and a pungent smell of animal urine. He swung the beam around what must have been a kitchen. Cobwebs festooned corners and the floor crunched underfoot with glass and detritus. Across the room, the beam alighted on a doorway, smudged dust on the frame. Smith had been here. Following his nose, Daley crossed the hallway into the back room of the ground floor. Swinging around, his torch spotlighted a sleeping bag and a rucksack, some water bottles and camping light, a small stove and a cool box. Smith was in for the long haul. Against the wall lay a shoulder bag in which Daley found Smith's laptop. A chair had been placed beneath a window. Through pinholes in the steel shutters Daley squinted out at the drive. This was Smith's vantage point. A safe place to watch for unwanted guests. To ensure he stayed hidden.

Outside the room, the stairs disappeared into the gloom of the first floor. Straddling the steps, fearful of rotten treads, Daley eased his way up, briefly startled by a pair of white pin-prick eyes which loomed large on the landing before scratching away. Upstairs, the sky paled the ceiling through broken laths and fallen rafters. There was a stench of guano and he could hear the soft warbling coo of nesting pigeons. To the rear of the house, the bathroom had been scavenged, bare walls and protruding pipes, whilst the main bedroom stood empty, festooned with fallen wiring and collapsing plasterboard and a single chair under the window. He peered through the pinholes.

Across the yard, the shed stood, padlocked and firm. From this room, Smith could watch the yard, monitor the comings and goings. Had Varsa told him what she had discovered? Had he discovered the farm and blackmailed Franks? No wonder he had fled. If Franks was prepared to kill Varsa then Smith was sure to be next.

The downstairs of this place was eerie, yet the upstairs was cloaked in a dark dread which had soaked into the walls and chilled the air about him. Some terrible tragedy had taken place here and every wall kept its counsel, protected its secrets and sat in silence, eyeing him with suspicion. Every fibre of his being told Daley that this was a place he didn't want to be. Taking a deep, musty breath, he turned to find the stairs.

The beam of his phone torch passed across something, a

flash of colour in the grey and a memory triggered. In the dimness, he recognised the print - *Tulip Fields with Rijnsburg Windmill, 1886* - it was a print he had seen before in his mother's house. He was familiar with it and it made him warm to watch the flowers sway as he ate his fish fingers and his dad talked about the nick and his brothers squabbled. But he had seen it before and a lot more recently.

"Keys." barked Daley, squinting against the glare of the November day.

Smith lazily raised a sullen head. "Piss off."

"You're in enough trouble. Just hand me your keys."

Smith canted his head, bullish. "Trouble? What trouble? What? Squatting? Trespassing? This is wrongful arrest and you know it. You wait till I tell your boss about you flipping out just then. Bloody Doolalley-Tap, you. I am in fear for my life here, you mad bastard."

"Oh, shut up or I really will flip my twig and tear you a new one. Now where are your bloody keys?"

Smith pulled the small back remote from his pocket. "I only have my car key. I haven't got a key to that padlock, if that's what you're thinking."

And there was the conundrum. Without a key, he could not unlock the padlock; without a warrant, they had no grounds to jemmy it off. Without a crime, he too was trespassing.

So Smith had hidden at the house, certain no-one knew he was there, picking rooms with vantage points over the drive and the yard. He knew who came, who unlocked the padlock. Daley would have to wait for Interview Room 2 and the opportunity to formally wheedle it out of the little scrote.

Chapter 47

Wembley, West London

Beneath the omnipresent urban rumble, Clarence Road was silent. The policeman by the squad car outside the apartment complex puffed out vapour trying to emulate the sound of a steam locomotive drawing away from a station but the steam from a funnel was thicker, fuller, so he gave up. Babysitting duty was mind-numbingly tedious. Most of the residents were at work so he was babysitting a pile of bricks. He had shared this view with the duty Sergeant and received a curt response.

He had been thinking of sausage and mash. More particularly, he had been thinking of the slight crust that would have developed on the mash back at the station by the end of his shift. At least on the beat, one could find a cafe or someone to chat to. People seemed at their most congenial during the day. The vibration in his pocket took his mind of the flaccid skin that would even now have settled on his gravy.

"John?"

"Hi, Chris."

"Did you see a bloke just now?"

"Thick-set guy, dark cropped hair? "Yeah. He just drove off. Dark coloured BMW estate."

"S'funny. He came up the stairs and looked as if he was walking straight at me. Then he seemed to panic. He said he left his paper in his car. I was expecting him to come back up."

"Nah, He drove off. Perhaps he forgot the milk or sommat?"

"I got the distinct impression that if I hadn't been here he would have been in the flat. D'you get a registration from the car?"

"No, sorry. I'll call it in anyway."

Chapter 48

Lambourne Road, Ealing, 12:00pm, Wednesday

Re-reading the email, Monaghan was gripped by a dilemma. The blood results from Ruparelia's flat, Smith's house and the van had been sent over. As expected, the traces found in Miss Ruparelia's flat were her own. No other person's blood had been found. Smith's house was clean, with evidence of vomit in the hall. The white van, however, was a positive genetic soup.

Unsurprisingly, substantial amounts belonged to Varsa Ruparelia, but what did surprise Monaghan were the other traces. Sherwood and Fletcher - two of Daley's *Zone 6* victims, with hair and skin samples matching Turner. Other traces remained unmatched.

Interestingly, at least to Dave Monaghan who revelled in the minutiae of life and death, were the ethnicity results. Varsa was a Ugandan Asian, her origins in the Indian sub-continent, a smattering of East Asian. Karen Sherwood and Diane Fletcher were broadly speaking European, having traces of Gallic, Germanic and Scandinavian heritage. Josh Turner was predominantly Irish with a small percentage of Middle-Eastern in his genome which, as Dave had discovered, was not all that unusual. Early Mesolithic settlers had followed the mammoth herds from what would become the bible lands before the great tsunami which formed the English Channel had separated the British peninsula from continental Europe. The other two unnamed samples were the puzzle. Both shared a remarkably similar heritage, originating from Israel, Lebanon and the Levant. There were no markers for Europe or the British Isles, leading Monaghan to deduce that these two people were either immigrants or visitors.

But none of this led to the dilemma which urged Monaghan to open his drawer and unwrap a humbug, an event so rare that he had to root around to find one. It was something considerably closer to home than some unidentified DNA.

If the van contained traces of Sherwood, Fletcher, Turner *and* Ruparelia, then the link between the *Hand in the Van* and the

Zone 6 enquiries was absolute. And that meant he had to decide whom to inform first and whom to piss off. Sucking on the humbug, he pondered upon the best way forward.

On the one hand - he chuckled at the unintended pun - he could phone the good news through to Whetstone, confirm that the *Hand in the Van* case was almost certain to be elevated to a murder investigation; that the resources would double, the pressure triple and the press conferences start, meaning Allenby would be on their backs, which no-one really wanted. On the flip side, he could inform Daley first, give him the news that his *misper* enquiry was now a murder investigation with pretty much the same effect.

Musing on Daley's ignominious return to a missing persons case, then under Whetstone's supervision, he felt more inclined to speak to him first. But if he was still popping so many Tramadol, was Scott Daley thoroughly fit?

As tends to happen on these occasions, the dilemma vaporised as the decision was taken out of his hands.

"Sergeant Monaghan. My office for a moment please?"

So engrossed had he been in the body of the email, he had neglected to spot Allenby's name in the *CC* list.

Chapter 49

Whetstone had resigned herself to a long hunt for Franks. Once the expletives and frantic radio conversation had died down, a sullen silence had descended and she expected a prickly drive back to Lambourne Road. She sat with folded arms as Keith craned his neck to peer down this side road or that driveway but the chase had gone cold. Pinner Road led to the A404. Franks could have turned left or right but if he had any sense he would go to ground.

"Look, Keith. It happens." Parrish glanced at Whetstone then back to the road. It must be a man thing, testosterone or maybe adrenaline, but Parrish was seething.

Perhaps going in cold had been a mistake but she had been worried Franks would run. Someone would have alerted him. Albin, or his wife, or even Smith, shit scared after the crash. No doubt a knock the next morning would have been a waste of time.

Now the horse had bolted. She had radioed in details of the car but there would be little chance of finding it. The only solution was to attempt to out-think Franks.

Then she had received the call from Corby.

"Sarge, Chris Patterson, the uniform at Varsa Ruparelia's apartment has just reported a male IC1 matching Franks description. Says he was acting suspiciously."

Whetstone sat bolt upright. "And did he arrest him?"

"What for? The guy turned up, walked past Chris, said he had forgotten his newspaper and walked back to his car. Then he buggered off."

"Jesus, Mike. He's just clobbered Keith around the head. Why didn't he stop him?"

"How was he to know that? And anyway, since when has forgetting a newspaper been an offence?"

Even as the last swearword had resounded off the interior of the car, the second call had come in, this time a tinny voice over the radio.

Grey BMW, Tango-whisky-one-two-xray-victor-charlie, spotted Mandeville Road, Northolt junction Eastcote Lane heading South West.

Whetstone looked at Keith as the two tried to pinpoint the location on their mental maps. "He's going to Smith's house in Southall. Can we get there first?"

"We can have a bloody good go." Parrish flicked on the lights and sound and downshifted. Whetstone closed her eyes as she sank back in the seat and the car hooked a right onto the Greenford Road.

Chapter 50

Chatham Woods Farm, Ruislip

Daley stared at the shining galvanised padlock. In his experience, open to the elements, the lustre dulls within a year. The lock was new. If it housed the van, if it was caked in Smith's prints, then he needed it examined pronto. Two vans, double the fun for your average abductor. He needed an excuse to remove that padlock.

He checked his watch. What was taking them so long?

Glancing back, Smith was contorting his wrist, twisting the cuff and wasting his time, so he walked across the yard and leaned a hand against the shed. The doors budged an inch or so. Squinting through the crack, there was nothing, black. He tried the torch app on his phone but the beam would not carry. His torch was next to his wellingtons in the Audi.

As he held it, the phone buzzed. It was the email from Dave Monaghan. There were signs that Sherwood, Fletcher and Turner had been transported in the crashed van. They were almost certainly dead. What was it that Franks and Smith were involved in? Sighing, frustration growing, pain sawing through his head, Daley strode across the yard and grabbed Smith's lapel, pulling the boy to his feet.

"What's going on here, eh? You're driving a van which has carried at least five bodies. You're hiding out at the scene of multiple abductions. Just what are you involved in?"

Smith cowered behind his one unfettered hand. "Five bodies. I..." In the nick of time, he stopped his racing mouth. "Is that how it works, these days? If I don't talk, you beat seven colours of shite out of me? Go on then, you nutter! Take the punch. You know you want to. Go on, right here..." Connor thrust out his chin and indicated the point. "Take a good punch. My brief will have a field day with you, you bloody lunatic!"

And he wanted to take the punch. He wanted to wipe the face off this cocky little bastard who knew everything yet told him nothing. He wanted to take it for all the wasted hours and minutes and seconds, for all the terrified victims and their families, for all the criminals who thought they were so clever they could outsmart him. For the train driver with the death of a woman on his conscience.

Daley felt his arm swing back, he felt the hammers in his skull and he felt immense anger for the people whose corpses lay rotting and hidden while this pitiful, good-for-nothing weasel played him for a fool. And he stilled his fist and he released the lapel. Turning, he marched purposefully across the yard, casting away the baying demons to follow in his wake. Grabbing a bar, he jammed it behind the padlock and summoned up every ounce of strength he had. He could feel the wood cracking, the sinews in his bad shoulder stretching and popping. He imagined his fists pummelling and punching at the soft round face of Smith until the blood spattered and the flesh tore and the bones shattered beneath his fists and the train howled around the corner and the ground vibrated but this time he would not flinch. It would need to go through him. He saw them on the tracks, He saw his hands drag the man away as the woman sitting zen-like exploded into a crimson mist.

And then he fell back in the mud, panting and retching. In front of him, the padlock lay torn from its mount and the doors sat tantalisingly agape.

Chapter 51

By the time Franks reached Southall, the rain had abated. He reversed into a space to afford a quick getaway and sat for a moment, considered his next move. Smith lived three streets away. By far the best approach would be on foot, protected by the maze of footpaths. There being no time like the present, he opened the door and headed off down the street.

Fuchsia Close was still, eerie in the commuter dead space of midday but still Franks eyes were on stalks. Smith's BMW, the smaller, rather effeminate Series one, which rather summed up the man, was missing from the drive. The house seemed deserted, windows dark and cold. Maybe no-one was at home? Or maybe, Smith was shitting himself in the back? And Franks didn't blame him. Where else would the police have gotten his name from?

Maybe he was not alone? Franks scanned the few cars about the Close but recognised none. Briskly walking down the drive, he was about to rattle the letterbox but thought better of it. Perhaps he should take a look around the back first? He retraced his steps up the close and down the alleyway which led to the rear of the houses. He found the gate for No. 9 and eased down the latch, which surprisingly yielded. He had been expecting to climb the fence. Thanking God for small mercies, Franks slid himself around the gate and into the garden. Beyond, he followed a line of slabs to the rear of the house, but again, the windows were dark, no sign of life.

Of course, they could be in the cellar. Did this type of house have a cellar? No, he doubted it. Concrete raft, solid floor. Frustrated, Franks slumped down onto the back step and pondered his next move. The police would have his house pegged and his usual gym was out of the question. Perhaps he should head back to Caz's house, conceal the car and wait for her to return? No-one was looking for him there.

Resignedly, Franks made his way back down the garden.

Parrish waited outside the gate, sensing the slow footsteps come nearer and nearer, sensing the right moment. Franks was easily twenty pounds of muscle heavier and he wasn't about to chew on that bag again. The paces slowed and shuffled to a halt. Franks was just behind the gate. Mustering all his strength, Parrish shoulder-barged the gate, renting it from its hinges sending him sprawling into the garden on top of a stunned Franks. Quickly regrouping, Parrish thrust his hand down onto Franks' chest and pushed the man onto the concrete as the latter struggled like an upturned tortoise.

"Just stay there...please! Steven Franks, I am arresting you for assaulting a police officer in contravention of The Police Act 1996 Section 89. You do not have to say anything but it may harm your defence if you do not mention when questioned something which you later rely on in court. Anything you do say may be given in evidence. Understand?"

"Bollocks to that!" Franks spat the words as Parrish's crotch exploded and the breath was driven from his lungs. Through a meteor shower of red and green sparkles, he pressed the button on his radio.

"Fuchsia Close, Southall, in pursuit of male, IC1, dark hair, six-one, wearing black T-shirt and jeans."

Franks high-tailed it from the alleyway and turned back towards the feeder road which would take him to his car. That blow in the nuts would buy him valuable seconds. The woman behind the corner was subliminal, a shape in the corner of his eye. Then, he felt the dull rap on his shin as the pavement came towards him. In an instant, he tucked in his arms and rolled onto his back feeling the gravel sharp through his clothes. Whetstone was immediately on top but Franks was too strong and heaved her off with a thunderous swipe across her face, which sent her backwards.

As Keith Parrish limped around the corner, Whetstone sat on the pavement clutching a bloodied tissue and Franks, once more, was gone.

Chapter 52

Chatham Woods, Ruislip, 1:00pm, Wednesday

Peering into the darkness, Daley's first feeling was one of deflation. Having flung the doors wide he had expected to see the silver eyes of a Transit Connect staring back at him and racks of stolen equipment. Instead, he saw an empty shed.

Behind Daley, Smith had stopped his adolescent whining and was staring expectantly into the void. The yard had stilled once more.

"What can you see, copper?" Had Smith ever been in the garage, or had he been witness to the goings on of Franks, the arrival and departure of the van, unable to see what happened when the doors were closed?

Daley briefly turned to Smith and raised his hand. *Not now.*

Around twenty feet wide and thirty deep, with a raked threshold and pent roof, the shed was probably meant as a double garage high enough for a tractor. For the first time, it struck Daley that this was a newer shed built on the site of a second dilapidated one that had been removed. A deserted farm was an ideal place to hide. Were the owners of the site aware? Protected from the elements, the floor was earth, dry and compacted; there were footprints and tyre tracks. The walls were hung with hoses and garden tools and shelves of various chemicals. Off centre in the floor, a wooden hatch, probably four feet square, lay flush with the ground. There was a familiar smell of cleaning fluid.

As, outside, Smith continued to call after him, Daley stared at the hatch, then back at the door. He estimated there was room for a van to reverse in, to close the shed doors and not be parked over the hatch. Somehow, as Daley reached inside his pocket for a handkerchief, as he draped it over his hand and grabbed at the small flush ring handle, he knew what he would find below this innocuous trapdoor. Steeling himself he heaved at the handle and raised the door vertically on its hinges and over to rest on the floor.

Beneath the trapdoor Daley found a void and a large round metal hatch, scuffed and rusted. A strong smell of bleach percolated through the ground around the hatch but it could not disguise the stench of carrion. Wrapping his handkerchief around the latch, he twisted and eased up the door with a graunching squeal. The smell was now overpowering and Daley could feel his stomach spasm. Taking out his phone, he clicked the torch app and shone it into the abyss. Suddenly the spasms became more violent and Daley could feel himself starting to retch. Dropping the hatch with a sonorous clang he ran to the door of the shed and vented his stomach.

Panting, he drew deep on the fresh moist air, now oblivious to the shouts and catcalls from Smith, oblivious to the teeming rain, his mind filled with a vision of which it could barely make sense. He found Whetstone's number and pressed the button.

"Sir? Franks has been leading us a merry dance here. The bastards given me a black eye and Parrish bruised nuts. Look, I am going to need you back here. You'll have to put your abductions on the back burner for a day or two. Anyway, you still out at that farm?"

"Deb. Just wait a minute, please." Daley was leaning on the side of the shed, the rain peppering his face, lungs full of icy air stemming the nausea. "Forget Franks. We need to put Smith in a cell for a while. Something's come up here."

"Oh, come on, Sir. Smith's been found, Franks is on the run. These are the last two people to see Varsa Ruparelia alive and you want me to wait a minute?"

"Section 41 gives us twenty-four hours. Allenby will almost certainly give us another twelve. Speak to Allenby. I need a full Forensics team out to Chatham Woods Farm now, the works. Get a car to cover the gate. We need to seal this place off. I think I have just found Varsa Ruparelia, Karen Sherwood and all the others."

Chapter 53

Lambourne Road, Ealing

Traditionally, Wednesday was quiet day for D/Supt Bob Allenby. An opportunity to plough through the paperwork that had accumulated on his desk since Monday. The hump day when he could make himself a cafetière of coffee, close the blinds and blitz the in-tray. And if he was lucky, slope off early and visit the driving range. With confirmation that the *Zone 6* killer may also be responsible for the death of Varsa Ruparelia and more, he was thrown into somewhat of a quandary, which could only spell trouble for his golf swing.

It didn't help matters that he had slept fitfully the previous night. With Whetstone seemingly chasing her tail and Scott Daley teetering on the edge, he needed to have a rethink. He could not afford this to backfire on him because of a rogue officer or botched investigation.

Fortunately, there seemed to be a media fog. The *Zone 6* abductions had been and gone from the front pages and a crashed van merited no column inches. However, it would only be a matter of time before some zealous cub reporter with an eye for detail put two and two together. For now, he hoped they could keep the DNA evidence quiet but, as always, it would only be a matter of time.

And for once, Daley had listened. He had even asked permission before revealing the blood results to the DI from Harrow. After all, it was her case, grateful for her cooperation and all that. Whetstone, though, was struggling. Following the rather chaotic fiasco with Steven Franks, she had been left out on a limb, seemly backing the wrong horse.

Then there was Monaghan. While Whetstone and Daley were out doing their Starsky and Hutch bit, it was Monaghan who managed the team, who marshalled Taylor, Corby, Smollett and the others. He was their senior in rank, experience and age and he who maintained their morale when things turned to shit. So now, it was Monaghan whom Allenby needed to reassure. And that would call for a measured response rather than the knee-jerks of yesterday.

Notwithstanding, even before the cafetière had been pressed, Monaghan had poked his head round the door and asked for a word, on the QT. So unusual was this that Allenby had waved an inviting hand before considering the consequences. Before the door had latched, the sergeant was filling him in on the situation with Daley, the pressures of coming back after six months away, the psychological effects of even a minor brain trauma. As he placed his palm on the plunger and eased down the press, Monaghan added more weight to his argument, that Daley was the best man for the job now the cases were linked, that the status quo needed to be resumed. *Status quo ante bellum* mused Allenby as the press had hit the bottom; if there wasn't a war right now, those two weren't far off one. And of course, there was that farm.

Soon, Allenby had switched off. There were too many words for a Wednesday afternoon before the first cup of joe. He dutifully nodded in the right places and promised he would sort it, reassured Monaghan that everything would return to normal. If he recalled, the sergeant had still been talking as Allenby had picked up the phone and feigned the need to make an urgent call, even as he left the office.

So now there were decisions to make. Firstly, murder was Daley's bag. Secondly, there was Whetstone's insistence on chasing Steven Franks. That would have to stop until he was firmly implicated. Then there was the thornier issue of Daley's fitness for duty. That was now about damage limitation. Dave was right, he needed to maintain the status quo but he needed to be seen to be acting. He would speak to Daley. A small sanction, neither severe nor prolonged. After all, the more action Allenby took, the more culpable he would appear when things turned South.

The other factor preying on his mind was Daley's Police Medal. Following the case that nearly killed him, Allenby had raised his head above the parapet and recommended the Inspector for the award, and the recommendation had been accepted. There was to be a ceremony after Christmas and Daley would be expected to attend, once he knew about it. The brown envelope had languished in Allenby's desk drawer for two weeks. The issue, of course, was that Daley could well be about to take a gargantuan shit on his own doorstep - *maverick cop rewarded for blunders*. Who knows what the tabloids would dream up?

The red light on his desk phone began flashing.

"What is it, Pat?"

"Scotland Yard, sir? Chief Superintendent Farmer." Pat was a civilian officer in the Comms. Room. A small woman with a rhythmic voice and under no obligation to use his rank. It was a coded signal to him to be on his mettle. Allenby sighed. His swing would be tantamount to an ostrich skipping on sheet ice, if these distractions kept up.

"Put him through."

Peering cautiously through the closed blinds, he watched Whetstone, seated at her desk, the receiver pressed to her ear, tentatively dabbing at a bloodied lip. Daley's chair was empty. He would fetch them both in when Daley returned.

And when the coffee had done its job and he had the faintest idea what to do for the best.

Chapter 54

Chatham Woods Farm

"You sure know how to show a girl a good time, Inspector. We must do this again someday."

Rounding the corner of the overgrown kitchen garden, DI Theresa Somerville raised a couple of takeaway cups and smiled nervously. The yard was a frenzy of organised activity and a wave of concern flashed across her face as she saw the open shed. Daley gingerly climbed down from the back of a flatbed trailer where he had been idly swinging his feet. His face was still the pallor of month-old cheese and, beneath a blanket, his clothes had dried to an uncomfortable crust. Smith had already been despatched to Lambourne Road. Allenby had reported that he was personally attending the site and Daley could feel the case sliding away.

"Looks like we could have found your missing persons. Oh, and careful not to mess up my crime scene, Inspector Somerville."

"*Touché.*" Handing the coffees to Daley, she looked back at the shed. "Mind if I..?"

Daley watched as she donned a white jumpsuit and disappeared into the shed, concerned that she should have to see, sure she was up to it. Arc lights now lit the inside as bright as day. She approached the hatch, tiptoeing across chequer plate, before peering down and recoiling sharply. After a second look, she nodded to one of the Forensic team and left the shed.

"You weren't wrong on the phone, Inspector. Kind of glad I avoided the cheese omelette at lunch." Even so, there was a greyness to her complexion. "Your guy estimates there could be upwards of thirty bodies down there."

Daley's mind saw the tangled, dismembered greying limbs, marbled flesh, round black eyes. He looked away at the tops of the skeletal trees, fixing on a more palatable reality.

"Scott. Please call me Scott. You know the van crash last Monday? Well, we've had the results on the blood in the back. It belonged to Karen Sherwood, Diane Fletcher and Josh Turner, so I am afraid there may be some difficult conversations soon. Once we have more to go on."

Somerville sighed. "I felt certain that Diane and Josh would just turn up, tails between their legs and begging forgiveness but I had kind of accepted the inevitable with Karen. Who leaves a two-year-old?"

Daley nodded. He could remember when his brother's boy had been an infant. Sunday afternoon visits, houses filled with a vague odour of digested milk and excreta, the constant din alternating between a grating bawl and a raucous yell, the hang-dog look of tired parents. He could easily see how someone could abandon a two-year-old. Somerville continued:

"What about Andrew Bryson?"

This was a question which Daley had been mulling over. He was the exception to the rule in many ways, having disappeared on a Saturday.

"Nothing so far. We were lucky to obtain the samples we did from the van." Daley heaved himself back onto the flatbed. "Tell me, what do you know about Medway Klein. It's a cosmetic clinic out towards Northwick Park."

"Cosmetic clinic?" Somerville furrowed her brow, sipped her coffee and considered. She jumped up onto the flatbed beside Daley. "Well, Karen Sherwood had some surgery following weight loss last February. I can check where she had that done."

"And the others? Anything which might connect them to the clinic?"

Somerville shook her head. "Not that I can think of. They barely connect to each other."

"What do you make of this place? I can't understand why such a prime piece of real estate has been derelict for so long without some property developer snapping it up."

Somerville turned her head distractedly. "Yes, I asked around the station when Josh Turner disappeared. Apparently, Chatham Woods Farm had been owned by the Blanchard family for four generations. Daniel Blanchard and his wife lived here with their two children. Blanchard had been a successful securities broker until his father had died. He took over the smallholding after burning out in the City, sort of therapy, back to the land.

"They appeared on our radar in 1990, paradoxically, when they disappeared. Milk and papers stacking up, post not being collected from the mailbox at the end of the drive. A patrol car attended and effected an entry. The house had been ransacked, most of the valuables taken. Basically, left a shell, as it is today. There were no bodies nor did the family turn up. The farm itself was closed off and has remained like this ever since. Until I mentioned it, our collator had forgotten it existed. Maybe there's a problem with Planning Permission. It is next to the Nature Reserve."

"And did the Blanchards ever turn up?"

"No, all four were declared legally deceased. In the absence of a legal heir, the farm and lands passed into the ownership of a holding company, Heligon Investments, representing the wider family, presumably to renovate or maybe develop, but that never happened. In the Eighties, land prices crashed. My theory is the owners are waiting to make a killing."

Daley looked towards the shed. "Maybe they got their wish." He recalled the sombre silence that had met him when he had entered the yard the previous day, soaked into the fabric of the house and the outbuildings for nearly three decades. He recalled the foreboding that had prickled at the back of his neck. Had some sixth sense told him of the memories etched into the walls, of the charnel house beyond the padlocked door? What intuition had brought him here in the first place?

As he sipped at the coffee, graciously ignoring the lack of sugar, Daley tried to drag all the pieces together in his head. A van that crashes and body parts are found. The suspected driver scrupulously cleans his home and comes here to hide out yet there is no blood at his house. A number of people from here or hereabouts simply vanish. If Varsa Ruparelia's hand had not been left in the van, she would have disappeared too. "Do we have contact details for the current owners?"

Somerville crooked her mouth apologetically. "Registered Office but it's an accommodation address at a newsagents. Still working to get a phone number. It wasn't important until now."

Reaching inside his jacket, Daley withdrew his phone, feeling the bruise from the impact with his chest in the tussle. He put it on speakerphone for Somerville's benefit.

"Monaghan?"

"Dave, it's me. I am out at Chatham Woods Farm, near the Nature Reserve."

"Sure, I worked that out all by myself, when everyone started running around like blue-arsed flies. You alright?"

"Few more bruises, bigger headache, hate-mail from the dry-cleaners, apart from that. I need you to find out what you can about the current owners."

"On it already. So, I googled the name and found only three in the UK, of which only one seemed plausible, as it was within walking distance of Josh Turner's home. A Land Registry check confirmed that the legal owner was a limited company, Heligon Investments. For whatever reason, their details are on suppression at Company's House."

Company's House can place details of a company on suppression for a number of reasons, such as the privacy of the owners, impending mergers and acquisitions, commercial sensitivity. The details are still available but Daley would need to apply to a court to get them.

"I don't think we have time for a court order."

"I am not that easily defeated, sir. I phoned my contact in Cardiff. Left a message. He will get back to me."

Just then Whetstone's face appeared around the corner. Her cheek had bruised to a merlot stain on a white rug and her lip still showed fresh blood. Her eyes blazed. Somerville self-consciously hefted herself from the flatbed, sensing gathering clouds. She turned to Daley. "Look, I'm going back to Harrow Central. I want to make a start on compiling a wider list of missing persons. See if we can identify more than just the ones we know already." Then as she strolled across the yard and turned the corner, she made the universal telephone receiver gesture - *call me*.

***

"What the Hell is going on with you, sir? Six months off sick and within days, you're baiting a witness, pissing off Allenby and running that bloody train of yours right through my investigation. And now, disappearing off without a word to God knows where and almost getting yourself killed."

"Smith? He's a streak of piss. He was no problem." Daley's

tone was nonchalant, despite the pain across his ribs.

In the shelter of the dilapidated byre, now that the cars had taken Smith away, Whetstone had decided that a rain-strewn farm yard was the right place to pull him down a peg or two. With his second-best suit clammy and cold against his skin and a blanket that smelt of cabbage about his shoulders, Daley couldn't disagree. Not that he would admit it without a fight.

"Streak of piss? Is that why you have blood all over your shirt? Jesus Christ! You're a stone overweight, with a broken shoulder and you're calling him a streak of piss? Look at yourself. You're a bloody mess."

Daley peered down. Across the lapel of his overcoat and staining the front of his shirt were flecks of blood. He reached up and touched his cheekbone and a shard of pain dug into his skull.

"It's nothing. I rugby-tackled him, that's all. I must have hit the ground. Honestly, it's nothing."

"Do you realise how long a fractured skull takes to fix? One tap in the wrong place and you're back in that coma for good. You're supposed to be easing yourself back in not tear-arsing around getting into fights. No wonder they call you bloody *Suicide Scott Daley*. I wouldn't be surprised to find Harrison has book open on how long you're going to survive."

"I told you..." Daley snapped back before catching himself. "I told you it's nothing, a graze, that's all. Come on, for heaven's sake. We got Smith and now we have the dumpsite!"

"More by luck than judgement. How am I supposed to run an investigation when one of my team is racing around North-West London with his own agenda, picking fights with my witnesses? I need you on my team, following my direction. For Christ's Sake, the only reason we have a dumpsite is because you broke the bloody lock off."

"Because it would take too long the trace the legal owner."

"And what would you have done if it held a vintage fire engine, or stored belongings from the farmhouse? There are any number of legal reasons why a door to a shed is padlocked. This maverick cop stuff has to stop and if it doesn't, I will ask Allenby to have you removed from the investigation."

So, she did want him removed. He had found Smith, He had

found the dumpsite and he was going to solve this whole damn thing. She simply couldn't face the competition now he was back. The pressure cooker was building to full steam.

"Just who do you think you are? Three months as Acting DI and you know it all? I was doing this job before you even joined the Force and you have the nerve to tell me how to behave?"

"Right now, yes I do! Allenby made me Investigating Officer and right now, you work for me. Whether you like it or not, you are on *my* team. You do what *I* say. This is *my* investigation and I will run it how I see fit." Whetstone was now being borne along by her own rhetoric.

"What investigation? You have a deliveryman with a hooky van and nothing you can pin on him, yet still you keep trying. You have lad barely out of short trousers who made a wrong decision and is shitting himself. You have no idea who is abducting and killing all of these people. And if it turns out those bodies belong to the *Zone 6* victims, *this place has nothing to do with you either*." Daley was throwing his arms about, almost on auto-pilot. Once more the locomotive was thundering down the track, the dead man's handle was jammed and the driver was away from the cab.

"It has everything to do with me. Half of your *mispers* have been found in Franks' van. For God's sake, what is Smith doing here if he isn't connected? Tell me!"

But Daley wasn't listening, his brain completely consumed by the rage that had been building for the last week. "I found the bloody farm and I arrested Smith. Without me, you'd be nowhere. You and Dave are floundering around in the dark with your thumbs up your arses while there's a killer preparing to strike again. If he hasn't already."

"Don't talk shit! Now we have marked his card. Everywhere he goes, everything he does, he will be looking over his shoulder."

"What? You think this is all about Franks?" Eyes wide Daley feigned incredulity. "Jesus Deb. He was nowhere near when Sherwood, Fletcher and Phillips went missing, when Ruparelia disappeared. Do you have any evidence at all that connects him with the crashed van? No! Of course you don't! It's not his van!"

"We have witnesses who placed him at the clinic arguing with

Varsa before she went missing."

"So what? I am arguing with you. Does that make me a killer?"

Whetstone turned away from Daley and looked across the barren yard, isolated, abandoned, forlorn. Even through his red mist, everything he said was true. She sighed and walked away, exasperated, feeling the chill rain spots across her face.

What options did she have? Should she make good on her threats and have him removed? Life would be easier. Monaghan was distracted, she was distracted, maybe that's why they were getting nowhere? She could have him removed for his own safety, if nothing else.

But there was no doubting he saw this case from a different angle; one that neither she nor Monaghan understood or had even contemplated. She stared up into the angry grey clouds and shivered. This place gave her the creeps. Swivelling on her heel she looked back at Daley. He was squatting on his haunches in the byre, He reminded her of an Argentinian *gaucho* wrapped in a poncho asleep, trying to block out the world for a few brief moments. She shouted across at him:

"You still here?"

Daley distractedly glanced up. His face was dirty and grazed and he was soaked through. He looked pathetic. "You've got the car keys."

"Come on then." Like a mother attempting to persuade and errant child to go to school, she reached out a hand and pulled him to his feet. "Let's get you back before you have another six months off with pneumonia." They walked back to the Golf in silence, a deep, all-consuming stillness which sent a shiver through her. There was something very wrong about this place.

"Look, Sir, things have changed around here. We have got used to coping without you. Now we have to get used to working *with* you."

As he collapsed into the passenger seat, he sighed, a long, careworn, weary sigh. "You're right. I know you are. I just hadn't realised how much has changed. For me, I stepped out of the office and I stepped back in."

"You just need to let it happen. You know like starting a new job."

"D'you know how long it is since I started a new job? Jeez, I have been kicking my heels for six months and then I am reading through missing persons files whilst you chase murderers."

"And how is any of that my fault?"

"I'm not saying..." Daley sighed. It was like a video on repeat. He didn't need to rewind. "Look, I'm flipping freezing. Let's get back to the station, I'll buy you a coffee and we can set about Smith."

"If you're buying."

Daley sighed again. The road to redemption was strewn with boulders. "It'll have to be the machine."

"In that case, I'll have the hot chocolate. The coffee is muck." Whetstone flashed a short vengeful smile. Hot chocolate was five pence dearer.

Chapter 55

Elstree

Tossing her bag onto the couch, Caz Albin raced around the house pushing through doors, checking rooms. It had been a matter of hours and Franks was gone. She had immediately noticed his BMW missing and it took her a moment to recall whether he had arrived in it the night before. Panicking, she doubted herself. Throwing open the French doors, running across the patio, she peered through the gap in the hedge. The space was empty.

Cursing her Walter Steiger shoes in the gravel, she removed them, padded painfully back into the house and cast them across the living room with an enraged scream. What was it with men and their inability simply to do as they are told?

Had she not expressly ordered Franks to stay put? Had she not stood semi-naked offering him more of the feast he had enjoyed the night before? Well of course not but the intent was there. Franks was controlled by his loins.

Finding her phone, Caz dialled the number that she knew Snowdon would answer.

"Nick? Look, Franks is gone."

"When? Do you know?"

"This morning, I suppose. Have you seen him?"

"I was here by 8:30am working at my desk. Have you tried his phone?"

The line collapsed to static, an exasperated sigh. "Of course. He's not picking up."

"Well, isn't this his day off?" Snowdon strode to the window and looked out over the courtyard. "His van is here. Looks like it's been here all night. Whatever he is up to, it is nothing to do with us."

"What about the police?"

"We left around 6:00pm and didn't see him return. What he gets up to in his own time is his own affair."

Caz mused at the choice of words. Less an affair, more containment. "What about between 6:00pm and when he arrived here. It worries me when things aren't where they should be."

Snowdon smiled. "You worry too much. See if you can track him down. Use your charms. He will be back like a rutting pig before you know it."

"What if the police find him first?"

"The police are interested in finding Varsa Ruparelia. What is Franks going to tell them?"

"What about the diary? Did you see it?"

"No, the police just mentioned it. I don't think any of that is important to Chronotech. They mentioned Franks, too. Seems that Varsa was trying it on with him too."

"Good luck with that!"

"Precisely. They were mostly interested in the relationship between Varsa Ruparelia, Steven Franks and Connor Smith."

"I don't know Connor Smith. I told them as much."

"The police mentioned Delta? They are bound to speak to Franks about it."

"Steve did the fetching and carrying, that's all. Whatever Varsa thought she had found out about him was basically rubbish and nothing to do with us."

"I hope so, Caz. That woman can cause us a lot trouble."

"How can it not be true? When they find Franks, he will tell them what he knows, they will cross-check the records at the clinic and at Chronotech and they will find nothing. The records are all meticulous and accurate. Anything Varsa wrote in her little black book will be supposition, discredited straight away. Right now, the most important thing is that Delta carries on as normal. There's too much at stake financially. It wouldn't hurt to make sure the clinic records are in order should the constabulary want to visit. Mind you, once they find Steve Franks, I am sure that he will keep them busy."

"Let's hope so, and quickly. For everyone's sake."

"Come on Caz. What can he say? Whatever they think he has done, you are each other's' alibi, and he knows it."

Then it occurred to her. That idiot Inspector had mentioned the farm.

Chapter 56

Lambourne Road, Ealing

The canteen was a morgue most afternoons, everyone preferring tinned catering coffee to a spotty barista on the fifth floor. But at least it was quiet and away from that bloody harridan Whetstone. Out of the suit and back into a tracksuit top and jeans, he felt more comfortable. The quack had assessed his bumps and bruises, berated him for stressing his weak shoulder and declared him fit notwithstanding. So, he headed up to the canteen for some peace and quiet.

Even though there was enough physical evidence connecting Smith and Franks with Chatham Woods Farm, the crashed van and the *Zone 6* abductees, it was all circumstantial. A higher process, invisible yet instrumental in everything, was at work. Daley suspected that interviews would be fruitless unless they discovered it. Their arguments contained more holes than a tramp's string vest. He needed to start darning and quick.

He couldn't help concluding that the clinic was central to all this.

Nick Snowdon and Caz Albin had been personable and willing to help but had also spoken economically. Not completely unexpected. Their work fringed on the edge of public acceptability. Cosmetic surgery, implant surgery, Frankenstein medicine. They would need a bent safety pin to winkle out any more information than was strictly need to know.

Daley's head was swimming and the pain behind his eyes once more threatened to shear off his scalp. He had kept that from the quack. Less ammunition for Allenby. Rotating the muscles in his shoulder he winced as it jarred. Six months and still agony. Not to mention his bruised ribs. He had rescued the pills from his suit, two days' supply. Surely without the pain, his head would be clearer?

He had asked the quack earlier, in a roundabout way, how many was too many and he was surprised, even ashamed, at the answer. Did Whetstone know? Did that explain the way she treated him, the way they all seemed to look down on him?

Daley was certain Varsa's diary held the answers. At least, piecing together Varsa's weird view of the world would keep him out of mischief for a while.

The book was a plain black notebook. Up until her disappearance, barely a day went unfilled. From the start, she had set out her stall.

23rd May 2012

I don't know how I will stick this horrible job. From my window into pre-op I can see them preparing and I wish it were me. I have been here three weeks and it is just like Charing Cross. Everyone is up to something and I am pushing around paperwork. When my tribunal is heard and I prove to everyone what sort of conniving, selfish people they all are, then they will get what is coming to them and I will be re-instated. It will be me the other side of the glass.

All I see are the walls of this stupid office. Three grey walls and that window so I can watch them all work while I type. I hate them all so much.

Anger stained every word. She blamed the world for her problems and it would need to pay. Daley flicked through the pages. Details of arrival and departure times, time lost along with initials of the miscreants, movements and liaisons. It was clear that Varsa was sizing up to start her blackmail.

18th July 2012

Today, I saw ME in a very deep conversation with SF over lunch. She was leaning across the table at him, their noses nearly touching. It is disgusting, she is a married woman. When she rose to leave she reached out for his hand. Maybe Derek needs to know?

And then again later in the book:

14th August 2012

ME and CS are getting really cosy now. Is she at it with everyone? Today I saw SFs car drive into the supermarket and they both got out. She took the garden path into the Hall and SF went along the road. I had to hide behind some people at the bus stop so he wouldn't see me. She is a common slut. One day he will look at me the way he looks at her.

Also, there were entries regarding Lorraine Lucas which began to show Varsa in her true light:

26th July 2012

LL is a disgrace to the clinic. She is obese and smells of body odour. Someone should tell her. It is a wonder the patients don't leave sicker than when they arrive with her sweaty bacteria floating around. How can she be allowed ward-side yet I am stuck in this prison cell? Don't think I don't know what she is up to. I am keeping a track of the stock. She thinks she has a perfect way of stealing drugs and no-one notices.

Well I notice.

3rd August 2012

LL took some more codeine pills today. She thinks I don't see that she prescribes more to the patients than she actually gives them. She is very clever but I am cleverer. There is a hole in the lining of her coat where she hides them. She will pay for her dishonesty. There will be a reckoning. Their gratitude will show I am worthy of being theatre-side again.

Daley kept the page with his thumb and leafed to the rear of the notebook where Varsa kept her lists. He found one headed simply 'LL'; around twenty entries. Hardly a capital offence, but enough to suggest that Lucas had a problem with drugs beyond larceny. He rubbed the pressure from his temples, felt the blister pack in his pocket. She was not the only one.

20th August 2012

LL took the drugs round again this afternoon. I could see her from my office, putting strips of pills into her pocket. Codeine, Tramadol. She even took a botox syringe. I confronted her. She seemed genuinely shocked I had seen her but, really, she was so amateurish. She threatened to report me for spying on her. I told her she needs to get up a lot earlier to get one over me and called her bluff. £100 a month to keep it quiet. I gave her a week to think about it or I will let NS sort her out.

22nd August 2012

That bitch LL told me to sod off. Does she think I won't carry out my threat? Really? Does she think I am only interested in the money? There is a principle at stake. Stealing is a sin. Fornication is a sin. They must be made to pay. If no-one else is going to police this place then I shall.

24th August 2012

I saw NS today, personally. I can't trust his minions. This place is a sewer of corruption. I told him all about LL and the drugs and how she is stealing from under his nose. She must be taking hundreds of pounds a month. I told him he needed to run a tighter ship. I had been in the NHS and seen these activities and no-one seemed to care. I showed him my notes. She is such a prolific thief I could never remember every individual incident without them. NS promised he would look into it. I have a mind to tell him about SF and CA. I might even tell CA about SF and ME. Talk about a *menage-a-trois*. That will put the cat among the pigeons :-)

29th August 2012

Surprise, surprise. Wonders will never cease. NS actually has a backbone and LL has been sacked. He is a lax manager and needs to step up to the plate and sharpen up his act. I wonder if I should tell him about CA and SF? Show him that he needs to open his eyes. Try and clean this place up once and for all.

So Varsa had squirrelled away information in her diary, awaiting her chance and when the blackmail didn't work she was prepared to go to Snowdon. But what had she done to cross Steve Franks? By October, he was arguing in the car park and perhaps worse. Daley flicked back to July:

13th July 2012

CA and SF are having an affair, it is certain. It just gets better and better. This morning, she drew up into the clinic car park in her Mercedes and who should be in the passenger seat but SF. His car was still there from the previous night. I could see him lean over to kiss her. As bold as brass. He nearly sucked her brains out. They live miles apart so he must have stayed over.

17th July 2012

Yesterday SF arrived as usual to go on his trip to Newcastle. He is a horrible man, always fawning over the women like he is the best thing since sliced bread. He is all hairy and muscle bound and has this vile tattoo of a monster on his arm. He even tried it on with me but I am having none of it. I stood with him at 4:30pm while we checked the stock into the van and I saw him lock up and leave the clinic. Yet here, at 8:00pm, two full hours after he left, his van is in front of the garage. There is no way he could get to Newcastle and back. I went down to the garage but it was locked up and he was nowhere to be seen. So, what is he up to while we all think he is in Newcastle? I bet he is seeing CA behind everyone's back again. That is the only answer.

This morning I came into work and the van was gone, so he must have had a quick knee-trembler and then rushed up to Newcastle for his appointment. That is all I can think.

But then a love triangle was not the only affair Varsa suspected Franks of being involved in:

29th June 2012

I have discovered a problem with the deliveries. Someone is pulling a fast one! I will keep a record and see If I can figure out who. I have looked back at the records and this all seems to have started when SF joined last year. Suddenly things do not add up.

At first, she had not pinned it down but soon she had shared her suspicions with Connor Smith, deepening her loathing for Steven Franks:

23rd July 2012

SF is definitely stealing from the clinic. He must be. The van is here when he is supposed to be away. I have told CS of my suspicions. He told me to keep my nose out. His language was vile. Why are these people so awful? He should have more respect for me, especially as I know about him bunking off early to be with the nurse from post-Op. I can forgive him his language as I am sure he is just a little boy really. Sometimes I see him in the ward reception, leaning over the desk talking to the nurses. Why does he not come and talk to me? No-one talks to me.

Of course, Smith would warn her off, if he was involved in the scam. Especially if he had been promised a cut. However, it was clear, she was still floundering in the dark.

31st July 2012

I still don't know what the scam is that they are involved in. I am sure that SF is at the centre of it. He must be. His van is here at odd times, loading and unloading even when he is away in Cardiff or Newcastle or even London. He is using the trips as a front for his stealing.

It is to do with the Delta project that much is clear but it could be others too. In July, there were five devices brought in but seven procedures carried out and. Seven units used. Two more visits to the farm. They are charging Chronotech for the extra procedures and skimming money off the top, I am sure. I will keep my list up to date and see if I am right.

Daley stopped and closed the book on his finger. So Varsa seems to have discovered an anomaly in the figures. He looked back at the table in the back of the book.

Date	Reg	Devices	Units	+/- units	Procs	Farm?
Apr 12	VH07 YMK	5	7	+2	7	7
May 12	VH07 YMK	5	7	+2	7	7
Jun 12	VH07 YMK	3	5	+2	5	5
Jul 12	VH07 YMK	5	7	+2	7	7
Aug 12	VH07 YMK	3	6	+3	6	6
Sep 12	VH07 YMK	5	7	+2	7	7
Oct 12						

So, *devices* referred to the equipment Franks controlled. *Procs* stood for surgical procedures. The table suggested that there were consistently more procedures than devices. How or where did the farm come into this? There was something strange in the language but Daley couldn't put his finger on it. His brain was becoming woolly. He sipped his coffee and read on.

17th August 2012

CS asked me out for a drink at lunchtime. I am foolish to ever believe he fancied me. He is a bastard. I could tell from the start he was there because he had been told to be. He warned me to stop taking so much interest in everyone and keep myself to myself. ME had complained to SF. Well, she can complain. She can just click her fingers and he will do anything to get his tongue down her throat. So, I am the latest victim. I told CS to piss off. He can't tell me what to do.

They are all bastards. They spiked my drink. I was in the toilet for an hour while they all laughed outside. From now on, my office door is well and truly shut. They have had their chances. Now they will pay.

As she repeated her foolish behaviour, the sins of her past were gathering in ambush around her. Snowdon was right. She should have heeded Smith's advice and let it drop. He was probably the closest ally she had, even if his motives were selfish.

In Varsa's mind, Franks was playing away with Edmonds and Caz Albin but again there was the question of the time line. How could Franks be in Newcastle and with Albin? If he had found a way to appear in both places at the same time, his alibis were meaningless. Was that what Varsa Ruparelia had stumbled upon?

Then there were the thefts. Varsa was adamant that she had seen the van at Medway Klein when it should have been elsewhere. Month on month, the table in her book showed small but consistent discrepancies yet it was vague about what was being taken. Maybe Franks was killing two birds with one stone; using the affair with Caz as a cover for the thefts, or vice versa?

Daley stretched in the creaking plastic chair. Who was most affected by Varsa's snooping? Franks obviously felt he had something to lose. Smith too, otherwise why the phone calls?

The diary frustrated Daley. It was like the trailer to an adventure film, seeing all of the action but none of the plot. Every entry in the diary was tantalisingly incomplete.

Chapter 57

Arthur Street, Wembley

For the second time in as many days, DC Mike Corby paused at the front door and sighed. Unlike the last time, the door was ajar and he was not being greeted by a malodorous, overweight, underdressed woman. The call had come through when the constable had found his card on the mantelpiece inside.

Earlier that day, the local station had been called to the house when the neighbour complained of the back door banging with the wind. There was no sign of Lorraine Lucas and the constable was concerned at the evidence of a struggle in the hall and through to the back kitchen. One of Lucas' slippers lay sodden on the back path. When asked if she had seen anything suspicious, the neighbour said that she had seen a white van parked in the alley out the back but thought nothing of it, until she heard the door banging.

Inside, the electric fire blazed two bars and the TV was on. The curtains were still drawn. With a lump in his throat, Corby dialled Whetstone's number.

Chapter 58

After an hour of reading and rereading, Daley summoned up his courage and headed for the team room. Whetstone was sitting in her chair, staring fixedly at her screen, simmering.

"Thought you might have become one of your own *Zone 6* abductees. Kind of hoping you had. It's been so quiet without you. Anyway, thought you should know, Lorraine Lucas disappeared sometimes yesterday evening. Just like Varsa. TV on, fire on, white van reported. But don't worry, *sir*, while you're hiding God knows where, doing God knows what, Mike Corby has your back. He's round there now."

Daley took a breath, refusing to bite. Lucas had a reason to kill Varsa, to seek revenge on Franks, Edmonds and maybe even Smith. Someone was clearing up.

"Have we got Franks yet? Where was he last night?"

Whetstone flicked off her monitor. "Leave it to Mike. Come on. We've got an appointment with Gascoigne. This time. I talk, you take notes. Oh, and best behaviour. *Bilko* has started taking an interest."

Daley made to say something, some repartee about sarcasm being the lowest form of wit, missing him when he was gone, or some such twaddle, but decided against it. He deserved the cold shoulder but this was giving him frostbite.

When they reached Chatham Woods, floodlights blazed over the yard. Despite the halo of white across the sky, Allenby had insisted on a blanket of secrecy. Off the beaten track, it might remain that way overnight but after that... It was an evens chance who would hear of it first; the Press chasing a story, or Scotland Yard to steal away the investigation.

Piles of translucent plastic boxes were being unloaded from a large black truck. Usually, a police or private undertaker would remove the remains discreetly once the body had been released. However, with so many potential victims, so many unidentified people, they were being removed wholesale. Whetstone imagined a smaller white van rounding the corner and reversing up to the shed doors, Franks alighting and furtively scanning the yard before opening the shed and transferring his gruesome load into the darkness. She imagined Smith, watching Franks through pinholes. She imagined the darkness returning as the remains settled and cooled.

Forensic Officers had begun bringing out sealed, labelled boxes and loading them. Daley mused ruefully that, whoever they were, they would be coming out of the shed the same way they went in.

Donning rompers, smearing menthol under their noses and following the line of chequer plate, the pair approached the hole in the centre of the floor. Under the glare of the floodlights, a head, shrouded in white, appeared and it took Daley a moment to identify Patrick Gascoigne squeezing his less than slender frame through the hatch. The man's voice was dour, life worn. "I am sick of this place. Shall we stand outside for a few moments?" He crooked a finger towards the door.

"That reek." Even from a couple of feet, Daley could still smell the odour of foetid flesh that had only just left his own clothes; that would be in his nostrils for weeks to come.

"So how many?" Whetstone's voice was subdued.

Gascoigne threw up his hands. "To be honest, I have no idea. I have counted at least twenty torsos but there are many more bones underneath. Could be upwards of thirty. Some have been there for a very long time. For now, we are cataloguing the pieces, boxing them up and shipping them out. We have had to organise a temporary cold store."

Whetstone sighed. "Are any of the remains identifiable, Patrick?"

"Well, I need to take samples, to compare blood and DNA but with the hatch sealed, and the effects of anaerobic decomposition, most of the flesh has macerated from the older bones. The sealed tank, constant temperature, they just turned to soup. Of course, there will be dental records. I suspect; however, your missing persons have started to turn up. There were fresh remains at the top which I suspect are the Lucas woman DC Corby just asked about. Some of the body parts have been dumped here recently having been refrigerated elsewhere. There is evidence of the same clinical dissection, a similar striated pattern on the ends of bones. Subject to confirmation, I would suspect you have found the body to match the severed hand and many others."

Daley looked back into the shed, empty for so many years, now heaving with forensic equipment. "So the bodies are dismembered?"

Gascoigne nodded, soberly. "More than dismemberment, I suggest. There is evidence that some of the bodies were tortured. I would have to examine them more closely..."

"Tortured? In what way?"

"Mutilated. Opened up. The flesh has been peeled away and the ribs cut and splayed out. It reminded me of a ritual the Vikings are reputed to have carried out - the *Blood Eagle.* They would open up the back, separate the ribs from the spine and splay them out like angel's wings, then the lungs would be pulled back through the opening and laid upon the shoulders. The victim must remain lying or kneeling until he dies. If he suffers in silence, he may enter Valhalla. But if he screams, he will be banished from it.

"The difference here is that the front of the ribcage has been opened. I believe the torturer wanted the victim to see what was happening."

Whetstone turned away from the shed as the images filled her mind. Defilement after death was sick. Before death was abhorrent. "Do you think that was done here?"

The Professor swilled down a mouthful of water. "The inside of the shed is too clean. Such a procedure would be extremely messy. The ground shows no significant signs of staining. My immediate thoughts are, as you suspect, the bodies were dismembered elsewhere and brought here in closed containers, deposited through the open hatch and then sealed in, any spillage confined to the area around the hatch."

"Could they have brought portable equipment, plastic sheeting?"

Gascoigne shook his head. "The ground is too smooth. Moving that type of equipment would disturb the earth. However, there is one interesting point about the floor of the shed. When I first arrived it was empty, the FIOs know better than to corrupt my scene, but there are subtle indentations in the floor. It wouldn't surprise me to find there are more water tanks under the floor which have been used and backfilled. I suspect our work here could take weeks."

Daley puffed his checks. The cases had collided and turned everything they knew on its head. At least there was a chance the families would know what happened to their loved ones, even if the knowledge was unpalatable.

"Have you been able to determine a cause of death for any of them?" Whetstone was already stripping off the overalls. One peek into the water tank had been enough to sear the image into her mind.

"Not as yet, Deborah. I will examine the fresher remains in the morning but for now we need to get these people out."

"Just do your best, Patrick."

As they turned to leave, a thought occurred to Daley. "Just one thing. Have you been able to identify Andrew Bryson down there?"

"Not as yet, Scott. Not as yet."

Chapter 59

Interview Room 1, Lambourne Road, 7:00pm, Thursday

With most of the mud washed from his face, Connor Smith looked vaguely presentable. His hair was a mass of matted spikes but at least now he was fed, warm and basically dry. The police doctor had seen to most of his grazes and cuts. He had made sympathetic noises when Smith had complained that Daley's roughness amounted to police brutality and written the requisite notes for the files, commenting that Smith was lucky to have been caught by Daley on a good day and that, from his examination of the Inspector earlier, honours were basically even. Now the boy was sitting in the chair, picking at a hang-nail, as a duty solicitor sat patiently by.

Scott Daley held the door open for Deborah Whetstone and sidled in behind her. He screeched out a chair, making Smith start, which was the intention.

Whetstone opened: "Mr Smith. You're a difficult man to track down. Anyone would think you were avoiding us." Daley cracked a brief disingenuous smile. "Now, you are not under caution and we are not recording this interview. We may decide to suspend the interview and bring you under caution. Is that clear?" There was no reaction from Smith. The duty solicitor nodded.

The generic white overalls, two sizes too big, made Smith look small and vulnerable. He continued to stare at the offending nail, refusing eye contact. Whetstone persisted. With a tenuous detente between herself and Daley threatening to take away her authority, she needed to prove herself quickly, that her approach was the right one. Who knows where Franks would be by now.

"Mr Smith. Monday night. The van crash. Tell us about that."

Smith raised his eyes and briefly glanced at each of them in turn, then at the solicitor, huffed and lowered his head once more.

"What caused the crash? Was it a blow-out?"

Smith made no response. She needed to kick-start him with a little white lie.

"Connor. We have DNA evidence from the van." There was DNA evidence, just not Smith's. "Tell us what happened."

"I can't."

"What do you mean, you can't?"

"Come on! Why d'you think I was hiding?"

"I don't know, Connor. Why were you hiding?"

"Because I crashed the van." Smith's tone was petulant. "How would you feel if I crashed your van?"

So Smith was driving the van. It had to be either Smith or Franks. Now they knew.

"Miffed maybe, but I'd get over it. It's no big deal unless, of course, you had filled it with human remains."

Smith leaned back in the chair and exhaled deeply. His voice faltered, anxious, confused. "Look, I didn't know what was in that van. I was just doing a favour."

"Favour for whom? Steven Franks?" Whetstone was swimming in a sea of half-truths and suppositions, great chasms in her argument which she hoped Smith would fill.

"Look, I can't say anything. Really."

"Connor, we've been round to your gaff. It stinks like a dry-cleaners. I reckon if we look hard enough we are going to find the bits you missed. That is going to prove that Varsa Ruparelia or the owners of the other unidentified samples from the van were in your house.

"Other samples?" Smith's attention was suddenly caught. "What other samples?"

"We estimate the blood of at least four other people."

Smith looked earnestly at the pair, then at his brief who sat unmoved. Enough rope could hang Smith but also trip Whetstone. There was desperation etched across his face.

"Look, it wasn't me. Varsa was never in my house and I don't know about any others."

Whetstone watched his eyes as they flicked back and forth. They betrayed him. Wild and scared, they showed a man who had been forsaken. A straggler at the rear, left to the wolves, sacrificed for the benefit of the rest. He also knew more than he was telling.

"Ok. Let me tell you what I think happened, shall I? Steve Franks is the only one who drives that van, the van belonging to Chronotech. Maybe he let you borrow it, maybe you have a spare key, I don't know but two weeks ago, you drive around to Varsa's flat. She lets you in because she knows you, she trusts you, then you murder her."

Smith's eyes were round and damp. He was shaking his head and his lips were flapping, unable to form words. The bravado had gone.

"According to our experts, you then dragged her across the carpet and into the bathroom and dismembered her corpse in the bath."

The solicitor sat upright. "Careful, Sergeant. We are straying into territory that would best be recorded. Mr Smith, these accusations are inadmissible."

Whetstone held up her hands. Once said, a thing cannot be unsaid.

"You have medical training, don't you?" interjected Daley. "We reckon she was still alive as she was dissected. How would one go about that? You know, just supposing. Would one just go right in with the *Black and Decker* or use scalpels? Of course, she would need to be stripped naked. How was that? Did it turn you on to see her naked?"

The duty solicitor raised his eyebrows but remained quiet, arms still folded.

Whetstone continued: "Afterwards, you went out to the van and brought in your equipment. Plastic boxes, cleaning products."

"I don't know what you are talking about. I've never... I don't even know where she lives."

"What happened then, Connor? Where was she for those two weeks after you killed her and before the van crashed?"

"Look, my client has already stated that..."

Daley cut across the solicitor. "You know, I can understand you wanting her out of the way. No-one liked her. I read her diary this afternoon. She was a venomous little witch."

"Yes, everyone wanted her out of the way but she was sacked. Why would I go around to her house?"

"But you just said you didn't know where she lived."

"I don't know where she lived. I'm just saying, if I did, why would I go around? She was gone already."

"Was she though? Judging by her diary, she had her claws into a lot of people. In my experience, that doesn't just stop. She had some something against you so she just had to go? Or maybe it was something else? Did you make a pass at her? Did she turn you down, make you feel like shit, so you took out your frustrations on her? Tell me." Daley leaned in to the boy. "Is that what floats your boat, Connor? Varsa Ruparelia, pain in the arse, nosey parker, all-round shit, lying in the bath stripped of her clothes. What about the others? Did you try it on with them too? Did they reject your advances?"

"I didn't kill her. I didn't kill anyone. Look, I told you, I was driving the van when it crashed. I was as surprised as anyone when I saw what was in the back."

"So why did you take her back to your house? We saw the hall carpet."

"I didn't. When the van crashed I didn't want any of that...that...stuff on me. I wanted nothing to do with any of it. I ran away, back home. I puked my ring, alright? Wouldn't you? I was just cleaning up, that's all."

"What about Lorraine Lucas, Connor? We found her this afternoon, too. What happened to her?"

Whetstone final words resounded from the walls and the room lapsed into silence. Connor put down his spade and stopped digging. The walls hummed with the plaintive moan of the air conditioning and a strip light flickered overhead.

Whetstone continued: "You do realise that you have been abandoned. Brownie points or not, you are well and truly on your own. How does it feel Connor? To know that they have all deserted you. Left you to carry the can. Do you think this is how Varsa Ruparelia felt? All those times she came to you for help?"

She leaned forwards over the table. "Connor, it's only going to get worse if you don't tell us. We know Varsa is dead. We know you were driving the van that night when it crashed and we know others were transported in the van. Now Lorraine is dead. Just tell us what happened."

"I can't!"

"Why can't you?"

"Because I don't bloody know!"

As Whetstone leant back, Daley tentatively took up the mantle. Earlier, with Connor in the pen awaiting their attention, Daley had used the opportunity to mend some fences with Whetstone, maybe even get her on his side. It had not gone well. Whetstone was still wedded to Franks' ultimate guilt, of a mass murderer who preyed upon lone travellers, abducting them, murdering them, then dumping the remains at the deserted farm. Then there were the inconsistencies in his location. It was enough to cast doubt on Franks' innocence.

Was it enough to prove his guilt?

Standard practice was to examine three factors - means, motive and opportunity. With Varsa's sharp tongue, whatever she knew threatening to come out, there was certainly plenty of motives forming. But there were the other *Zone 6* abductees. Seemingly no connection between them except their rough geography. What motive could Franks have for killing them? The evidence pointed to a single killer or group of killers. Daley had to believe that the *Zone 6* killer was choosing, abducting and killing his or her victims completely unchallenged, that Varsa Ruparelia, maybe Lorraine Lucas, had stumbled on it and been murdered to protect the secret. Means was problematic, yet Franks had been known to be violent in the past. Opportunity was a circumstantial minefield. ANPR camera stills were popping up everywhere, except where the van was known to be. Even after the accident, cameras had flashed the van in Newton Aycliffe on Tuesday morning, then at Tibshelf and the Target Roundabout in the afternoon, all of which indicated Franks returning from Newcastle. Then others picked it up near the Madjeski Stadium in Reading, on the M4 East of Slough and again near West Drayton. Unless Franks had sourced a TARDIS with a bloody big carport, there had to be two vans, and therefore two drivers.

Could Smith be the other driver? Daley examined him across the table. He cut a pathetic figure, which Daley believed was genuine. He was only the gofer, the wide-eyed acolyte trying to climb an increasingly greasy pole.

And that pointed back to the diary.

All along, something had been niggling at Daley. Gascoigne had remarked on the clean, almost surgical dissection of the hand, and again at the dumpsite. That pointed to someone with medical training. It pointed to the clinic rather than Chronotech, to someone other than Franks.

"Tell me about Steven Franks."

"He's a delivery driver at Chronotech."

"We know, Connor. What sort of man is he? How you know him?"

"He's just a work mate. I oversee the devices being loaded and unloaded, report any failures to him, that sort of thing. I sometimes help him load and unload when he turns up at the clinic."

"Is that all? Just loading and unloading? Nothing else?"

"I am not allowed to do anything else. Look, I can't talk about the clinic. I signed a confidentiality agreement when I joined."

Daley leaned in closer, conspiratorial. "So, here's the thing. All of these trips that Franks has been making, you know, delivering and collecting, we think he has been siphoning off a little for himself. No wonder he can afford the *5 Series* and you have a battered old *1 Series*."

"That's nothing to do with me."

'But you wanted in, didn't you? I mean, watching the consultants arriving in their top-of-the-range Beemers and Audis and Mercs, leaving your old baby BMW on the drive. Then when you get there, toadying for them while they sit in their plush offices and you are left to share a desk with Varsa Ruparelia. You don't want to be a Junior Surgeon forever."

Smith shrugged. "Still young. These things take time. I'm not doing so bad for myself."

"So, is that what happened? You ask for a chance. Just the one. On the Friday, you see him at the clinic, loading up the van. Maybe you think that's weird. Late on a Friday and Franks is still here. You get nosey and he gets on his high horse. You have a row. Franks tells you to piss off, to stop following him around, pestering him. Then finally on Monday, he throws the keys at you. If you want to drive that van, get on with it."

Smith looked up, his eyes flicking left and right as he processed his thoughts. "No! Not at all. You've got it all wrong. I..."

Daley came straight back, keeping up the impetus. "So how was it, Connor? Tell us. Right now, you are in the frame for Varsa's murder and maybe the others as well. I don't see Franks here looking after you, now. Do you? Come on, help yourself for a change. Tell us what happened."

"OK. Look. Like I said, I was driving the van. Just driving it, that's all. When I got to the clinic, it was already loaded up. The key was under the wheel arch. I had just been told where to take it, to wait there and help unload, that's all. Then I had to return the van to the yard and go home. That's all and no-one would be any the wiser if that pillock hadn't cut me up."

"So, what, you swerve and the van crashes, bursts into flames? Was Franks following you?"

"When I saw what was in the back, I just ran. They just needed me to drive."

"They? Who are they?"

But Connor Smith was in full flow and was not to be diverted. "The doors must have come open in the crash. Some of the lids had come off. It was like a butcher's shop. I was having nothing to do with it. Nobody told me about that. I ran across the fields and back home. As far as I knew we were just dumping clinical waste on the sly. Someone would call the police and the council would clear it up. No real harm done. But that. I could never do *that.*"

The duty solicitor leaned forward. "Can I suggest we take a break now? Stretch our legs?"

"Tell us about Varsa." Whetstone cut in.

Smith's brow furrowed, confused at the abrupt change, his mind looping the horrific images of the night.

"Spying on us. Telling management every time one of us stepped out of line. Of course, it just meant everyone avoided her. She never got invited to the pub. No-one sat with her at lunch. Then Lorraine got sacked and we knew it was her. A couple of the male nurses wanted to take her out and punch her head in. She just didn't seem to get the message."

"Then?"

"Well, this one morning Caz - Miss Albin - told me I needed to sort her out, you know, like, talk to her. She was causing too much strife. So I had a word. I told her she needed to shut up or ship out. She told me to piss off."

"Did you know she mentioned you in her diary? By all accounts she held a torch for you, fancied her chances but you rebuffed her."

Connor's eyes widened, aghast. "I never did anything of the sort. She could be OK...now and again...when she wasn't being unpleasant. But that was all. I didn't fancy her."

"Maybe she got the wrong idea?"

"Look, what I did, I did because I was asked to. Varsa was just an interfering cow who could have sabotaged the project, even ruined the company. She was trying it on with everyone there. We were all relieved when she left."

"And Steve Franks? What angle did she have on him?"

"Franks? How should I know? Ask him for Christ-sakes. Look, I can't tell you anything I don't know."

More and more, Daley was certain he knew what Smith was capable of, and what he was not. What had Marion Edmonds called him? Just a boy? He was a boy who had the ear of management, whom they came to when Varsa needed to be spoken to. Maybe they came to him for other errands too?

"Tell me about the farm."

"Wh...what? The farm? How do you..." Smith's eyes widened to the size of footballs and his lower lip wobbled like a tent flap in a gale. Then he twigged. "Chatham Woods? I was hiding there. It's the one place no-one will look for me."

"Why's that? Because of the bodies?"

"I knew nothing about any bodies. Look, you were there. You found them. You must have seen I knew nothing about them."

"Then why were you there?"

"Because that's where I was told to take the van. They knew I had seen inside, so the last place they would expect to find me was there. When I saw the old farmhouse, I broke in and hid."

"Who, Connor? Who won't look for you there?"

Connor Smith shuffled in his chair and looked around the room for salvation. Daley got the distinct impression that now his cover had been blown, Smith was more scared than ever. The boy hunkered down in his chair and folded his arms.

"OK, Mr Smith. We're going to take five. I suggest you use it to speak to the duty solicitor. Can I get you another cup of tea?"

As Daley and Whetstone rose and gathered their notes, Smith gazed up, brow furrowed, his face a map of confusion. He nodded weakly. He seemed to be as in the dark as they were.

***

Stepping into the viewing room, Daley peered through at Smith. He was cradling an empty cup, which he had held throughout the interview, perhaps it's tangibility helped ground him in the other worldly environment of the interview room. Beside him, the duty solicitor was whispering conspiratorially. At the door, PC Ron Cooper stood with his arms folded.

He was shit-scared of something or someone, that much was clear. Just who were *they*?

"He's not the man, Deb. He's too scared. We have six people missing possibly murdered. The killer is meticulous and ruthless. Someone capable of planning a murder, covering their tracks. You heard Smith. As soon as he saw what was in the van, he ran."

Whetstone nodded, reluctantly conceding the point. "He's just the gofer. So, what was he doing at the farm?"

Daley had been startled when Smith had leapt out that morning but not surprised. Smith had packed a bag and left to hide out. "Hiding in plain sight. I suppose he thought the one place he would never voluntarily go, where no-one would look for him, would be the farm. So that's where he went."

But Daley was troubled. When he had asked Smith about Chatham Woods there was genuine fear in his voice.

"Whatever has been happening has been going on for years according to Patrick."

"Yes, but I believe Smith only drove the van once, last Monday. Whoever left those keys knew that Smith would become implicated if anything went wrong. Maybe that's what all this is about? Ensuring there is always someone else to take the fall if anything goes wrong."

"Who, Franks? If that water tank is anything to go by, he's been getting away with this for years. He must have been convinced nothing would go wrong. Surely the first place Franks would look for Smith would be the farm?"

"No, Deb. It can't be Franks. Every time he wants to kill, he borrows the company vehicle? It just doesn't work."

"There are obviously two vans. I get that. The legitimate Chronotech van and another van which he has cloned."

"For God's sake!" Daley huffed and looked to the ceiling tiles for inspiration. "Van one, legit. Franks is driving it to Newcastle, Cardiff or wherever. Van two, clone. Smith is crashing it in Greenford."

"Yes?" queried Whetstone. Daley was stating the bloody obvious.

"What about the van that ANPR caught in Reading while Franks was in Newcastle and we had the crashed one in Loughton Street?"

Whetstone sighed long and deep. "Well, Franks obviously wasn't in Newcastle, was he? Maybe he started back earlier than we thought. Maybe someone else drove his van back, I don't know."

Just then, the door opened and Bob Allenby's face peered around, then through at the small figure seated at the table playing with a cup. The pair stopped and tried to assume an air of decorum.

"Monaghan said I would find you here. Connor Smith, Chatham Woods. Tell me." Daley and Whetstone both nodded unnecessarily. It was always bad when Allenby came down to the sharp end.

"Sir. I was looking for an alternative route out of the nature reserve. I figured Josh Turner and Tom Phillips were taken through the farm rather than back through the car park. Anyhow, Smith reckons he has been hiding out there since yesterday morning."

"...which again connects the two cases." *Bilko* was smarter than he looked, mused Daley. "So, what are we saying? Is he implicated in the *Zone 6* Abductions?"

"Don't know yet, Sir," added Whetstone. "He wouldn't say. We asked what he knew about the farm and it was as if we had killed his granny."

"I got a similar reaction from Marion Edmonds," added Whetstone. "I dropped the farm into our conversation yesterday. She definitely knew something."

"And Varsa Ruparelia? What has he said about her?"

"No more than we already know."

Allenby sighed. "Solidify the link between these two cases. When you have, pool your resources, co-operate with each other." The senior cast Daley a long, hard look. "Whetstone. You lead. I want a daily report. Oh, and catch Franks this time. No more *Keystone Cops*, you two. Is that clear? What actually do we have on Smith? Anything?"

Whetstone considered the past half an hour. Had they gleaned any more from Smith that they didn't already know? "I suppose driving without due care, maybe trespass. We could have him as an accessory once we know what he's an accessory to."

Allenby scratched his chin. "Scotland Yard are on my back to take over. Pull your fingers out and start making some real progress and fast. I have the Chief Super on my back. Both of you in my office 8:00am sharp tomorrow."

Whetstone turned to Daley. "What about Smith?"

"Let him go." The other two eyed Daley curiously and for a brief moment he enjoyed being the centre of attention. "He was told to drive a van. He crashed it. He found out what the load was, then he ran. He has betrayed someone's trust badly. The only saving grace is his determination not to reveal who they are but they don't know that, which is why he was hiding at the farm. I reckon we release him and see where he leads us."

Allenby looked at the pathetic form.

"Have we processed his car?"

Daley nodded.

"Well, drive him back to it and tell him to find a hotel. He's not to go back to his house, to work or to Chatham Woods. Get someone to watch him."

Chapter 60

Budapest-Keleti Station, Budapest, Hungary

As one's train pulls into the monumental railroad station, one cannot fail to be overawed by the sheer scale of the architecture, the rambling, endless platforms shepherding trains into the colonnaded, grandeur of a cathedral to a bygone age of rail travel. The immense arched windows owe more to French Gothic revival than the iconoclastic modernism of Hungarian unification. This was a true 19th century station in every sense of the words, vast canopies seemingly defying gravity, easily rivalling the ornate Italianate Gothic revival of Chhatrapati Shivaji Terminus in Mumbai, even the Neo-Gothic splendour of St Pancras or the amalgam of Art Nouveau, Art Deco and Egyptian revival which gave Milano Centrale it's playful quirkiness. One might even compare it to the sheer towering audacity of New York's Grand Central.

That was, if one had time to appreciate the building as more than simply a stop on one's journey West.

For Satya, it was a luxury she did not have. Time-wise, there was no distinct rush. Arriving a few minutes late, she still had an hour and a half to kill and, given what she had learned about railway departure boards, Budapest-Keleti was easily navigated. No, Satya's problem was a lot closer to home.

She had dozed most of the way from Vidin, under her overcoat, occasionally surfacing when cramp or boredom or urination got the better of her. It was on one of those forays that she noticed the man under the coat. Initially, it was just a poke in her memory from the previous night. Maybe the man was travelling to Budapest too. On the next trip down the aisles, she had examined the man, still covered, recumbent across two seats. The trousers and shoes looked familiar. Yes, this was the same man. There didn't seem to be any luggage, no overnight bags nor briefcase. So, it was a troubled Satya who resumed her seat for the last fifty miles of the journey. Then she was struck by a terrible, gut-wrenching realisation.

She was being followed.

Who could it be? The secret police? She had heard the stories in Syria. Associates of her father had disappeared. Would they venture this far out of Syria for a single illegal? Was it the Turkish authorities? But why cover his face? She would not be able to tell a policeman from a pork butcher. What did it matter if she saw his face? Staring out at the suburbs, watching the graffitied walls and run-down apartment blocks slide past, suddenly she knew.

This was the man from Sofia.

Grabbing her things, Satya headed forward, away from the man. There were few hiding places on a moving train but she found a toilet cubicle, rank with use, and locked the door.

Was this the man from Sofia? Would he travel half way across Europe after her? She had heard of prostitution rings and drug gangs. Vasil had warned her to be careful? It was the Makarov. She had made a terrible mistake thrusting that into his chest. She could have acted, been flattered by his advances, bluffed her way out. But the gun had changed everything. Maybe his gang were on the train too? But surely, she had checked every carriage?

Then again, maybe he was secret police. Perhaps he knew she was an illegal and he was sent to follow her. Follow the pawn to take the king.

Holding back the fear, she waited anxiously as the train slowed, hearing doors bang, people chattering as the platforms filled with disgorged passengers. Gingerly, she eased the door open and peered around the jamb. To her left, the snake of people had almost disappeared from the corridor exiting to the front. To her right, a queue in the next carriage waited to leave. Would he have walked forwards to her carriage? Had he spotted her empty seat and assumed she had already left the train? Was he on the platform lying in wait?

She headed forwards, through each carriage, ducking to study the platform through the window but there were too many people. If he was there, he had the advantage. Finally, the last remaining carriage door stood agape. The platform crush had now subsided as the snake of travellers reached the ticket barriers. Reaching for her ticket, Satya quickly jumped down from the train and sprinted towards the barriers. With mutterings of missing her connection, Satya teased her way into the throng and towards the gate.

"Fiatal hölgy. Kérjük, tudok pár szót?" *Young lady. Please can I have a word?*

Even before she had slowed, she felt the hand clamp down onto her shoulder and drag her to a halt. Turning, she saw a tall, wiry guard eying her suspiciously.

"Kis türelmét kérem." *Please wait for a moment.*

Satya shrugged her shoulders, answering in English. "Sorry, I do not understand."

The tall guard turned to his colleague and raised his eyebrows. "Please step this way so not to block gate. Please, Miss."

In her pocket, Satya's right hand reached the Makarov, her fingers caressing the safety. Theatrically, she huffed. "My train. I have to go."

"Just one moment. That is all." Grudgingly, she followed him a few yards to the side of the gate. A knot bunched her stomach. Was this a counterfeit ticket? Maybe the traffickers who provided her papers were sloppy? Maybe now they had her money she had been abandoned?

"Passport please, Miss."

The guard was wearing an earpiece, a small coiled worm sliding under his ear. Had they wired a description? Surely not this deep into Hungary. Why would they care?

"Please may I see your passport." The voice direct, insistent.

Satya dug into her breast pocket for the maroon booklet. Did it look genuine? She had barely glanced at it. She watched as the guard opened it, checked the Turkish visa stamp from Kapikule, the entry stamp into Europe. He twisted it and eyes flicked from the photo to her face. The photo taken by the Imam in a closet in the mosque as she had steeled herself against the terror she had witnessed.

"What is the purpose of your journey."

She had barely glanced at Vasil's paper. "I am a student in Sofia. I am travelling back to my family in Paris for the holidays."

"In November? Is that not early for the holidays? What do you study?"

"Mechanical Engineering. Lectures are finished. I am taking assignments home where I can work in peace."

Looking down the guard frowned. "No books? No luggage? No laptop?"

"I, er. My work is online. I have reserved books at the Bibliothèque principale in my Arrondissement. The library. I use my father's computer." Impressed by her own inventiveness, she glanced backwards towards the platform. "My train?"

The tall guard lazily looked at the ticket. "You have plenty time. Don't worry." He tucked the ticket into the passport and made to hand it back. Then, as she reached for it, he withdrew it sharply.

"We have many migrants in the station. More by the day. They are camping outside. They are like leeches. They steal your money, your luggage, your ticket. Anything to get to Germany. You should not be travelling alone. Please Miss, keep your bag close to you and be on your guard."

Satya smiled her gratitude, hearing Vasil's words from a different face.

He held out the ticket and passport. "Platform 6 is to your right. Oh, and boldog Karácsonyt" *Merry Christmas.* The guard chuckled to his colleague at his own wittiness.

"I, I need WC?" So many eyes were upon her now, her heart was beating through her ribs and her hands were shaking. Somewhere, her pursuer was biding his time watching this pantomime.

"WC for ladies on the right in cafeteria. You must buy."

Holding her breath, her quivering fingers grasped the documents, thrusting them deep into her coat. Composing herself, Satya strolled as nonchalantly as possible away. Hurrying into the WC, buying water from the cafe on the way, she locked the door, falling against it, exhaling deeply. The toilet cubicle was identical to the one in Sofia. She was still running, still hiding, still struggling to keep one step ahead.

The ticket collector was wired. If it were the police, he would have recognised her, surely? It must be traffickers. Someone had figured she was worth a few thousand euro, a ransom?

Her mouth felt dry. She drained the bottle of water, warm and unrefreshing. Outside the cubicle she could hear trays banging, chairs scraping. Life went on outside her bubble. She was safe behind this locked door but sooner or later she would be forced to return to the station if for no other reason than to check the clock.

Quickly using the toilet, running cold water across her face, Satya once more stepped out into the late evening throng. People were standing and chatting, corralling luggage, hugging tearful reunions and painful goodbyes. Squinting at the departure board she could see her train. Platform 8 but not for another forty minutes.

Out along the tracks, beyond the cafés and the newsagents, beyond the colonnaded waiting rooms and bars, she could make out the far end of the platforms, swathed in darkness unbroken by the weak orange sodium lamps, a mist of fine rain diffusing the light into an eerie glow. They were empty and quiet. She could melt into the brickwork for a few minutes. Satya skipped smartly to the first bar, and then the next, ducking under the arches, seeking every shadow until she reached the end of the station buildings where she slipped around the corner, completely invisible to the rest of the station. Following the signs, she arrived at a deserted platform 8.

Like a sliver of light through an open door, the man eased himself from the shadows. A hand clasped around her face, stifling the helpless whimper. A second arm came around her waist trapping her arms against her side and, unable to resist, she was dragged back into the dark.

Chapter 61

Alperton, North West London

Take-out in hand, Scott Daley slipped the security chain into the bracket on the door jamb, reminding himself that a fortnight ago, Varsa Ruparelia had done the same. He recalled her apartment. The chain limp, the jamb undamaged, and there was a spy hole, just like his own. The entry had been unforced.

After an afternoon getting to know her, sensing her venom, he was convinced that Varsa would consider all of the people in her diary as enemies and would have locked herself in at night...or lock out those she had crossed. She knew her killer, trusted the person who had called that evening.

With a shudder, he checked the chain on his own door.

For Ruparelia and Bryson, for Sherwood, Fletcher and Turner, and now maybe Tom Phillips, their lives fell into that dark, stinking abyss, and they languished at the bottom waiting for someone to pull them out.

Now it was up to him to ensure no-one got away with murder.

Switching on the hall light, he threw down his overcoat and made for the kitchen. In his mind, threads had begun to form but they were many and frayed, tangled and knotted. Varsa had uncovered an affair, she suspected thefts, she had even shopped a colleague. Which one of these had led to her death?

In the old days... The old days! Six months ago before the accident. It seemed a lifetime ago. In the old days, he rarely enjoyed the luxury of a free afternoon, uninterrupted, thinking about an investigation. A chance to mentally arrange the cards, running through the permutations, seeking out the epiphany or the cul-de-sac. Daydreaming could lead to the lightbulb moments that could turn a case. But today, answers had remained tantalisingly elusive.

It reminded him of a game show where contestants had to uncover a picture, one tile at a time, and guess the phrase it represented; the 'random' computer always missing the key square which gave the game away, leading to apposite yet hilarious answers. And, though infinitely less amusing, so it was here. Franks away but seemingly not, thefts from the Hall yet no-one shouting about it, a van turning up where it shouldn't be. Even Caz Albin's affair with Franks yet no-one seemed any the wiser. How could Varsa know all of this yet everyone else keep their counsel?

Settling onto the sofa, Daley thought about Varsa, about her apartment, about her life. A lonely, embittered woman who needed help that she never received. He saw her sitting in her tiny, cramped office, as he had, in this room or that, for six months and he felt an overwhelming sadness as the darkness closed around them both and a night of silence stretched ahead.

Closing his eyelids, he allowed his thoughts to meander across the landscape of his imagination. Soon, he stood on a hillside with Varsa Ruparelia, looking down to the Hall and the courtyard lit bright as day. She had a clipboard, recording every movement, ticking off names. As she turned pages, Daley could see writing underneath but he could not read it and a frustrated rage filled his mind. As she tore out each page, she thrust it into her bag before his flailing arms could grasp it.

There was a coach in the yard, a squat chubby Bedford OB liveried in white with a red sweep along the side. Across the yard and back out through the gates a queue snaked, Varsa pointed out Fletcher and Turner and Sherwood and many more, waiting patiently to board, their faces etched with concern. And all the while Franks stood, driver's cap askew, back to the coming hoard. He was deeply engaged in an act of carnal pleasure with Caz Albin, ignoring them as they boarded.

Then he was puzzled. The queue disappeared into the coach and reappeared on the other side, snaking across the courtyard and up the steps into Medway Hall. Beyond, the serpentine curve of people stretched across the lawns and out towards the gates of the farm. Varsa was ticking off the names of each person as they trudged across the farmyard towards the blackness of the shed. But she was not ticking them off as they boarded the coach but as each in turn was consumed by a raging beast which prowled the dark chasm inside the shed and their screams of torment rang across Daley's mind.

For six weeks, alone in the toxic blackness, the monster had stalked him.

Panicking, Daley tried to fix the details in his head as he was pulled further from consciousness. But the courtyard and the snakes of people and the monster began to echo and blur, becoming smaller and more distant until his eyelids met and his fingers let them slip.

Chapter 62

Budapest-Keleti Station, Budapest, Hungary

"Hello again, Miss. It's me, Gregor. We met in Sofia." His face was a shadow but she could smell the man's breath, warm and pungent, thick with coffee and tobacco. She could feel him pressed against her. Was that the hunger he needed to sate? She struggled to speak, but the hand clamped harder. She remembered the reek of oil and salt in the cabin of the boat to Şarköy, the same pungent breath moistening her neck and immediately she was annoyed. What was it with men and their dicks?

Then suddenly he had turned her. A forearm crossed her back and pressed her face against the rough brick. Beside her, her bag dropped to the floor and her hand fell to her pocket and the grip of the Makarov.

Satya's breath faltered as the panic took her and the noises of the station faded away. "What do you want with me?"

"You? Nothing. You're just a little diversion, something for me to while away a boring Wednesday evening." His accent was strange, German maybe. His English was good but his tone was mocking, arrogant, dismissive. "We have been following you from Edirne. We want the people who are transporting you."

"I don't know who that is. I was hitching. They picked me up, they brought me to Sofia."

The arm tightened across her back, crushing her ribs and the voice spat at her neck. "Don't be stupid. The blue Skoda that brought you across the border, dropped you at Sofia, gave you the passports and tickets. Of course you know."

She had to think quickly. The train would soon be here and she needed to be on it. Her mind fogged as the pressure on her neck sent red spots prickling across her eyes. She saw Vasil and Pietr. She saw the blue Skoda and the ramshackle cottage and she saw Maria, smiling beyond the sight of the Makarov.

"Look, I know nothing. I am a student. I have an English passport. I am going home to Paris for the holidays."

The arm in her back leaned further on her spine sending sparks down her legs. She could feel tendons ripping in her shoulders.

"You must know their names. Tell me or this is going to be a long night."

Vasil and Pietr, Maria, Şarköy. Just tell them and the pain would stop.

Behind her the tracks started to sing and the tannoy echoed. Her train was arriving. How could she reveal their names? There were twelve people in her truck from Aleppo, and after crossing the border there were ten. She only identified five of her party on the boat across the sea and now she was one. And without Pietr's strong arms hauling her from the water, she too would be gone. Surely one person freed from tyranny was something to be thankful for? How could she yield so easily? How could she destroy everything *The Brotherhood* had built?

"I-I don't know. They put me in the car, gave me the papers." Then she yelped as her arm twisted up her back and her shoulder threatened to pop. Resistance was futile, the man strong. How could she buy herself time? "Please," she pleaded, "you're hurting me. Let me go and I'll tell you what you need to know." Reluctantly, her hand left the Makarov and slid behind her to the hardening mound in the man's jeans. "Then I will make it worth your while."

The pressure on her back eased a little as the man considered his options. She shut her eyes and gritted her teeth as a hand reached around and under her coat, fingers like tentacles exploring her shirt, pants of hot breath on her neck. Then she felt the point of the blade pressed into her spine.

As on the boat, she had made a wager with the Devil but, as then, she had no intention of paying. Anyway, what did she really know about her transporters? Anonymous men taking her to the border at gunpoint, Maria, Vasil and Pietr and their cottage with the secret room. And the inside of a tired blue Skoda. What else could she tell him? He knew of the Skoda. He must already have traced Vasil and Pietr.

Slowly, she turned to face her attacker, feeling the trace of the blade around her midriff, the tips of fingers on her flesh, the glint of orange from the blade. She could now see that this was Gregor, the man from Sofia. Even in the shadows, she could sense the hunger in his eyes.

He used the word 'we'. How many more were around the corner? Maybe they rode with the guard, or the driver or boarded the train later? Unless he really was the sleeping man under the coat.

In which case, he was alone.

"My father paid before he was killed. I was put on a lorry in Aleppo and shown a place to cross the border." She policed her words carefully. Just enough information to survive.

"Where was that? Çanakkale, Dikili?"

She had to buy more time. Behind the man, the cyclops eye of the train was slowing down into the station. Her hand played with the crotch of his jeans. "No, I was sent inland. To a road with a culvert. I followed a stream."

Panting, the man released her slightly and she watched the blade glint as he reached into his pocket for a cigarette. She saw the flash of a lighter, stark across his face and the warm orange of the tip. Through a cloud of smoke the man asked: "And where was that?" His tone told her his mind was elsewhere.

"It was dark and I was in the back of a truck, you idiot!" A hand impacted her cheek and crying out, she reached up to cover the burning skin. *Reckless bravado, Satya!* The train was now less than a hundred metres away and she was having to raise her voice to be heard over the boom of the motors. "I was in a truck all the way. How would I know where I was being taken?"

Pushing her hand from his trousers, the man held out a palm, the cigarette bobbing between his lips. "Give me your papers. Come on! Give them to me!"

As the headlight beam tracked across the platform, briefly illuminating the doorway, silhouetting the man, Satya's eye caught something familiar, a shape etched into the frame of the wood. Her heart leapt to her mouth. Inside she was consumed by a desperate longing for a home to which she could never return and for people who were gone.

And she knew now was the time to act.

Digging into her bag, she pulled out the postcard album and offered it to the man. Her arm was crooked, he would have to stretch. As his hand reached, she dropped it, mumbled apologies and bent to retrieve it, her hand mechanically drawn into her pocket. Cursing loudly over the noise of the train, the man bent to pick up the wallet. Satya thrust out her other arm and grabbed the man's wrist, yanking it down, causing him to stumble, her knee impacting his jaw. Now the train was pulling into the platform, it's huge electric motors beating through the air, sending vibrations through the platform. Drawing the Makarov from her pocket she jammed it into the man's skull and squeezed the trigger.

The safety! Damn!

Recovering his balance, the man swung an arm, sending the gun clattering into the doorway. Satya saw a flash of the steel as the knife travelled in an arc from above her head, then gold sparks as it impacted the wall behind her. Briefly sent off balance, the man reeled. She saw her opportunity and swung her foot as hard as she could into the man's shin.

"Bitch!"

And once more the blade arced, sweeping past her face. Satya grabbed at the arm, straining to hold it aloft, to hold the knife away. The man towered over her, his strength twice hers. The muscles in her arms tore. She could feel her strength ebbing as the man pushed the tip closer to her face. Pressed into the doorway, she was inches from the etched mark. The shape of a Western Letter A with and Arabic ah running through.

Alaam.

Digging deep beyond her own strength, she made a plea to the migrant beast who had protected her thus far. The blade turned, pulling the arm down and out to her side. *She saw Alaam sitting in the backyard of their shop carving with his penknife A-Lah-m.* The sinews in her wrists burnt as the man rallied, folding the knife inside. *A-Lah-mmm. Her brother mouthed the words as tip of his knife dug at the wood.* She could feel the ridge of the blade at her stomach, she could see Alaam's sign in the wood. Staring deep into the shadowed face of the man, with a primeval growl, the migrant beast pushed the blade.

Suddenly, the air around her froze. The noise from the train became an echo and the night collapsed into darkness. With a short, stilted grunt, the man fell to his knees, his eyes pinpoints of orange. The glow of the cigarette tumbled to the platform. Then he was on the floor. A small dark pool began to spread, glistening orange in the lamplight.

The train was now stationery. Further along the platform, doors were banging and feet were running but here at the far end, she hid in the shadows until the stragglers left. What had she done? Something primal, basal, the beast within had held the soldier's face beneath the waters as his mouth gaped and frothed and now it had forced this man's hand against his stomach and the knife through his flesh. She felt acid rise to her mouth. Turning away, she ran to the opposite platform and vomited. Her body started to quiver uncontrollably. Looking about her she was completely alone. She had to get a grip.

Alaam was here. Right here. He was in this doorway.

There was no time for self-pity or sentiment. She needed to be on that train. *Alaam had been here and she needed to follow him.* Quickly, stemming the urge to retch, she dragged the lifeless corpse into the doorway and stripped off his overcoat. She pulled him up into a seated pose and draped the overcoat about him. Hopefully he would be ignored, a sleeping hobo, a migrant like herself. She saw the snail trail of glistening black and wondered for how long that would be.

Alaam. He too had passed this way.

Grabbing her bag and the postcard album, Satya made for the train.

The Makarov.

Returning, she hunted in the darkness until her hand alighted on the gun, still warm from her pocket. Then another thought struck her. She leaned over the repulsive shape, willing herself not to look into the staring eyes. Feeling her diaphragm spasm once more, she peeled the fingers from their death-grip on the hilt of the knife and withdrew it, wiping the blade on the man's coat. Then, as the tears streamed down her face, she lifted the man's arm and removed his watch. Inside his jacket, she found his wallet. She thrust them all deep into her pocket. Now she truly was damned to the blazing fires of Jahannam. Twice a murderess and stealing from the dead.

Suddenly, there was no emotion. The primeval beast once more soaked up her guilt. Once more, she sank beneath the raging seas of her conscience and she flicked a switch, became a machine. Against the darkness of the platform, the empty carriage was stark and bright and it took a moment for her eyes to become accustomed. It was then she saw the stain, deep and crimson, across her beautiful skirt. Folding her coat about her, she headed for the rear of the train, which would become the front. Reaching into her pocket she checked the watch. 20:30. Ten minutes until the train left. Ten minutes for the body to be discovered. The coach was still deserted. Making for a cramped toilet, she quickly stripped off the top, skirt and tights, taking care to fold the blood away from the floor and donned new clothes from her backpack. Then she opened the window and let the garments drop to the tracks. Then, taking a seat, she pulled her coat over her head and feigned sleep, just like the man had.

But once more her hand was on the Makarov, flicking the safety on and off.

Chapter 63

Ealing, London

Deborah Whetstone leaned her head into the living room. 10:30pm. Maureen Whetstone was seated, as every night, in her husband's old chair, cradling a half-full glass while the television flickered unseen.

"Just me, Mum. I'm going straight up." Whetstone was in no mood to socialise.

"Would you like something brought up? I have a pizza in the fridge. It's pepperoni, the one you like." More a plea than a question, Deb instantly felt guilty. Walking over, she kissed her mother on the forehead and sat next to her. She held her hand and stared at *Newsnight*, forcing out stilted, meaningless conversation. Since Louise, Deb's younger sister, had left for university, Maureen had been alone a lot. At thirty-three, Deb should also have flown the nest, but with house prices, the job and a million and one other excuses, she had stayed despite the claustrophobia her mother's dependency brought.

Roy Whetstone had been hit by a car. Picking up a loaf of bread on his way home, he died alone on a cold, rain sodden street. The *Tesco Express* had run out of medium sliced that Friday evening, so he had nipped across to the Asian shop opposite. He never made it. Nick Vaughan was reaching for a CD in the glove box. He never made that either. At that moment, the world went about its business, Mannion Street froze in time and Roy Whetstone's life ebbed away.

For her father, death was inconsequential. There was no pain and he knew no loss, because loss is a curse of living. Deb lost a year trying to come to terms with the emptiness. Her mother had yet to do so. One cannot recoup the loss; one only loses more in trying to do so.

At fourteen years old, she was initially overwhelmed. There were no tears. Those close to her worried that she hadn't accepted her father's death; fearful of a cataclysmic breakdown. But her logic was simple, pragmatic and measured. Change was inevitable and had to be embraced in order to benefit from it, or at the very least, not to be consumed by it.

For Deb, a body wasn't a person. It was an object – the shell of a hermit crab, the cast skin of the snake. Was there an afterlife? The prospect of reincarnation was a mixed blessing. A pragmatic middle ground was to believe that all we have is now; born from nothing, returning to nothing – a simple transformation of molecules. The soul disappeared, whether in the slow decay of electro-chemical processes in the brain or the melodramatic escape of ectoplasm, it did not matter. So that meant that any service she gave, any debt she owed, was to the living not the dead.

Half an hour later, muttering feeble excuses, she finally hauled herself up the stairs. These days her room was the only privacy she had and she guarded it jealously, preferring to work long hours than bring it home with her.

Yesterday, with Daley's return from his enforced leave, she prayed the weight would be lifted from her shoulders yet today it felt redoubled.

Today she felt defeated.

In her pocket, her phone burred. It was Keith.

"Hi Babe. How you doing?" She sat on the bed, knees up.

"Hi Debs. Freezing my 'nads off in a Beemer, if you must know. Wanna come and keep me warm?"

"Nah. Mom's cooking me a supermarket pizza. Then I am putting on a onesie and crying to a film."

"Onesie, huh? Just a onesie?"

She giggled, feeling a tingle in her groin. "Filthy bastard. If you must know I will be wearing skimpy white knickers and bunny slippers too.

"*Jesus H.* You prick-tease! How can you do that to a man with another hour left on his shift?"

"Easily after what you did to me. I reckon I will have a right shiner." She glanced out of the window. It was cold and foreboding but the central heating had warmed her room. A tired world-weary face was reflected back. "So what do you want apart from some dirty phone sex?"

The line went silent for a moment. "Look, I just wanted to

say sorry, you know, for this morning. He's built like a brick shit-house."

"Two goes, Keith! Two attempts to catch that guy and we let him slip. I just hope your nuts are hurting you as much as my eye is hurting me. If he hadn't kicked you, I bloody would have."

"Come on, Deb, like I said he was a big lad. Knew how to handle himself."

She imagined the unmarked BMW parked across the road from the hotel Smith had been billeted in, Keith *The Uniform* and an aluminium police issue thermos. It was punishment enough but she wouldn't tell him. He would need to earn his reprieve.

"Look, Keith. I got to go. I got to call my other boyfriend."

"Scott Daley? What's he got that I haven't?"

"Rank, Keith. Rank."

She said goodnight and killed the call. Before the desperation to call back consumed her, she speed-dialled Daley's number. 8:00am tomorrow. That would be when Allenby would remove her from the case. When she would sink back to Sergeant and all her good work would be blighted by Steven Franks and Scott *Bloody* Daley.

"Daley?" The voice grated like nails in a blender.

"Jeez, gov. You sound rough."

"Yeah. Been asleep. I think I have a bug or something."

Whetstone wondered if it was the pills talking. "Well, keep it away from me."

"Apart from checking on my general wellbeing, what's up?"

"Keith just phoned. Was it you who got him to stand in the rain outside Connor Smith's hotel?"

"Might have been. No need to stand. He has an unmarked Beemer and a flask."

"Yeah. No expense spared."

"Bit of a dive that hotel, though. More cockroaches than residents. They rent rooms by the hour, full of tarts. Never know it might grow Smith up a bit."

"So, what do you reckon? You think he is involved in any way at all?" Since the interview, Whetstone had started to doubt herself, coming more around to Daley's way of thinking.

"Doubt it. Like I said, he's a streak of piss. He would use someone else's."

"You what?"

"Nothing, a turn of phrase. Smith just drove the van. Someone put him up to it."

"Franks?"

"Maybe."

"What about the van though? If you're right and there are several vans..."

"If?"

"OK, let's assume there are several vans, Franks has to be driving one of them. Who's driving the other?"

Outside the bedroom, Deb heard a tray clunk against the door and suddenly realised how long ago she had grabbed a sandwich from a newsagents. She held the phone between her ear and shoulder, opened the door and dragged the tray inside. On the line, Daley had gone quiet. Whetstone filled the void.

"Look, I still think Franks is in the frame. How he manages to be in two places at one time..."

"TARDIS with a carport, Deb."

"What?"

"Nothing. Continue..."

"Somehow he is managing to disguise his movements as business trips. Perhaps he takes the real van, parks up somewhere, swaps into the clone and stalks people. Then, when he is sure he can get away with it, he strikes."

"So, he has abducted someone, drugged them or killed them and thrown them in the back of the clone van. What then? Gascoigne said there was evidence of refrigeration, mutilation. There were no freezers at Franks house nor any sign that he had dismembered bodies."

"I don't know, wherever he parks the van, I suppose. And the other driver. Maybe that's his wife, Jill. Maybe they are in it together? There is certainly something wrong there."

"Seriously? Keith said she was a right nutcase."

"Six known victims, maybe many more. I'd say they were both nutcases, wouldn't you?"

"Look, it's just not hanging together well enough for me. I think you're right. Franks is never where he should be but I am not sure he is the killer. And where is the second van?"

The line went ominously quiet. The sort of silence that preceded a bombshell from Daley.

"Deb, there are some things I need to take care of before we see Allenby tomorrow, so I may be a little late. Stall him."

"Scott!" Whetstone's tone was plaintive, like a schoolchild kept back. "How the Hell am I supposed to do that?"

"I don't know, Tell him a joke, dance naked on the table...on second thoughts, not naked... I just need to get Steve Taylor and Mike Corby started on a few enquiries. I'll be minutes late, seconds even, no more."

"What enquiries? What is so important that you have to stand up Allenby? You going to share?"

"Look, it's just a hunch at the moment."

"For Christ's sake, sir. You could at least pretend to be part of this team."

"Just ten minutes, that's all."

Chapter 64

What sort of a man is Steven? Would he take matters into his own hands?

Marion sat with her legs up under her dressing gown. Derek was engrossed in his football. The TV was on but she didn't see it. How much did she really know about this man, Steven Franks?

She and Derek had met at school, although for the first five years, he was just another boy, all testosterone and teenage acne. She had been nineteen before they had started properly going out. The romance had come much later, slower than donkey with rheumatoid arthritis in a strong headwind. Even then, it had never been torrid, bodice-ripping lust; they had just settled on each other. But at least it had taken time. By their first full-blown sexual encounter she knew him well. She knew his secrets, like how he picked his nose when he thought no-one was looking and how he hid the gadgets he bought so she wouldn't chastise him over the cost. How he struggled with the mortgage payments but wouldn't let on.

And she knew how far he could be pushed before he snapped.

What did she know about Steven?

Thinking back to their conversations, had he ever revealed anything personal? True, they had spoken a lot of her family, of troubles with teenage kids, the boredom of life as a working mother, but never about himself. She didn't even know where he lived.

Could she trust him?

She picked up her phone and scrolled through the read messages, finding Margery, Manicure, her code for his number. A conversation from Tuesday.

Keep a low profile. Police

Police will have to wait. Just say u know nothing.

What about the farm?

I will see u there. For now, u know nothing. Keep it simple. U don't know where I am.

What about Connor?

Leave him to me.

OK. Text me again. I am v worried.

And there had been no more texts.

Of course she could trust him. She had been sharing his car for months. Would he take matters into his own hands? She only saw him for a few short minutes each day and this time of year it was in darkness. He was pleasant enough at work, though again they kept their distance and conversations were matter-of-fact.

He said he would deal with it.

Had he? The police were suggesting he had killed Varsa. There was a rumour his van was involved. She hovered over the keypad. He had not appeared on Wednesday as arranged. Maybe he didn't get the text.

Maybe she was wrong about him.

The words had to be right. Circumspect but to the point. If the police got hold of the calls...

Steven. I need to speak to you. I need to know what is going on.

A quarter of an hour later, she had discreetly checked her phone what seemed like a million times to no avail. Dropping the phone into her dressing gown pocket, she tapped Derek's arm. "I'm going up, love. I am going to read for a bit. Let you watch the match."

Derek made an unintelligible response and she rose from the sofa and headed upstairs, checking the screen once more as she peed and again as she propped up her pillows. Less than quarter of an hour and already her patience was wearing thin. She needed to put her mind at rest. She found the number and clicked call. It went to voicemail.

"Steven, it's Marion. Marion Edmonds." Her voice was quiet. The Script boomed out from Katie's room so she knew she couldn't be overheard. "Did you get my text just now? We need to talk. The farm. As soon as you can."

Cradling the phone, she watched the screen die. These were foolish notions. She would know if he had, as the police put it, taken matters into his own hands, wouldn't she? And why wasn't he answering?

She jumped as the door opened and Katie's face peered around it.

"Who you talking to, Mums? Your fancy man?"

Did she look that guilty? Had Katie overheard?

Katie smiled and trotted over to the bed and threw her arms around her mom, planting a kiss firmly on one cheek. "'Night, Mums."

"'Night, Kates. Oh, and could you remind your dad I will be late in tomorrow. I am seeing Margery for a manicure."

"Oooh, is that what you oldies call it these days?" Katie giggled. "I'll make him some tea, don't worry."

Chapter 65

Alperton, London, 00:00am, Thursday

Daley awoke to a car alarm, a howling daemon vaporising as the room turned black and the eyes of the TV and DVD player glowed green. Great squares of amber flashed across the walls.

Varsa's pad. He was clutching at air as she thrust the torn sheets into her bag.

What did that mean?

Shuffling wearily to the bathroom, Daley swilled his face and rubbed some life back in with the towel. Then, with a sudden realisation, he grabbed Varsa's notebook from the sofa and disappeared out through the door.

The synthesis of ideas was still skulking in his brain but they were snatches of detail, notions rather than images. Had Varsa kept another secret diary? She tore off pages and thrust them into her bag.

More importantly, had her killer missed them?

Clarence Road was very different to his first visit on Tuesday. The Saharan heat had dissipated and apart from the regular chirrup of a mantel clock, it was silent. Fingerprinting dust carpeted every surface and there was a smell of metal and must in the fine motes which danced around the vague light from the window.

Varsa Ruparelia had died for something far worse than the theft of a few drugs or an expenses fraud. Some deadly confidence which needed to be protected. The image returned, Franks was turned away, his arms on Caz Albin as she knelt before him. Opening the diary, he reread the pages that had sent him into a fitful sleep, trying to recover the swathes of memory that had drifted away.

Turning to the last entry, Daley reread:

23rd October 2012

Tonight I stayed around till 7:00pm. I sat on the top corridor in the dark and waited. At first, I thought he was not coming but he is always so regular, I can set my watch by him. Sure enough, he came

> and opened the garage. It was dark but it had to be him, only his car was left in the courtyard car park. He parked the van close to the garage doors again, but I think I counted five boxes being loaded. Then he closed the garage and left.
>
> Next time I will follow him and see where he goes with his boxes. This man must get his comeuppance.
>
> I will get to the bottom of this but it scares me. I thought I saw him look up to my window. The face stared at me and I knew he had seen me. I need go home and I need to lock my door.

He checked the date on his phone - 23rd October was a Tuesday. *He is always so regular, I can set my watch by him.* Whatever was going on, it was in the knowledge that Franks would not be there, yet still she saw him.

Next time I will follow him and see where he goes with his boxes.

Had she followed the van? If she had, why had she not kept the diary updated? Why did it suddenly end?

Daley flicked backwards and forwards in the book. There had to be something. He examined the front and back inner covers for pages tucked behind the bindings, but nothing. Then he noticed something strange. Flicking through the dates, most of April and part of May 2011 were missing, notes taken long before Varsa had been at the clinic. She was fastidious. Why omit these months? Turning the diary, he looked at it end on. Just an ordinary commercial product, a number of folded booklets strung together with thread and glued between the covers to make a complete lined notepad. With his finger, he traced the line of the missing pages across the end of the spine and smiled to himself.

Varsa had torn out the final entries and with them the entries on the opposite sheets.

Daley switched on the main light and scanned the room. In a haze of white dust, disorganised piles of papers and shifted furniture, the evidence of a thorough search by Corby and Forensics Officers was all around. Had Varsa outsmarted them all?

Examining mattresses and skirting boards, furniture plinths and picture frames, carpet edges and window sills, Daley systematically searched. After an hour, he stood in the centre of the living room and sighed, exasperated. Perhaps this search was in vain? Perhaps, when Varsa was taken, so were the pages?

He sipped at the take-out coffee he had brought along and grimaced. Cold. He placed the cup in the microwave to warm, listening to the leisurely whir. The amount of electricity Varsa had used in the last few days, no-one would miss another few watts.

Then his eye caught something and he wondered if it could be that easy to hide something in plain sight. Reaching down, he grabbed the corner of a folded piece of paper stuffed under the foot of the washing machine to stop it vibrating. Frustrated when it wouldn't budge he leaned a shoulder against the machine, wincing as his injury ached, eventually tugging the paper out as the microwave behind him pinged. Unfolding the paper, he smiled, as he saw Varsa's last diary entry.

Chatham Woods Farm.

Chapter 66

6th November 2012

Nobody knew I was there in the car park. They walked past my car and didn't even notice me.

They might have sacked me but they have not seen the last, I assure you. I will expose them all. I will find out what SF is up to and I will bet you, dear diary, that whenever he tells them he has left for Newcastle, he comes back here at night.

Ha ha. I won again! The van came. He waited until everyone had left. SF is supposed to be away yet there was the van in the courtyard by the garage. He is as bold as brass, that man.

He is also clever. I could not see what was happening in the garage as he blocked the opening with the van. I had to walk over and go in. There was no-one inside but the rear door was open and plastic boxes were stacked in the back room. Before I could open one, I heard him coming back. I ran back to my car pretty sharpish. There is a smell of bleach and something horrible in there.

When he drove off, I followed for half an hour and nearly ran out of petrol. It is the middle of nowhere. Chatham Woods farm. I hope he didn't see me following. The road is really quiet. He parked by the gate and I drove past, pulling up further on. Once he had gone, I walked up the drive after him.

7th November 2012

I looked on the map. I found Chatham Woods farm. The farm has been derelict for years. What can SF want with that place? Unless he has a drugs den there. Maybe he is like Breaking Bad and there is a meth lab or a marihuana farm?

SF arrived back from Newcastle today. Like he actually went in the first place. I took the inventory and his receipts as normal, then I asked him why he was back at the Hall yesterday. He told me to mind my business. I asked him what was in the boxes. He ignored me and shut the van in the garage.

8th November 2012

It is Friday. I saw SF again today and I challenged him to tell me what was in the boxes. He was mad with rage, swearing and shouting. He told me that my nose would get me into trouble if I wasn't careful. He grabbed hold of my arms and told me he was warning me. He cannot assault me and get away with it. I will tell CA.

Enough is enough! I decided to go to NS. I marched right in to his office and told him that SF is a thief, a liar and an adulterer. It was best he knew it all outright. I also said that I have seen him here when he should be in Newcastle. I told him I knew about the farm. This can't happen under his nose. He asked me all about the boxes, what had I seen. I don't know what I had seen but it must have been drugs equipment or even crack cocaine or something. He must have a major business right under NS's nose.

NS told me he had put his trust in SF and this betrayal was a tremendous shock. He was visibly shaken and distraught. I told him I also thought that SF and CA were at it behind his back. For one minute, I thought I had said too much but the truth is the truth. NS said he was grateful that I had come forward. He said he would sort this all out once and for all and that I should stay away. SF was not the sort of person I should be arguing with. Now that I had told him everything, I should leave it to him. He would look to reinstate me for my loyalty, even after I had been sacked. He is a good man. He is the only person in that whole stinking place who has shown me any kindness. I know I can trust him.

***

Date	Reg	Devices	Units	+/- units	Procs	Farm?
Jan 11	VH07 YMK	3	3	0	3	

Steve had not joined. Units from HTA?

Date	Reg	Devices	Units	+/- units	Procs	Farm?
Feb 11	VH07 YMK	3	5	0	5	
Mar 11	VH07 YMK	3	3	0	3	
Apr 11	VH07 YMK	4	4	0	4	
May 11	VH07 YMK	3	3	0	3	

HTA ended & SF Joined. Units? No HTA!

Date	Reg	Devices	Units	+/- units	Procs	Farm?
Jun 11	VH07 YMK	3	5	+2	5	5
Jul 11	VH07 YMK	5	7	+2	7	7

Too many units!

Date	Reg	Devices	Units	+/- units	Procs	Farm?
Aug 11	VH07 YMK	3	5	+3	5	6
Sep11	VH07 YMK	5	7	+2	7	7
Oct 11	VH07 YMK	5	8	+3	8	7
Nov 11	VH07 YMK	5	9	+4	9	7
Dec 11	VH07 YMK	5	8	+3	8	7
Jan 12	VH07 YMK	3	4	+1	4	5
Feb 12	VH07 YMK	5	7	+2	7	7
Mar 12	VH07 YMK	3	6	+3	6	6

64 units in the farm since SF joined, 25 extra procs & 25 extra units. Where do they come from?

Date	Reg	Devices	Units	+/- units	Procs	Farm?
Apr 12	VH07 YMK	5	7	+2	7	7
May 12	VH07 YMK	5	7	+2	7	7
Jun 12	VH07 YMK	3	5	+2	5	5
Jul 12	VH07 YMK	5	7	+2	7	7
Aug 12	VH07 YMK	3	6	+3	6	6
Sep 12	VH07 YMK	5	7	+2	7	7
Oct 12						

Chapter 67

Monarch View Hotel, Greenford

The street was running rivulets of rain. Keith *The Uniform* Parrish had kept station across the road since 8:30pm. It was 2:00am and relief was supposed to have arrived hours ago but Despatch seemed totally uninterested. Plain clothes, unmarked motor. He was beginning to think they were unaware of the request from DI Daley. By now, Deb Whetstone would be asleep, yet again their elliptical orbits keeping them apart.

He had watched a string of couples entering and leaving the hotel. Visits measured in hours, some in minutes. Now, under a dim porchlight, a slim girl shivered as she smoked, bare legs, stamping her feet against the cold. Every half an hour she had ventured out. Her skirt was impractical, his mother would have said more a belt, and she was wearing a loose strapped top even though the gauge on his dash read 3°C. Even at this distance he could see her nipples taut against the fabric of her top. Eventually, she bent down to extinguish the cigarette, her top hanging like a hammock from her chest. At this distance it was more imagination than titillation.

A confirmed singleton, with a wake of one night stands and short relationships, Parrish had been told it was time to settle down. He and Deb had met in the Spring; he had been assigned by chance to drive her. They had been together ever since, off and on. However, with Deb it was more off than on. They rarely met and when they did, she was either barking orders or biting huge chucks out of him. With Deb still living at home, privacy was rare and she seemed lukewarm to the idea of a flat.

Thank God.

Another woman arrived at the doors of the hotel, another man paying in cash. Maybe that was the way to go? Less complicated, easier to manage.

Had he grown bored of Deborah Whetstone?

Franks had not shown up nor had Smith attempted to leave, yet his flask was empty and his bladder full. Leaving the BMW and cresting the steps, he creaked through the door into the lobby. To his left, the slim girl sat hunched over her phone behind a pockmarked counter. She looked up and idly turned her head to the office behind.

"Dimitri! Policja!" Her tone was one of disinterest. This time of year, police visited more than punters. From the back, a tall man wearing a two-tone blue tracksuit, lazily rounded the corner.

"No, love. WC? Can I use your toilet?" Parrish glanced up at the man, shaven head, wide-shouldered, impassive, sending a warning shot across the bows. The man shrugged and pointed along a dark corridor, before disappearing back into the room. Behind the counter, the girl sank back down into the chair and resumed whatever she was doing with her phone. As she crossed her legs, the belt-skirt rode up exposing an expanse of thigh. Feeling himself react, Parrish turned and headed down the corridor. A strong smell of sweat, faeces and vegetable fat forced him to mouth breath as he relieved himself.

Returning to the reception the girl was still there, the door to the office closed. As he approached, she leaned forwards and smiled. Her top had fallen away and her small breasts hung free.

"Can I get some coffee?" Parrish waved the flask he had earlier left on the counter.

She nodded, indicating back down the corridor. Parrish grabbed the flask and turned away.

Then he turned back.

"You want to help me make it, love?" In his chest, his heart began to pound and his mouth dried, a line crossed. He nodded towards the back and waited a heartbeat. The girl concentrated on her phone and did not move.

The kitchen was squalid and basic. Parrish filled a kettle and spooned some coffee from a Polish catering tin into the flask. Then he waited.

From behind, he heard the soft click of the door latch and, spinning round, saw that she was leaning against it. Her legs were long and the front of the skirt was creased. Her toenails were painted blue, her expression detached and disinterested.

"Twenty." She held out her hand. "Twenty pounds. No kissing, no penetration, just blowjob."

Parrish felt himself harden. An anonymous room, what was there to lose? Her hair was tied back and the landscape of her white neck stretched down to the small shadow of her cleavage. The top hung from the stud points of her breasts. Her lips were thin and red.

"And for penetration?" Parrish's heart was beating fit to burst as the roar of the boiling water sounded louder behind him. Teetering on the point of no return.

She smiled and held out her other hand. There was a small silver packet. "Fifty for penetration but you use condom." Her eyes had darkened to emotionless black and feint tracks of maroon coursed down her forearms. Her life would be short and insignificant. He dug into his back pocket and drew out his wallet; his hands were shaking so much he could not separate the notes.

Behind him the kettle clicked off and the room descended into a still silence.

Transaction completed, the girl tore open the condom and handed the flaccid rubber across. Parrish fumbled with his flies and soon he was ready, as the girl mounted a worktop and spread herself. He was assaulted by an overwhelming odour of scent and sweat and her smell.

Then he was on her, forcing her back into the wall, thrusting himself awkwardly into her, hearing her faint sigh, watching her impassive eyes, imagining the fist against Steven Franks' face. He pawed inside the top at the small breasts. Slipping an arm around her waist, dragging her back onto him, harder and harder he pushed against her, a fist pummelling a jaw, tearing flesh and breaking bone, and he felt the explosion and rush and a warmth and weakness subsumed his body.

Behind Parrish, high in the corner, a small eye blinked red. The manager smiled, checking the numbers moving on the digital display as the recorder captured the grainy images of the police constable and the fourteen-year-old Irina. Everyone needed an ace up their sleeve for the day Vice came calling. Something to up the ante.

Seeing the reception empty, knowing the policeman had left his watch and was otherwise engaged, Connor Smith hauled his bag out of the front door of Monarch View and headed to his car, three streets away. He needed to get to the farm quickly.

Chapter 68

Lambourne Road, Ealing, 8:05am, Thursday

Whetstone lowered herself gingerly into *the throne of doom*, a fabric and chrome chair selected to make visitors to Allenby's office feel vulnerable. She checked the clock on the wall. 08:05am. *Thanks, Scott, thanks a lot!*

Allenby had been there at 07:45, obviously, emphasising the importance of the meeting, which should have been self-evident to Daley given the events of the previous day. The D/Supt puffed irritatedly and sipped his tea.

"So how is DI Daley settling back in?"

A question so open, thinking about it gave her vertigo. She wanted to say he wasn't ready, wasn't fully fit, that he was insubordinate and an obstacle to her investigations. She wanted to request he be removed from the case, that he had lost his touch.

"Fine, sir. A little rusty but OK." She cursed her inability to put truth before loyalty.

"I heard he was out at Chatham Woods Farm on his own? That tussle with Smith could have gone badly wrong. What was he playing at?"

"*Zone 6* case, sir. Another missing person. I was busy after Team Brief so he went alone."

"You thought that wise? I asked you to keep an eye on him for a few days."

Whetstone sighed. She wanted to say she was not his keeper, he was a big boy now. "He didn't tell me he was going. He just left."

Allenby leaned his elbows on the table and locked eyes with her.

"Look, Sergeant. I'll get straight to the point, shall I? There is a murderer on the loose and you two seem to be having a lover's tiff. You've had six months to experience the responsibility of command. Sometimes it's as much about diplomacy as it is about discipline. You knew it was going to difficult when Daley returned, both for him and you."

"To be fair, sir, the Inspector has been making things quite difficult..."

"So tell him. Sort it out. You spent half of yesterday chasing your arse trying to bring in your main suspect, and now they tell me Connor Smith has done a bunk from his hotel and could be bloody anywhere. Meanwhile Inspector Daley seems to be making all the progress. He has found a link between the two cases and a dumpsite. He's even found your body for you. However difficult he may have made things, he is out there on the ground working the angles, while you seem to be chasing ifs, buts and bloody maybes.

"I have put my faith in you over the last six months. I am proud of how you transitioned. Now the *Hand in the Van* investigation looks like going stratospheric so you will need all your colleagues behind you." Allenby paused and settled back into the leather. "Look, I have to manage expectations and right now, it is of a small team unable to cope with what we found yesterday. Don't cock everything up now. Find a way to work with Daley not against him. And for God's sake, if he is going down, don't let him drag you down too."

Whetstone made to speak but thought better of it as Allenby reached once more for his cup.

"You've got your Inspector's exam. When is that?"

"January, sir."

"You're a bright woman, a good officer. When it comes to recommending you for the step up..."

"Yes, sir." Whetstone checked her watch. It had crawled on another few meagre minutes yet her career had slid headlong into the crap. She remembered a nursery rhyme about a wise old owl. *The more he heard, the less he spoke, the more he spoke, the less he heard.* She let the uncomfortable silence suffocate her.

There was a knock at the door and Daley finally poked his head around. Allenby made a point of twisting his wrist and scrutinising the time.

As he sat, Daley was aware of Whetstone's eyes burning a hole in his temples. "Sorry, I am late, sir. I had to wait for DC Taylor to arrive. I need him to check some things out for me."

"What things, Inspector?" Allenby leaned back in his chair, ready for a yarn.

"Out of context, it sounds bizarre but I want him to check out the Medway Klein clinic, its finances, the type of work it does. There are connections with the white van and with Karen Sherwood who had cosmetic surgery. I have asked Steve to check if it was done at Medway Klein. It might be nothing but..."

"And Steven Franks?"

"That's Sergeant Whetstone's call, sir. There is enough evidence, albeit circumstantial and with him running, we should bring him in. The alibi he set up is either bogus or covering for someone."

Allenby rested his chin on the point of his fingers. "Ok. I'll level with you. The Chief Super thinks this case is way too big for us. Scotland Yard are champing at the bit to take over and he is on my back to let them. Ray Kramer is coming around later to discuss it. Ray *Bloody* Kramer!"

Allenby raised a hand as the pair muttered their discontent. "Now... I can hang onto it for now but that's all. Show me significant progress and soon. Daley, ask Inspector Somerville to compile her evidence as we will be sequestering that as part of our case. Whetstone, make sure our house is in order."

Daley's head fell to his chest, a rather too obvious sign of insubordination. Whetstone made hers even more obvious.

"Sir! This is our case. We are that close...," she indicated proximity with two fingers, "...to arresting Franks."

Allenby cut across her, in no mood to argue. "It's out of my hands. The Chief Super has spoken. "You have until the end of the week to conclude whatever lines of enquiry you can. However, before you hand anything over to Scotland Yard, I wish to personally review everything. How ever long that takes, if you get my drift. Right, carry on."

Chapter 69

Zürich Hauptbahnhof, Zurich, Switzerland

Gregor Wolfe.

Hunched into an alcove towards the back of the Burger King, Satya stared at the face on the card. It was younger than she remembered from Sofia or Budapest, the hair trimmed smartly for the photograph. The stiff, staring corpse a thousand kilometres away had been twenty-three years old when he had died. When she had killed him. It would have been his birthday in two weeks. Cards bought, presents wrapped, families planning parties.

But Gregor Wolfe would not be there.

Instead there would be another phone call, another mother wailing on a doorstep, another girlfriend crying in her room. Satya had completed another leg of her trip and he was dead.

Travelling overnight from Budapest, Satya had remained huddled beneath her overcoat, propped in the corner of the front-most carriage. She could hear the driver and conductor talking, the bells and alarms in their cabin. But she could not sleep.

She recalled the days before ISIS, before the rebels. The noise and bustle of the old town, stifling in the heat. Long days when she and Alaam had stayed out from the grey amber of dawn through the last embers of golden dusk, howling through alleyways, screaming and yelling under the ice-cold fountains, playing in the rocks of the Guensrin Garden until their knees bled and their clothes were tatters. She and Alaam would weave in and out of tired traders hauling their trolleys back from their stalls, past sly hosts inveigling tourists into restaurants, sure that there would be fattoush and falafel, and if they had been really good, rich, sweet basbousa. Sure that they would drift to sleep in the arms of their father as he puffed on his narghile.

Then there had been puberty and the hijab, the air-strikes and the rebels and suddenly everyone in the old town hid. A constant state of apprehension. The streets were empty, derelict and ruined. Houses became prisons and often tombs. And the rest of the world watched from the safety of their Western armchairs as her home imploded.

Less than a week ago, she had lain in her mother's blood praying for the bullets to stop, unable to scream, unable to cry. She had allowed herself to be spirited away so that, whilst others died, she could live. And her family were dead, the guard on the bridge was dead. And now Gregor Wolfe was dead.

What justification could there be that two should die so she could live?

Sliding up her sleeve, she looked at Gregor Wolfe's watch. It was a Seiko. The strap was too big for her wrist. He had been dead for thirteen hours.

In the back of the Renault truck, she had sought to separate herself from the primeval beast that had held down the soldier's head and felt the bones crack. And as Gregor Wolfe had fallen to his knees, it was not she who had pushed the knife, nor she that had looted him of his possessions, it was the beast. A vestigial twin, hitching a ride across Europe. Soon, the time would come when she could kill the beast and Satya Meheb could once more run freely through the streets.

She replaced the ID in Gregor Wolfe's wallet. The money had long since been taken. One hundred and twenty euros. Blood money. There was a photo of him and his girlfriend, sepia and overexposed, taken in a booth. She was pretty, pulling a face, laughing. Would she ever know how her boyfriend had died, cold and alone on a station platform? Satya would shed no tears for her, nor for the girlfriend of the soldier. They had no tears when her mother and father were cut down. Why should she cry for them now?

Finishing her meal, she prepared to find yet another platform, yet another train to take her nearer to England, where she could finally shed her migrant skin and live again.

Across the busy hall of the station, the automatic doors wheezed open as the cigarette was extinguished with a heel of a shoe. The girl was still sitting in the restaurant when he returned to his vantage point on the corner. Still sipping her drink through a straw, still pawing at the food she seemed to have no desire to eat. Since Budapest, since she had murdered the *Grepo agent,* she had let down her guard. He had walked to her carriage, watched her sleep. Even when the conductor had asked for tickets and passports, she had not noticed him, beneath his coat, three rows away. She had assumed the *Grepo* was alone. The *Grepo* never acted alone.

As Satya Meheb disposed of the detritus of her food, along with the wallet, she looked around her. She had the strangest feeling that she was being watched. With the Makarov now nestling in the calf of her boot, she felt inside her coat for the knife. Reassured, she left the restaurant and mingled with the stream of people heading towards the platforms.

One hundred metres behind her, the man pulled his overcoat about him and headed after her.

Chapter 70

Northwick Park

The supermarket car park in Teasdale road ran alongside the grounds of the Hall. Marion Edmonds had told of a footpath which allowed entry at the rear of the gardens. As Whetstone and Daley were not expected, they decided an unannounced visit would avoid the rather rehearsed affair from before. They would use the unofficial shortcut to take a look around first.

The pair had assumed and uneasy detente that was all too common in their professional relationship. Despite their infantile and rather embarrassing bickering, Allenby had made the situation crystal clear. Use it or lose it. Scotland Yard was nipping at their heels.

They had grudgingly agreed that they needed to return the clinic. If possible, they would speak to Snowdon and Albin again, to discover more about Franks.

After a moment or two, Whetstone spotted the gate into the Hall gardens, disappearing through a hawthorn hedge. A muddy, worn footpath edged the Hall's vast dew-soaked lawns, past crows, cawing and dancing, to the rear of the building, unearthly through the leaden mist. Daley placed his feet carefully to avoid the slushy puddles, scowling at the mud on his trousers. He was running out of smart clothes. Whetstone glanced down at her shoes and huffed at the ridge of mud around her heel. "Jeez, I'll never get these clean." Somehow that would be Daley's problem too.

Behind the Hall, the path stepped up to a terrace. Shaded under conifers, mottled by lichen, the yard felt dank and claustrophobic, home to a couple of rusting benches and pile of cut logs under an ancient log store. The block bricks snagged underfoot as the ground heaved with the wet winter. Above, an angular steel fire escape contorted down the side of the building and spilled out into the yard.

"Through here."

An old iron gate was propped open with a rake handle. Daley

guessed visitors to the Hall never made it this far. Passing through, the vista changed dramatically. The Hall stood haughty and proud atop layered beds of wintering shrubs and flowerless bedding plants. Sentineled by two lions rampant on their brick-built pillars, limestone steps lead to the enormous Baroque building, boasting four stories and an austere porticoed front door.

Across the courtyard, a row of vintage limousines was parked, boasting maroon and cream coachwork and crests on the doors. Amongst them, skulked a more modern Mercedes, an old Ford and a Volkswagen at odds with the faded grandeur of the house. The gravelled yard was strewn with confetti and tiny tinsel numbers, a sign of the financial depths to which the Hall lowered itself to raise a bob or two. To their left, the driveway passed onto the main road through more lionesque pillars and an overhanging bower of trees, skeletal against the gunmetal clouds. To the right, an archway between two rows of muse building led through to the clinic.

Whetstone pointed across the courtyard. Fifty yards away on the other side, against a set of panelled doors, a white Transit Connect sat covered by a fine blanket of dew. Whetstone pulled out a fob and depressed a button. The Transit blinked an amber greeting. "Franks wife gave me his set of keys. That is the van he claims he was driving. Says he parked up at 5:30pm on Tuesday."

"Wrong number, Deb - *RN08 DVB*. Franks is yanking your chain again."

Whetstone was momentarily confused. She stared at the car, hands on hips. Road-stained and grimy, the car certainly looked as if it had been to Newcastle and back. Peering through the window, the cabin was a mess, strewn with coffee cups, chocolate wrappers and other detritus. Donning latex gloves and opening the rear doors, she found the load space empty and clean.

"Suppose it makes sense," offered Daley. "If *VHK* was wrecked, he'd need a new van. I'll have Dave run the number. He hunched down and ran his fingers across the top of the licence plate. "Look Deb. These have been changed since the van returned." The plate had been screwed on slightly askew revealing a line of clean black plastic bumper.

"Maybe he thought it wouldn't matter if he was somewhere else in the country, then changed them when he got back yesterday. Might account for the evening. If he had to source new plates and then change them before going home."

"Possibly." Still, it puzzled Daley. How quickly could one source a white Transit Connect, of roughly the right age and specification, especially overnight? Most dealers would want funds to clear, preparation time, a day to tax the vehicle, insurance. "Let's get the FIO to take a look anyway. I'll clear it with Snowdon."

As Daley pulled out Snowdon's card, a notion flitted through his brain too quickly for him to fix. Above him, the skies blustered but at least the sleet had abated. Across the courtyard, Medway Hall stood tall, mocking his incompetence, his inability to see what was right in front of him. What exactly was he missing?

"Snowdon?"

"Hi, Mr Snowdon. It's Scott Daley, Metropolitan Police. I am at Medway Hall."

"Inspector? Yes, I know. I am told a DC Taylor is with Joan Thompson? She is Varsa Ruparelia's replacement." A man that liked to be in the know.

"I am sure he won't take up too much of her time. Is there any chance myself and my sergeant could have five minutes?"

"Unfortunately not. I will be away for the next few days and need to leave soon. Is it anything I can help you with over the phone?"

Distractedly, Daley cast his eyes around the yard, unable to scratch the mental itch, to draw out what was bothering him.

"We are in the Hall courtyard, sir, by the white Transit van Mr Franks uses."

"Yes, Inspector."

Daley suddenly felt uncomfortable. Snowdon's tone flat, emotionless, a statement. Was he looking down on them, as the Hall seemed to look down on the courtyard, upon the row of cars, the Daimler limousines like a pair of identical twins? Looking around, there were CCTV cameras everywhere.

"We need to remove it for examination."

"The van belongs to Chronotech rather than the clinic. I will square it with Caz. How long do you think you will need it? If it helps your enquiries, I am sure we can source a replacement for a few days."

"There is something else that you can help me with. Varsa Ruparelia seemed to think there was something untoward, possibly illegal going on. Maybe concerning Delta. What can you tell me about the project?"

As Daley stopped speaking, the line lapsed into silence. Eventually Snowdon spoke.

"The phone you are using? Are the calls recorded?"

"No, sir."

"Hang up and I will call you back."

Daley raised his eyebrows and watched as the call dropped. All of this cloak and dagger, secret squirrel stuff. His phone vibrated, caller number withheld.

"Daley?"

"Sorry. There are no patents yet for the Delta products. I have to be careful. If the information I am about to give you leaks out, I shall know where it came from."

Again, Daley raised his eyebrows.

"Caz Albin outlined the nature of the project?"

"Yes, bionics, Steve Austin."

"That's fiction, Inspector." Snowdon's tone was derogatory. "Delta is backed by a number of influential international governments. It's a big deal, a very big deal. We operate under agreed confidentiality protocols from the Ministry of Defence.

"I am sure you have seen prosthetics before? Where a person wears a false arm and by connecting implants into the brain, they can move the prosthetic, grasp objects? Delta is similar, except that it is bidirectional. Basically, Chronotech has built a device which is implanted deep into the brain to control peripherals or indeed to control the person based on external stimuli. It connects to the central nervous system to stimulate muscles and the optic and auditory pathways to receive a feed of what the person sees and hears."

"Control the person? I am not sure I like the sound of that. Shades of Big Brother."

"Or a quadriplegic or amputee living a near normal life. Restoration of sight, hearing. The therapeutic applications are limitless. But think on this. Missiles fired in the time it takes a military spotter to see the target, soldiers who can dodge bullets, that they have no awareness of."

Rather than shades of Big Brother, the implication was far more serious. A military grade weapon.

"So, the device. It requires surgery?"

"Ultimately yes. The device itself is a multi-part unit. Each of these has an array of electrodes and sensors embedded around the subject's body."

"That implies a certain amount of invasive surgery. Who are the subjects? Are they volunteers, army personnel?"

"No, Inspector. It's purely research and development at the moment. Currently our work is confined to the stimulation of discrete muscle group, and the interpretation of responses. Decoding of sight, for example, is fraught with complications. Then we need to consider rejection, compatibility, toxicity, battery life and charging before the project can be considered a success."

"Varsa records in her diary that she suspects Franks and/ or Smith of stealing from the clinic. Would you know anything about that?"

"Impossible, Inspector. Any discrepancies would be obvious. Both Smith and Franks have our utmost trust. Can you be more specific?"

"She mentions devices and units?"

Snowdon paused. "To my knowledge, and I keep a close eye on everything, there is no evidence of loss or theft."

Thanking Snowdon, Daley closed the call and nodded to Whetstone. Words were in short supply today. She had called Ealing and a Forensic Officer was on his way with a low loader.

"Can I help you?"

The pair wheeled round as small man, coat flapping came from a door in the corner of the courtyard, eying them curiously.

Daley smiled broadly, thinking on his feet. "The Daimler DS420. My wife and I had one when we got married." The mental itch was solidifying, becoming more tangible. Perhaps a distraction would help it form. Whetstone, her investigation being hijacked again, doled out the rope for Daley's neck, took the cue and sidled off.

The small man smiled and thrust out a hand. "Arnold Evans. I look after the vehicles. Beautiful aren't they?"

Daley took the hand, invited the sales pitch. "We want to renew our vows so I am looking to hire the same type of vehicle. Feigning interest, forcing the thought patterns, Daley asked "Are they up for hire?"

"You would have to speak to reception, sir. We have four DS420s, two pairs. The black and white pair are ex-Royal fleet. The maroon and cream pair come from Monaco, the Grimaldi estate. We brought them back a few years ago. The Grimaldis drive without registration plates, so these retained their British registrations and we were able to simply screw plates back on. Come and look at these. If you and your wife want something special..."

There were stables around two sides of the courtyard, broken only by the arch into the clinic yard. At the left-hand end, an open woodshed played host to an old tractor, a couple of vintage carcasses and a plethora of assorted spares. Evans pulled out a mammoth bunch of keys and creaked open two of the garage doors.

These are Rolls Royce Silver Wraiths - a '49 and a '51. Next door there are two Phantom Vs from the same era."

"What do you think, dear?" Daley looked over at Whetstone, who was peering through the windows. She turned and scowled, still too cold to melt the permafrost.

"Of course, they are notoriously unreliable. We have two of each in the same livery. If they order a Phantom, they want a Phantom, and in the colour they ordered."

Like a stranger appearing from the fog, at first amorphous, featureless indistinct, Daley's mind urged forward a thought, knitting together disconnected notions as it became more and more solid. *They don't care about the exact car...* Daley counted the stables in the courtyard. The van, the number plates, the crash.

"This isn't the van, Deb."

***

Snowdon watched the two detectives. Daley stood a hundred yards away, stock-still save for bouncing the corner of his phone off his chin, deep in thought. Whetstone bobbed in and out of sight as she gazed at the cars in the open garages.

So, Franks and the white van were their main focus. How long would that last?

Should he suspend Delta? With Franks and Smith now unavailable, not to mention the undue attentions of the police it was probably the right thing to do. The project had already been pared to the bone and with the Hall needing so much renovation, he could virtually hear money being sucked through the ancient pipework.

Snowdon retrieved a mobile, and dialled the only number stored in its memory.

"Hi Nick." Caz Albin's greeting was edged with concern. "Have you seen Franks? He left a message on my mobile. The police are after him."

"Have they arrested him?"

"No, he gave them the slip. Even called around here first thing. Banged on the windows for a few minutes and got the message. God know where he is now. Apparently, his alibi isn't good enough."

"And what is that?"

"That he left for Newcastle on Monday evening and didn't get back until yesterday night. What else would he tell them? He knows where he stands."

She was right. Franks knew which side his bread was buttered.

"He's a big boy. He can look after himself. Look, Caz, there is nothing we can't handle here. Nothing that will connect us with anything Franks is up to."

"Are the Police at the clinic?"

"Yes. There's someone in with Joan Thompson. She will keep him in check. I think the poor boy is scared of her."

"She terrifies me, Nick!"

"Hmm. And I also have the two detectives poking about in the courtyard. They are taking a close look at the van. What about you? Have they sent anyone to Chronotech?"

"Not as yet but the constable is going to swing round after he has finished with Joan."

"Nothing you can't handle, dear. I'm certain."

"What if they find something, Nick?"

"What can they find? Like you said yesterday, the books are in order. They will spend a couple of days chasing their tails, walk away with a skip-full of photocopies and be buried in that for months. Look, when they catch up with Franks, he will be the one doing the explaining."

"But Delta? What happens to Delta?"

"You find a replacement driver and I look for agency staff. We carry on as planned without missing a beat."

"Is that wise with that Inspector nosing around?"

"Seems more interested in the vintage fleet than catching a murderer. Perhaps I overestimated him. What I took for deviousness, maybe it's just dumb luck. Oh, by the way. He wants to drag Franks' van off to CSI or something. I said you would be OK with that."

"Can I stop him?"

"Why would you want to? They have a crashed van full of incriminating evidence. Now he has a new one, it will be as clean as a whistle. I read an article once that said however hard you clean a car, it will still carry the traces of everyone who has travelled in it. That will keep their labs happy for weeks. And you know what? There is not a trace of you or me. Maybe a fingerprint or two on the outside. After all, I seem to recall admiring the new van."

"I believe you did." Caz smiled to herself.

"I must have run a finger or two over it, maybe even hugged the shiny paintwork."

"Come on now, Nick. This is serious! What happens if they come over here?"

"Let them. Just leave them to it. They will chase their tails for a few weeks, everything will come to a dead end and it will all point to Franks."

"Perhaps, Nick, but maybe now is the time to start considering damage limitation?"

***

The low loader was taking an age to arrive. That was OK. Daley was sure it was the wrong van but it needed to be eliminated. The mud under the wheel arches would eventually do that.

There were twelve identical panelled doors around the courtyard. Each garage, along with its neighbour housed a pair of vehicles. The Wraiths, resplendent in brilliant white, dusty from storage. Similarly, the Phantoms; a '49 and a '51 in gunmetal. Two 1967 Alvis Three Litre drop-head coupés. The four garages where the Daimlers slept.

Everything in pairs. If one wasn't available, they could use the other and no-one would notice the difference. Maybe Varsa didn't notice the difference?

"And these?" Daley thumbed at the remaining two.

"They're used by the clinic, sir. Not my responsibility."

Daley reached into his pocket and held up his warrant card. "Let's make it mine, shall we?"

Despite her reluctance, Whetstone had resolved that there was nothing to be done until Franks was in Lambourne Road, so she gave Daley his head. She had seen him like this before. Searching for the last edge in a jigsaw box. This was the one percent inspiration which may change the course of the investigation.

Evans visibly started before anxiously looking around the yard, seeking a higher authority which avoided his gaze. Flustered he searched for the correct key. The first garage was empty, a breeze sending crisp, brown autumn leaves skittering across the dry concrete. Hardly a garage, this was more a storeroom large enough for a car and more besides.

"So what? The van is parked in here, the stock off-loaded, then taken through the corridor at the back?"

Evans shrugged. "I suppose so. The equipment is stored in those lockers. It's all very confidential. I don't come down here. None of my business." He was having no part of this.

"Yeah, you said. And that door? Where does it lead?"

"To the corridor, Sir. All these garages back onto an old covered alleyway which leads along the back to the corner where

I came out. My workshop's just through there."

Daley peered through the door but all he saw was a dark unlit space stretching left and right. Resignedly, he closed the door, somehow disappointed that dismembered corpses had not littered the corridor. Now he was even more satisfied that they had the wrong van. He looked towards Whetstone enquiringly but she shook her head. A casual poke about had again revealed nothing.

"Can we look at the last one?" It was Whetstone, now somewhat bored. Now she wanted to move on. Her cursory check of each garage had found nothing but a stray cigarette end and some congealed *T-Cut* in the corner of a windscreen. These foetid automotive dinosaurs just didn't float her boat. She liked her Golf. Trustworthy, reliable and just like her, cheap to maintain if slightly boring and a little past it's best.

Evans sorted the final garage key. Everything in pairs. They could use the other and no-one would notice the difference.

"Do you mind if I open this one?" Daley was playing a hunch.

Bemused, Evans handed across the key. As he inserted it into the lock, Daley asked: "How many keys are there for each lock, do you know?"

Evans shrugged.

"And these two?"

"Dunno. Don't think I've ever been in this last garage."

As he eased the door open, Daley was hit by the smell of cleaning fluid. He turned back to Evans. "Looks like you're not going in now either. From now on this is a crime scene. Do you understand? Deb, get onto base. We need a team here." Gently he closed the door slid the key from its ring.

Chapter 71

1986

The tulips dripped shining dew and the scent filled my nostrils, masking everything real in my world. My mind sees the stripes of red and green, undulating, stretching to the horizon, to a place that wasn't here. The small wooden cabin with the log fire and the stout lock, the windmill surrounded by empty skies and silence. Where the world is beautiful and the sun shines down. Where the screams and the sobs and the pleadings are echoes on the whistling breeze.

Where he is not allowed to do these things to children.

Then the room caves in, dark and still. The world once more turns real and the log shack and blue lined horizon beyond the colours have drifted back into the picture. Outside the window, the rain raps on the sill, streaks of grey silhouetted across the walls. In the prison of my own Hell, the shadow prowls and the voices mumble. Unheard excuses and meaningless apologies as I whimper in my own wetness and he enjoys the sleep of the righteous.

She has to know, she really does, but at breakfast, he will be there and she will be there, the toaster will surround her in its electric force field and hold her tongue. His x-ray eyes will burn the memories from her brain. She will smile and pour the milk and he will read the paper and I will sit as still as I can and hope that they can't see me.

Lina will play with her dolls and I will join in. Don't play at the table, Dom. I would need to be punished, but Lina can get away with anything. She is daddy's little girl. Surrounded by the toaster force field. Protected by a smile, a gossamer thin veneer of childhood that he can remove in a caress. Maybe he visits her too? Does he do to her what he does to me? But her eyes are different. They are beacons and her cheeks are red and her smile is wide. Behind the eyes, the innocent still plays without the need for fields of colour, of endless skies and stout locks and the wind-blown solitude beyond the horizon.

I pull up my pyjamas beneath the sheets, smelling the vinegar sweat in the cotton, feeling the gnawing pain, and the warm moisture creeping and seeping into the mattress. I stare at the tracks of rain scurrying down the window and I know that in the morning she will blame me.

Then, the shroud of sleep is dragged away once more as footsteps cross the groaning boards. I hear the metallic pop of the door handle and I am instantly awake, alert. Terror releases my bladder. I feign sleep whilst all the time watching for the shaft of light to widen in the door frame but I hear voices. There are never voices. This is an act of silence, of obedience. I strain to hear the words but all I can hear is sound. It is him...and Lina.

Her time has come.

So absorbed was he that he sees nothing but I see everything. I see the pawing hands which should never touch flesh like that on one so young. I see the puzzlement, the sudden dawn of fear on her face, as the hand slowly creeps below the bedclothes. I see the blue grey spray of brains as the face of the cricket bat tears away the back of his skull. I see his eyes roll back before the spatters hit the wall.

Then everything hushes to heartbeat, a quickening of breath. Lina sits with her eyes covered and the hand still up her nightdress. I scoop her up and take her to my room, away from harm. Away from the blood and the horror. Then I take up the bat and I walk to my parents' room.

Mother is sitting on the bed. She is swaying backwards and forwards and the rosary is swinging in her palms. I ask her why she allows this but her mind is filled with the glory of God and the Virgin Mary. How can she sleep whilst I cry to myself in a pool of urine? How can she let him back into her bed? Why does she love him more than me?

But her ears are closed as she mutters her meaningless prayers.

And she sways to the Hail Mary, Mother of God. She looks at me and her eyes are full of hatred for the devil spawn that has destroyed her family, the evil that is dragging her to the deepest levels of purgatory.

My hand raises the bat, still glistening, and I bring it down on her. Again and again, I strike as the holy prayers fade away to the sounds of breaking bone and renting flesh. Never again will those eyes look and not see. Never will those ears listen and not hear. As the arm rises and falls, the wind beats on the sails and the windmill rumbles and creaks and the tulips sway to the rhythm of the breeze.

And Lina is there and she is smiling. She reaches up and takes my hand. A tacit understanding. Before it was us and them. Now we are one.

Chapter 72

The Goldfish Bowl, Lambourne Road

Detective Chief Inspector Ray Kramer fidgeted in the uncomfortable chair in Allenby's office. A young DC placed a tray of coffee down on the mat and smiled. Kramer turned to DI Phil Dodds.

"Nice office." Kramer was admiring the cabinet stacked with awards and memorabilia. The walls teeming with golfing artefacts, pictures of Allenby pressing the flesh with the great, the good and the not-so-good. The eleventh floor at Scotland Yard was a bland affair, much like the Team Room outside. Aluminium and glass, industrial carpet tiles, white formulaic office desks arranged in barracks. He had always coveted the homelier feel of the Chief Super's office. Now he coveted this.

"S'pose." Dodds billet in the barracks made his opinion moot.

Kramer had attuned himself to the chirrup of the clock above the door. More a whirr-click. He imagined the small motor gathering momentum, storing energy for the last push which would force the gears on another notch, the briefest of pauses, then onto the next. Over and over. And over.

What was keeping that Superintendent anyway? As much as Kramer respected the rank, from what he had heard, *Bilko* Bob Allenby was a bit of a stickler. A jobsworth they used to call people like him but Kramer played the long game. The lion stalking the herd from the long grass. Sooner or later the time would be right to move in. Now Dodds, on the other hand, was a bull in a china shop. He saw it, he went for it, then dealt with the consequences later.

Much like the celebrated Detective Inspector *Suicide* Scott Daley.

Kramer huffed. He reached for his coffee, pleasantly surprised at the quality. Filtered, rich, the only perk to a meeting with a senior grade, or maybe a diversionary tactic. Whilst they were holed up in this bunker, he knew Allenby was negotiating a rear-guard action which would prevent them taking the case. He would be pacing the Met blue carpet of some sixth-floor mandarin, in deep soliloquy about how well his officers had performed, about the seriousness of the case, of the excellent record of his team. Well, at least that's what Kramer would be doing in his position and always with the same result.

Failure.

The case had exploded the previous day. Kramer and Dodds had been called into a conference room and shown photos of the shed, of the charnel house it contained. They had reviewed the scant notes from Lambourne Road and concluded that the North London Homicide Unit kept things so close to their chests there was a danger of the print rubbing off onto their skins. There were few details of potential suspects beyond the driver at the tech company and the Junior Surgeon at the clinic. The Farm seemed to be the anomaly. Derelict for years. Seemingly no connection yet stuffed full of corpses. This was a meaty case and Kramer could not wait to begin work, to unravel the mess these provincials had left it in.

Where was that bloody superintendent?

In answer to his invocation, the door opened and Allenby breezed in, thrusting out a welcoming hand.

"Sorry to keep you waiting, gentlemen. Ah, I see you have coffee. Now, the *Hand in the Van.*"

Kramer stifled a smile. There was a quaintness about the description. When a case reaches the level of seriousness that dictated a significant level of resource, CID teams would request a name for the investigation and one would be allotted. *Operation Nimrod* or *Lemongrass, Diablo or Thoroughbred.* Random and meaningless but adding gravitas. These plods were a throwback to the old millennium.

"Sir, as my Chief Superintendent stated in his email, you are requested to hand over the investigation to the Serious Crimes Squad and make all documents and evidence available to us. DI Dodds and I are here to begin the process as soon as possible." Straight in, no messing.

Allenby smiled and placed himself into his chair, safely behind the metre or so of walnut veneered oak. "No problem. No problem at all. I have just spent a few minutes with my Chief

Super. We agree it would be in the best interests of the case for Scotland Yard to become involved."

Kramer shared a glance with Dodds, inwardly stunned. They expected at least some degree of resistance, even if ultimately futile. "We appreciate the co-operation, sir." He tried not to sound too condescending but that was a skill he had not yet mastered. The Superintendent behind the desk, however, was more observant than he looked, judging by the expression.

"DCI Kramer. Don't think I am happy with this outcome. I have argued vociferously for my team and ultimately had to accept the decision of my superiors. Less than a week into this investigation, my officers have made tremendous progress and it is a slap in the face for them when the *prima donnas* from Scotland Yard waltz in and take over because ultimately, we know who will get the plaudits when the case is solved. So, Monday morning, the case is yours."

"But the Chief Super..."

"Take it up with him. I will arrange a room on Monday at 9:00am where DI Daley and DS Whetstone will present their findings so far."

"With all due respect, sir..."

"Funny how that phrase usually precedes something entirely disrespectful. By all means take it up with the Chief Super. You might just catch him before he leaves for Northern Ireland. I believe he is back on Monday at, oh, 9:00am."

Allenby lowered his glasses and peered at Kramer. “Don’t I recall you and Scott Daley falling out over something? Federation dinner?”

Kramer shuffled in his chair as Dodds smirked undiplomatically. He fixed eyes with the senior officer for a long moment, much as a lioness would a huge patriarchal wildebeest. His claws were sharp and bite fierce but Allenby had the high ground and weight. If it had to be Monday, then Monday it would be. A kill is still a kill, even if it takes time coming.

Chapter 73

The yard was crawling with police now. There would be no chance of retrieving his phone or the jacket. God, he loved that jacket. Franks watched through the archway as his Transit Van was winched onto the flatbed.

Having given the police the slip the previous day, he had spent the evening shivering in his car, afraid to venture too far. A quick recce had established that the house was being watched and that bitch of a wife would just love the opportunity to deliver him to them on a plate. So, he had driven North towards Elstree. He knew there were plenty of hiding places there, mysterious copses, dense woodland, a man could disappear there and, if he didn't want to be found, he wouldn't.

Calling at his home, towing the van, a car chase for Christ's sake! Why were the police putting so much effort into pursuing him?

He replayed the voicemails from Connor Smith in his head. An accident! What kind of accident and what the Hell had any of this to do with Varsa Ruparelia? *Help me, Steve.* That still sent a shiver up his spine. For weeks, Smith had been pestering him, Ruparelia had been interrogating him. It really was none of their business what he or Caz got up to in their private lives. She was the best thing that had happened to him in a long while and all they sought to do was to turn it into an opportunity.

Well, no! Thousands, if not millions, of people have illicit affairs; sure, they might eventually end messily but what of it? The male of the species was designed to spread his seed.

Unless it was not about that at all.

Having laid low until darkness fell, Franks had ventured out of the security of the dense copse and risked the drive around to Caz's house. There was no-one in, or if there were, they were not answering the door. For months, they had been lovers but, at the first inkling of trouble, she was nowhere to be found. He knew he was in deep shit with her. She had urged him to remain at the house. Yet, still he had left.

Then there was the text from Marion. *Keep a low profile. Police.*

Now he thought about it, that sounded ominous. It had to be the farm. Had the police found out? Well, if they had, surely that's a good thing. Ultimately.

He had thought back to the mysterious lost days in his calendar, the fictitious appointments. On those days, his profile was so low as to be subterranean, gaping holes in his life. If the police took an interest in his whereabouts on all of those lost days he would have no alibi. Unless Caz provided it.

Now he had been determined to have it out with her. Whatever the police were investigating, whatever they thought they had on him, he needed to be sure he could count on her. He had skulked around the first floor of the Hall for three hours, dodging cleaners, looking out at the courtyard, but she had not shown. He had even considered going to the farm but then all hell had broken loose. He had spotted the sour faced sergeant hanging around the yard along with another policeman. A large box van had parked up next to his Chronotech van and a couple of guys in jumpsuits had begun crawling all over it. His phone, and that beloved jacket, had been bagged. Now he watched as the winch tightened and the Transit crawled up the ramp of the flatbed.

"Too cold for a smoke but hey."

Leaping out of his skin, Franks turned as the tall, slim, bespectacled man paused the cigarette before his mouth and smiled.

"Yeah, I suppose." He returned to drama unfolding in the yard.

"Excuse me but are you...Steven Franks?"

Irritated, Franks turned and glowered at the man. "Who wants to know?"

"Detective Constable Steve Taylor, North London Homicide."

Homicide?

Franks turned and ran through the archway. There was a narrow corridor devoid of coppers around the front and off through the garden gate to the gardens beyond. But he would have to be quick. Behind him, Taylor shouted "Ma'am, Steven Franks!"

Deborah Whetstone spun towards the shout and saw the robust form of Steven Franks bounding across the courtyard towards the gate into the back garden. She indicated to a uniform to radio ahead and dashed after him, leaping instinctively as the rake doorstop clattered below her feet. Ahead she could see Franks, kicking up dew as he headed for the footpath to the supermarket. She leapt down the steps and onto the grass, once more thanking God she had left the Jimmy Choo's at home. From behind, a large black figure jumped from the patio and puffing like a train crossed the lawn, launching himself at Franks. The two landed in the muddy grass with a painful thump.

As blue and green stars filled Franks' vision and he tasted blood, Whetstone dragged his hands behind his back and the cold of the cuffs bit his wrists.

"Don't test me today, Sir, I have been bollocked by my boss, bollocked by my Inspector and I am in no mood for games." She pushed on his back. "Just don't move."

Chapter 74

Gare de Strasbourg, Bas-Rhine Department, France

How could it be? He was dead.

Satya grabbed her wrist and felt the solid case of the Seiko beneath her sleeve. How could it be him? She saw the knife arc, felt the resistance and the yield as it pushed to the hilt into Gregor Wolfe's abdomen, she smelt the warm, metallic odour of the blood as it seeped into her clothing, smelt the tobacco on his breath as he exhaled his last. She felt the sting as she had ejected the contents of her stomach onto the tracks. There was an inevitable reality about the last twenty-four hours.

So how could it be him?

Leaving Zurich, hidden within the flow of passengers heading for the train to Basel, she had the feeling she was being followed. She had turned, feigning a glance at this sign or in that shop, hoping to catch a glimpse.

And once she had seen the man.

It was a fleeting glimpse, a figure, one hundred metres back turning on his heel a split-second too late. He was about her height, wearing jeans and a dark overcoat, the hair was short but the face... She was too far away. Was this the man under the coat?

Her blood froze and the footsteps around her echoed like salvoes. Should she duck into an alcove, allow the man to catch up, blow his cover or would one of his colleagues simply take over the pursuit? No. She would bide her time, tighten her shaking hand on the knife in her overcoat.

The train to Basel had been sparse, the passengers spread out. She lost sight of the man but she knew he was there.

We he had said. *We want the people who are transporting you.* Gregor Wolfe was not alone. His accomplice had followed her from Budapest under his overcoat.

Drawing up at Basel, she had joined a small but significant number sprinting for the change to Strasbourg. Safety in numbers. This time she had been fortunate. Her favoured seat, with her back to the cabin bulkhead, had been free. Studying the boarding passengers, she had not seen the man but she knew that somewhere on this train, he would be reporting back, arranging for her to be followed until she met her contact in Paris.

She had only closed her eyes briefly, a cat-nap but that was enough. Now, nearing Strasbourg station, it was the shoulder of the overcoat in the seat two rows ahead which held her attention.

Around her other passengers collected their things. Laptops were closed, bags zippered and coat sleeves flapped like scarecrows' arms. The overcoat stayed seated. Arms and bodies bobbed this way and that, obscuring her view. She rose with the swell and stood amongst the queue waiting for the train to stop.

Outside, the platform was a procession of people. She could see uniforms, perhaps station guards, perhaps police. She could not draw attention to herself in so public a place. For now, she would need to follow. Sooner or later, the overcoat would turn to assure himself that she was still there. Then the next move would be hers.

Finally, the queue vented through the doors. The overcoat was three metres away, collar up. By the time she alighted, the man was forty metres in front, heading for the exit.

Satya placed her hand on the hilt of the knife, quickening her step, trying to gain ground as the man entered the main hall. Suddenly she was in a melee of people, milling this way and that. The overcoat stopped briefly, getting his bearings, before carrying on across and towards the small flattened arch above the exit doors at the far side. She needed to find a way to intercept him before he reached them. Adding half steps into her gait, she skipped quicker until she was within a metre of the man. She would ask the time. Ahead the winter sun shone through the entrance and, temporarily dazzled, the man stopped. Satya seized her opportunity. She withdrew the knife, held it beneath her coat and stealthily walked up behind the man. She would press the knife to his back, force him to one side.

"Harrald, Rene!" The man raised his hands in greeting and sprinted out into the vast domed courtyard. Beyond, two figures similarly dressed raised their arms. Quickly covering the knife,

Satya was confused. Now she could see. This man was fifty if he was a day! The three exchanged handshakes. What would she have done, when she had dragged the man away? Would she still have slit his throat? Could she have apologised and run off? She pocketed the knife. She spun on her axis, panicking, scanning the crowds, dark overcoats everywhere. He wasn't stupid. He would be watching this charade, phoning his friends and laughing at her.

Feeling the anger welling inside her, Satya followed the exit into the vast sweeping arch of glass that encased the station building. As the crowds thinned, seeking taxis and the streets, as the man and his colleagues chattered and strolled away, Satya crossed to the departure boards and looked for her next train. This was to be the final journey and it couldn't come soon enough. Her shoulders sagged as she spotted it, way down towards the bottom. She had another hour and a half. Finding a bench with a view on the exit, she settled down to wait.

She was so tired of travelling, bored with watching her back, of uncomfortable nights on anonymous trains and characterless platforms. She was tired of stale clothes, of tasteless fast food and feeling grubby. She thought of the places through which she had travelled. Of Sofia, Budapest, Zurich, Basel and now Strasbourg, crossing eight countries, yet since leaving Turkey she had seen nothing of them. The greatest adventure of her life and she was no more than freight, a human parcel transported across Europe by faceless individuals who enjoyed the comfort of their ill-gotten gains, whilst she huddled in corners and sheltered under coats, continually afraid, hopelessly alone.

Outside the vast glass atrium, the world beckoned. She could walk out of here now, find a job, somewhere to stay. She had a European passport. To all intents she was a citizen. She still had one hundred euros of Gregor Wolfe's money. In order to throw off her pursuers maybe she needed to do something unexpected, off-plan?

But then there was Alaam. Reflexively she checked the bench, like every door frame, every seat back, but his mark was not there. Had he even made it this far? Or had he had second thoughts and ended up a waiter in a bar in Zurich or Berne or Hamburg? Would she ever find him?

Disconsolately, she leaned back her head and closed her eyes.

She could feel the tears coming. Tears of weariness for the long days past, tears of sadness for her parents but most of all tears for the loss of her life in that split second when the rebels struck. Her tiny, comfortable bedroom in the house on the bustling side street in Al Jalloum, where she could read her books, flick through her postcards and be at peace. Looking to the skies through the vast glass roof, she asked what she should do. Should she take the train, *TG 2358*, into another unknown, blindly following the crumpled itinerary? Or should she walk through the atrium and out into the daylight of Strasbourg and make her own itinerary, find her own way?

As the weak winter sunshine parted the clouds and warmed the vast greenhouse of an atrium, Satya shut her eyes against the world. Twenty metres behind her, a man in an overcoat stood behind the ticket machines. The stream of lunchtime travellers entering the atrium was thick but the girl was alone on the bench and the space around her was clear. Maybe now was the time to seize the opportunity he had been waiting for since Sofia.

Chapter 75

Medway Klein, Northwick Park

Suddenly for Daley, logistics had become a problem. Who would have guessed that Franks would literally fall into their laps?

Whetstone wanted to remain at the Hall to supervise the forensic team. He needed to get back and check in with Monaghan but his car was at Lambourne Road. Of course, one solution, perhaps not the most diplomatic, was to borrow Whetstone's Golf and suggest she hitch a lift with Taylor. Another might be to commandeer a mobile unit. Then he had a brainwave. Steve Taylor's Astra. He could make it an order and suggest the lad rode back with Whetstone. Problem one solved.

Then there were the logistics of Franks' movements. If the van had been spotted in Newcastle and Newton Aycliffe, as well as on the A40, the A33 and at West Drayton at the same time, there had to be several vans, that much was now clear. It was also clear that the van disappearing on a low loader was the van that went to Newcastle, it was VH07 YMK and had been all along until the previous evening when someone had changed it to RN08 DVB. So where was the other van, the real RN08 DVB, and who was driving that?

After a little cajoling and even offers to pay for the bloody petrol himself, Daley had hijacked Taylor's old Astra and within forty minutes was drawing into the car park at Lambourne Road. His first port of call was Sergeant Harrison on the desk, who told him that Franks was ten minutes away. More than enough time to speak to Dave Monaghan, or so he thought, right up to the moment he pushed through the double doors to the Team Room to find D/Supt Bob Allenby waiting for him.

Chapter 76

Inside, the garage was humid and the starched fabric mask adhered to Whetstone's cheeks in a most unpleasant fashion. Cosmetics and forensics were sworn enemies. Taylor had already texted three times reminding her not to leave without him. The fourth text from Monaghan she was trying to put out of her mind. She suddenly felt very alone.

With the SOCO halogen lights still being erected, it was pitch black, save for the splinters of light around the door frame and the beam of her torch. Shorter than the garage next door, this one was empty and had being routinely scrubbed. With her untrained eye, she counted three overlapping purple smears although it was hard to tell. There could have been more. Maybe this was where Varsa had been brought after she was spirited away from her flat? Maybe Sherwood, Fletcher and the rest met a grisly end here. And who knew how many more.

She stepped through a door in the back of the garage, where the Forensic team were working away.

"Have you found any actual blood, Ramesh?" she asked out loud. Masked and dressed in white the robots all looked the same. She couldn't decide who was the team leader until a torch beam swivelled towards her. A muffled voice responded. "Yes, ma'am. Along the bottom of the cabinets where the doors shut and there are traces on the table and in the freezer."

"How many?"

"Hard to tell at the moment."

"Guess."

"I'd rather not."

"Try."

"More than five."

Directly opposite the doors, there was a chest freezer and a couple of Bisley office cupboards, easily two metres tall, brown with cream double doors.

"Can we open these?"

She watched as Ramesh picked the locks and swung the doors wide. A couple of flashes went off as the contents were recorded. Whetstone scanned the shelves but there were no machetes or daggers or pistols, just shelves full of neatly folded surgical smocks, boxes of latex gloves, wipes and plastic containers of cleaning fluid emblazoned with orange diamonds and black crosses. The freezer was empty.

"So, after he kills them, he brings the van back here, where he can slice and dice, packing everything away, perhaps using the freezer until he can take it away to Chatham Woods. That would certainly explain the mess we found in the back of the crashed van." She half-turned to Daley, momentarily forgetting he wasn't there, still concerned about Monaghan's text. Ramesh nodded behind her, not really listening.

Beside the cupboards, a sink dripped incessantly, a muddy stain etched into the enamel, and leaking through an ill-fitting U-bend and onto the floor. Training her torch in front of her, she held her breath, feeling the bile rise. Most of the left wall was taken up with an old woodworking bench, striated with vicious grooves where saws and chisels had maimed its surface. Here and there were yellow numbered markers, identifying the blood samples, she presumed.

It was a butcher's slab. Glowing a surreal spectral violet, awash with blood. She imagined Varsa Ruparelia lying on the table, Franks leaning over her, attacking her flesh with an electric handsaw, grinding as it hit bone. Quickly, she turned her head as the cleaning fluid bit her throat. Taking care not to antagonise the white-suited minions, she carefully picked her way through yellow markers to the small door at the rear of the room.

"Can I go through here, Ramesh?" she asked out loud.

"Yes, but careful what you touch as we haven't processed in there. Oh and don't come back in."

The corridor was absolutely black. With her torch, she picked out the wall to the left which she assumed formed the boundary with the woodshed. A dead end. Swinging the light around, the beam shone fifty or so feet. She could pick out five slits of light sliding under the doors of each of the other garages. At the far end, another door stood shut, a faint yellow light squeezing below it. Trying the handle, it was locked. Whetstone sighed. Not for the first time today there seemed no way out.

Frustrated, she hammered on the door and waited. Presently, she heard a shuffling of feet and a rattling of a key before the door opened and the site supervisor stood with a bemused smile across his face.

"Hi, Mr Evans. Is this door normally kept locked?"

"Yep. Can't remember the last time I used it. When I heard you knocking, I almost shit myself. Usually quiet in here."

"And who else has a key apart from you?"

"Search me. This one is kept in my drawer."

"And is the drawer kept locked?"

"Not usually. No-one ever goes through here."

"Just one last question. You got a brew on? I'm parched."

Chapter 77

1990

Ferdinand sits in the chair. It is his chair and we respect that. After all he has given us, how can we not? He has taken us in, looked after us. We are grateful that sometimes he allows us to enter his room, his sacred ground in this huge house. We are allowed to read his books, look at his pictures.

Mother and father have gone. Lina and I moved them to the shed where they could be together in the darkness forever. Perhaps then father will share his secrets and mother will hear them. Perhaps, the Holy Spirit will pierce the lid and offer them both redemption, but we doubt it.

Then we became them. We forged their signatures, we paid their bills, we lived their lives. It was perfect. Lina and I and no-one to come between us. Once or twice, people tried. They came to the farm, knocked the doors and left. Sometimes they were more insistent. They remained in the shed. Sometimes at night we could hear them scraping at the metal lid, treading in the slime of those that went before, pleading to be let out. Which, of course, would never happen.

No-one comes between us.

But all good things must come to an end. Eventually the money ran out, the furniture was sold. All we had was the farm, empty and stripped bare, and the memories it held.

We needed somewhere else to live, someone else to provide. A new benefactor. So, we chose Ferdinand.

We had seen him walking in the park. He has a small dog, a spaniel or a terrier. His house is large and empty, his visitors few and his proclivities made me attractive to him. Lina's smile is broad and warm and soon he had invited us for tea, some cake, some television. We stopped and talked and he told us of his life, of his success, of his loneliness. Afterwards, he walked us back to the park. Whilst Lina fussed the dog, I tossed him off in the woods and we said goodbye. It was not long before the trips to the woods became less and the visits to the house became longer. Soon we had a new roof over our heads. Lina and I under one roof. We were happy to pay in kind for the benevolence of our new host. We would both cook and clean and I would provide other private services.

The house was enormous, a rambling Victorian country house. It was far too big for Ferdinand, far too big even for us. What does he need with such a rambling pile? Mortgage paid off, no family or friends, he lives alone in this mausoleum to a life past, with nothing but photographs and memories, his antiques and the money he has amassed through decades of not spending. He was content with his books, his dog, with his clothes washed and ironed and his food cooked. There are plenty of mushrooms in the woods behind the house. Ferdinand likes mushrooms.

And now he sits in his chair. His eyes are wide and lifeless. His bank accounts are ours and the letter tells me the house has sold. Soon the last of the antiques and paintings will be taken away. He was the host and we are the parasites, slowly devouring him from the inside. Now he needs to be taken to the farm, along with his dog, to join the others in the shed.

Even now we have found our next benefactor. Another loner on the fringe, with money to spend and no-one to spend it on. A city full of rich, lonely people.

Chapter 78

As Daley closed the Goldfish Bowl door, Allenby squared his elbows on his desk, leaned forwards and flashed a brief, forced smile, totally betrayed by the thunder brewing behind his eyes. Beneath the elbows languished a yellow lined pad, the sort that Monaghan and Taylor used and, if Daley wasn't mistaken he recognised Monaghan's writing, even upside down. Allenby already knew something he didn't.

"So, Scott. Steven Franks?"

"Well, Sir. Like I said before it's Whetstone's angle."

"Humour me. I want to hear it from you."

"Well, there are inconsistencies over the whereabouts of the van he was driving at the time of the crash and on many other occasions before, including when Miss Ruparelia disappeared. He is known to have argued with her shortly before and he has form for ABH."

"And your *Zone 6* victims? How are they linked to Franks?"

The question annoyed Daley. The van had only just been recovered from the Hall. How could he possibly have assimilated the data that quickly? It irked him that Monaghan would have done so already and that Allenby knew the answer.

"Off the top of my head... Franks was away often. His trips roughly coincided with these people's disappearance."

"Roughly? So what? You suspect that Franks argued with all of these people and killed each one? Seems a bit far fetched. What evidence do you have?"

Daley's temples began to ache. What evidence could he possibly have, faced with Allenby's ambush?

"Smith and Franks are seen arguing on the night of the crash, then Smith disappears leaving suspicious forensics at his apartment."

"Which turned out to be vomit...not blood."

"Yes, but the van is caked in Ruparelia's blood, with significant traces in her apartment building. Not to mention the severed hand."

"And Franks fingerprints?"

"Not...as yet, sir. We have matched Franks' trips to the *Zone 6* disappearances. Franks claims he has an alibi for each of these occasions; he was in away on business. Yet Sergeant Monaghan has located ANPR images of the same van on the A40, A33 and M4 at the same time. He can't be in two places at once."

"So basically, you have nothing that actually places Franks at the scene of the crash or the abductions?"

Well, not yet but when we get him in..."

"The Director of the clinic," Allenby glanced at the yellow lined pad, "...Snowdon. He phoned me personally. For God's sake what were you thinking? Whetstone told me you two nearly came to blows."

"I'd hardly go that far, sir."

"What, so she's a liar? Right now, *she's* the investigating officer, yet she tells me she feels more like your secretary. Couldn't get a word in edgeways as you forged on with your own personal bloody agenda."

Daley puffed out his cheeks. His mouth was parched and he suddenly felt incredibly tired. He took a glass of water from the desk. Thanks, Deb! What other tales had she told Allenby? How often had she squirrelled away this gem, that titbit in her own little notebook, waiting to plunge the blade between his shoulders? Measuring his breath, forestalling the annoyance that was building, Daley placed the glass onto a coaster. His hand was shaking and try as he might he couldn't steady it. Deliberately, unwisely, he set about defending himself.

"Look, Franks is playing Whetstone for a fool and she is letting him. She's pussy-footing around while he's laughing at us. You know we have to lean on people sometimes, otherwise they would never say anything. Everyone thinks they are cleverer than us bumbling *plods*. Snowdon certainly did. And Franks. How can the van he was driving be in two places at once?"

"The van, Scott, not Franks himself." Allenby exhaled loudly, pitching the volume of his response to counter Daley's excitable tone. "Firstly, two vans. It's not unusual for a vehicle to be cloned. For all you know, this could be some chancer who has picked the number off a parked van to avoid driving penalties.

And secondly, maybe the reason he can't answer the questions is because he is innocent? Face it Scott. The van could be anywhere but Franks might just be telling the truth."

"Or lying to cover up some other misdemeanour. Seriously, sir? How can he be in Newcastle and Greater London at the same time? Who is he, David *bloody* Blane? Look, it's becoming more and more obvious that there are two vans. There has to be, but it doesn't alter the fact that someone else is driving the other and Steven Franks is *lying through his teeth*. Surely you can see that?"

It was Allenby's turn to huff. He had rarely seen Daley so animated and he was having difficulty following thought patterns that resembled a Red Arrows aerial display.

"So first he's our killer, then he's not. Then he's driving the van, then he's not. Do you have any idea at all what you are playing at?" Allenby paused, feeling himself teetering on the edge of Daley's abyss. "So where was he? Franks? Have you even established that? Before you go in *all guns blazing* would it not be politic to check his alibi, or do we shoot first and interrogate the corpse later?"

"We're waiting for the hotel to get back to us. Look, if he has killed this many people, he is not going to hang around while we have our thumbs up our arses. Look at yesterday, the slightest sniff and he was off."

"Bollocks! You've just got it into your head that he is guilty. Even with the van on *Candid Camera* three hundred miles away! You need to get a grip and start answering your own questions before gunning after Franks. How can he possibly be in two places at one time?"

"And that," asserted Daley waving both hands towards Allenby, rather too energetically to demonstrate his point, "is the question he's coming in to answer, sir! Varsa is saying she has seen him but he's hundreds of miles away. ANPR sees him in two places. Whatever was happening with that original van, he has to be sure they won't both be in the same place at the same time. He *has* to be complicit. Even if we accept that he was in Newcastle, I am sure we will find that his alibi has more holes than a block of Emmental. It's so straightforward, why can't you see it?"

Allenby slammed down his pen and threw himself back into

his chair. Catching himself, he took a deep breath, slowly letting his chest fall. "I don't want you interviewing him, Scott."

The words falling like an autumn pheasant, Daley was briefly stunned. He sipped his water, feeling the pain redouble in his temples. He cursed Building Services for cranking up the heating at the first sign of cold weather as a trickle of sweat meandered down his spine. "What, sir? Of course we have to interview him!"

"No, I mean I don't want *you* interviewing him. Leave it to Whetstone. I am leaving the case with her, at least for now. Look at you! You had a pop at the owner of the clinic yesterday. You're even having a pop at me, for Christ's sake. I want you nowhere near any of them until you have calmed down. For now, you sit and build a proper case. When you have one of those maybe, just maybe, you can put it to your suspect."

Daley had had quite enough of *Whetstone this* and *Whetstone that*. The golden girl who had seized her opportunity as soon as his back was turned. And now Allenby. Was this a ruse to move him sideways? To declare him unfit, farm him out to some hick backwater? His vision started to blur and he could feel the adrenaline tingling in his neck. He grabbed the glass from the desk and drained it but his throat instantly parched. He wanted to shout at Allenby, to challenge him, to expose the collaboration. He wanted to punch Allenby's supercilious round arse of a face.

Raising a finger, he stabbed it into the air in front of Allenby. "You...you..." Then he felt himself tugged back by a gossamer thread of self-preservation. "Look, I can't do this right now, OK?" Gritting his teeth against the hordes of demons baying for blood, against the throb in the narrow veins of his temples, Daley rested both hands on the arms of the chair and hefted himself up, spinning around to the door.

"Sit down, Scott...*Sit down!*" The room rang as Allenby barked the command. Through the blinds, the team room had frozen and all eyes were on Daley. He was consumed with rage, barely able to keep his body standing. With the demons screaming for him to leave the room, leave the building, leave the Force, he reluctantly sat.

Allenby had grabbed his pen and began distractedly leafing through some papers, angrily scribing through sentences, adding pithy corrections, regaining his composure. Behind Daley the subdued hubbub of the team room had resumed and the world still spun but now his place in it was different. He raised the plastic cup, but it was dry and he didn't feel safe to replenish it.

After a full minute, Allenby broke the taut silence, his tone purposefully measured and avuncular. "What's going on, Scott? You and me, we've had our disagreements, God knows we have. I've always believed that we could hold a difference of opinion, have a really good debate and still remain friends, and I respect that. But this? I can't have all-out war every time I challenge your view of the world." Daley made to speak. "No, Scott. Your foot is already in your mouth. Just leave it there and let me finish. You know I answer to higher authorities than you. It's my job to challenge you, to play devil's advocate and that's all I was doing today. And here you go, off like a bottle of pop!" The senior officer lowered his pen and rose to stare out of the window. Daley suddenly felt an overpowering sense of doom descend. Policing was all he had ever known.

"Monaghan tells me you're still taking tablets. Tramadol?"

Daley rolled his eyes. Was nothing safe from their prying eyes? He thought he knew the Irishman, such were the hours they had spent together over the last four years but now it transpires the bastard was spending more time investigating his own colleagues than he was putting into his caseload.

"Well?" Allenby leaned across the desk, the challenge in his eyes redoubled.

Daley nodded lamely, incapable of anything else.

"Look, Inspector. I am going to level with you. I cannot have this kind of atmosphere in my team. Before the accident, I had a cohesive, experienced unit I could rely on. You left a huge hole and Whetstone and Monaghan have proved more than capable of filling it. If you are not fit to return to full duties, then you may as well not be here at all." Allenby rose and paced across to the windows, easing apart the louvre blinds and looking out onto the street below. "You don't know how hard I am working to keep this case in Lambourne Road. I have the Chief Super on the phone every three or four hours. I have SCD1 all over me like a cheap suit. Book another appointment with the Force shrink. It's quite clear you're not over the accident and I apologise if I allowed you back too early. I'm sorry, I really am."

Daley sensed a but. *But I don't want you in my CID room, but I have to refer you to a disciplinary panel, but I need your warrant card, you're suspended...*

"But..." continued Allenby. Daley gulped. His heart raced. "...I am going to give you the benefit of the doubt on this occasion. Sort yourself out. Take a breath and think before you speak - and stop taking those bloody pills." Turning from the window, he locked eyes with Daley and pointed a finger. "Just...just keep your bloody head down because, as all of those nosey bastards out there are my witnesses, I will bloody have it if you *ever* speak to me in that tone again."

***

"Come on Tinkerbell. Get a move on!" Whetstone stood impatiently outside Joan Thompson's office as Steve Taylor agonised over the best way to carry an inordinately large pile of photocopied documents, bag his laptop and put on his coat. There was something terribly ungainly about the young constable, like a foal attempting to stand for the first time, except that Taylor was in his early twenties. He had mastered the finger-on-the-keyboard-thinking part of the job, but actual locomotion was taking much longer. It's a good job they only employed him to think.

The text from Monaghan had read *Daley in meltdown. Allenby ballistic. Need you back here*, so she abandoned Ramesh and his team, collected Taylor and set off for Lambourne Road. Taylor was not one for conversation, which suited Whetstone fine. Mending fences with Daley was more important right now, especially as she and Monaghan were about to interview the prime suspect without him. She plugged in her headphones and dialled Monaghan's number but he didn't pick up. She hovered over Daley's number. Would clearing the air help? In truth, she had no idea why he was so angry with her. It wasn't the first time that she had remarked on his truculence and it certainly wasn't unique for her to report their cases to Allenby, warts and all. She was Investigating Officer. Usually, there would be a slanging match, the dust would settle, but this time there was more going on. Monaghan had used the word *meltdown* - not *furious* or *incandescent* even but *meltdown*. That couldn't be good. And *Allenby ballistic*? She left Daley's number untouched, that battle would have to wait. Instead she found Monaghan's number and started a text - *Meet me in the car park. We'll find a room to prepare for Franks interview. Need to avoid D&A for now. Let the dust settle.* As the Golf turned into Lambourne Road her phone pinged - *See you in five. Avoid fourth floor.*

***

"Sergeant. Meeting room 99. Now."

Monaghan sighed and slowly turned to peer at Daley, stone-faced, a world-weary expression of one who had seen it all before and had the scars to prove it. Puffing out his cheeks, he rose and indicated that Daley should lead.

On auto-pilot, Daley left through the double doors, down two floors and out into the fire escape stairwell on the opposite side of the building. Descending to the basement, he unlocked a steel door and passed into a breeze blocked anteroom lined with conduit and neatly pinned wiring. The room hummed with machinery and fans and smelt of mould and dust. Meeting Room 99 was a code for the boiler room, the only place in the building one could speak without anyone eavesdropping. Daley had purloined a key and everyone coveted it. The room was just large enough for an old desk and chair. On the other side of the small space, a ship-grey fire-door led to the basement, a maze of pipes and racking which extended across the width of the building. The small room was uncomfortably warm and lit only with emergency lights, adding to the apprehension Monaghan already felt. He perched onto the edge of the careworn table, watched as Daley flipped the latch and awaited the onslaught.

Chapter 79

Gare de Strasbourg, Bas-Rhine Department, France

At first, Satya had not heard the footsteps behind her, gradually turning from a slow purposeful stride to a sprint but then some sixth sense, developed in her days on the road, alerted her. Alarmed, she grabbed her bag and jumped off the bench, just as the hands of the assailant bore down on her back. She caught a glimpse of flailing black as the overcoat billowed like an untied canvas. Then she was running down the side of the station building back towards the main hall, dodging and weaving through the other passengers, shouting *pardon* as she collided with an arm or a briefcase. If she could make it to the platform, the sheer weight of people would hide her. Safety in numbers. Behind her, above the noise of the people and the sounds of the hall, there was a shout.

"Satya, stop, please!"

Her name. How did they know her name? She had assumed she was a small, meaningless link in a chain of trafficking.

"Just please stop running!"

No way would she stop. Not until she was locked behind a door in Tower Hamlets. Not until she and Alaam were together again. With her lungs straining in her chest, she jogged across the hall trying not to look too conspicuous, towards the platforms. Through the human obstacle course, she could feel the pain building in her legs, stealing her speed. Then she was consumed by the crowds of people bunching together for the gates. Subliminally, she could tell he was still there, matching her stride for stride. In front of her a small stout uniformed SNCF guard stepped out.

"Billets, s'il vous plaît, Mademoiselle."

Gasping for breath, she reached inside her pocket, fumbling for the tickets, feeling the man edging closer through the thickening crowds. She sorted through the tickets cursing her laziness at not disposing of the used ones. What use were they now? She tried to look cool, not to panic, mustering as much of a smile as she could.

"Vous savez que vous devez avoir un siège réservé?" *You know you must have a reserved seat?*

Satya shrugged. Something about chairs. Her French was poor. Maybe waitressing in Strasbourg was not a good idea. Behind her she could hear the voice excusing himself as he pushed past indignant passengers, edging nearer. She willed the guard to hurry with his checks.

"Satya for God's sake, stop!" There was a distinct tone of frustration in the voice.

Barely looking up from the ticket, the guard peered over his glasses at the man.

"Connaissez-vous cet homme, Mademoiselle?"

Satya turned and the man loomed over her. Her heart almost leapt from her mouth as he spoke.

"Désolé monsieur. Elle est ma cousine, Satya. Je l'ai perdu dans la foule. Nous sommes plus tard pour notre train."

"Et votre billet, Monsieur? Vous devez avoir un réservation?" As Satya stared at the face, the man handed over his ticket. The guard studied it and returned it, eying the pair curiously. "Plateforme cinq. Vous avez beaucoup de temps."

And with that, the man grabbed Satya's arm, steering her through the barrier, and disappeared into the gloom.

Chapter 80

Even before the latch had fully turned, Daley launched into his tirade.

"Jesus Christ, Dave. I thought, of them all I could rely on you to back me up. Instead you're telling tales to bloody Bilko every time my backs turned."

"That's a little unfair, sir. You know as well as I do..."

"Unfair? I'll tell you what's unfair. Standing in front of your senior officer and being called a junkie. That's unfair."

"I'd hardly say..."

"Seriously? *Monaghan tells me you're still taking Tramadol. Oh, yes Sir and I'm snorting lines in the bogs, too.* He'll be looking for track marks up my bloody arms next. What is this? Some deliberate attempt to derail my whole career?"

Monaghan exhaled a deep sigh. "Come on, Scott. Surely you know me better than..."

"Don't you bloody Scott me, Sergeant." Daley spun on his heel and thrust a finger at Monaghan. "You need to remember who the senior *bloody* officer is around here."

Without a flinch, Monaghan retorted: "You are, Inspector Daley! So why don't you get a grip on yourself and bloody start acting like one?" The Sergeant's left eye twitched. A sign he was irritated.

"What the Hell is that supposed to mean?"

"Well, cracking jokes in Team brief, deliberately undermining Deb Whetstone at every opportunity, picking arguments with interviewees. Then this case. First, it's Smith, then it's Franks. You change your mind like a politician's breakfast order. Jeez! Just look at you now, flouncing about like a two-year-old because you can't get your own bloody way."

"I don't have to justify myself to you. If I want to lean on a witness, I bloody-well will. I don't need your sodding approval first."

"Really? Deb says you pissed off that clinic owner so much

that he was ready for a fight. Then after Team brief, you just buggered off. Where the Hell would you have been if Franks had decided to lamp her one?"

"*Deb says this, Deb says that.* And then you're squealing to Bilko. What is it? *Write an Essay on the Inspector Day*? Varsa Ruparelia isn't the only one with a bloody diary!" Even Scott Daley could hear how pathetic he sounded, how asinine, but not even he could stop himself. And deep down, he had no idea why he was behaving this way.

"So, what would you have done? If Franks *had* taken out his aggression on Deb? Where would that have left you then? Another bloody six months suspension and then you'd be packing shelves at Sainsbury's. You want to think yourself lucky you have a boss like Bob Allenby. When Chris Mercer over at Hounslow was shot in the shoulder, he was back in a month and still found himself moved to the evidence room. Within a year he'd quit. At least Allenby has enough faith in you to keep you in the team."

"Oh, yeah, He's got faith in me alright. While you and Whetstone chase the murderers, I get to look for strays."

"Until we got those blood results back, there was no murder. Did it not occur to you that the white van was the only tangible bit of evidence we had? Allenby thought all along your *Zone 6* victims were part of the same case. He was trusting you to prove it - which you did. C'mon, man! We're all on the same side here, surely."

"Well, I am on the same side. I don't know about the rest of you. Who got the phone call about the ANPR photos?" It wasn't me! Then who gets told about the bloods? Not me!"

"It's Deb Whetstone's case!"

"I am the senior officer, Sergeant."

"Not on this investigation, *Inspector!*" Slamming the table with the flat of his hand, Monaghan rose from the chair and turned his back on Daley. He drew a hand across his scalp and across the knots in the back of his neck. "What the Hell is wrong with you? You're back three days. You've pissed off Deb. You've pissed off Allenby and now you've even managed to piss off me and believe me that takes some doing but you, Scott Daley, have - *bloody* - *managed it!* You can't blow in here off the breeze and expect everything to be as it was. Jesus Christ, we weren't all sitting around here with our thumbs up our arses waiting for you to return. You have to find a way to fit in or fuck off, it's as simple as that." Monaghan rounded on Daley and locked eyes. "As much as you would like it to be, this is not all about you. This is about a woman who has vanished off the face of the earth, about five people who started out for home and never arrived. And you know what? It's about the next wife or husband, son or daughter, father or mother who is out there just waiting for Franks to strike again. That's who it's about!"

Daley's heart was pounding in his ears fit to burst as Monaghan's finger pointed outside towards a big, wide world full of victims. They all seemed to be getting a better deal than he right now. They had taken away his wife, his house, his health and now their hands were on his career, the very essence that defined him.

Monaghan lowered his hands with a slap against his legs. "Look, I can't be dealing with this. You might want to wallow in your own self-pity but I have a suspect to interview."

"Well, bloody good luck with that because it isn't him."

"Oh, yeah? And why's that, *sir?"* There was a smugness in Daley's tone that disconcerted Monaghan. A smugness that on any other day he might try removing but one police officer with his career down the toilet was enough.

"Because he was in Newcastle when they all went missing. He isn't the one. Can't you see it?"

For a good part of the previous day and most of the morning, Monaghan had been assembling a folder of information which Franks would need to answer. There was no way he was about to be derailed by Daley's latest pet theory. "Whether you like it or not, Deb Whetstone is running this investigation and her money is on Franks. And right now, I am inclined to believe her."

Pushing past Daley and turning the door lock, Monaghan rounded on the senior officer and jabbed a finger at his face.

"You need to take a good hard look at yourself because if you don't, God help me, I bloody will."

Chapter 81

On the ceiling, every thirty seconds or so, a strip light made a loud rhythmic hum, a series of clicks and then went silent. Like everyone who sat in the room, like Smith before him, Franks, puffed his cheeks irritably and glanced up at the light. Then he stared down into his lap, arms tightly folded grasping his biceps, the dragon tattoo sleeping fitfully as his forearms tensed. Due to international legislation, most forms of torture were frowned upon these days. Long gone were the overnight cleaning crews slopping blood from the walls and medics were rarely called to suspects who had fallen down some steps but that strip light, with it atonal buzz and arrhythmic click, that was still legal and right now Franks nerves jolted with every one of them.

He twisted his head and checked the time - 2:40pm. He had been in this room in an anonymous police station in a crap part of London for nearly two hours with only a coffee and a sandwich.

Behind him there was a sonorous clunk, which made him jump. The door opened and in walked the dour faced sergeant and another guy, slightly older.

"Mr Franks. Thanks for your patience. I am sorry we have kept you waiting so long but it's been a busy day." Whetstone beamed an ingratiating smile, as it happened fruitlessly.

"Not brought the uniformed gorilla in with you then? I could feed him this sandwich and watch him dribble. Who's he?" Franks cast a glance at Monaghan. This would be piss-easy. They didn't look like they had a backbone between them.

"As you know, I am Detective Sergeant Deborah Whetstone and my colleague is Detective Sergeant David Monaghan. You are not under caution and we are not recording the interview. Is that OK?"

"Yeah, whatever." Franks unfolded his arms and wiped a hand across the bridge of his nose and down his face. The room was claustrophobic, starved of all but a meagre slit of natural light that shimmied through a small window high up on the wall.

"So, Mr Franks," began Monaghan. "Please can you take me through the trip to Newcastle from the point you left Chronotech on Monday afternoon?" Monaghan smiled broadly, disingenuously.

Franks huffed at the imposition and shuffled his backside in his seat. "I left work around 4:15pm. I collected the van and set off for Newcastle. Non-stop I arrived around 10:00pm, maybe a little after."

"How much after? The timing is really important, I'm sorry."

"Maybe five minutes, oh and not non-stop. If your being picky I stopped at Watford Gap for a slash and a coffee. Maybe five minutes there too."

"And then?"

"Checked in, went next door to the restaurant for a bite then hit the sack. Probably around 11:15pm."

"And your room number?"

Franks smiled at Monaghan. He would have to get up a lot earlier... "Room 9, ground floor. I always have the same room. It's on the receipt."

"Thanks. So, the next day, er, Tuesday?"

"I slept in late, went to the restaurant where I had a full English, checked out at 10:00am. I drove straight around to Medical Logistics Limited where I picked up the stock, filled in the paperwork and sat in on a logistics meeting. That wrapped up around 1:00pm."

"So 1:00pm Tuesday. Where did you go then?"

"I started back."

"Did you stop along the way?"

"Yeah, Tibshelf."

"And you arrived back at 5:30pm."

"Yeah." Franks slouched back in his chair. Pick the bones out of that.

Whetstone leaned forward. "Why did you run Mr Franks?"

Franks' foot was bouncing under the table. "I don't know. Me and the wife had just had an argument. You were banging on the door. I panicked."

"Some panic. You left home, drove round to Varsa

Ruparelia's apartment then on to Conor Smiths house. Can you account for the rest your movements between 5:30pm on Tuesday evening and 1:00am today when we picked you up?"

Franks preferred silence.

Whetstone organised her sheaf of papers and took a deep breath. Franks had been calm and assured and his timings were off-pat and precise. A couple of hours in the cooler had given him time to gather his shit. What would Daley ask? More specifically, what stick would he poke Franks with?

"Mr Franks. You had an argument with Connor Smith at the clinic around 5-5:30pm on Friday 9th. Could you tell us what that was about?"

Caught off guard, Franks performed a mental regroup, eyeing Whetstone suspiciously. "It was nothing. The little twerp has ideas above his station. He has been on at me for weeks to let him drive the van. Said he could ease the load and do some of the driving. Well, apart from the fact he's not insured, the last thing I wanted was him in the cab for four hours. So, I told him no. He got lippy called me a twat or something so I gave him a shove and told him to grow up."

"Just a shove?"

"Yeah, just a shove. For Christ sakes, he's just an idiot."

"Then?"

"Then nothing. He buggered off with my foot up his arse and I went home."

"And the argument with Varsa Ruparelia. Was that about driving the van too? "

"No!" Franks' tone was indignant. "Look, you've done some digging. You know what Varsa was like, nosey bitch. Well, she started sniffing round me so I warned her off."

"What, with just a shove?"

"OK, maybe not just a shove but I didn't hit here."

"Exactly what was the, er disagreement, about Mr Franks?"

"Me thieving from the clinic, basically. She'd been taking notes, put two and two together and decided that I was stealing stock."

"And were you?"

"Maybe a paperclip or a pen but not what she was alleging. Now if the company sold laptops or hand tools, there may be something to steal but the devices Chronotech developed are niche. No resale market."

"Yet," intervened Monaghan. "Competitive market, commercial secrets. Valuable stuff, surely? Doesn't have to be hardware."

"Is this that nurse, Marion? What has she been saying?"

The question fell on deaf ears, Dave Monaghan pulling them back to the point. "What's the registration number of the van, Mr Franks? The one you used for the trip?"

Franks cast his eyes to the ceiling. "VH07 YMK - white Transit Connect Mk 2 Long wheelbase. It's on the diesel receipts."

Monaghan reached into a pack in front of him and pulled out a photograph of the crashed van. "This is VH07 YMK taken in Greenford while you were in Newcastle. We found traces of Varsa Ruparelia in the back. Do you want to change anything you have told us?"

Franks brow furrowed as he examined the photo. Smith's text had mentioned Varsa and an accident. "No, I drove that van to Newcastle. I know I did." But behind the stubborn eyes, there was a glimmer of something else creeping in.

Fear.

"Look, do I need a brief?"

"This is all off the record, Mr Franks. If we need to make it more formal, you can make a call, don't worry."

Monaghan pulled out a second photo from the pile. It showed another grainy picture of a white Transit Van. "Let's try this one. Time and date stamp 13:30pm on Tuesday 13th, in roadworks on the M4 Eastbound in Slough. 60 miles per hour in a 40 section. VH07 YMK, the van you claim was parked outside Medical Logistics in Newcastle."

Franks again studied the photo, then each detective in turn. The colour had drained from his face. Whetstone was discomforted by it. In her experience, there is a tipping point beyond which the evidence becomes undeniable. A suspect either coughs up there and then or flatly denies any involvement, forcing the police to establish proof beyond all doubt. Franks seemed genuinely confused. She gathered up her papers into a neat pile, tamping them on the table. "Steven Franks. I am arresting you for obstructing a police officer in the course of his or her duty under Section 89(2) of Police Act 1996. You do not have to say anything, but it may harm your defence if you do not mention when questioned something which you later rely on in court. Anything you do say may be given in evidence." Winking she added: "Might need that brief now Steve, don't you think?"

***

Now that Dave had abandoned him to interview Franks, Daley had no option but to face the team room. No option except procrastination. Hiding in the bogs, he stared at his face in the mirror, taken aback by what he saw. His skin was pale and his tongue resembled a matted sheepskin rug. Boggling his eyes, he examined the tube map of veins turning the whites to an uncomfortable shade of pink. Serves him right for coming back to this foetid, scabrous bunch of misfits.

He suddenly felt incredibly hungry. Would the canteen still have food at 3:00pm? He reached in his pocket for some coins. No more procrastination. Chocolate from the machine would have to suffice.

Rinsing his face, he centred his tie and smoothed down his hair, took a deep breath and headed to the team room.

If Franks had actually taken the van to Newcastle on Monday and was away until Wednesday, there had to be a second van. That meant a second driver. Had Franks been using Smith to establish an alibi?

Then again, was Franks telling the truth? Smith took the van to dispose of Varsa, crashing in the process with Franks in an identical van in Newcastle.

So, who was driving the vehicle that pulled up behind the crash and helped clear up? There had to be someone else. A third person who had not yet shown up on the radar.

Apart from the crash, whatever happened on Monday night was not a one-off. In that year, there had been eleven trips to Newcastle, roughly one a month. Each time Franks had stayed away from Monday night to Wednesday afternoon. Each time, supposedly returning to the clinic with the van. As Varsa had noted in her diary, the trip was routine, planned, dependable.

Behind him the kettle clicked off. He watched the grains of coffee dissolve into the dark, murky water.

"Sir, that's my cup." Taylor had crept up behind him, agonising over whether he should speak, given the precarious state Daley appeared to be in.

Daley started. He studied the cup disparagingly from a number of angles. "Jeez! It's just a cup. What does it matter?" He caught himself. "Sorry, Steve. Unforgivable. Crap day." Then, like a cryptic puzzle, a seemingly insoluble anagram, pieces started to swirl unconsciously in his mind, gaining momentum but not yet a direction. He placed Taylor's cup side by side with an identical one.

"Tell me, why does it matter to you so much? Why that one, not the other. Humour me. I am just thinking something through."

"Well, it's my cup, sir. I like my cup. It's familiar. I've had it for ages." Taylor resembled a naughty spaniel hiding behind a curtain. He needed this ordeal to be over.

"And this other one? Holds the same amount, looks the same, weighs the same, same slogan, same tea stains."

"But it's not mine. I would know if I had the wrong cup."

Daley smiled broadly and clapped Taylor on the shoulder, an action the latter clearly found distasteful. "If Franks had been driving the wrong van, or it had been switched, he would have noticed, even if they appeared identical. The van at the clinic was filled with all kinds of rubbish; Franks' rubbish. The van he has been driving for a year or so has never changed until last night, after he had left it at the clinic, when someone switched the registration plate. But it's still the same van." Daley grinned. "Right now, we have the wrong man in custody and the wrong van in Forensics."

***

When Monaghan and Whetstone returned to the interview room, Franks was deep in thought, cradling a cup of tea and staring at the now stale sandwiches. Next to him was Deirdre Brown, the duty solicitor. Mid-forties, a thin, drawn woman with a viper's stare and very little patience. She was busy imparting what sage pieces of advice she could, presumably involving saying nothing and admitting nothing. A uniform sat beside the door, trying unsuccessfully to blend into the architrave.

From the viewing room, Scott Daley looked on. Four CCTV monitors showed Franks, head bowed, his foot bouncing rhythmically below the table. Daley had felt it politic to stay that side of the glass. Franks was almost certainly not their man but there had been enough confrontation for one day. He had to let this particular drama play itself out.

Whetstone began: "Mr Franks. You have your solicitor so this interview will be recorded under caution. OK?"

In the absence of a response from Franks, the brief gave a slow purposeful nod. The machine whined as the tapes initialised, everyone introduced themselves and Whetstone read the caution, explaining the situation for the benefit of the tape. Then she replayed the whole show. This time, whether by design, or under orders from his brief, Franks restricted his responses to a monotone yes, no or no comment. After ten minutes, Whetstone decided to lean on Franks slightly harder.

"Mr Franks. October 23rd? You had an argument with Miss Ruparelia in the clinic courtyard before you left for Newcastle. Can you tell me about that?"

Franks folded his arms, the dragon snarled but his lips remained closed.

"And November 9th, last Friday, you had an argument with Connor Smith. Can you tell me about that?" Again silence.

"Varsa Ruparelia has disappeared. What do you think happened to her?" More silence.

"You didn't like Varsa very much, did you?"

Franks smirked, unable to hold his tongue. "And? Nobody liked Varsa."

"Why was that?" Franks reclined back in his chair, arms folded, lips once more sealed. The dragon hissed and sat back on its haunches.

"I think she found out what you were up to. She wrote down everything in her diary; the times you turned up at the clinic, when you left, what you were carrying and what you shouldn't have been carrying."

Franks looked up, challenging. "Oh, yeah, and what shouldn't I have been carrying?"

Whetstone let the question hang. They were on the back foot. Like Smith, she hoped he would inadvertently fill in the blanks. Franks was shrewd but she knew Monaghan was shrewder, biding his time.

"What was the last straw? Was it the blackmail? Was that when she had to go?"

Franks sniggered, wise to the game. "She was just a pain in the arse. If I killed everyone who was a pain in the arse..."

"So, you are preparing the van on 23rd October and she turns up, you have words, she threatens to expose your little scam. Soon afterwards she disappears."

"Yeah. You said that before." Franks folded his arms and stared at the table, whilst his brief wrote copious notes.

"And Smith? Was he after a cut of the action or did he threaten to expose your little scheme, too?"

"You keep going on about my little scheme. What scheme? Varsa was a busybody. I told her to piss off. Connor was a nuisance. I told him to piss off too. It was nothing."

"Was? Past tense? We've read the texts on the phone. He mentioned an accident, Varsa Ruparelia. So what happened, Mr Franks? Can you tell me?"

Franks sat upright. His eyes questioned his brief, her inaction. "Nothing happened. I gave him a slap and told him to piss off. Look, what exactly is this about?"

Finally, the penny dropped and Deirdre Brown set about earning her corn. "Yes, Sergeant. What is this about? If you have a point to make, please make it." She cast a glance at Franks, who rolled his eyes. *Is that the best you got, woman?*

"Thank you, Ms Brown." Whetstone cast a professional smile at the solicitor. "OK Let's cut to the chase, Mr Franks. I don't think you were in Newcastle on Tuesday night."

Franks dander began to rise. "Of course I was in Newcastle. Check with Brian Davies at Medical Logistics Limited. Check with the places I stopped at. Check with the Travelodge. There's has to be twenty people who saw me. Check the CCTV. You could probably follow my van all the way up." Deirdre Brown placed a steadying hand on the dragon's head as it reared and bucked. Calm down.

This was true. Franks had been tracked every step of the way by hundreds of cameras but Whetstone was prepared for the bluff and immediately called it. She pursed her lips and exhaled the stress, like a trumpet player whose instrument had been stolen.

"You see Steve, we did check. We looked at the CCTV." She shrugged and glanced across at Monaghan, who took his queue.

Monaghan was not so good with human psychology, so he didn't mind being kept in his box at Lambourne Road. Looking at Franks across the table, thick-necked and taut, eyes burning, tattoos rippling, Monaghan felt he had made the right choice. With Daley excluded, however, he had been forced out of his comfort zone. He glanced up at the one-way mirror sure the senior officer would be there. He opened the folder, in his periphery, sensing the sedentary bulk of the strong-arm by the door, and prepared for what could end up a bloodbath. He began speaking in his quiet, measured Irish brogue, as if explaining a terminal diagnosis in extensive medical detail to an elderly female patient.

"Mr. Franks. My role is collection of evidence, connecting fragments to create a continuous picture. Like assembling a jigsaw puzzle, only I don't have the box lid to work from. I'll just need a 'yes' or 'no' in the right places and we can move on. No cross-questioning or interrogation. That's not my bag, so I'll leave that to my colleagues. So, 'yes' or 'no', is that clear?" Franks shrugged almost imperceptibly and Deirdre Brown glared.

"For the tape, Mr. Franks. Like I said you have to answer 'yes' or 'no'."

"Yeah."

"Here's a few photographs." For the tape he added, "I am showing Mr. Franks photo DM1. This camera is over the main entrance to Watford Gap Services on the Northbound M1. Here you are coming out of the toilets. Do you agree?"

Franks crouched and scanned the pictures distractedly, safe in the knowledge that the dates and times proved he was where he should have been. "Yep."

"Thank you." Dave Monaghan cracked a business-like smile

and exchanged the photos with two more. "Photo DM2 the *Road to Newcastle* series shows an ANPR camera at Newton Aycliffe at 13:45 on Tuesday..." the sergeant ran his finger along the date and time stamp in the lower corner. "DM3 is a camera over the entrance to Tibshelf Services at 15:34, you, er, *taking a slash*. Then the final image, DM4. This is another ANPR camera. This time on the Target roundabout A40 Eastbound at 17:15 on Tuesday. Shouldn't be using your phone whilst driving, eh, Mr Franks?"

Franks shrugged. "So I was where I said I was."

Deirdre Brown pulled herself upright in her chair. "I agree with my client, Sergeant. The images appear to show Mr Franks travelling to and from Newcastle on the times and dates he has freely provided." Brown, unsure exactly what challenge to level, felt it necessary to intervene in order to stop Franks' brain exploding.

"Sorry, Ms Brown. Just a few more items before that becomes clear." Monaghan's fleeting smile and Irish charm did not wash with Brown who had seen it all before. Monaghan delved into the plastic wallet for the three remaining photos, which he laid out in a similar fashion to the others.

"DM5, Madjeski stadium, Reading, A33 Southbound, VH07 YMK. DM6, M4 Eastbound Slough, VH07 YMK. DM7, M4 eastbound at West Drayton. VH07 YMK.

Franks' eyes scanned from one photo to the next.

"VH07 YMK. Is that your van; the one you drove to Newcastle? The one you left at Medway Klein on Tuesday evening?"

"So? Someone has cloned the number plate. Must happen all the time."

"Your van was recovered from the clinic earlier today. A VIN check came back with an entirely different number - MK07 LYN. The van you were driving was the clone, Mr Franks. Meanwhile the real VH07 YMK appears to be travelling the M4 corridor and crashing on the A40."

I would know if I had the wrong cup.

From the other side of the glass, Daley caught that elusive expression in Franks eyes. Fear. Fleeting and gone. The solicitor saw it too, immediately picking up her pen and scribbling notes.

Franks considered a moment and sat upright. The room had fallen silent once again, the atmosphere warm and oppressive. He ran his hand across the back of his neck and waved his head from side to side, cracking tired sinews. The noise of meshing gears from his over-revving brain was almost audible above the ticking of the strip light. Franks glanced anxiously at Brown, who shrugged. *You're on your own. They have photos.* Facts would always out. Whetstone decided to fill the void.

"OK, Mr Franks. It really doesn't matter what was going on; what you were stealing. Varsa Ruparelia had discovered your secret. You take the real van round to her flat, murder her and bring her body back to the freezer in the garage at the clinic. Then, last Monday, an accomplice takes the clone up to Watford Gap Services for your photo opportunity and on up North. To all intents you have travelled to Newcastle. Then you set about dumping Varsa's remains at Chatham Woods. Even so, your story needs to be tighter than a duck's bum and so you ask Smith to drive the van to Chatham Woods. But he crashes on the A40 and runs, leaving you to transfer the contents into your BMW and dump it yourself before driving up to Newcastle, swapping cars with the accomplice and attending the meeting next morning. How does that sound?"

Whetstone paused briefly but Franks remained motionless, arms folded, dragon lying in wait. Franks leaned over towards his solicitor, who inclined her head, and they whispered a few words between them. Deirdre Brown whispered a response, and Franks nodded. Better to keep one's mouth shut and be thought an idiot than to open it and remove all doubt. Franks resolutely leaned back and refolded his arms. "No comment."

The furrows in Franks brow could have swallowed a Massey Ferguson. The muscles in his folded arms flexed and the dragon swayed like a polar bear at Regent's Park. In the viewing room, Daley could see that even Franks thought the case against him was compelling but *who was the accomplice?*

Or was this just an elaborate smokescreen?

"I didn't know about the crash until Connor texted me."

"You arrange an alibi, even arranging a cloned van and you expect me to believe you know nothing about the crash?"

"Honestly, I went to Newcastle."

"Then why did you run?"

"Unless you can prove it is material to this case, does it matter why he ran?" Deirdre Brown had reached the limit of her patience.

Franks slouched back into his chair and looked around the room for an intervention. He wanted out but he knew these stupid plods could eat up many more hours before they got tired. He looked at the errant light, the high window mottled and yellow as a tree danced beneath the yard light, hoping for fire, flood, nuclear war, even a mild heart attack, any unwelcome obtrusion which would free him.

He was in luck.

Deirdre Brown had also seen quite enough for one day.

"This stops now, Sergeant! You have nothing to connect my client with the death or otherwise of your alleged victim. Even with two or more vans sporting the same registration plates, anyone could have carried out the alleged crime while my client was on lawful business in Newcastle. If the van he was driving had been unlawfully cloned, then he was unaware and you should take that up with the clinic. Of course, if you do find a single shred of evidence which suggests he may, in any way, have broken the law, I am sure he will cooperate further, but for now, I believe this interview is over." Brown closed her leather folio with a slam which rang off the walls and impressed itself on the still whirring magnetic tapes.

"Ms Brown," countered Whetstone. "I think we have shown your client wasn't where he should have been. He has questions to answer." She cast her hands towards the file of photographs. "Even you have to admit that he cannot fully account for his whereabouts on Tuesday, surely?"

Brown folded her arms and leaned her elbows on the table, her eyes flicking between Whetstone and Monaghan. "Indeed, maybe he does have some explaining to do but you have absolutely nothing that puts him anywhere near Miss Ruparelia beyond the argument of the 23rd October. Do you have the accomplice with whom my client allegedly conspired? Do you have any forensic evidence? Any CCTV of him near the victim on the day of her death? Now, either you charge Mr Franks with something or he and I will be leaving right now. Have I made myself clear?"

Whetstone sighed and held Brown's steely glare for a long moment, and then clearly defeated, she flicked her gaze to Franks, head down, wearing the slightest of smiles. Round one to you, caveman. "Interview terminated..." She glanced at the clock on the wall, "...17:03pm."

***

"What a bloody car crash!" Whetstone harrumphed and placed her armful of papers and cassettes on the table.

"If you'll pardon the pun, Deb." Monaghan flashed a smile but he too was incensed.

She looked back through the mirror glass at Franks and his solicitor. With the uniform outside the room, Franks arms were flailing like windmills as he explained something to his brief. Then Whetstone noticed in the corner of the mirror, a piece of paper had been attached to the glass with Blu-tack.

Deb, this is not about Franks or his van. He is the cover for something else. He was in Newcastle. Where was he on Tuesday night and Wednesday morning? Compare Varsa's figures with those Corby and Taylor brought back. It is Varsa's diary that disagrees. You will have to let him go if he doesn't tell you where he was. Don't sweat. A bad penny always turns up.

I am going to take some time out of the office as I have some things to sort out.

Daley.

Handing the sheet to Monaghan, Whetstone made her excuses and raced down the corridor to the lift. She had to catch Daley before he disappeared.

Chapter 82

Le Café du Rendez-vous, Gare de Strasbourg

Satya found the corner of a red PVC bench, her mind a pinball of disparate thoughts. In the subterranean gloom of Strasbourg station's lower level, people passed the door like wraiths in a dream, customers sat drinking coffee and gossiping but Satya had closed her bubble around her and was unaware. Through its invisible shell, her eyes were fixed on one person as she struggled to process last few minutes. Across the shop, he paid for drinks and turned, beaming a mammoth smile and for once her urge was not to leap from her seat and make for the exit. For the first time since a boot had kicked in the front door of her home and changed her world forever, she felt safe.

Pietr Lazaro placed down the coffees and sat facing Satya, staring at her for a long moment. Her face was drawn and tired, her eyes moist and bloodshot, loss and loneliness etched deep into her skin. She looked very different to the girl who had left the car at Sofia.

"What are you doing here, Pietr?"

"I wanted coffee!" His snicker ended abruptly, her face remaining stony and serious. "OK. Look, it wasn't the coffee. I was worried about you. When you got out of the car in Sofia, when you looked back... I was worried, that's all. I thought you might need help."

"What? Like I am a poor privileged girl who can't cope with such hardships? Like I need a man by my side to validate my decisions and keep me out of trouble? She scrunched up her nose. "Why me, Pietr? What's so special about me? Do you think my family is rich and will pay you more?"

Pietr sighed deeply, hurt. "No! I watched as you left the car. It was something in your eyes. Something different. Look, I was worried, that's all."

Satya wielded a tiny wooden stick, viciously stirring copious amounts of sugar into a thick brown syrup. "I have managed though. Weak little me. Did you not think I could?" She wondered whether to speak of Gregor Wolfe, or the soldier on the bridge, of the capacity within her that had surfaced. The capacity to kill.

"No. It's not that. I have travelled the road between Şarköy and Sofia so often, that blue Skoda knows the way all by itself. I have parked the car in that same space at Sofia station twice a week for the past year. That's over a hundred people that Vasil and I have personally carried into Europe and it dawned on me. I have no idea what has happened to any of them. We simply turned around and headed back to Dikili or Canakkale or Lapseki or Örtülüce to wait for the next call."

"Why should you care? You were paid. Once I left the car, I was not your responsibility."

"But that's it. I do care. I look around my town. All I see are strangers, travellers, migrants. Most are just ordinary people, like you, who have bought passage but in amongst them, there may be drug smugglers, assassins and murderers, even terrorists. If I get too involved, if I see the merchandise as people, then I will see them strapping on vests and blowing themselves up in Paris. I will see them begging on the street or sold into sex. I will start to concern myself with who I carry, with whether I should carry them at all, whether I should play God with their lives.

"Vasil tells me to ignore them all; they are just cargo. We have our own problems. He says if I stop to dwell too long then I may as well get a job in the fish market."

Then Satya understood. She understood the thief confronted by a victim of their crime. The politician watching drone strikes on a big screen. The murderer facing the victim's family across a court room. She understood that Pietr had found something precious.

A conscience.

"So why do it, if it makes you that unhappy?"

"What else can I do? Running guns from Russia and the Ukraine, moving drugs from the Middle East and now people are big business. Like my father and his father before him, this is all I know how to do."

"So why me? Out of all of these people you have transported, why did you follow me?"

Pietr looked away, to the window. He took out a cigarette,

tamped the ends on the table and held it unlit. "We carried your brother too."

"Alaam?" Satya felt her breath catch in her throat.

Pietr nodded. Pulling out a pen, he drew the symbol on a napkin:

"This was on his forearm about here." Pietr slid up his cuff and indicated just above his watch. "I recognised it when you traced it on the door at Edirne. Then he had the other tattoo, that bought him passage. I didn't ask his name."

Satya reflexively rubbed her arm through her coat. She had forgotten the brand she would carry forever. "He came this way?" Suddenly, the tiredness drained away. So Pietr had seen Alaam. Looking round she began scanning faces. Was he still here?

"He was at a truck stop in Lapseki. There were three people. We took them to the coast and across the straits to a safe house near Gallipoli. Then we drove him to Sofia just like you. Someone else took the other two. That's all I know."

"Was he heading for Paris too? Was he going to England?"

"He was taking this same trip two weeks ago. If he made it, he will be in England by now."

Satya took out the crumpled piece of paper, running her finger down, stopping at Strasbourg, tracing back the lines to Budapest and Vidin and Sofia, her mind replaying the endless miles of track, the deserted early morning platforms. Had Alaam's journey been easier than hers? Had he been able to avoid the State Security. Had he been forced to kill? Then a thought occurred to her.

"Pietr. Have you followed me all the way?"

Pietr fidgeted in his chair, toyed with the cigarette. He nodded. "I saw what happened at Budapest."

"The policeman?"

"He was *Grepo* - State Security, not police."

"You watched me take a life and you are arguing about his

job title? Why did you not help?"

"You were coping well enough on your own."

"I stole someone's life from them. I have to live with his face in my mind until the day I die. How can you talk of someone else's life so cheaply?"

Pietr leaned over the table, grabbed Satya's arm and lowered his voice. His face was stone, more serious than she had seen him. "Because that's how we stay alive. Your life is meaningless to anyone but you. Every day people around you die and do you care? No. But faced with your own death, you are prepared to do anything to avoid it, even kill. In that moment when you pushed the knife into that man's belly, your thoughts were not for his family, his girlfriend. They were for yourself. And the border guard? It was you or him."

"He raised his rifle. He almost took my head off with his bullets."

"Word is he was shooting at someone else and you saved them. Makes you the hero?" Pietr cracked a broad grin, the sort Satya had seen on television when the detective figures out the case and exonerates the suspect and all in half an hour minus ad breaks. "From what I saw you only killed the policeman in self-defence."

There was a glibness, a disregard for the seriousness of her crimes, for any moral code she held dear. "You think anyone will care about self-defence?"

"He also had fifteen grammes of heroin on his body when they found him. They are not looking for you."

"You...?"

"Maybe..." There was a twinkle in his eye. Our job was finished. Vasil told me I would compromise the whole of the *'akhuww* network if I were caught. I had no choice but to hide under my coat when you came down the carriage. I thought you saw me once in Zurich."

She recalled the overcoat, the blue jeans and black shoes that were so familiar. She recalled the vague, almost palpable sense of recognition as the man turned away. "Why did you not show yourself earlier? Even though the policeman..."

"State Security..."

Satya glowered. "Even though the policeman was gone, I thought I was still being followed. I have been watching my back ever since and all the while you were there and you never thought to do anything?"

"No-one has been looking for you since Sofia. They don't care about one migrant. Anyway, you are the girl who killed the border guard, aren't you? You can look after yourself?"

Frustrated with his off-handedness, Satya raised her coffee and sipped. It was thick and tepid but she let the sweetness hang in her mouth and subsume her for a brief moment. She looked again at the itinerary. There were only a few more uncomfortable hours before she would reach England and Alaam. Soon, very soon, she could shed the bubble, consign the migrant beast, Gregor Wolfe and the soldier to her past. Soon she could be Satya Meheb again.

Chapter 83

Monaghan was away from his desk interviewing Steven Franks, a collar which DC Steve Taylor had chalked up to himself, even though no-one else had. That allowed him space to scrutinise the Chronotech and Medway Klein accounts without the distractions of a busy team room.

It had not taken him long to find a problem.

Beside him, he had the page from Varsa's diary which Daley had found in her apartment. Her table dated back to January 2011 long before either she or Franks had joined Chronotech. Up to the point Franks joined, the numbers all agreed but then things started to go awry.

Date	Reg	Devices	Units	+/- units	Procs	Farm?
Jan 11	VH07 YMK	3	3	0	3	
Steve had not joined. Units from HTA?						
Feb 11	VH07 YMK	3	5	0	5	
Mar 11	VH07 YMK	3	3	0	3	
Apr 11	VH07 YMK	4	4	0	4	
May 11	VH07 YMK	3	3	0	3	
HTA ended & SF Joined. Units? No HTA!						
Jun 11	VH07 YMK	3	5	+2	5	5
Jul 11	VH07 YMK	5	7	+2	7	7
Too many units!						
Aug 11	VH07 YMK	3	5	+3	5	6
Sep11	VH07 YMK	5	7	+2	7	7
Oct 11	VH07 YMK	5	8	+3	8	7
Nov 11	VH07 YMK	5	9	+4	9	7
Dec 11	VH07 YMK	5	8	+3	8	7
Jan 12	VH07 YMK	3	4	+1	4	5
Feb 12	VH07 YMK	5	7	+2	7	7
Mar 12	VH07 YMK	3	6	+3	6	6
64 units in the farm since SF joined, 25 extra procs & 25 extra units. Where do they come from?						
Apr 12	VH07 YMK	5	7	+2	7	7
May 12	VH07 YMK	5	7	+2	7	7
Jun 12	VH07 YMK	3	5	+2	5	5
Jul 12	VH07 YMK	5	7	+2	7	7
Aug 12	VH07 YMK	3	6	+3	6	6
Sep 12	VH07 YMK	5	7	+2	7	7
Oct 12						

But what did the figures represent?

First off, Taylor checked Chronotech, soon honing in on Delta project, where most of the expenditure was occurring, quickly linking *procs* from Varsa's table with procedures run under Delta.

Delta project was consuming vast amounts of money. The turnover approached quarter of a million a month. Any discrepancy could be expensive, or lucrative.

Chronotech was living off some sizeable research grants and private sector funding which were drip-fed regularly every quarter. Against them a string of costs was set; staff costs, theatre overheads, other petty costs. However, Taylor's eye was caught be two specific recurring entries - Device Supply and Maintenance and Unit Supply and Maintenance. Comparing the figures from Varsa's table and the numbers in the accounts, the proportions exactly agreed. Looking at the OR Logs, he correlated the number of procedures involving Delta Team with the *Procs* column in Varsa's written log. They too exactly agreed.

So, the clinic carried out exactly the same number of research procedures that Chronotech paid them for. Each procedure used a unit and a device. The books were square.

Yet Varsa's table suggested that since Steve Franks joined, there were more units being used - the +/- column.

Taylor scratched his head. Units, devices? What was the difference? Why were they being accounted for separately? Checking further, he found the records for devices. They were supplied by Medical Logistics and serviced by Pontypridd Pharmatech; again, everything seemed to agree. Unit costs were attributed unerringly to a single company. Limewood Holdings.

Perplexed he turned back to the notes Varsa's written log. Soon after Franks had joined she too had resolved *too many units.* Then in April, *25 extra units. Where do they come from?*

Was that what Franks was stealing? Units?

Temporarily baffled, suddenly number-blind, Taylor put the papers aside with a mental note to speak to Daley in the morning. Meanwhile, he set about finding a needle in a haystack - a specific taxi driver at a specific time in a specific place.

Chapter 84

Le Café du Rendez-vous, Gare de Strasbourg

"I have always wanted to go to Paris," mused Pietr.

"I have never thought about it." Satya lied, gazing distractedly around. "There was never any real prospect of seeing any of it."

"Yet here you are. Sofia, Budapest, Zurich, Basel, Strasbourg and soon Paris and London. Quite the adventurer!"

She scrunched her face and eyed him reproachfully. For all his raffishness, dangerous, charming, yet magnetic, Pietr was the type of man her mother would have warned her about. Mind you, Satya's mother would have warned her off any man under fifty and a few older ones too. "I have seen the inside of stations, Pietr. Hardly Marco Polo."

"Yeah, but if anyone asks, at least you can say you've *been* there."

Pietr studied Satya as she sipped her coffee. For the first time since he had pulled her from the sea, she had started to relax. Below the hastily fashioned boyish fringe, her deep brown eyes shone in the neon bright of the cafe. For the first time, he was truly alone with her. Emboldened, he handed back the itinerary.

"You have a whole day in Hervelinghen before you are picked up. Why not spend it in Paris with me, instead? We could be tourists. I will still get you to the rendezvous in plenty of time."

Satya feigned astonishment. "You are not *mahram.* You should not even look at me. Yet you ask me to consort unchaperoned for a whole day in Paris?"

"And two nights. Don't forget the nights. Allah will explode with apoplexy!" Pietr raised his eyebrows, leaned back and laughed. "Seriously? We have one life. Why squander it? We have faith in a supreme being for whom there is no evidence and we ground ourselves in outdated traditions. What is God other than an abstract concept invented by man so he wouldn't feel so alone in the universe? What is culture and tradition, if not the mistakes of our forebears like a millstone around our necks? Do you not look in the mirror and see how beautiful you are? Do you not wonder why selfish men forced you to wear the burkha?

"And where was your God when that soldier raised his rifle or the *Grepo* pulled out his knife? Yesterday is the prison of the soul and tomorrow is an undiscovered world. Today, you are here and no-one knows you. You can be whoever you want, do whatever you want."

The stick had stopped stirring but her mind was racing faster than the TGV she would soon be boarding.

"Oh, come on. Live a little! We can go to Paris together. There is a safe house." He held his hands up in defence. "Separate rooms, of course! Then we can see the Eiffel Tower and the Statue of Liberty, the Champs-Elysées. We can even take a ride on the Ferris Wheel at the Place de la Concorde. They say you can see the whole of Paris from up there."

Satya glanced at Gregor Wolfe's watch. Her train would be leaving soon. Her own reticence, the inhibitions of her past, however much she wanted to rail against them, would linger longer. "No, I can't."

"Why not? I'm going to Paris anyway!" With a flourish, Pietr produced his tickets. "I have followed you this far. Do you think I am going to abandon you now?"

Suddenly she was affronted. "Abandon me? I am doing perfectly well on my own."

"Yeah, but it would be better with a little company." And he flashed his most disarming smile as she smirked behind her coffee cup.

Chapter 85

With an apologetic call to Margaret, which met with a stony silence, Monaghan headed North to Alperton. He had to clear the air with Scott Daley but more importantly, bring the warring factions together to prevent further damage.

The solicitor was correct; the interview with Franks had been a disaster. The evidence, or lack of anything to the contrary, put him in Newcastle.

However much it annoyed, they had *jack*.

Then there was Daley. Whether by luck or judgement, or his maverick scattergun approach, he had stumbled onto something. Right now, he was several steps ahead, convinced that Franks was not their man. Yet the friction with Allenby and Whetstone meant he was keeping his cards close.

Taking a deep breath, Monaghan leaned a finger on the door bell and waited. As the door opened, he raised a bottle and carry-out.

"Olive branch?"

Daley nodded noncommittally and stepped aside. "You let Franks go then?"

"No choice," huffed Monaghan. "The smarmy git even got us to pay for his taxi."

Daley grasped the olive branch. "Look, about this afternoon..."

"Let's put it behind us and move on, eh?" Monaghan's smile was as warm as he could muster. He had to work with Daley for the foreseeable future, even if that was measured in hours. Daley nodded and set about tidying the room.

Monaghan surveyed the living room, hands on hips. There was a chaotic frantic manner about the room; spotless, tidy, un-lived in, except for the confetti of white. "You been busy." An open statement.

Along the skirting beneath the window were a series of A4 pages which appeared to represent trips to Newcastle dating back to April. Above them a single sheet with the word *Franks* taped to the wall. Dotted about the floor were three cut-outs of what Monaghan took to be Transit vans. There was an easy chair for Chronotech and a sofa for Medway Klein, each bearing a piece of paper on which sat a number of what looked like breakfast bars.

"There are too many disparate strands, so I made a model. Just a theory, right now." Daley had been home since 5:30pm. Returning to Alperton, he had scattered his thought across his living room. "Just a theory, Dave. Could be nothing."

"And that is?"

"Nothing yet, it's just numbers in my head. The number of trips to Newcastle since the abductions started, the number of vans needed to cover all bases. The number of drivers. Then there's all those Wednesdays. What was Franks doing when he was supposed to be in Newcastle. There must be something and I don't know whether it is connected with the plastic boxes or whether that is the other thing..."

"Hey, hey, hang on! Slow down. So, one thing at a time. Food." Monaghan sat himself on the chair that had been Chronotech, resting the food and drink on a side table. Ideas were rushing around Daley's head likc rats in a thunderstorm."

"It's just that I am sure I have missed something."

"Look just stop for a minute! It'll come. It always does. You just got to give it time."

"We probably don't have time. Right now, another victim is being stalked."

"And without a flash of enlightenment from the Almighty, what do you expect to accomplish tonight? It will keep."

"But..."

"It - will keep, Scott." Dave Monaghan leaned forwards on the easy chair, stretched out a steadying hand. "You know on a plane, the safety briefing? They say put the mask on yourself before your baby? I need to know you are alright before we look for another victim."

Daley sat, suddenly exhausted. Was he alright? He was sleeping poorly, his appetite had deserted him, his temples were throbbing and the tremors had yet to fully subside. He shrugged his shoulders.

Monaghan grabbed the bottle from the table. "Tullamore D.E.W. 12-year-old single Malt Whiskey. Named after Daniel E. Williams. Now, that's a very Welsh name for an Irish master distiller but we'll let that go. Take a sip of Ireland's best. It'll do you the world of good."

Daley raised hand. "No Dave, I can't."

"Sure you can, after the day you've had."

"Not that you were listening."

"Definitely not listening. As Federation rep, making notes for the tribunal." The sarcasm was almost lost on Daley. "Now, find some glasses before I crumble to dust."

"Dave, I'm on tablets. No alcohol. It'll make me go loopy."

"You, loopy? I would pay to see that after this afternoon."

"Not that you were listening." Daley disappeared into the kitchen and returned with tumblers.

Pouring two shots, Monaghan shook his head earnestly. "Jeez, boss. You're a hopeless case. Let's get the Tube to CentrePoint and I can help you jump off. Less paperwork than a Met tribunal and a guaranteed outcome. Unexpected overtime for the clean-up crew and more in the pension pot for the rest of us. Everyone's a winner!"

Daley smiled weakly. "Sounds fair. Probably hurt less too. Every muscle aches and I just can't shake this damn headache."

"If it's any comfort, they're still knocking the dent out of the train. Nobody would begrudge you an extra couple of days, least of all the prat you pulled off the tracks. And those pills. How many have you taken today?"

"I was fine on Monday," he lied. "Quack checked me and signed me off. He said the headaches would gradually subside but they get worse every day."

"Yes, Scott, but what's with all the arguments and fighting? Look, we've know each other a long time. You always know when to push and when to back off, but Deb said you were nearly exchanging blows yesterday. Then, earlier with Allenby. OK, he's a dickhead but you nearly tore him a new one. What's going on?"

Daley cradled the glass in his hands. "I don't know, Dave. Every time I hear a noise, I see the white lights, hear the horn. I have to catch myself before I scream out loud sometimes. I risked my neck to save that guy. Sometimes I wish I'd never bothered. And Deb Whetstone has pretty well taken my place in the team. I feel like a spare part, like I don't fit any more." He could feel the cracks appearing in the dyke which held back an emotional torrent. "Right here, right now. I am on those tracks and there's a bloody great train coming. Why doesn't somebody save me?"

Monaghan sipped the whiskey and felt the bite on the back of his throat. In his chequered career, he had seen inspectors come and go. Faced with the worst in life, one could either sink or swim; many were dragged under anyway.

"Let me tell you a story, Scott."

***

"1978, I was sixteen, just out of school with the summer to myself. Anyway, one day, my mate Sammy MacIlroy and me are hanging around the back of the pub acting hard, drinking poitin, smoking tabs like James Dean and larking about. It was the height of the troubles in Northern Ireland. We were Provos who hated the British and threw V-signs at the passing Land Rovers, all teenage angst and testosterone.

"Now, a local hard case by the name of James O'Riordan comes out of the pub. He listens to our posturing and he smiles to himself. He tells us to be outside the Post Office at 7:00pm that evening. So naïve are we that we say yes.

"So, later, we end up in the back of an old Granada. We were so up for the craic, tanked up on booze, in with the big boys, singing songs of glory and telling crude jokes about the British. After an hour or so, we swapped into a Land Rover to cross the border to a place called Crossmaglen. As soon as I saw the signs I began to shit myself.

"About a mile out of town towards Newry, they pulled the Land Rover off the road into a field next to a farmhouse. Jimmy and the others put on ski balaclavas. More than anything that's what freaked me out. Suddenly the pictures on TV became real. They shoved us aside and removed automatic pistols and an Armalite rifle from under the rear bench seats. Jimmy threw us a couple of pairs of field glasses and pointed over the hedge to the yard. Then they marched off, black shadows against the dusk towards the farm. The whole world closed in on us as we sat there. My heart was pounding fit to burst and I could hear Sammy's breathing, tremulous like he was freezing cold. But he was just terrified.

"Eventually, an outside light came on in the farmyard as three black shapes strode towards the farmhouse door. The hall light came on, the door opened and a man appeared on the doorstep. He jerked a couple of times and then fell to his knees as two fire cracker sounds crossed the fields to our Land Rover. Then another figure appeared at the door, I guess his wife, and threw herself down on her husband. As the men turned away, there was a scream and another two cracks. For a full five minutes, I could not take my eyes from the shapes lying still in the halo of the light from the hall. Next to me Sammy was moaning - No, no, no - over and over like he was in deep shock. I am not ashamed to say I pissed myself and on the way back, I noticed Sammy had too. After that, we steered clear of the pub, steered clear of the troubles, steered clear of O'Riordan and his mates. Looking back, I suppose that was the intention.

"Just a month earlier, the Provos had kidnapped an RUC officer at Crossmaglen and killed another. The British Army had used the farm as a base in the wake of the kidnapping and farmer and his wife were seen as collaborators.

“Now, me, I could rationalise their deaths in some weird way, just like we do every day, but Sammy was different. He spent most of the summer in his room. When I saw him he was sullen and argumentative. What he saw fundamentally altered him, yet even as his closest friend, I didn't see it. Then one day in August, I went to meet him at McCaskill's barn. He was hanging from a beam.

"Hardly a day goes by that I don't tell myself I should have done more. The fact is, I knew what he had seen and we never talked of it. I knew how it had affected him and I did nothing. He died alone and I will carry that burden for the rest of my life.”

***

Dave took a swig from his glass, reaching for the bottle and topping them both up.

"Look Scott, you can't change what happened, you can only

change how you relate to it now. Tell me - he's on the tracks and you see the train coming, but you stand aside and do nothing, just like I did with Sammy-boy. How would you feel then? Knowing that you didn't even try?"

Daley cradled the glass and stared down at the amber swirls. Monaghan was right. As he had approached the tracks, fought off the woman, fought off the terror, there had not been a second where he had considered abandoning the man to his fate.

"Scott, this job grounds me. It shows me the world is a crap place, not just for me but for everyone and I am no different to the rest. You're no different. You - we - have just got to find a way to handle this, to put it in a box. It will still be there but at least you can keep the lid on.

"Every day, I am on that track beside you. Every day, I choose to step off the line. You can't let this thing eat you up, Scott."

Chapter 86

Gare de L'est, Paris, France

"So, will you stay here in Paris or are you taking your lift to Hervelinghen tonight?"

Satya had forgotten the car would be waiting.

The vast cobbled yard of the *Place du 11 Novembre 1918*, stretched out into the darkness in front of her and beyond it the rumbling ribbon of lights on the *Rue du 8 Mai 1945*. Aside from one hundred metres in Sofia at the start of her trek, this was the first time she had been outside a rail station for over two days. Still, she was disappointed that *Le Tour Eiffel* did not dominate the skyline, that Paris in the dark looked like any other city.

As the train had drawn into station, she had thought on Pietr's offer. Had they been alive, her parents would have been apoplectic at her even considering it. What if they had known of the soldier on the bridge or Gregor Wolfe? But they were dead, hell fire had not rained down and the world still turned. Would one day alone with a man be so terrible? Fifty percent of the population were male. Across the world, non-Muslim *kuffār* people lived their lives without consequence of their unbelief. In Aleppo, it might be said that hell fire was raining down on those who believed just as much as those who did not.

Pietr nodded at a red Citroen DS4, misplaced amongst the other *Taxi Parisien* vehicles. "You can either drag your old life with you and reach nowhere, or let it go and head for a new destination. You have to make a choice."

He sidled over to the car and took out a cigarette.

"qad yakun barakat al'iikhwan ealaykum" *May the blessings of The Brotherhood be on you.*

"walbarakat ealayk eshrt 'adeaf" *And blessings on you tenfold.*

A hand reached out of the car and a small flash lit the cigarette. The two men began talking and laughing, plumes of smoke rising into the moonless sky. Pietr glanced briefly at her and smiled then turned back to the driver. He was giving her space to make the decision.

Of course, Pietr was right. If the rebels had passed by her house, if the Imam had not pushed her onto the truck, given a choice, would she still have travelled to the West, abandoning her life, her heritage, her culture? The dreams she had were of a new life in the West, not simply her Eastern one supplanted. Travelling did mean reaching a new destination, not just physically but spiritually. Al Jalloum was now desolate and filled with hate. Should she reconstruct it in the heart of London? What she sought was change and change often meant sacrifices.

She turned to Pietr. "Tell him he can go." She hoped she would not live to regret it.

Chapter 87

Elstree

"You just open the bloody door and let me in, you bitch!"

The alcohol now unsettling his balance, he fell back a pace as his foot kicked at the door. On a hiding to nothing, he backed away and gazed up at the plate glass. Through the louvre blinds and deep grey of the tint, he thought he could make out a vague orange glow.

"Look, I know you're in there. I can bloody see you! What do you think I am, stupid?"

When the taxi had dropped him off earlier, Franks had swaggered up his drive with the supreme arrogance of a man who had made the Metropolitan police look stupid. He had even suggested to the duty solicitor that she should sue for loss of earnings and the inconvenience, however she had pointed out that he had not lost earnings and there were still questions over his whereabouts on those specific Wednesdays. She had drilled into him with those weaselly eyes and suggested he should quit whilst he was ahead.

Still, convinced he had scored a significant victory, Franks had resolved to celebrate at the Railway in Pinner until, for the second time in as many nights, he had been turfed out in the early hours. Unable to persuade a taxi to take him home, unsure of the reception if he had, he had set about the two hours walk to Caz's house. He would keep banging on the bloody door until they opened it and then she would explain just what the Hell was going on.

Of course, he had known he was being used but it had taken a few weeks to cotton on. The first month of the affair was torrid, secretive, frenetic and frankly exhausting. Even the thought of her slipping her dress to the floor, unhooking her bra, could excite him. Fully clothed, she was gorgeous but undressed, she was a goddess. Tall yet full figured. Amazonian. How naïve he had been?

Pausing to catch his breath, for the world to stop spinning, he leaned against a dwarf wall and thought back to the start. Less than a week into the job, returning from a trip to Cardiff, she had been there, startled him, the stark automatic spotlights emphasising the line of her jaw, the length of those legs, silhouetted against the light. Small talk had lasted as long as it took him to open the garage and close the doors behind them. Hard and breathless she had pushed him to the wall and their lips had met, animal and frenzied before he had hoisted her to his waist, sating a hunger that he knew would either enslave him or engulf him.

But as quickly as it had started, it turned stale, predictable and sordid, meeting out of habit or rather, as he began to suspect, by design. Regular Tuesday nights following his trips to Newcastle, Sunday afternoons. Always her schedule, always Tuesdays and Sundays, like clockwork. Only ever at her house, her turf.

And once he had seen the van.

Then there was the farm. The unwritten pact. Never spoken of. If he finished with Caz, then secrets would out. OK, so he had embroidered the truth a little for the police. He had been foolish to lie about Wednesday but if they had found out where he had actually been, would that not have been worse?

He knew she was in there. He thought of the number of times, naked and hot, they had lain spent on the thick sheepskins, staring out at the gardens, safe in the knowledge that no-one could see in. Once it made him horny just to think of it but now, it made him angry.

"Come on. Open the door. This is pathetic." The cold was beginning to seep through his beer jacket.

Staggering back, surveying the expanse of glass, Franks stumbled over the steps and fell backwards onto the path. However much he was paid was nothing compared to what they made. Did they not think he would do the maths?

Surely, they would know that someday, someone would find out about the farm?

Now in the chill cold of the night, through the miasma of drink, his mind was finally clearing. At last he knew what he had to do. Groping around as he sat on the path, his hand alighted on something hard and cold. He grabbed the pot and threw it, enraged as it shattered impotently against the mirrored window.

Chapter 88

Lambourne Road, Ealing, 8:00am, Friday

Room 3 was the room of last resort. Monaghan was fiddling with the little box behind the door. There seemed no connection between the buttons and the vents in the ceiling but still one played with them with the dexterity of a chimpanzee showing off. As Whetstone entered, she half expected to see penguins rubbing their sides. At the very least she expected to see Scott Daley. Punching him would have kept her warm.

Monaghan turned and smiled; she had coffee. Outside, a sliver of blue and gold inched over the buildings opposite. He reached a hand towards the ceiling vents, withdrawing it as an icy blast bit his fingers.

"So, what are we to do?"

Whetstone puffed out her cheeks. "I want to go back to bed. Cover myself with the duvet and scream."

"Not the only one. Thank God it's Friday." Monaghan's head ached. He had gone easy on the whiskey but these days, late nights didn't agree with him.

The previous afternoon, they had summed up the interview with Steven Franks as, broadly speaking, a pile of crap. Their case was as weak as a priest's handshake and the duty solicitor had run rings around them. Then Daley's note had rubbed salt into the wounds. Worse still, Franks had smirked his way into a taxi. The smile on his face would prove a challenge should they need to wipe it off.

Whetstone sipped her coffee and pulled her coat about her. "Ray *Bloody* Kramer. He won't let up until he has the case." She paused as Monaghan once more rose and ineffectually played with the box. No matter what he changed the outlook remained cold and bleak. Monaghan considered whether playing in some of Daley's theories might help. After all, he had not been sworn to secrecy and technically Whetstone *was* the senior investigating officer...

"What is our take on the white van, Deb? You still think

Franks accomplice drove it North, then swapped over?"

"Not a clue. We now have two vans; one with bits of Franks all over it but no blood and one with blood all over it but no bits of Franks. There has to be some forensics somewhere to link him in - a hair, a skin cell but was it Franks driving or the accomplice? Every time we hear of a van, we have no idea which it actually is or who is driving."

"And you think the accomplice is Connor Smith?"

"Who knows? His wife? Connor Smith? Doctor *bloody* Who? Maybe he does have a TARDIS with a carport..."

"Beg your pardon?"

"Nothing."

"Not that Franks fits my idea of a psychopath, Deb. He is quick to annoy, loses it too easily. In my experience, they are usually ultimately in control. During the interview, it was his brief who was holding him back or we'd all be in Intensive Care."

"Could all be an act?" She sipped her coffee and gazed out at the morning. "Let's say it is. Let's say Franks is Hannibal Lecter reincarnate..."

"Can't really reincarnate someone fictional, though, Deb. Of course, Franks' trips to Newcastle could be genuine and someone else is using him and his van for cover." Monaghan held his breath as Daley's conjecture slid onto the table. It felt like a betrayal.

"Let's...just say." Whetstone scowled, ducking the curve ball. "Ok, so he cruises the area for an easy target, he incapacitates them and bundles them into the van. Or maybe there's a sexual motive? He befriends them, takes them to his love nest. Then he incapacitates and kills them. He uses the van to transport them to the garage where he can work with impunity before dumping the bodies at Chatham Woods. Using the two garages at the Hall, he can have two vans; the clean one and the dirty one, and no-one notices as they both outwardly look the same... as long as they aren't seen together.

"But that could equally be Connor Smith, and Franks trips to Newcastle provide some degree of alibi. If Franks consistently uses the cloned van, that would leave Smith free to drive the other. All that clean-up at his house, maybe that was him taking precautions after the crash? Why else would he run?"

"That, Deb, is the $64,000 question, But Smith? He hasn't got that *X Factor* that makes him a killer. Can you see a man like Franks covering for someone like Smith? Jeez, as soon as Varsa pointed the finger at Franks, he would be round to demolish the wee shite. Nah, there has to be more.

"Anyway, to fit in with the Newcastle trips, surely the victims would need to be abducted on Tuesday evening or Wednesday when everyone assumes he is in Newcastle." Dave leafed through the packed folder, pausing at a couple of pages as he went. "The *Zone 6* victims were abducted on...a Monday evening, except for Andrew Bryson. He disappeared coming back from a Saturday Premiership match."

"And Franks wouldn't be in Newcastle on a Saturday?" Dave raised his eyebrows. An exception to prove a rule?

"This is all a bit risky, though. The clinic is manned twenty-four hours a day. He has to get the victim to the garage, then he has to get the body parts back into the van and out to the farm, all without being seen."

"Yes, but that internal room in the garage makes him virtually invisible. And anyway, he was seen - by Varsa Ruparelia."

"True." Whetstone drained her coffee and shivered. "This isn't getting us anywhere, Dave." Checking her watch, she wondered if Daley had turned up yet. He could always be relied upon to cut through these inconsistencies. Maybe he had been right the evening before. Perhaps this was nothing to do with Franks and the van.

"Look, I am going to chase Gascoigne. See if I can bully him into rushing the blood analysis. If we can identify as many people as possible who ended up in that garage, then maybe we can tie them to Smith or Franks. See if you can find out what they were carrying. Oh, and let's see if we can trace more pictures of that van."

"Sure, if you have a broom, I'll sweep the floor too." Daley had left him enough work to do without this.

"Thank God it's Friday, eh Dave?"

Chapter 89

Alperton, North West London

A trouble shared.

Daley had often used the phrase over the years, usually as a plea to a witness or a suspect - *It will be worse for everyone if you don't tell us, a trouble shared.* But today, Daley regretted confiding in Monaghan. He vaguely remembered Dave wishing him a good night, after which he had waved a glass in the air and promptly fallen into unconsciousness on the sofa. When he had awoken, jack-hammers pounded on the inside of his skull yet the whiskey bottle was still half full. He had been hung over before but lately, with the pills...

Raising himself from the sofa, Daley felt old before his time, small guttural utterances his father used to call *old man noises* as he eased himself to his feet. Reaching in his pocket, his fingers felt for the blister pack. He needed pills. The pocket was empty. Of course it was.

You can't let this thing eat you up, Scott.

Hauling himself up the stairs, he checked his secret caches but they were empty. Monaghan had performed a thorough search the night before, leaving only over-the-counter remedies which would be neither use nor ornament. Last night, caught up in a heady outpouring of alcoholic evangelism, he had promised the Irishman that a line would be drawn under the previous three days. A new dawn.

That there would be no more pills.

Dawn had already risen without him, and no-one had told his pounding head, or his guts which heaved like a boiling tar-pit. An alien grey face grimaced from the bathroom mirror. He grinned back, which was still more terrifying.

"Nothing that a good shave won't fix, eh?" The alien face wasn't impressed by the snake-oil smile and insincere optimism.

Pouring a glass of water, Daley downed a maximum dose of ibuprofen and paracetamol, glancing at his watch, keeping a close eye on the time of the dose. He needed Tramadol. The feel of the tablets between his fingers, the security of the foil pack crackling in his pocket.

He was running late but today he didn't care. In the living room, his phone pinged insistently. It was Whetstone. She could wait. He needed to be at Harrow Central for 10:00am and he needed to be sober, if only in appearance. Anyway, there were ideas he had kept to himself. If they thought him unstable yesterday, they would have sectioned him today if he revealed any more.

He arrived at Harrow Central around fifteen minutes early. Somerville was otherwise occupied, so he was ushered through to the canteen to kick his heels for a while. Outwardly, Harrow Central was considerably more modern than the pre-war warehouse that now housed the North London Homicide Unit, yet inside the decor was depressingly familiar, begging the question why did he traipse across the county to speak to Somerville when he could have phoned?

He needed to talk to her about the bloods, even discover if there was more to tell regarding the sightings of the van. He needed to know where the other van was and who was driving it. And he needed to speak to her about Andrew Bryson.

But most of all he wanted to see her.

Through the swing door, DI Theresa Somerville cast her eyes around the canteen, a short pony-tail bobbing behind as she did. Daley resisted giving an over eager wave, deferring instead to a professional nod.

"Buy you a coffee?" Daley offered as she placed a folder onto the table.

"Freebie card, Inspector. Perks of Harrow Central. You didn't pay for that, did you?"

Daley looked down at his cup and frowned. "Didn't get the memo but if you're buying, flat white." Somerville laughed and snaked her way to the counter, leaving him to sink the remainder of his scalding coffee before she returned.

In his pocket, he felt the edge of the blister pack recovered from the glovebox of the Audi. A tanker-load of caffeine and the headache was a buzz behind the temples. There had been no Tramadol for over twenty-four hours. There were ten pills in the unopened blister pack. Enough for around three days, not counting yesterday when they would have only stretched to one and a half. Maybe Monaghan was right, he had become too reliant on them. Could he ride it out with just optimism and coffee? If he were to take one now, then push the next until the evening, that was OK? It was a reduction, a movement in the right direction. This was something he could control. Something he had to control.

Guiltily, he looked up as Somerville returned.

"So, what can I help you with, Inspector?"

"The Brysons? What did you make of them?"

"I had the feeling that Mr Bryson ran the house like a tight ship. Nothing was out of place. Even Mrs Bryson knew when to speak and when to keep quiet."

"Apart from the cabinet in the living room, there was a barely a sign they had a son. And the motorbike. Restored to pristine in that empty garage. They were like shrines."

Shrines? For Daley, there was something obsessive with the cabinet and the bike; something which spoke volumes about the Bryson's relationship with their child but probably much more about how he ruled the house. "Do you think that Andrew Bryson was railing against the system?"

"There were arguments. They were disappointed that his football career had ended so early. They believed his job was beneath him. He was under their feet. I got the impression that he was looking for somewhere else to live. Interviewing his friends, he had asked if any of them had a room to rent, or they knew anywhere."

"Could he have found somewhere? Moved away to spite them?"

Somerville shook her head. "Living and working in Moor Park there weren't many options. If he had moved out, he would have kept the job to pay for the new digs, references would have been sought from his old employer. Anyway, his bank accounts have stagnated. His phone and cards have stopped being used." Somerville looked anxiously at the clock and smiled apologetically. "Look, I'm sorry but I have to go..." She drained her cup and collected her things.

"How are you fixed later this morning?"

"Is this a date, Inspector? And me dressed in this old thing."

Her eyes sparkled, her teasing instantly forgiven.

Feeling his cheeks blush, Daley quickly elaborated. "No, I want to have another chat with the Brysons. I would like you to be there. You being the IO and all."

"Shame. I was looking forward to cocktails. 11:30 OK?"

As she rose, he asked: "I know this is entirely unprofessional and joking aside, but do you fancy a drink later? I'll get you that cocktail."

"Ah, that explains the new suit. I thought you had a tribunal hearing upstairs."

Daley squinted down at his jacket, somewhat abashed. With the likelihood of another ear-bashing from *Bilko*, and the Damoclean sword of an appointment with the shrink hovering over him, the selection had been anything but random. Blue suggested reliability and trustworthiness, someone not prone to spontaneity or impulsiveness. Traits Daley wished he had in spades but didn't. Maybe the suit would make the man and in a rare flash of clarity Allenby would soften. Somehow, he doubted it.

"You like it?"

"Like is a bit strong. Ambivalent. Yes, ambivalent. I think that's the right word. Still it's better than the grey suit you wore on Tuesday or the brown one on Wednesday."

Daley furrowed his brow. "Ouch! And I selected it specially from the nearly new rail at the Oxfam shop. Anyway, do you?"

"Hmm, let me think, Washing my hair? Waxing the dog? Saddo meal for one? All very compelling. Then there is the mould around the bath..."

"So yes, then?"

Somerville smiled and her nose wrinkled. "You must be some detective when you get warmed up, DI Daley. Meet me at Andros, on the High Street at 7:00pm. Don't wear the suit. Oh, and you'll need to book. It is reassuringly expensive."

Chapter 90

When Monaghan returned to the Team Room, Taylor had his head in his hands and a pencil, almost chewed to extinction, between his teeth.

"What's up, Stevie. Lost a sixpence?" Dave nudged his shoulder. "C'mon, it's Friday. *POETS* day."

"Can I ask your advice, Sir?"

"'Course you can. I need something to cheer me up. What is it?"

"Well, the Inspector asked me to analyse the accounts from the clinic and Chronotech and I think I have found an anomaly."

"Good for you, son. So, why's that a problem?"

"The Inspector gave me this." Taylor handed Monaghan a photocopy of Varsa's extended list. Monaghan scratched his chin, mildly irritated. He studied the extra rows, the cryptic notes, the references to the farm. This would have provided a talking point yesterday, perhaps something Franks would not have been able to wriggle out of. But essentially, it was still a list of numbers, contextless. "And?"

"Well, this list shows devices used, units used and procedures performed against Delta Project since January 2011. You can see that from the point Franks joined, there are always more units and procedures than devices. How can that be?"

"Your show. You tell me." Preoccupied with Daley and Whetstone, Monaghan had yet to look closely at the list.

"Chronotech pay Medway Klein for each procedure, a flat fee to cover a number of costs including device and unit. So, from June 2011 they are suddenly performing more procedures, using more units and charging more without using more devices."

"And?"

"One unit, one device, one procedure. Why does that suddenly change? I thought a device could only be used once before it needs replacement or refurb. The Inspector told us that."

"So he did, Stevie. So he did." Monaghan usually had trouble following Taylor's logic but today, he had little enthusiasm to do so.

"I reckon some procedures must be doubling up on devices, or they are fiddling the books to exaggerate the number of procedures and units used. Or they are acquiring devices off the books."

"So, what is actually worrying you?"

"Well, Sir, by March 2012, that equated to twenty-five extra procedures and extra units without any more devices being used yet they were billing Chronotech for complete procedures - devices and units.

"Ah, a little fiddly-diddly going on. Good spot!"

"Not so little, sir. In ten months, the clinic earned an extra three quarters of a million pounds and the company supplying the units, Limewood Holdings, has taken one hundred thousand. Seems like fraud."

"And can we link this in any way with Steven Franks?"

"No, but that's not what's worrying me, Sir."

"I'll ask again. What is actually worrying you." Monaghan was beginning to lose faith. Undoubtedly Taylor was intelligent but sometimes he hid it extremely well.

"Since Steve Franks joined there have been 38 extra procedures."

"Yes."

"And 38 extra units used."

"Uh-huh."

"I have no idea what the procedure is. I don't know what a unit is and..." Taylor searched for a magic third, "...I don't know who Limewood Holdings are."

Chapter 91

Moor Park, Baldwin Avenue

Drawing up at the Bryson's, Daley spotted Malcolm Bryson's Mondeo on the drive. Ringing ahead, he had spoken to Irene, who had been reluctant to meet whilst her husband was at work. So he was disappointed when Malcolm opened the door. He had been hoping to speak to Irene alone, uninfluenced by her constant chaperone.

"Ah, Inspector Somerville. Do come in. Any news on Andrew?"

"No news at this stage, I'm afraid, Mr Bryson."

Daley followed Somerville and the Brysons into the time capsule that was their front room. Elsewhere, a television played to itself. Malcolm rubbed his hands together, the room cold, unused. "What can I do for you?"

"Just a few loose ends, Mr Bryson," began Somerville. "Could you tell me about the 29th September. The Inspector and I would like to get the timeline in our heads."

Daley caught the subliminal glance to Irene before Malcom started. "What again?" Bryson huffed. "We went off to Sainsbury's at 9:00am, as usual. When we got back Andrew had left for the match. He met his friends for a drink near the ground. We never saw him again."

"And the previous evening he had been out with his mates?"

"Yes, to the Anchor."

"Returning at...?"

"2:00am. Something like that. We are light sleepers at the best of times. I looked at the clock."

"He was still in bed when you left for the supermarket?"

"He tended to waste his Saturdays." It was Irene.

"May I have another look around his room, Mrs Bryson?" Daley rose with Irene, leaving Somerville with Malcom. Not for the first time, Daley detected an undertone of anxiety as Irene rose, as if separation from her husband was a step too far.

The bedroom was unchanged from Daley's previous visit, except for a fresher smell of polish. Daley opened the wardrobe and made a cursory check of the racks, opened drawers. Nothing had been moved, still he looked for something that had caught his eye on the previous visit, yet not registered.

Somerville was sitting on the edge of the sofa, stifling the need to sneeze. Motes of dust disturbed by the infrequent visitors played in the faint sunlight. Malcolm lit his second cigarette since they had arrived. He cracked a guilty grin. "I am only allowed to smoke in here or outside."

The front room was a Seventies time warp except for the glass cabinet. Over a tiled fire place, a Tretchikoff-esque Spanish flamenco dancer stood frozen, arched back and castanets, looking over her shoulder. There was no TV.

"How was Andrew coping since the accident?"

Malcolm shrugged. "As well as can be expected, I suppose. The job was not what he wanted to do but since the accident..."

"Since we last spoke, has anything else come to mind? Anything that might have been worrying him?" Somerville was playing her part, stalling for time, leaving Daley with Irene Bryson.

"Not that...look, we been through this before, Inspector."

"Yes, but since then, we have found some new evidence, so we are re-examining what we know."

Malcolm nodded. "He was always a lazy boy. He could have made so much more of himself. We told him he needed to start thinking of the future. Working in a supermarket was all very well but he needed a proper career."

Daley followed Irene back into the room and nodded briefly at Somerville. Soon all four were seated and an uncomfortable silence had descended before Daley ruptured it.

"So, tell me Mrs Bryson. What was the argument about?"

Irene and Malcolm looked at each other. Daley might have expected confusion, even concern at such a direct question. God knows Nick Snowdon was quick enough to mount his high horse.

But their faces were stone.

"Argument?" It was Malcolm.

"Yes. After he came back on that Saturday?"

Irene caught her breath and turned to look out of the window. A tear welled in her eye but she quickly brushed it away, regaining her composure. Malcolm remained motionless, stoic.

"He didn't come back. He left while we were at the supermarket. On the morning."

Daley persisted. "So, what happened? He rolls in at God knows what time, second night in a row, drunk and mouthing off?"

"I've told you, Inspector. He never came back."

"End of your tether, I suppose. Two nights running, pissing his cash up a wall. Little consolation for the 2-1 drubbing Manchester City had inflicted on his beloved *Whites*. You're already in bed, or maybe watching a film? He comes through the door, gobbing away, disturbing the peace and quiet?"

"No, he didn't come home," Malcolm spat through gritted teeth. "For God's sake man! Our son is missing."

Daley flicked a glance at Somerville. Her face was etched with concern. He knew his reputation preceded him. She nodded. *Continue...carefully.*

"The house is tidy, you're settled in. Then Andrew comes in, slamming the door, probably rifling the fridge for something to eat, standing in the doorway telling you how crap Fulham were again. Meanwhile, the peace is shattered, the film is ruined. And not for the first time."

Malcolm huffed. "I'm not sure what you're getting at Inspector. Andrew didn't come home." He looked over at Somerville, for salvation. She sat quietly, letting the drama play out.

"Except," continued Daley. "Ali Hussain of A1 taxis distinctly remembers picking Andrew up from the Tube and dropping him off here."

"That's impossible. The man is mistaken. He must pick up hundreds of people a week."

"He remembers Andrew because he was drunk and bemoaning the pitiful performance *The Whites* gave that afternoon. Drawing 1-1, holding them to the eighty-sixth minute before Riise's poor header allows Dzeko in to score the winner. I remember watching it myself on *Match of the Day*."

"Andrew can't be the only Fulham supporter in Moor Park, surely..."

"Maybe not, but Andrew dropped this in his cab." Daley drew a black and white bobble hat out of his coat pocket. Irene Bryson drew a deep breath. Malcolm stared at Daley puzzled, unflinching, unblinking.

"No, must be someone else's."

"Mr Hussain was adamant. One of my officers showed him a photo."

"There must be any number of black and white bobble hats. A lot of Andrew's friends were Fulham supporters."

"Still one heck of a co-incidence that a man matching Andrew's description took a taxi from the Tube to your house wearing a Fulham FC hat on that night."

"Co-incidence! Co-incidence!" Malcolm Bryson became animated and his face began to turn crimson. He locked eyes with Daley. "You come into my house, *my bloody house*...I don't know what kind of stunt you're trying to pull..."

"So, am I right? Coming home at all hours, dropping his stuff wherever it landed, disturbing the evenings. Out all week trying to keep a roof over your head, while Andrew just seems to do what he likes. No regard for the future. No attempt to make anything of himself."

"Look, I have had quite enough of this..." Bryson made to get out of his seat, show the pair the door.

"What happened? Were there words? A row? Did it get violent? After all, what right has he got under your roof...?"

"You just get out of my bloody house right now." A finger was thrust towards the door.

"It wasn't like that!" Irene snapped and the words rang off the flock wallpaper.

Daley leaned back in the easy chair, rubbing his temples. His head was hurting. Against his hip, the edge of the foil packet dug into his flesh. Thirty-six hours since the last tablet and a monster was growing in his mind, exploiting the moment, exploiting his weakness. One pill would not hurt. Surely, he had earned it?

Somerville leaned forwards and spoke quietly. "What really happened that night, Irene?"

Malcolm Bryson's eyes widened and he willed his wife to keep quiet but Irene was in need of catharsis.

"They were rowing all the time. Every time Andrew came home these days, something was wrong. His job, his bike, his life. What are we supposed to do? He's a grown man. He needs to look after himself. But still he's tapping his dad for a few quid here or there, making us fetch and carry for him, treating this place like a bloody doss house."

"And is that what happened that Saturday?"

"He came in at 1:00am," interjected Malcolm Bryson, now defeated, resigned to the inevitable. "He stunk the place out with booze and curry and started mouthing off about the match. I'd watched *Match of the Day* too. I didn't want it all over again. We had words in the hall. He turned around and walked out again. We haven't seen him since."

Daley remained unmoved. He dug into his pocket. "So, how did his ticket stub for that match get into his drawer?"

Bryson's shoulders dropped "He dropped it. I put it away."

"Where is he now, Malcolm?" Somerville was not to be distracted so easily. "What really happened?"

"I told you..."

"No, Malcolm." Irene dragged a handkerchief from her sleeve and dabbed an eye. Then resting her hands in her lap, she faced Somerville.

"The two of them were pushing and shoving, shouting and swearing."

"Irene..."

"I'd had enough so I went upstairs, just to get away. Just for some peace and quiet but Andrew followed me, ranting at me for not sticking up for him, always taking his dad's side.

"Irene!"

"He could be a spiteful boy, just like his father." She cast Malcolm a searing glance. "I turned and next thing I knew he was at the bottom of the stairs. It was an accident, honestly. I just couldn't stand any more of the shouting." Irene Bryson hid her face behind the tissue and shook as the tears came.

Malcolm Bryson dropped his head and stared into his lap. As his wife sobbed, he tentatively reached over and cradled an arm around her shoulder.

"Where is he now, Malcolm?" pressed Somerville.

"In the garage. In the pit underneath the bike. I- I didn't know what else to do. It was an accident, plain and simple? I saw the *Zone 6* abductions in the paper, it just seemed a lot easier to believe he had not come back that night. Ever since his accident, things had been strained. I just wanted everything to return to normal."

Chapter 92

North Harrow

Whetstone glanced over to DC Steve Taylor who had a hand braced against the dash. She tried to recall the last time she had arrived at the office before him or left after. She was concerned he may be allergic to fresh air. Or a vampire, which was more likely. So, it was a surprise when he had approached her with a request to leave the building during daylight hours. She had listened distractedly as he had repeated his analysis, his confusion over the devices and units. He had bravely suggested that she and Monaghan should stop making stuff up, hoping to hit the mark, and ask the right questions. After throwing him a withering scowl, she had suggested they learn from the horse's mouth.

Marion Edmonds was not on shift on Fridays. She lived on a smart terraced street of ex-council houses in North Harrow. Cheaper than the average for the town, they were paradoxically better maintained, as owners valued their investment more. Marion and Derek Edmonds end terrace was ecru stuccoed and UPVC glazed, maybe the sign of a zealous improvement programme, as the council sought to dispose of the properties. The driveway ran along the side of the house to the rear, where a small hatchback sat in front of a garage, a prized asset in the area.

Though dressed in a navy tracksuit, Marion Edmonds still had that edgy nervous way about her, her hair still an unruly flop of curls today allowed to hang free about her sun-lined face. She flicked a brief purposeful smile as she opened the door and waved the pair through to the rear of the property and a kitchen diner which looked out onto a tiny yet immaculate rear garden.

"What can I help you with. You said, on the phone, the clinic?"

"Yes, Marion. We have been looking through Varsa Ruparelia's diary and it has raised a few questions which you may be able to help us with."

"If I can. Fire away." Resting her hands in her lap Marion seemed smaller, diminished.

"Can you tell me about Delta? What is it about, on a day to day basis?"

Marion shifted in her seat and her eyes flicked between the pair. "I don't wish to be obstructive. We have all signed a confidentiality agreement. We have been advised not to discuss Delta. I would need to..."

Whetstone sighed. "Marion. We are not actually interested in Delta project from a commercial perspective. I am afraid we have found a body which we believe to be Varsa Ruparelia. This is now a murder enquiry."

Marion raised a fist to her mouth and stifled a gasp.

Whetstone sighed at the theatrics. "Tell me about Delta."

"There is a roster. Twice a week on average. Usually Monday, Thursday and Friday, or maybe Saturday if the OR is busy. The procedures can take upwards of twelve hours but I am not required for the whole of that. Usually I will arrive at 8:00am and scrub up and then assist the theatre staff and consultant to prep. The OR is already prepped, the necessary equipment has been arranged. That is Connor Smith's job. He's the Junior Surgeon. Joan...or Varsa...would be outside in the admin room checking the details of units, devices and other regulated equipment required for the procedure.

"Then, around 9:00am, the procedure would start with the consultant leading and I would assist. There is an audio link and Varsa would remain in the Admin suite, transcribing what was said."

"And afterwards, when the procedure was completed?"

"The reverse. There is a debrief in the OR, equipment is taken to the sluice room and checked back in by Varsa, the device is placed into a hermetically sealed container and checked back in, then the unit is removed from the OR and returned. I will supervise the primary clean of the OR pending the professional cleaners."

"Who is the consultant?"

"Nick Snowdon. This is his show." Marion's eyes flicked left, closing a door in her mind.

Taylor shuffled in his seat. "The procedure? It's a surgical procedure?"

"Yes. This is part of a wider project. We are developing techniques to be used when the project goes into clinical trials. Everything has to be as it would be in a real OR situation."

"So, it's invasive?" Taylor's brow was still furrowed.

"Oh, yes. We implant the two component parts of the device, and over forty separate electrodes and sensors. Then when we have finished and debriefed, we remove them all again."

"And this happens each time a procedure is carried out?"

"The procedure varies as it is improved, made more efficient but broadly speaking it's the same."

"And do you ever reuse equipment - devices, units?"

"The equipment and the OR are professionally cleaned each time. We can re-use the device and the electrodes but only after they have been refurbished and repacked. We either use a new one or one which is exactly like new."

"And the units?"

"We use a fresh one each time because of the nature of the procedure. No unit can ever be reused. There are strict requirements regarding the age of units. If they are too old there is nerve degradation and the process does not work."

A sudden realisation hit Taylor and he shuffled uncomfortable. As if all of the pieces had finally slotted into place but the image they formed was obscene. "So, the units are...bodies?"

Marion looked taken aback. "Yes. I thought you knew. This is a medical research project. We use medical cadaver units. We need to use them within 48 hours of the circulatory system being stopped or they will not react effectively to stimuli."

Whetstone glanced nervously at Taylor. He had stopped writing and was thinking. "Where do you get the, er, units?"

"Not my department. Chronotech handle that side of things. When we arrive, there is already a unit waiting."

Marion turned her head to gaze out of the window. A timid sun had broken through the winter skies sending dim shards of yellow across the white lawn. Suddenly everything she did seemed so alien, so grotesque, modern day Gothic. Her face was lost to a thought.

Whetstone caught the expression and pressed: "What is it, Marion?"

"Oh, nothing. Sometimes I think I walk into that clinic and real life is suspended until I walk out again. Each cadaver is a tragedy that has befallen a family, the only blessing that they can be of some use even after they are gone. The least I can do is care for them."

"Marion, I think you should know that, on Wednesday, we found a mass grave out at Chatham Woods Farm, near the Nature Reserve. Varsa Ruparelia was amongst the dead. We believe that the grave is in some way connected with Medway Klein and Chronotech. There are upwards of thirty bodies."

Marion Edmonds eyes flicked left and right, her brow furrowed. The fist returned to the mouth.

It was obvious to Whetstone that she already knew.

Chapter 93

1995

There is a special moment in everyone's life. If one is unlucky, one will be unconscious when it happens. It is the moment when the life leaves. A brief, transient moment when everything vaporises into hopelessness. For the victim of the moment, it has mixed blessings. There is a sudden clarity, an epiphany, when the whole meaning of existence is revealed. When everything that one has ever strived for, everything won and lost, becomes futile. Friends, acquaintances, relatives, enemies no longer matter. All that is important is life itself. For the fleeting moment that it remains.

Lina and I met that moment many years ago. Only for us, we watched the life drain from our parents. We watched the moment that they realised they meant nothing. In that briefest of seconds, they gifted their life to us, a life without scruples and inhibitions, without rules and restrictions. That fleeting moment that we would steal from them and hold for a lifetime.

Janey and Doug are at that moment now.

We met them by chance, looking for a car. On the forecourt, a sunny afternoon, they were holding hands and full of happiness. Lina used her charms. At seventeen, she was beautiful, tall, slim, with a rounded face and deep auburn hair; the only one I would ever need. Within quarter of an hour, we had befriended them, two couples perusing the lines. They had chosen the Lexus, and we knew we had found our new hosts.

We chose the ancient Maestro van, white, anonymous. It suited our needs.

Their house is in Twickenham, next to the river, modern and airy, stretching down to a jetty and a small boat. They had bought it following success in the City. The city was Philadelphia and they had moved to England bringing their money and their glorious, childless isolation with them.

By now, this was our sixth host. We had grown accustomed to the routine. A well planned, slow, insidious devouring of a being, of everything they are and everything they own. Every other host had been a singleton. Less risk. Either a man for Lina or a woman for me, although it didn't much matter. When pushed, most people would plumb the depths of any depravity. We could share the seduction or swap roles. The prize was literally in the kill. However, this was our first couple. We made love that night, our excitement intense, knowing that these people, this particular consumption was something we could share.

And so it was over the next few months. The casual acquaintance, the slow, easy dance into friendship, the edgy paso doble as we sized each other up, the seductive rumba of passionate sex.

And now the sudden frantic tango of death.

Janey's breasts are hard and full as I sit astride her, naked and sweating, her hands and feet tied to the bed frame, the halter about her throat. She likes it that way, tense and perilous, in the raptures of asphyxiophilia. Her eyes are insistent and her lust animal as the halter tightens. She urges me on, harder and harder, deeper and deeper, tighter and tighter. Beside, Lina is riding Doug and his breath rasps and grates, the sweat pours from his chest as the bonds hold his hands from her naked flesh and his neck bulges as his own noose feeds his adrenaline. Her body is mine and mine is hers but we will allow this for as long as it takes. We have shared each other with Janey and Doug for two months, gradually gaining their confidence, learning their practices. They are big on shared experiences, little knowing that this will be their last. Soon, it will be just us again, they will be in the shed and once more Lina and I can be exclusive.

And then the room changes. Their eyes widen as the halters continue to tighten, the gasps turn to choking. Small haemorrhages redden their cheeks and their bodies stiffen, fibrillating muscles.

In that moment, I look into Janey's eyes and Lina looks into Doug's and we see in them the realisation that all is lost, the utter hopelessness and inevitability. Then I see something else, something unexpected. As Janey's eyes flick sideways towards her husband's, as they catch his twitching, taut body, as they see Lina holding pressure on the chain around his throat, the ecstatic whimpering, I see sorrow. And I know it is not sorrow for her but for the husband who will die with her, for his pain and loss.

It is the look of my mother as the bat crushed her skull.

Then it is over. Janey and Doug lie still next to each other, and the room is silent, prickling and close. Lina climbs from Doug's priapismic member and comes to me. We make love between the corpses, energised by the life leaving their bodies, drawing it into our own, augmenting the explosive climax.

As we part, exhausted and spent, Lina whispers in my ears.

"I want to look inside."

Chapter 94

Baldwin Avenue, Moor Park

Daley and Somerville stepped aside as the black Transit reversed into the drive. With the discoveries at the farm, Andrew Bryson would take second place as he probably had for most of his life. The pathologist from Harrow had brought along his own team, who were currently erecting their tent across the open garage doors. Somerville had summoned a DC from Harrow to take formal statements from neighbours.

With so much going on, Daley had almost missed the Fulham home shirt in the wardrobe, the woollen hat in the chest of drawers. The ticket stub amongst a collection. How could they be there if Andrew had not returned? Of course, the hat had not been left in a taxi. Amin Hussain worked at Daley's local Indian. It was a hunch. This time it had paid off.

The case was to be formally passed back to Harrow. Theresa Somerville would take it.

In his pocket, his phone buzzed. It was Whetstone.

"Deb?"

"Taylor and I have just been to see Marion Edmonds. Units are bodies. The procedures at Medway Klein are performed on cadavers. They need a fresh one for each procedure. Too old and the nervous system has died. She doesn't get involved in transportation of cadavers. Someone else does that."

"Franks?"

"She has no idea where they are coming from, she just takes the next on the list."

"There has to be a ready supply of fresh bodies. Given the clinic had a limited legitimate supply, someone is augmenting it."

"*Zone 6* abductions? Surely not, sir. They were plastered all over the news. Sooner or later, someone would recognise a face."

It was true. The body would be identifiable if it were Ruparelia or Lucas, or any of the *Zone 6* victims. Varsa was killed because she found out there were too many bodies and did the maths. Daley visualised the tangle of body parts in the tank. This had been going on a lot longer than *Zone 6*.

"I'll meet you back at Lambourne Road. You and I need to talk. We need to settle our differences. Then we need to find out where these bodies are coming from."

Chapter 95

Lambourne Road, Ealing

Scott Daley had decided that the canteen was the safest place to speak to Deb Whetstone. In the afternoon, the place was quiet and most of the objects lying around were small and would inflict little damage if she threw them at him. There were a few too many knives, though. He sat and fidgeted as Whetstone stared dejectedly at the pile of papers she had brought ready for the Team meeting in the Conference Suite later. Where to start? Prevarication.

"So, how's it with you and Keith *the Uniform*?"

Whetstone glanced up at Daley. She had seen that look before. It was combination of mock concern and of someone attempting to relieve a stubborn bout of constipation. How were things going with Keith? Since the farce with Franks, they had barely spoken. Even in the brief moments that they found together, she felt another presence. Keith always seemed pre-occupied. The relationship was floundering. She was clinging on to the wreckage for fear that she would sink without him or be stranded alone and lost at sea forever. These days, she plied a lonely route.

"Oh, he's OK."

"You?"

"OK." But she really wasn't OK. She was embarrassed by dressing down she had endured from Allenby and angry with Daley for his juvenile behaviour, but the last few minutes in the Conference Suite had left her incandescent. Taylor and Monaghan were spending more time following Daley's whims than helping her. Yet even that was nothing compared to the anger she felt over how she had failed herself. Even now, she was no nearer understanding what Daley had seen, obtusely holding onto the fading shreds of the case against Franks, stubborn in the belief that if he was lying, then he must be guilty. Liars seek to protect themselves. They have good memories. Franks movements, his alibis were so precise that he had to be guilty. Didn't he?

Then she found herself speaking. "Look. I am not OK. I am really just...not OK." She reached for the coffee to stem the flow, sensing a torrent that could drown them both.

"That makes two of us, Deb." Daley picked up the salt and upturned it, spilling a fine strand across the table. "There's the line. It's drawn. Whatever our differences, there is a killer who is going to strike again while we argue niceties. Added to that I am buggered if that smarmy bastard Kramer is going to march in and take over. Do you know he hit on Lynne once at the Federation Dinner?"

"Yes, by all accounts you decked him."

"It was a tap, but all the more reason to tell him to do one."

Contrition had to start somewhere, so Daley took a breath. "Look, Deb, I'm sorry. I'm sorry for the way I have behaved, for the way I left you in the lurch. I am sorry for everything." Apologies were not Daley's strong point but he had to try. "I admit, I am probably not fully fit. My heads all over the place and I bloody well deserved the bollocking I got from you and Allenby and especially from Monaghan. I should have been there to help and I wasn't. I have let you all down and you deserve a whole lot better."

"I could have been more understanding too..." Whetstone knew it was an appeasement, that she should have been throttling the life from his worthless carcass.

"No, Deb. This is on me. As senior rank, whatever the situation, whatever the provocation, I should lead by example. Even if the investigation was formally yours. When Allenby ordered me not to interview Franks, I threw a strop. Instead I should have sucked it up and fallen in behind you. We have to be able to work together, debate, to argue but there's the line." He cast a thumb at the strand of salt. "We all know where it is and however many times you tried to pull me back, I kept on crossing it."

"Like you say, sir. A line. Sometimes it was easier not to argue. Sometimes I just wanted it the way it was before the train, before six months as Inspector. It was easier to let you go off on your own than to rein you in."

They lapsed into an uncomfortable silence. There was a lot

more that could have been said, a lot more that would reduce them to quarrelling children but nothing that would make the situation any easier.

"So, explain what's going on in your head?" Whetstone leaned over, smudging the line, brushing salt from her sleeve. "What do *you* think we are investigating?"

"I don't know, Deb. It's like a cut gemstone. Every way you look at it, a different facet, a different view of the same things.

"Take the van. We have a crashed van and a clone. Is Franks orchestrating this or is he, what did Snowdon say, Just a patsy? He goes about his business, oblivious to the other van. Or did he simply set himself up to help with alibis later? I just don't know.

"And Varsa, her diary, the people she had crossed. Maybe she blackmailed someone and they finally snapped, hacked her to pieces and stole the van to dispose of her?

"Then it occurred to me to turn this on its head. What if Franks appearance on the scene is not the start but the point when things became easier?

"Long before he joined Chronotech, they have a Transit van for deliveries and collections. Only there is another with matching plates which our killer has and keeps hidden. Franks drives the same van all the time, oblivious to the fact it is a clone. Who checks VINs apart from us? Smith crashes the hidden van. Franks genuinely is in Newcastle in the other.

"Our killer has to source a new van and disguise it as the old one until Franks gets back, at which point the killer replates both vehicles to be the new van - RN08 DVB. Still two vans, Franks is a clone of the real, hidden one. ANPR shows the same van in two places. Which is genuine? Who knows?"

"...All the time the real van is still out there somewhere whilst we fixate on Franks."

"Precisely, and with two garages next door to each other, Varsa could have easily mistaken which van she saw and which garage. I got lucky. I looked about that car park, saw two of each vehicle, even Taylor, who could identify his cup amongst loads of identical ones. Of course, Franks would notice if someone else used his van. That's why there always had to be another. Two by two."

"And Franks in the frame."

"Precisely."

"OK. So, Chatham Woods Farm. How did you know Connor Smith would be there?"

"I didn't. I was following up on the *Zone 6* abductions and he jumped me. Same with Varsa's diary, the missing pages. I follow a hunch and get lucky."

"Next time you place a bet, let me know, sir." Again, the leaps of deduction which Whetstone felt she could never have.

"It's all just luck."

"It's anything but luck. Whether it's mental synthesis or connecting the dots, I have no idea how you do it. These are just random ideas but somehow you manage to pull them together. I just see what's there, a jumble of disparate facts, no discernible pattern. It's like a crossword where the answers are obvious if you can read the clues but they are all in code."

"OK. Tell me what you see? What do *you* see as obvious?"

"We have upwards of thirty bodies including *Zone 6* abductees, Varsa Ruparelia and countless others stretching back who knows how long."

Daley cut in. "And according to Marion Edmonds, the procedures at the clinic have been going on for ages, involving recently deceased bodies, lots of them."

"How do we know they are the same people?"

"We don't."

Whetstone huffed. "What *do* we know?"

"Do you really think there are two crimes here, each involving a mass murderer?"

"I don't know!" She was beginning to think Daley was making this up as he went along.

"The killer uses the hidden van, with Franks as cover, abducts and kills his victims and transports them back to the garage in the clinic. He or she has to keep Franks and his van out of the way whilst scouring homeless refuges, picking up strays, anonymous bodies? Anyone that realised what was going on, simply ceased employment with Medway Klein and disappeared into that tank."

Daley leaned back, creaking the chair. "I just don't buy the Franks double alibi, double bluff. His solicitor was right. There is nothing to link him to the deaths apart from working with Varsa. But even she could have riled the *Zone 6* Abductor quite separately from everyone at the clinic."

"So, Franks is the unwitting cover for someone else who is committing the *Zone 6* Abductions and many more?"

And finally, thought Daley, she is on the same wavelength, now just to tune in the station. "A research project uses a large number of cadaver units and we have a large number of bodies in a mass grave. Let's assume Patrick Gascoigne will link the two. That's the starting point.

"Originally, the clinic had a legitimate supply of cadavers. The project ramps up and they need more. Maybe they find a few innocent dog walkers and joggers. They use the elaborate ruse with the vans leaving Franks to explain it away if anyone starts nosing about. Meanwhile as long as the paperwork matches, cadavers keep turning up in the clinic freezers and disappearing afterwards, everyone's happy."

"Until Varsa starts nosing about."

"Either our killer wanted to kill or needed a body. I don't think they cared about who as long as they were in the right age bracket and fit and well."

Whetstone raised her eyes to the ceiling. Each time she understood, another layer peeled away. "So, you're saying whoever is supplying the bodies to the clinic, that's our killer?"

"Uh-huh."

Whetstone felt like her head was ready to explode. That was quite enough for one day. She decided to change tack. "Anyway, what's with you and Inspector Somerville?"

"Terri? Nothing, just a colleague."

"Not good enough, Scott. The way she was looking at you yesterday. In this new-found spirit of honesty and openness...?"

"We are having a meal out tonight. *Andros* in Harrow."

"Jeez, either it's love at first sight or she saw you coming. That place is well outside my price range. You must have it really bad."

"A hint of jealousy, maybe?" Had he got it bad? Maybe. In a

world full of people, of concentric lives, and unreasonable expectations, he had learned to manage his. Lynne had been the only woman he had really cared for and she had deserted him. Perhaps that was the anchor that kept his expectations low. Since Lynne, no-one had come close; he had made sure of that.

"Anyway, that explains the suit." Whetstone smirked. "Still it's an improvement on that threadbare grey one you wear."

"What? You like it?" You're not, er, ambivalent towards it?"

"Eh?"

"Oh, nothing."

Chapter 96

La Basilique du Sacré Cœur de Montmartre, Paris.

There are days when time seems to slow to an absolute crawl. Lazy days with nothing to fill them but time itself. During her endless train journeys, Satya had willed time to pass, frustrated when the miles dragged and sleep would not come. But now she willed the opposite. Time could drag its heels all it liked. Even Gregor Wolfe's watch appeared to be broken, it moved so slowly.

As she and Pietr, sat on the steps of La Butte Montmartre, with the magnificent facade of the Basilica behind, the urgency which controlled her existence had suddenly disappeared. She felt at peace, the warmth of the weak afternoon sun on her face, the background sounds of people and traffic about her. With her arm linked around that of Pietr's, she sketched the flat panorama of Paris in her sketchbook, the twin fingers of Montparnasse and Eiffel pointing skywards.

The previous evening it had been very different. Having resolved not to travel on to Hervelinghen, she immediately began to regret the decision. To be stranded in France, penniless, homeless would be a disaster. She had broken the contract. Would they still honour the connection? Even now, she could reach Hervelinghen, to find herself cut adrift. Was the least worst option to be abandoned in Paris, or a village in an unknown part of France?

Then there was Pietr. Brash, impulsive, boyish, turning up out of the blue, solving so many of her problems. The relief at knowing there was no need to run. The comfort of knowing she had someone to catch her when she fell. Of course, she had spotted from the very beginning that he was in love with her. The way he looked at her, occasional awkwardness, how he flushed when he said something too forward. Or at least she kidded herself she had.

But the problem was, she thought she was falling in love with him. This mad, bad *kuffār*. A thief, a black-marketeer, maybe even an assassin. He was exciting, dangerous even, and since leaving Sofia she had prayed that she would see him again.

The debate between Pietr and the driver of the red Citroen became louder, hands were waved, the Arabic more profane. Eventually, Pietr had waved her over and together they bounced around in the back as the driver took out his frustrations on the streets of the city. Pietr spoke quietly in English.

"He is annoyed with us. He lives in Hervelinghen and was looking forward to his own bed. Now he has a detour before he can warm his feet on his wife."

The Paris safe house was East of the city, in the suburb of Montreuil. Their rooms overlooked a small claustrophobic courtyard. Drawing the drapes, Satya had consigned herself to another night before she would see the city. True to his word, and much to her chagrin, Pietr had left her to the large bed and taken the other room. Exhausted, she had fallen instantly asleep.

When she opened her eyes, Gregor Wolfe's watch said 07:30am. The room was bright and Pietr stood silhouetted against the window. Beside her was a plate of cured meats, cheese and a curious croissant with chocolate pieces. The aroma of fresh coffee filled the room.

Pietr threw out his cigarette and turned from the window. "You slept well? At one point, I had to check your pulse, I thought you had died."

"You came in here during the night?"

"Well, more accurately, in the morning. I sat in the chair and watched you sleep. I could not believe I had found you again." Pietr lowered his eyes to the floor, embarrassed.

Sitting up, gathering the sheets about her, she was both affronted and elated. "So much for separate rooms! You are obviously not a man of your word."

"We have separate rooms. Mine is along the corridor but the boiler is the other side of the wall and the pipes creak. I gave you the best room. You should be grateful."

"So, the pipes creak and you came in here to take advantage of an impressionable Syrian girl, innocent to the ways of the world?"

"Something like that, yes but you were asleep and I was a gentleman." He smiled and took a piece of cheese. "Eat. We have a long day."

Chapter 97

When Daley and Whetstone returned to the Team Room, news of DCI Kramer's visit had become common knowledge and the mood was sombre. Unless they made the breakthrough, they would lose the case. Monaghan, Taylor and Corby had sequestered the conference suite and were waiting. Their faces were as long as the night they had all spent trying to connect the pieces before SCD1 did.

Earlier, Allenby had restated the solid deadline of 9:00am on Monday. He had also asked for an update. Daley had suggested Whetstone would be more appropriate. Allenby had insisted he wanted it from Daley. Then he knew that the case was effectively back under his wing. He had won.

But it was a Pyrrhic victory. Over thirty bodies and they were still nowhere near understanding why. Daley had more or less stumbled on the dumpsite and there was the chance that, despite the previous hour, the relationship with Whetstone may have been irrevocable damaged. Not to mention the executioner's axe of Scotland Yard sweeping ever lower over their heads.

Shoulders were down and spirits even lower. Daley needed a performance worthy of an Oscar to bring these people together.

"Guys, it's been a rough week. We have not really covered ourselves with glory and, yes, I include myself in that, but I believe that somewhere in our vast pile of notes, in the facts swimming about in our heads, we have the answer. We just haven't joined all of the dots. Let's see if we can make that happen.

"As you know, DCI Kramer from Scotland Yard was here yesterday and Allenby has promised them the files on Monday at 9:00am sharp. Until then, let's keep this on a need to know basis. We don't want them swanning in at the eleventh hour and taking credit for our hard work."

"Didn't you deck Kramer at the Federation do?" It was Monaghan?

"That's the guy."

"Supercilious twat."

"Indeed. So, files on local servers and don't leave paperwork around. This is our case and we are going to solve it. OK. Rousing speech over. Deb?"

Whetstone steeled herself. "Dave, Chatham Woods Farm?"

Monaghan opened a folder. "According to my man in Companies House, the Farm is owned by Heligon Investments, a Holding Company. Its registered office is a private address out towards Elstree. In turn, Heligon Investments is owned by another holding company, Limewood Holdings, same address."

Taylor sat up. "Limewood Holdings is the organisation that Chronotech pays for the cadaver units they use."

"And what do we know about them?"

"Nothing beyond the invoices and remittances. Regular monthly payments into a UK bank account. Still waiting for the details of the account holders."

"What about supply of the units?"

"Nothing, ma'am. They are bulk invoices."

"If Limewood obtained the units legitimately, there would be some history of the transactions." Daley looked across at Whetstone. Financial forensics was not his bag but a movement of stock usually left a trail, especially if it concerned human corpses.

Taylor shrugged. "There was nothing but I am still looking. If they have hidden the details, I will find them."

Whetstone sat up. "When we spoke to Marion Edmonds, she suggested that the cadavers had to be particularly fresh for the procedure to work, which would tie in with someone, maybe Franks..." Whetstone cast a sly glance at Daley, "... maybe someone else, abducting and killing to order, maybe using Limewood as a front to make the transactions appear legitimate."

"And Limewood, Dave?" asked Daley. "Is that the top of the tree?"

"Yes, sir, and this is where it gets interesting." Dave grabbed a marker and paced over to a paper flip chart board.

"So, we have Limewood Holdings up here..." He drew a blob and started a hierarchical chart. "They own Heligon

Investments, which in turn owns Chatham Woods Farm. So, then I looked at Medway Klein and Chronotech. It turns out that they are also owned by Limewood Holdings."

"OK, ultimately, Limewood Holdings owns Chatham Woods Farm, Chronotech Biosciences and Medway Klein cosmetic clinic."

"Who owns Limewood Holdings? Can't be Franks, surely? It would take massive funding."

"So, Limewood Holdings is wholly owned by its two directors, Nick Snowdon and Caz Albin."

"OK, surprise me. They live out near Elstree.'

"Sir. In a house named *Limewood*."

Chapter 98

Paris.

Having breakfasted and dressed, Satya and Pietr headed out into a bright Paris morning. The sun was threatening to make an appearance as they descended the steps to the Metro at Mairie de Montreuil. Yet another train but this was a wonder, deep underground, the smells of electricity and rubber, the howl of the motors and the rhythmic tap of the tracks. Station names flashed by - Robespierre, Voltaire, Republique, Saint Denis - stirring in Satya the romance of Paris that she had read in books, or seen on television. After forty or so minutes, they left the carriage and began the ascent to the streets. As trains came and went below, she felt the inrush of the cool air against her face, dispelling the clamminess of the underground. Soon, full of anticipation, she could see the sky above the steps.

"You need to shut your eyes and trust me."

"I can trust a *kuffār* who sneaks into my room and watches me sleep?"

"I sat in the chair. It was dark." His tone was dismissive, impudent.

"I was practically naked under those sheets."

"I didn't look much as I tucked you back in, don't worry!" Pietr laughed loudly as she stared dumbfounded. "Anyway, I too am completely naked under these clothes!"

But still she closed her eyes and gave him her hand.

After a while stumbling across pavements, tripping up kerbs and steps, he pulled her to him.

"I wanted this to be your first sight of Paris. Open your eyes."

Then suddenly she was there. The breath was robbed from her body as she gazed, wonderstruck. Either side, the colonnades of the Palais de Chaillot towered above with their honour guard of gilded statues, arms beckoning her forwards. As she walked across the geometric tiles, the Hill of Chaillot gave way and the Trocadero gardens rose from below, stretching out across the river, through the Champs de Mars and down to L'école Militaire, misted and ethereal in the distance. But dominating her vision, legs akimbo, Le Tour Eiffel stood tall and proud, commanding the sky, touching the very edge of the low clouds.

She stood transfixed. She was actually here. So many images, so many stories distilled into a single moment. She could feel the tears welling in her eyes.

"I knew it would be like this, so I got you these." Pietr dug into his pocket and pulled out some tissues. "Women are far too emotional." She turned and glowered but she knew he was kidding.

"I also got you these." He handed her a small sketchbook, a box of pencils and a disposable camera. "You can add more pictures to your album. But with these you will actually be able to say 'I was there'."

"This is the best day of my life."

"So far." And he pressed the shutter and captured the smile which had eluded him for days, for which he had chased across Europe, which he had gladly abandoned himself to.

In an instant her arms, were around him and they were kissing. She didn't care about the itinerary, about the soldier, about Gregor Wolfe or the migrant beast. She cared about the moment. She didn't care about gun-running, the Makarov in her boot or human-trafficking. Not even Paris, freedom or happiness. Pietr was right. She cared about the moment. However long it was to last, at least she was here now.

She had sketched the view, sketched Pietr, consigned them to her book before he had whisked her away back into the Metro, to Charles de Gaulle – Étoile, to the Avenue des Champs-Élysées, the immense boulevard stretching down to the distant Ferris wheel on La Place de la Concorde, framed by the might of the Arc de Triomphe. Together they strolled hand in hand, like friends or lovers, taking in shops, drawing breath at the prices. They bought crepes from the vendors, and stood for pictures under the street signs.

And, as Pietr had promised, she saw the whole vista of Paris from the top of the Ferris wheel.

Chapter 99

Daley's energetic phone calls to the clinic, Chronotech and the numbers which Nick Snowdon had left on his phone had yielded nothing. In true Friday fashion, everyone, seemed to have *pissed off early*. The M1 was a car park and the A5 crawled Northwards like a wounded dog. It would be another hour before they reached *Limewood*. The house was deep in the countryside between Elstree and Borehamwood, an anonymous gateway, on a rural road. Not for the first time that week, Whetstone was musing that someone valued their privacy.

The drive opened out onto a gravelled forecourt alongside a modernistic angular house, a single storey letterbox of concrete and glass supported at one end by blocks and pillars and at the other by a precariously flimsy wall, as if it had all fallen from a child's toy box. It overshadowed a paved patio surrounded by planted beds of tall reeds and box hedges and a slate block inscribed with the name *Limewood*. At the time, it had probably been some architect's wet dream but now stood anachronistic against the natural beauty of the countryside. Except for a double garage and a few outbuildings, which Daley mused should have been called *under* buildings, there was an acre of open space on all sides of the house.

Two Mercedes sat in front of the garages; an estate and a convertible belonging to Nick Snowdon and Caz Albin respectively. Daley pulled up behind them, hampering any potential getaway, though he doubted that would happen. Looking up, the bustling grey clouds were reflected in the glass and Daley wondered if there were eyes watching them arrive.

Alighting, he knocked on the door and leaned on the bell, finally giving up and heading clockwise around the building as Whetstone travelled anticlockwise.

"No sign of life, gov. There's a broken pot in the back garden but other than that..."

"They're away for the weekend. Nick Snowdon said something about crossing to the Continent. They must have left already. I had no idea they were an item."

"No, but it makes sense. Limewood Holdings, Chronotech, Medway Klein. All interlinked."

"I thought I saw a movement in the house around the back. Could be burglars." Whetstone lied.

"Did you?" Daley played along.

"Not sure, sir. Could have been a trick of the light. Still, if the householders are away..."

Whetstone pulled a large granite fragment from the rockery.

"Hang on. You can't go breaking in."

"Me, sir, no sir. The window on this back door has been...broken." Behind her there was a dull thud and the clinking of glass on tile. "With both cars on the drive, I fear they may be in danger. Least we can do is check."

"Fair enough. Let's hope they're not in."

The house was dark and cold, immaculately tidy. No sign of life. This was becoming an annoying pattern too. Checking the rooms in turn, Whetstone returned from the hall and shook her head.

"Looks like we've missed them."

A light blinked on a panel. "I estimate fifteen minutes max before local plod responds to that silent alarm. Let's see what we can find before they do."

At the end of the hallway, looking over the forecourt and the drive beyond, there was an office. Daley rooted around amongst the paperwork, household bills, circulars and a few documents with clinic letterheads but could find nothing of interest. He found few receipts - groceries, diesel, some in French. The *Carrefour Cite* in central Calais and a Boulangerie and wine shop in a place called *Ardres*. There were Eurostar stubs and a few menu cards, again in French. Casting his eyes around the room, he struggled to find a flavour of the man. The walls bore certificates - a medical degree from Imperial College, several diplomas for surgical specialisms. There were vocational certificates and photographs of Snowdon at conventions, or seminars, forced smiles and handshakes. No family pictures. No kids with jaw wrenching grins and gappy teeth. The whole room screamed about what he did but said nothing about who he was.

"Suitcases are missing. They've left for the weekend already."

Whetstone was peering around the door.

"Look at this room Deb. What's the first thing that strikes you about it?"

"It's like the rest of the house, sir. Completely impersonal. No wedding pictures, no family pictures, nothing. It's like a show home. There's something else too."

Whetstone retreated back into the hallway, a small square lobby which led to each of the bedrooms.

"I think they slept apart. Look in here. Makeup, duvet, curtains. All feminine. Two bedside tables but one completely empty. Wardrobe. Women's clothes." She turned to the room opposite. "Clothes in the wardrobes, cufflinks, watches, shoes, all masculine. Each of these room has its own ensuite. They could live completely separate lives."

"Perhaps he snored?" He poked his head into the room. He could smell aftershave. Then his attention was captivated by a picture over the bedhead and everything started to fall into place.

Chapter 100

Lambourne Road

How easy was it anyway? To spirit away dozens of people in plain sight? If it were that easy, Monaghan would have spirited away half of Traffic by now. Especially the car that habitually sat at the end of his road. People are missed. They leave a hollow in the universe which, sooner or later, someone notices. And a regular supply of cadavers? With no idea how one would go about that, Monaghan called a contact at Imperial College and asked a few hypothetical questions.

For the price of a pint, he was told about the Human Tissue Act 2004, which governed the distribution and use of medical cadavers. On average 600 whole people were available for tissue research each year under the Act. At the rate Medway Klein seemed to get through them, that was none at all. Of course, his contact had quipped, one could always obtain them outside of the Act but someone might notice. Monaghan had allowed the man a moment to compose himself. Although he obviously didn't get out much, he was probably incredibly near the mark.

Again hypothetically, he had asked about neural degeneration. His contact told him that neural degeneration after death is swift, chemical changes within the brain and the nerves would affect neural transmission and render them useless within hours. In any case, it was rare for the complete cadaver to be used; usually it was tissue samples, specific organs.

Then he asked how one would become a licensed handler of human tissue. The Human Tissue Authority apparently kept a register. The contact offered to email the logon details. The bribe rose to a bottle of Irish, *none of the cheap stuff*, and reluctantly Monaghan had agreed.

Now as he typed in the names, Heligon, Chronotech, Medway Klein, Limewood, he had a fair idea what he would find, or rather what he wouldn't.

Chapter 101

2002

Once done, a thing cannot be undone.

Once my father had violated me, it could never be the same. As my mother ignored me she had become complicit. As they had died, our future had been pre-ordained. As we explored the bodies on the bed, organs and muscles, sinews and nerves, our futures changed yet again.

By now, the pattern had become routine. After Janey and Doug, there was Liz and Chris, Helen and Paul, Justin and Lawrence and… The list has grown so long I cannot remember them all. Each time, we enjoyed the seduction, enjoyed the kill and the defilement. Then we set about dismantling every part of their existence until we became them and ultimately everything they were became ours. Which in itself created problems.

By the turn of the millennium we had become, what could officially be described as, wealthy. Successive houses sold for cash, successive accounts raided and made our own, furniture, assets, all had conspired to swell our bank account beyond that which we needed to survive. Successive bodies consigned to the shed and the darkness below the hatch.

Kath and Jo Robshaw had been a couple for ten years, eschewing civil partnership for the hope of a true same-sex marriage. As it turned our they would never be legally joined, which would be fortunate for us, as Lina could become Kath. I had neither the demeanour nor the physiology to become Jo. From the moment that we met them, that they took us back for dinner, we knew that the house needed to be ours. Isolated and secluded, of all the houses we had invaded and occupied, taken and sold, this was the one which we wanted for our own. Where we could be private and alone away from the world.

Limewood.

But for us, life had also moved on. After Medical college, my skills, both legitimate and otherwise, gave me greater scope when a trespasser strayed too near the Farm. Lina's prowess as she progressed through her Business degree strengthened our hand and we looked towards putting our skills to good use, to add some legitimacy to our personal endeavours. We invested our money, assumed our new personas, found new outlets for our talents, nurtured our alter-egos.

One weekend, Kath and Jo took us to their home in France, to Ardres, where we holidayed in hedonistic abandon, where Lina and I thought of our plan. An endless supply of fun.

So, Lina and I began to befriend, to inveigle and seduce until each one was turned against the other. And each began their slow descent into the shed.

Chapter 102

Elstree

The local plod were nice guys, even shaking Daley's hand after he confirmed he was indeed the same DI Daley who had been struck by a locomotive. At first, they were sceptical about the whole break-in ruse, curious about why the pair had travelled so far off their patch. Still, they had silenced the alarm and admired the gardens as Daley and Whetstone concluded their fruitless search of the property. Then they had reported *Limewood* as a suspicious break-in and headed back to their car.

The Friday afternoon traffic was still a bitch, everybody leaving early and ultimately being defeated by their own cleverness. Daley was anxious to avoid being late for his rendezvous with Theresa Somerville and measured each mile in painfully slow seconds. As yet another queue slowed at yet another roundabout, Daley's phone rang and Monaghan's voice came over the Bluetooth.

"Sir. It's highly unlikely that those cadavers are legit. Varsa thought that there was an HTU license which expired in May 2011 but there is no record of one ever being issued to any of the companies we know, nor any or the individuals. I have a call out to the HTA direct but being Friday..."

"Whatever has been going on at the clinic was happening long before Varsa arrived."

But what was actually going on? Was this an evil killer satisfying a need for blood, whilst Chronotech and Medway Klein unaware? Or was death just a consequence? A cold hard financial transaction, syphoning hundreds of thousands into the mysterious Limewood account?

Was this about money or about death and mutilation?

"If the cadavers aren't legitimate, then where are they coming from?" Whetstone interjected. "There are nowhere near enough abductees to fill those water tanks."

"According to the blood samples," continued Monaghan, "the greater proportion so far, from the van, the preliminary findings from the water tank, these came back distinctly Middle Eastern. The *Zone 6* Abductees may have been killed because they found Chatham Woods and started nosing around."

"If this has been going on for years, why has nobody noticed before?"

A clinic operating illegally, perhaps unknowingly, under the radar of the Human Tissue Authority for years. Why had nobody, apart from Varsa, noticed? Had everyone assumed a license was in place? No-one outside the clinic would know to question. When anyone came too close, the problem was removed.

Daley edged the Audi into the traffic jostling for position on the roundabout before seizing the opportunity to turn right onto the comparative emptiness of the London Road. Time was getting tight. Would he be able to get back to Lambourne Road, then back to Alperton to change and out again to Harrow in time to meet Terri?

Distinctly Asian? Was that important? Was this a matter of ethnicity, or had someone tapped into a ready supply of humans that wouldn't be missed? A place where faces were anonymous, a river, transient and endless. If someone goes missing they are simply replaced by 3 or 4 more.

"Dave. Put in a call to British Transport Police and the Dover Harbour Board. See if they can trace the van, RN08 DVB leaving the UK sometime Thursday. More importantly put out an all-ports. It will be returning later today or tomorrow morning. We need to pick it up as soon as it enters the country."

Daley had never seen the transit camps of Northern France. He could only imagine the plight of refugees, the terrors they were fleeing, risking everything for the promise of a better life.

"What about the clinic?"

"No, Deb. My guess is that nothing is going to happen there until the van returns. We need the element of surprise. We need to wait until that van gets back."

Chapter 103

La Basilique du Sacré Cœur de Montmartre, Paris.

She could have stayed on the steps forever.

Behind Satya, the majesty of the marbled Basilica held court over the gradually thinning groups of tourists, tired office workers returning home and excited gaggles of students just starting out. At her side, Pietr sat, his arm intertwined with hers, flicking through her photo album. The warmth of the sun had deserted the bright November day and she was beginning to feel the chill of evening.

She didn't want it to end.

Enchanted by the city, captivated by Pietr, his smile, she thought back to the Trocadero, Le Tour Eiffel, to the distant spike of Montparnasse against the flatness of the horizon.

But Hervelinghen was always there.

"One day we will visit these places."

She hugged him closer. "We can take tea at the Ritz."

"We will stand by Nelsons Column and the gates of Buckingham Palace. We can creep up behind the sentries and try to make them laugh, or knock off their bearskins."

As he talked of a future, she wondered if that could ever be. Tomorrow, she would be on a ferry bound for new, very different adventures. He would turn back towards Sofia and finally, their time together would be over.

Below them, the sky had turned crimson and the darkening city had come alive with twinkling amber stars.

"We must go now." Pietr untangled his arm from hers and stood, stretching the fatigue from his cold legs. Sombrely, she closed the small box on her pens and placed them with her books into the bag that Maria had given her.

They travelled in silence to Gare de L'Est, to a red Citroen. She sat in the back, leaning on Pietr as the car drove into the night, street lamps pulsing past the window and Paris becoming smaller and smaller behind them.

Chapter 104

Andros Bar & Grill, Harrow

It had been aeons since Scott Daley had been in a restaurant, let alone with the top button of his shirt fastened. The tie was stifling him and totally incongruous, given what the other diners were wearing. Following the earlier debacle over the blue suit, he had consigned it to the supermarket dry cleaners, along with the brown one which had also drawn Somerville's criticism. The grey one had been sponged off and would have to do. The balance of his wardrobe was sadly scant. Having discounted any item which would have opened him up to further ridicule, he had settled on a pair of brown corduroys and an ecru shirt with a maroon tie. He looked like a G.I. on furlough. Still, brown implied honesty, a down-to-earth quality, friendly, approachable, genuine and sincere, or so Google said.

Even at thirty-eight, Daley felt himself a dinosaur compared to the other clientele who seemed mostly pre-pubescent. The music was five notches too loud and sounded like someone hitting a sewer pipe with a cat. Every surface was mirrored, as if to emphasise what a twat he looked.

It was all so casual these days. He and Lynne had eaten out but that had stopped with the divorce, or rather six months before when they even stopped eating in together. Nowadays, the nearest he got was a rowdy curry night with some of the misfits at Lambourne Road but, as alcohol featured more than food, that could hardly be considered eating out. Staring into his lukewarm glass of tonic water, Daley tried to recall his last pukka date with a woman, but couldn't.

Obviously, in common with all ageing men he deluded himself that he was down with the kids, that a smile from a young blonde PC was tantamount to an animal longing for his sexual experience rather than shallow sympathy for a harmless avuncular. Deep down though, he knew he hadn't a hope and he hadn't a clue. Once, there had been a Victim Liaison officer he had taken a shine to and he had mustered the courage to ask her out. She had let him down gently, bless her, remarking only obliquely that the age difference was enough for him to be her father, mathematically at least.

And there was the problem. In his head, Daley was twenty years old and it was still 1994. Stuck in a limbo of Oasis and Blur, of Blairites and Sunday Trading, of exhortations that *things could only get better*, but for him they had stayed the same. Immersed in the Force, consumed whole and insulated from the world. Even meeting Lynne had been a fluke. She had picked up his wallet on a tube train in Shepherds Bush and he had returned the favour by picking her up. Paradoxically, he had put her down when he could stand no more of her putting him down.

The traffic through Stanmore, Harrow and Wembley had been horrendous. Much to the amusement of Whetstone, he had delayed the restaurant booking, then called Terri Somerville asking her not to rush. Predictably, the divine Law of Sod had intervened to part the sea of cars and now he was half an hour early. He checked his watch and sighed. There was little chance of it moving since he last checked it a moment ago.

After an anxious ten minutes, finally his guest arrived. Theresa Somerville was wearing the same chocolate brown coat he remembered from Chatham Woods on Wednesday but now her hair was down, she was made-up and wore a skirt. Her face beamed a broad smile which wrinkled her nose. It occurred to Daley that until she had walked through the door, he had been unable to recall what she looked like.

"Good to see you again, Inspector." Her voice had that same lyrical quality that he remembered, as if announcing the next free sales counter, or an arrival at Glasgow Queen Street.

"Scott, please. We are off duty, I hope."

"In my experience, Scott, I am never off duty, especially according to my D/Supt. Call me Terri."

In one of those cripplingly embarrassing moments where the mouth derails the brain, Daley found his saying: "Terri Scott, that's really quite funny when you think about it. Terri...Scott?" Folding up inside, Daley cursed himself. What an opening line. He wanted to curl into a ball and roll under the table.

Somerville glared. "I can see this is going to be a long evening." But she still gave him a sympathetic smile. "I see you decided against the blue suit?"

"I decided that ambivalence was not my colour after all."

"We should be thankful for small mercies, eh? Remind me to come along to Oxfam with you when you choose a new one." Somerville raised her eyebrows and Daley felt himself flush. "Oh, and please lose the tie. You don't need to impress me by tying a tiny noose around your neck."

Daley frowned, loosened the tie and unfastened a top button. He couldn't help feeling she had his measure already.

They were shown to their seats, a small table near a window which overlooked Harrow High Street. Soon they had drinks and had sent the waiter off with their orders.

"So, to what do I owe this pleasure, Inspector, er, Scott?"

"Does there have to be a reason?"

"In my experience, yes." As she sat opposite resting her elbows on the table, the flame from the tea-light sparkled in her eyes, captivating Daley. "Let me guess. Either you've found some more bodies or you've had another flash of inspiration or Tom Phillips has been found still running round the woods having lost his way. Or maybe my virtue is under threat?"

Daley did not want to talk about work. So much was circling about his mind, some would invariably come tumbling out. This meal was set to cost him a small fortune. He needed to get shop-talk out of the way so he could attempt to enjoy the rest of the evening.

"No more bodies. I think well over thirty is enough. And if Tom Phillips is still running, none of our coppers have the stamina to keep up with him."

"So, you were simply enchanted by my charismatic charm and couldn't live a moment more without me? I will check the lock on my chastity belt."

"Harsh, very harsh. Would that be so bad? Must happen from time to time." Perhaps she was a better detective than he gave her credit.

"Hey, Inspector, don't push it. I haven't eaten since lunch. I am very particular to whom I show my charismatic charm."

"Charismatic charm aside, I have been thinking about *Zone 6* and Chatham Woods Farm. Apart from their addresses, all within a few miles of each other, they have different backgrounds, different routes home, no reason to effect their own disappearance."

Somerville nodded. "Truly, it's the tabloids that linked them, and then only because they went missing recently. I looked back over the last twenty years and I was surprised to find around forty people within a twenty mile radius of the farm have gone missing."

"Is that a lot? Two a year? Missing Persons is not my speciality."

"For a relatively small area, around twenty square miles, it's above average. Date-wise, there were more earlier than more recently. It seemed to have eased off until earlier last year."

Daley's brow furrowed. Since Franks had joined.

"Is that significant, Scott?"

"OK, Terri. I suspect that starters will arrive in..." He tilted his wrist, "...ten minutes. Then we stop discussing work. Until then... We have a cosmetic clinic and a technology company developing a biomedical device. Both are owned by the same two people and it seems that this is a cover for syphoning off large amounts of investors' cash. OK so far?" She nodded.

"Which is brilliant, except that the research requires human tissue trials and there is a finite legitimate resource of cadavers, and a licence must be obtained."

"So, they bump off dog walkers and courting couples in the park? Seriously?" There was a look of incredulity on her face.

"Well over thirty bodies, forty people gone missing and never returned? It's an avenue?"

"Yes, but that degree of crapping on one's own doorstep. Someone is going to smell it sooner or later."

"Well, my *Hand in the Van* victim smelt something. Maybe others like her from the clinic did too? Maybe Josh Turner smelt something when he saw the van in the car park at the nature reserve?"

Somerville smiled. "Reminds me of when I was young and we played in Holyrood Park. There was this old trampy woman. She used to sit for hours on a bench by St. Margaret's loch, staring at the water, with some stale crumbs between her feet. Sooner or later, a brave pigeon would venture in too close. Then he was away into a sack she carried. The first time I saw it I couldn't believe my eyes. Onc moment the little bugger was pecking crumbs, then in a swift movement, she had grabbed him, wrung his wee neck and stuffed him in the sack, barely a feather shed. When she had a sackful she would away, only to return the next day."

Daley was once more captivated by her eyes, by the lilt of her voice, falling into dialect as one does when returning home, to a place one felt comfortable. "For sack, read van. It makes a degree of sense."

"I just get the impression that the research projects at the clinic are somehow immaterial, a front. As far as everyone involved is aware, they have legitimate cadavers and are just doing a job."

"Evidence?"

Daley nodded. "One of my DCs has discovered anomalies in Medway Klein's figures. The *Zone 6* victims may not be the only ones that have going missing. Maybe you're just about to mop up many more missing persons than you imagined."

Daley glanced up as a small woman carrying a tray strode through the tables, blonde ponytail flicking left and right. He tried desperately to remember what he ordered, though he had no idea what half of the courses were. He hoped that Somerville would recognise her meal first.

"Look, I have loads of theories and not a lot else. Would you be up for helping me go through it all tomorrow? Maybe we could grab some lunch?"

"Whoa! Slow down, cowboy! Let's see how this evening goes first, shall we, eh, Scott?"

Her smile, her body language, told him it was already going fine.

Chapter 105

Hervelinghen

This was not how it was supposed to be.

The tiny gîte was tucked away behind a caravan park, anonymous, invisible, cold. When they had arrived, it had reminded Satya of the ramshackle cottage on the banks of the Sea of Marmara. She had wondered if there was a bookcase, a secret room.

As she stood taking in the bland walls, blood red floor tiles and tourist kitsch, she wondered how it was supposed to be. What had she been expecting after nights in a train seat, cold platforms, uncomfortable chairs in fast food restaurants?

She expected it to be like Paris. Carefree and lazy but instead it was cold, hard and very real. A staging post in her travels. The last in Europe. The last where she could be with Pietr.

Though it had been less that thirty-six hours since he had grabbed her shoulder on a concourse in Strasbourg, it felt like thirty-six years. They had become closer in that short time than she had even been with another boy, even those her father had known nothing about. But did that matter? There would be others. She had had admirers in the past, albeit ones too frightened of her parents to venture too close. There would be plenty more in England. She was a good catch, wasn't she?

But Pietr was special. He had become special. Until tomorrow when he would once more be a memory. Whether she liked it or not that was what Allah had ordained for her. How could a God be so hateful, so spiteful?

Closing the door behind him, Pietr crossed to the mantelpiece and searched briefly for car keys.

"When you wake in the morning, I will be gone. It has to be like that. There is a car out back and I will leave for Sofia early. You must go back up the lane to the church and stand under the cross. Now we must get some rest."

She walked the five metres to the bedroom as if it were to the gallows. Pietr locked the front door and plumped cushions on the couch.

The bedroom was small and cold, plain walls, beige carpet, a rag work counterpane the only colour. Outside was deathly quiet and she longed for the noise of Paris, the neglected safe-house of Montreuil, it's flaking plaster and must. She longed for another day with Pietr.

Settling under the counterpane, all she could think of was him. Her mind traced the route from the couch to the corridor, from the corridor to her door and from the door to her bed. She willed him to come, to lie with her and hold her and not be a gentleman. She willed him to take her in a frenzy, to hurt her and defile her. To leave her hating him. To make the parting that much easier.

Her mind traced the route from the bed to the floor, across to the door and down the corridor to the couch. Should she go to him? She yearned to be with him, wherever that might end. Would he think less of her if she made the first move? She thought of the Quran, on the hundred lashes it ordained for fornication and she wondered whether fornication was so bad when set against theft and murder.

Above her the ceiling gave way to the roof and the roof gave way to the clouds and the clouds gave way to the heavens. And Allah was conspicuous by His silence.

Quietly she pulled back the counterpane and crept to her door. Along the corridor the couch was empty. He was framed in the doorway smoking. He turned as she put her arms around him.

"Stay with me tonight," she whispered.

"Is that what you want?"

"At this moment, yes. It is what I want."

Pietr took her hand and led her to the bedroom. They kissed, deeply, passionately, for a long moment before she climbed into the bed and he climbed in beside her. She felt his arms around her, a cradle, a cocoon and it felt like the arms of her mother or father keeping her safe from the nightmares and the demons. He leaned his head into the back of her neck.

"Satya. You told me of Sofia Station. When you were lost and called on Allah yet it was your father who answered you. How he told you to treat the journey as a series of small trips. Each trip is an adventure. You have had many adventures this week and you will have many more. Me, Paris, the past twenty-four hours. Tonight, I have you and you have me. This is just one adventure. Don't look back on it with regret, look back with the happiness you had when you saw Paris for the first time."

She turned and folded herself in the warmth of his body, as sleep overtook her thoughts.

This was not how it was supposed to be but Satya was happy in the moment.

Chapter 106

Andros Bar & Grill, Harrow

Daley waited for the PIN number prompt. Even the card machine was having trouble processing such a colossal amount for such meagre, delicate plates of food. At one point, he had searched beneath an asparagus spear for fear the rest of the meal was hiding. Mid-month was never a great time to spend money. There would have to be some financial sleight of hand before pay day but he figured it had been worth it.

When the food had arrived, they had pushed away all thoughts of work and fallen into easy conversation. Inevitably, talk had turned to relationships, or their lack. Somerville too had been married. An early, ill-thought out mistake after university, hasty, over almost before it began. That had been a long while ago. Since then, much as with Daley, loneliness and career had been uncomfortable bedfellows.

The chap behind the counter handed Daley the receipt stating that he hoped they had enjoyed their meals.

"Yes. It was great, thanks. Once I had found it on the plate." Daley smiled sardonically. "The lobster was actually really good."

As Daley caught sight of Somerville returning from the washroom, the man went on. "They are cooked to order. We have a little farm out back so chef can keep them fresh until they are ordered."

Daley nodded and held out Somerville's coat. The night had turned cold.

"Where are you parked?"

"Oh, on my drive. I live three streets away." Linking arms, she turned him around and the pair headed North and away from the Friday night bustle of the small town.

"Terri. May I ask you a question?"

"Ooh, that sounds ominous, Scott."

"Could you see yourself doing anything else. Aside from policing?" The situation with Allenby had been praying on his mind. Should he jump before he was pushed.

"I have a degree in Economics. Once, I wanted to be an actuary, you know, births, deaths, marriages, diseases, epidemics, incidence of, likelihood of, but by the time I had finished at Southampton, I had developed an allergy to spreadsheets. Brought me out in hives. You?"

"No, nothing. My father was a policeman and his before him. I often wonder how I would have gotten on if I had taken up a different career."

"Milkman? Scott Daley and your Daley pinta? A vicar? Give us this day our Daley bread?"

Daley turned to her and frowned, desperately trying to think of a rejoinder. "Ah, Slimming instructor, Terri-lean? Or proprietor of the ghost train in the fair, Terri-Fying? Rubbish matador, Terri-bull?"

"Laugh a minute, Scott Daley. This is me."

Daley looked up at a small town-house. Neat, well presented, compact and self-contained. The epitome of Theresa Somerville.

"I've had a great night, Scott. Despite everything, my misgivings were unfounded." She winked mischievously. "I shall tell the guys at the station they were wrong about you."

"Uh?"

"Joke. Just a joke. Seriously. It's been great."

"We could do it again, sometime?" The words had slipped out even before he had realised and he was glad. One thing tonight had shown him was that he put too much time into thinking and not enough into doing.

"I would like that." She stretched up and pecked him on the cheek, then their mouths met and he was holding her like the last lifebelt on a sinking ship and he felt her arms holding him. Tacit recognition of the years of nothing and an island of hope in a stormy sea.

After what seemed like forever, she was looking up into his eyes. "Do you want to come in for coffee?"

Imbued with subtext, the question hung heavy in the night air, any response capable of derailing a perfect evening. There were butterflies in his stomach. Insane! He was an adult yet still he writhed in a senseless juvenile turmoil. Feelings were surfacing he had allowed to lie dormant, even suppressed for so long, he was unsure how to behave. With so many other things going on in his head, should he even contemplate this right now? He felt like he was on a precipice, peering over the edge at the wreck of his marriage, the years of pain and arguments as sense and reason slowly lost their grip on his shirt.

Then there was sex. These days coffee meant sex, right? Or did it? He was out of touch with social mores and etiquette, not to mention out of practice. He had enough performance anxiety over his job, his life, without introducing further complications.

We have a little farm out back so chef can keep them fresh until they are ordered. Why did that resonate?

"You know what? Yes I would. I would love a coffee. I've really enjoyed tonight myself and, I know it sounds crass, but I don't want it to end. Unfortunately, I have a busy day tomorrow finding this psychopath before Ray Kramer takes over the case."

"Ray Kramer of SCD1? Hang on, didn't you and he have a scuffle at the Federation dinner? Slimy sod."

"Might have done."

"Well, off with you then."

He caught a brief flash of disappointment in her eyes and he understood. They kissed once more and it disappeared. Then he added: "Tomorrow evening? 7:00pm? I'll pick you up?"

"I would like that very much, Scott Daley." And she kissed him again.

As Somerville turned up the path, he felt as though she was dragging his heart with her. He hoped she would turn and persuade him he needed coffee, that his heart would rule his head, that he would change his mind.

As she opened the door, she turned and smiled.

"It really has been great, Scott. Great Scott. Now that really is funny!"

For the first time that evening, it occurred to Daley that his head was not hurting. He had been without painkillers for two days. Maybe things were looking up?

Her door closed leaving the chill damp air to descend around him. He watched the hall light shine yellow through the pane in the door. Then he turned back towards the town centre.

Was this the change? Was this the start of the rehabilitation he had craved since the divorce? As his shoes lightly measured the steps back to his car, it occurred to him that he really didn't care. This was the moment and he was happy in it. Even if the price was extortionate, the company was good and the lobster was sublime.

We have a little farm out back so chef can keep them fresh until they are ordered.

With the pendulum beat of his footfalls on the pavement, Daley's brain echoed the words of the waiter and he was disquieted. Why were those words so important? Why specifically would it matter? But somewhere in the morass of facts and conjecture, it did.

Chapter 107

Rue de l'Église, Hervelinghen, 6:00am, Saturday

Satya pulled her greatcoat about her and stamped her feet on the brick path, trying to warm her legs. Behind, a Christian cross towered above her, scant protection from the freezing morning. Aside from a few hardy crows, the place was still and the air was damp and cold. She spread her fingers in her pockets searching for change. The notes had long since gone and now she had only four euros and some unidentifiable small copper coins. What did it matter? The shop in the campsite opposite had long since closed for winter.

Gregor Wolfe's watch said 07:45. She prayed the car would arrive promptly.

Last night they had shared a bed and they had shared each other. She had abandoned herself to him and to the moment in the full knowledge that it would be their last together. This morning, she had woken to an empty bed and the smell of Pietr's cologne on the pillow. Now she too was empty, retreating once more inside the migrant beast of which she thought she had rid herself.

And already she missed him.

Still, she had made the rendezvous. To her right the fingers of a signpost pointed out her route to Calais. One step nearer to England. One step nearer to the end of this journey. A new life without fear, without hunger and without the beast.

But for now, the beast would be her guardian. Cunning and ruthless, a dispatcher of men. She would sit, safe inside until this ordeal of death and fear and love was over.

To her left, she heard the sound of an engine and froze momentarily as a small corrugated truck carrying milk passed without slowing. Her eyes tracked the flatbed as it slowly sidled along *La Rue Principal* and disappeared beyond the cawing of the crows and the feint tap of brittle branches.

Then her eyes alighted on the tall signpost, white paint and peeling, and there she saw the fresher wood of a rough-hewn mark. An A with a vertical line.

Alaam!

Her finger traced the shape of the letter, imagined an hour like this two weeks earlier when a man, older than her yet with the same eyes, had waited for the same white van. Just a few kilometres and she would see his face again.

But the joy in her heart was bittersweet, torn between the yearning for Alaam and the clawing loss she felt for Pietr. In life, there were debits and credits, checks and balances.

Chapter 108

Alperton, North West London

Unable to sleep, on a high from his evening with Terri, Daley had made himself some coffee, strong and earthy. An extra spoon in the filter so that now he was awake, he would remain so, despite tossing and turning half the night.

Had he made the right decision? Recalling the dismay in Terri's eyes, the mental turmoil he had suffered for the remainder of the night, he doubted it. Maybe that one moment of reluctance, fear of flying, would doom the fledgling romance before it even began?

Upstairs, the alarm caterwauled. 6:00am. On a normal Saturday, he would assault the button with such venom that his hand would still be stinging as he dragged it back under the covers but today, it could howl.

We have a little farm out back so chef can keep them fresh until they are ordered.

Then he saw Smith's face, a sudden panic in the interview when they had asked about the farm. There had been terror in his eyes, a secret discovered, a confidence betrayed. As Daley stared out at the benign streets, dark windows and sleeping automobiles, the last piece of the jigsaw tumbled into place. Hardly able to believe it himself, he wondered if something so grotesque could really be happening below the radar. And now he knew the deadly confidence that Edmonds and Smith, and maybe even Franks, had held, he felt exposed, as if a million eyes were searching his soul. What sort of twisted individual could carry out such an atrocity and why would so many allow it to happen?

He dialled Whetstone's number. It was 06:15am. There would be words but he had to cut through all that. A new train was bearing down on them all.

"Deb, it's Daley. We need to get to Medway Hall."

"Do you realise what time it is, sir? Don't you ever sleep?" Whetstone's voice was barely coherent.

"Yes, sorry. Can't be helped. You have to meet me at Medway Hall as soon as you can."

"Can't it wait until later?"

"Not this time. I don't know how long we have but there might just be a chance of preventing another murder."

"This better be bloody good. Dragging me away from my beauty sleep on another of your whims. Are you going to tell me what's so damn important?"

"Let me put it this way, if I am wrong you can lie in all weekend and report back as DI on Monday because Allenby will kick my arse from here to sunset."

Whetstone let the silence hang, waiting for Daley to fill it. The time for rhetoric was past.

"Ok. So, the farm, Deb."

"What about it?"

"You remember the story behind Chatham Woods Farm? City Broker and his family disappear? The Blanchards?"

"Yes, but I didn't see any relevance. It looks like a convenient dumpsite for our killer."

"That's what's been puzzling me. Maybe we have been looking at it the wrong way round? We have been so busy chasing a killer, chasing a kidnapper, that we missed the biggest puzzle. Why was Chatham Woods Farm allowed to rot?

"Remember the interview with Smith. I asked him about the farm? A straightforward enough question, as he was found there. It was as if I had murdered his dog. I clarified I was talking about Chatham Woods and suddenly he was back to his bolshie self. Like a switch flipped."

"And? Maybe he knew we had found the dumpsite and he was going to get the grief as soon as we opened the shed."

"Yeah but why hide there? There must be a thousand better places to hide."

"What are you saying?"

"He meant a different farm, Deb. You remember the prints on the walls of Nick Snowdon and Caz Albin's offices? And the one over Nick Snowdon's bed?"

"A windmill, Holland? Impressionist paintings. Nice. What of them?"

"I saw the same print on Wednesday. On the wall of one of the bedrooms in the farmhouse at Chatham Woods."

"Slim connection. Must be thousands of those prints, millions."

Daley still considered it a coincidence. "I dug out the files on Chatham Woods. What happened there. Daniel Blanchard and his wife Helena. Second generation French. Their two children, Dominic and Lina. The whole family disappeared. No traces were ever found. What if they are not dead? Dominic and Carolina - Nick and Caz?"

This was a stratospheric leap for Whetstone. Her world still revolved around Steven Franks, Connor Smith, around kidnappings and murders, of a squalid garage and a derelict, forgotten dumpsite.

"And Smith? He's not involved? He was at the farm keeping an eye on them?"

"Best guess."

"But what does that have to do with the clinic, with the *Zone 6* Abductees?"

"That's where you're going to have to trust me Deb."

Chapter 109

Rue de l'Église, Hervelinghen, 8:00am, Saturday

Tracing the grooves gouged into the post, Satya closed her eyes and pictured Alaam at the kitchen table, his head in his books, sighing at the weight of his studies. She imagined him strutting about the small shop, rearranging the shelves while his uncle stood hands on hips, bemused at this new broom sweeping clean.

How would it be when she knocked on that door?

Cousin Fatima worked in the shop but she only wanted a husband and children. For her, faith was paramount, duty to family above all. She wore the burkha and hijab dutifully and with pride. Cousin Yara was a freer spirit, capricious, a worry to her parents, yet still they were proud. Having graduated, she had a job, her own flat and many disappointed admirers. Yara had an ability to sift the old ways, the old traditions. To respect the philosophy of her faith without being constrained by it. Satya admired Yara and had always modelled herself on her.

Fatima and Yara had been born in England. They could never comprehend the enormity of the scars she bore nor would she enlighten them. She still rode the back of the migrant beast, she still looked into the glassy eyes of Gregor Wolfe.

Behind her Satya heard the bee-buzz of another distant engine from the *Rue de l'Église* to the South. She watched the white van draw up next to the squat red hydrant along the churchyard wall.

Inside, a small knot of doubt began to form. Since Aleppo she had been borne along on a swell, trusting to the plan, trusting to Allah. She had stolen, killed, loved and lost, all in the space of a week. As the van's engines died and the knot tightened, she wondered whether life truly lay at the end of this journey, or somewhere on its route. She picked up her bag and ran her fingers over Alaam's mark one last time, imprinting the texture on her fingers. Once more Satya Meheb trusted to the protection of the migrant beast.

A man and a woman stepped out of the van. They were both tall and slim, pale, expressionless. Satya stood and stared, colder than the hoar frosted graveyard beyond the wall.

Briefly the man studied her. His face apathetic, featureless. "I am Franks, Steven Franks. This is Jill."

"Show me the tattoo," barked the woman.

Satya rolled up her sleeve, past Gregor Wolfe's watch. The woman grabbed the wrist, her nails digging into the flesh and she twisted the arm, scanned the rough drawing, edged red and still sore. She nodded to the man. The man nodded back.

The woman dragged her to the rear of the van and opened the doors. A yawning, empty load space made Satya panic, voices in her head screaming for her not to get in but the beast felt Gregor Wolfe's knife and the Makarov.

"This is where you ride. Remember, any trouble, we will kill you. If you try to run, we will find you and kill you." The woman yanked at Satya's arm and she felt her elbow twist, a shard of pain.

"Wait. What is that?" The man grabbed hold of Satya's coat which had fallen open revealing the knife in her belt. The man seized the handle, pulling it free and examining the keen blade.

"What are you, a fool? They have metal detectors at the border. Do you think you would get through carrying this? Do you want to spend six months in detention because of *this*?" The man raised an arm and hurled Gregor Wolfe's knife over into the graveyard.

She recalled the tar pushing her down into the dark cabin, Gregor Wolfe holding her in the shadowed doorway. This was all wrong. But then when had it ever been right? She had trusted the sailors on the boat, Vasil and Pietr, but their trust was measured in dollars. Could she ever really feel safe? The Makarov pressed against her calf. It would stay there for now but she would need to lose it before the metal detectors.

"Look, girl," The man stared directly at Satya for a brief moment, eyes hard and emotionless. "We were promised three and were provided just one. The amount we paid for you, you should have gold-plated tickets."

Paid?

As the hand pushed, she tumbled onto the hard plywood

floor and her world turned black as the doors closed. In her ears, her heart pounded. Already the air in the van was warm and stifling and she fell against the wall as it drew off onto the road. With no sense of direction, she became disorientated, suddenly lost. It was the feeling she had experienced in the fields at the Turkish border, the rifle trained on her back, on the banks of the Sea of Marmara, sensing the bodies hiding in the dunes. A sudden feeling that everything she knew meant nothing. The amount he had paid for her? Was not the fare settled? Then why would this man need to pay?

The Makarov. Metal Detectors.

In front, the engine of the van hummed laconically, devouring kilometres of empty tarmac. The rear doors rattled and squeaked and her vision saw only grey.

Feeling her way around the empty space, she found the edge of piece of plastic trim. Clawing behind, popping the clips, she drew it back and felt a small crevice, between the outer skin of the van and the frame. If they found the Makarov on her, she would be arrested. If they found it in the van, she might argue she had no knowledge and still be arrested. She might as well be hung for a sheep as a lamb. Wrapping the Makarov in her scarf and dropping it into the space, she pushed back the clips and smoothed the trim with the palm of her hands. It was dark. She had to hope she had done enough. She had to hope they had not heard.

Chapter 110

Medway Hall, Northwick Park

Parking in the supermarket, it took a quarter of an hour to reach the clinic gates by road. Even with her coat and a thick jumper, Whetstone was feeling the chill as Daley forged ahead around the streets. They need to avoid the car park. There may be automatic floodlights and footprints would linger in the damp grass of the Hall lawn. The clinic car park was deserted except for a few small cars, cold and wet. Behind blinds, a few bulbs burned, night lights on slumbering wards. Ahead, the archway into the courtyard of Medway Hall, was still and quiet.

The Forensic tent stood outside the garages and each door was sealed with tape. Their visits were now common knowledge, although the grim discoveries behind the doors had been kept quiet. A single squad car had been stationed in the courtyard to keep an eye on things. Daley rapped on the window and once the dozing copper had recovered his wits, asked him to drive away, just do it, he would square it with the duty sergeant. He needed to make it look like police had moved on. Together, they set about removing the tent and the tape and bundling it all into the lean-to. Soon, apart from the presence of two detectives, huddled in the shadows, the yard was empty and quiet.

"So, come on, sir. Exactly what are we doing here."

"Waiting for Nick Snowdon and Caz Albin to turn up."

"Couldn't we just come back later?"

"No, we need to be here when that van returns."

"Franks' van?"

Daley wheeled round and glowered at Whetstone. "No, not Franks' van. We have that. This is the van... Oh, OK."

Whetstone was smirking. Daley puffed. His sense of humour was still under the duvet.

Behind them, a faint creak and a crack cut the night. A door slamming. The pair wheeled around, trying to fix the direction in the gloom of dawn. Medway Hall stood silhouetted against the grey sky, monstrous and foreboding, gathering its coat tails, guarding its secrets.

"The garden?"

Whetstone followed Daley around the perimeter of the yard to the dilapidated gate. Away from the main courtyard the garden was a dark grey moonless sea.

"Must have been fox at the bins or something." But then she saw the light, almost hidden behind the parapet wall. At the base of the metal fire escape that scaled the end wall, a thin band of yellow. Stealthily, the pair descended the four stone steps to the door and Daley eased down the handle, hearing every pop and crack of the springs.

Inside, a small emergency lamp cast a dim glow over a long dark corridor, stone and brick, lime leached, strewn with cobwebs and dark mould stains. A network of lagged pipework skirted the ceiling running off, fading into black. The air was chill and it sent plumes of vapour billowing about them. Whetstone found a torch in her bag. Daley steadied her hand before she could illuminate it, his eyes slowly becoming accustomed to the gloom. They were in the basement of the Hall, a maze of brick built columns partitioned into rooms and corridors. As the silence descended, every sound was amplified tenfold, a mouse or a rat scurrying, cracks from the pipes, the noises of the night, their own hearts beating. Daley listened to the silence roaring in his ears, the prickling colours of darkness in his eyes. Far ahead along the corridor, electricity hummed. Another sliver of light under another door. He and Whetstone began to walk towards it, their footfalls thunderous on the stones.

Then there was a movement down the corridor, an intake of air and once more Daley knew the figure was running at him from the darkness. Whetstone flicked on her torch and temporarily they were all blinded in the whiteness. A scream of anguish rang as the figure raced along the corridor. Sinking against the wall, Whetstone trailed a leg and the body impacted her shin and, with an almighty *Ooph*, slid to a halt on the stone floor.

Blinking as his eyes adjusted, Daley sighed, reached down and hauled the man to his feet. "We really have to stop meeting like this, Connor. Even my Sergeant here is starting to talk."

Chapter 111

Route des Estuaires, near Peuplingues, Calais

She could prise open the doors, hurl herself onto the road, roll out onto the carriageway, then run before the man could catch her? But the van must be doing over 100ks. Even with the coat she would take off most of her skin, maybe even break bones. No. The moment would come and she would be ready. In the past week, one thing had kept Satya alive.

Fear.

From the unease of trusting to strangers, to the horrors of the soldier and the boat and Gregor Wolfe, to the sixth sense of being followed, of seeking the safety of boltholes and restrooms, her body had attuned to an undercurrent of fear. Reflexes sharpened. Somehow, she felt more alive. She had heard of Post-Traumatic Stress Disorder. A feeling of loss, anger, isolation following some deep traumatic experience. The inability to rationalise, to adjust to, normality. Would she be able to return to normality? Would she be glad the adventure and the agonies were over, or would she miss it?

Yesterday, with Pietr and Paris, she already missed it.

She could have stayed with Pietr, travelled to England another day. Pietr had said that the ferry ride was easy with a European passport. He could have driven her to the port himself. A few more precious hours together. Instead she chose to abandon herself again to strangers. Soon this small trip would be over and the next by ferry would begin. She would keep her wits about her and trust Allah.

The van had become suffocating. *We will find you and kill you.* Would they really? Once she had her tickets, once she was aboard the ferry, she could slip their clutches, find a place to hide, bide her time until it docked and then blend in with the crowd. If they kicked up a fuss she could shout louder. After all, if the tickets were good, if her passport was good, she would be in England. She would have rights. At worst, she could hitchhike to London.

Chapter 112

The Farm

> *I remember him as if it were yesterday, as he came plodding to the inn door, his sea-chest following behind him in a hand-barrow — a tall, strong, heavy, nut-brown man, his tarry pigtail falling over the shoulder of his soiled blue coat, his hands ragged and scarred, with black, broken nails, and the sabre cut across one cheek, a dirty, livid white. I remember him looking round the cover and whistling to himself as he did so, and then breaking out in that old sea-song that he sang so often afterwards:*
>
> *'Fifteen men on the dead man's chest— Yo-ho-ho, and a bottle of rum!'*
>
> *in the high, old tottering voice that seemed to have been tuned and broken at the capstan bars.*

Easing through the doors, Whetstone gasped at the sight before her. The space, about the size of the team room at Lambourne Road, illuminated by a restful half-light, was warm and dry, like coming home. Around the windowless walls, machines beat a rhythm, slow and purposeful. There were beeps, monitors displaying numbers and bouncing lines. Between them, rows of beds, like a dormitory, each with a patient, quiet and still except for the mechanical rise and fall of their chest. At one of the beds, Steven Franks, glanced over before returning to a patient. At the far end, behind a desk sat Marion Edmonds, a stark lamp casting a white glow over the open book. Briefly, she raised her eyes to Whetstone. They were filled with emotion, deep and clawing anguish. A grief beyond words that she had seen in many eyes before. Behind them was a calm, a professional detachment and relief that the deadly confidence was now broken.

"Sergeant. I knew it would not be long before you worked it out. We've just started a new book. *Treasure Island.* You've not missed much." Her eyes returned to the book and she continued reading.

Then he rapped on the door with a bit of stick like a handspike that he carried, and when my father appeared, called roughly for a glass of rum. This, when it was brought to him, he drank slowly, like a connoisseur, lingering on the taste and still looking about him at the cliffs and up at our signboard.

'This is a handy cove,' says he at length; 'and a pleasant sittyated grog-shop. Much company, mate?'

My father told him no, very little company, the more was the pity.

'Well, then,' said he, 'this is the berth for me.

Suddenly unable to stand, Whetstone found a chair, her mind struggling with what she was seeing. She could feel tears in her eyes, the rows of souls lost, of lives awaiting deliverance or destruction. Beside her, Daley bustled through the door dragging Smith by the lapels. Whetstone glanced up as he too froze.

"The farm, sir?"

Daley turned to Whetstone and nodded sombrely, again recalling the words of the waiter the previous evening:

We have a little farm out back so chef can keep them fresh until they are ordered.

***

And once more the TV breaks into static and the sea of turgid slime yields to distant voices. Behind, the monster cowers. Whilst the sounds and images drift across the limitless seas, the monster cannot strike. I am safe. I can hear the sounds and recognise the words. The Inn, the boy. Detached and dissociated they still mean something in the miasma of black and blinking lights and the steady beating sounds. I hear a voice and it screams to be heard, to be noticed. It is my voice, I am sure but there is no mouth, no breath, no conscious words formed. Just the notion of a scream.

See me. Hear me. I am not gone. I am here, just beyond your vision, just beyond your consciousness. I am that notion that once thought is forgotten, the dream, dangling from a fragile thread and, once woken, fragments to nothing.

I will concentrate on the voice, amplify the sound until, at last, it breaks through from this realm of ghosts and into their world. They may not see me but I am still here.

Chapter 113

Port de Calais

As the doors opened Satya blinked away the whiteness. The woman and the man were standing behind the van.

"Give me your documents." A flat palm extended, fingers flipping. "Hurry!" The man's eyes were cold and hard.

Moving to the edge of the van, Satya found the ticket and the passport. She could make a run for it, through the doors, into the hall. There would be security, crowds. Immediately the woman snatched them from her.

"Now you are no-one, just like every other mongrel that descends upon this port looking for a better life and, like every one of them, you will fester here in the camps unless you do exactly what you are told."

She felt the panic rise. The passport was the one asset that meant anything. Except for the Makarov but that was behind the trim. Until she could retrieve both, she would have no choice but to go along.

Beside her the woman barked "Out, now. Gather your things and follow me. When we get to the Border Control, I will give you your ticket and you will board as a foot passenger. You will journey across alone. If you get stopped, we will deny knowing you. If you run, we will find you and kill you. We have people on the ferry who will be watching you, so behave yourself. No-one will miss you if you fail to reach England. When the ferry docks, wait by the Customs point. Is that clear?"

Satya nodded meekly. Now was not the time for heroics. With the man in front and the woman behind, they crossed the Departure lounge. Ahead Satya could see the glass kiosks of the border control booths, the armed border guards, their berets angled and their eyes darting, their fingers bridging the trigger guards on vicious assault rifles. Over her shoulder, her passport appeared. She grabbed it and flicked to the identification page. The likeness was excellent, the forgery good. Was it good enough?

With barely a nod, she was waved through. Amid barked orders, she took of her coat, belt and boots and placed them on the conveyor alongside her bag and Gregor Wolfe's watch. Then held her breath as she passed through the metal scanner. On the other side a dour woman in a khaki blouse, knee length skirt and severe shoes, waved her off to collect her things. Then she and the woman parted, consumed by the crowds, transported away towards the mouth of the ferry and the prospect of England.

***

Daley released Smith, who rather than break free, walked quietly across to Franks and began to tend to a patient.

Marion placed a finger on the page to mark her place. "Connor and I found out about six months ago. Varsa had been mouthing off as usual. She started questioning the procedures, the number of cadaver units, somehow believing Steven was murdering people and bringing them to us to experiment on. She used to catch me over lunch and explain her theories. How Steven was disappearing on his trips and coming back with bodies."

Connor purposefully stepped to one of the beds, pressed a button, checked a cannula. "It became staff room gossip. We all just ignored her at first but then she remarked on the HTA licence, how it had expired. Without it, where did all of the cadaver units come from? Of course, she had no idea what was really going on, even when she started shouting her mouth off, but somehow there must have been some truth in what she said. One, maybe two a week. When we discovered the farm, we dropped it into the conversation, you know, as a joke. She never cottoned on, though."

Franks paused for a while. "You were right, Sergeant. I was with Caz while Nick set up the farm, filled it with units - people. All those missing days when I was with her, I had no idea what their game was. Then I started to smell a rat. First it was Varsa keeping a record of my comings and goings, adding two and two, making five, demanding money to keep her mouth shut. I told her to piss off. I knew I was doing nothing wrong. Then Connor, outside the garage."

"Varsa started her snide comments about Steve. He was at the clinic when he shouldn't be. The van in the yard. I was convinced that there must be some truth in what she was saying. No smoke without fire, so I confronted Steve."

"And what could I say but what I had told Varsa. OK." Franks held up his hands. "I might have been a bit rough but I was fed up with feeling like a criminal when all I had done was play away once in a while."

"I know, Steve." It was Whetstone. "When we figured out the van, that there was another one, another two. Another driver. That was who Varsa had seen."

"So how did you find this place?" Daley gazed around the ward, brick walls, gothic, incongruous against the monitors and machines.

"You work somewhere for years, you think you know everything about it, then this, right under your nose." Marion had slipped into the second person, dissociative, remote. "Connor came to me. Initially, I thought he was mad but the more I thought, the more I listened to Varsa... In September, I was working a night shift and I rang Connor. Together we decided to have a little nose around. Only the van arrived and we watched as the load was brought around to the side of the Hall."

"It wasn't Steve." Connor looked up to Franks, perhaps hoping for approbation or vindication. "Anyway, when the van drove off, Marion and I found the fire exit. I knew a way into the Hall basement from the other side. It wasn't long before we found the farm."

"But you must have suspected something, earlier. The sheer quantity alone...?"

"The projects we were involved in, the cadavers we used, they were just delivered and taken away. Just like the devices, the equipment, the laundry, they just appeared and were removed. We were cogs in a machine. We had no reason to suspect they were anything other than above board. We knew that even brain stem dead, the bodies would need to be kept fresh, as if alive but it never occurred to us that this..." Marion swept a hand across the ward, "...existed. Until Varsa started."

"Did you not question where they were coming from, how so many could be found in such a state and with such regularity?"

"It's a cruel, unforgiving world, Inspector. I like to believe that, regardless of the circumstances that brought them here, they would eventually be of some use. That we could offer them some degree of dignity."

"The paradox, Inspector," continued Smith, "is that Varsa knew that something like the farm must have existed but she never found it. It was she that gave it its name."

Daley counted the beds, the bodies lying on them. There were ten beds; only seven were occupied.

Marion continued: "Connor, Steven and I, we take turns to keep an eye on the wards, look after the patients when we know Nick is away. I like to think they can hear the stories. Even after Connor had warned Varsa off, she kept on taking notes in her diary, making half-empty threats. We were worried she would catch on for real."

"So, you killed her?" returned Whetstone. Daley cocked his head; not even Whetstone believed either of these two had the mind for murder.

"No Sergeant. There is more than enough killing. We just warned her off. Our only thought is for these people here. We have to look after them, preserve what little humanity they have left or lose our own."

As Marion continued the words of Jim Hawkins to the sea of beds, a crew of lost souls, there was nothing to do, nothing to say, just to listen.

"What can be done for them?"

Daley walked along the ranks of beds. There were no notes, no charts, medication regimes, no personal belongings on bedside tables. Each body still and silent except for the steady inrush and outflow of air, anonymous in their face masks.

Connor looked up earnestly. "Nothing, Inspector."

"And this cannot be reversed?"

"No. Technically they are no longer alive, but their bodies function as if they were. The machine still runs even though there is no-one at the controls. Technically they still circulate blood, digest food, excrete waste. If left long enough, brain dead children would grow, become sexually mature, their wounds would heal. Females could even gestate and deliver a baby."

"Could they not just be in a coma?" Daley thought back to

his recent hospitalisation, the centuries of half-life, the black tar of unconsciousness and the mirages of reality which bled through like conversations heard on the wind. He recalled the wild torment as the monsters of his own making stalked the inky molasses waiting for death to come.

"No, Inspector. We know the routine. A new one arrives every Wednesday and maybe Saturday. Most of them are foreign, we think, Middle eastern. They all have the same tattoo on their left forearm."

Daley reached for a forearm. It was warm, living, like Terri's arm as he held her the previous evening. On the inside, just below the elbow, there was a mark, an Arabic monogram. It reminded him of the tattoo that his barber had; numbers ascribed for an equally sinister reason.

"We check each new patient for brain stem reflexes, dilation of pupils and of course pain stimuli but they are all gone. They are checked again in theatre before the procedure."

"But all these people, tens of individuals over years. How could they all have suffered this fate?"

Smith shrugged his shoulders. "Chemicals, Inspector. They have all taken or received massive doses of barbiturates. Look, this one is the latest arrival. You can still see the hypodermic marks." He eased back the top of the bedclothes. The patient, a male, had two angry puncture wounds to his neck. "We think one of the injections sedates the person and the next..."

Daley peered at the wounds. He looked at the short cropped dark hair, the prominent chin, the aquiline nose. A lump came to his throat and he felt nauseous. His mind began to swim. Reaching up he clicked on the lamp over the bed and stared at the face.

"Deb. This is Tom Philips. Went missing Tuesday night at Chatham Woods."

***

Grabbing a coffee, parting with the last remaining euros, Satya headed for the prow. There were around twenty people, fair skinned and wrapped against the chill, laughing and shouting and pointing, all embarking on their own personal adventures - and the woman, never more than a few yards away. As the boat inched from the dock and out towards the breakwater, Satya's mind drifted back to the previous day, to the streets of Paris and the adventures she had seen. To Pietr's smile and the warmth of his hand in hers, the warmth of his body against hers.

Opening her bag, she withdrew the small book with its scrawled notes and sketches, belonging to a different time, already separate and distant. She found the strip of photos, Pietr pulling faces and she laughing. Just like Gregor Wolfe and his girl and she longed for a time when her life would not be punctuated with loss. The black Renault was moving further away along the Autoroute towards Strasbourg, smaller and smaller as the distance between them grew immeasurably. By the time the boat docked in Dover, Pietr was a dot on a far-off horizon and Satya had closed the book forever.

Leaving the boat, through the corridors and halls and towards the border control, she felt empty, burdened by the sacrifice. Was freedom really worth the loss of everything she held dear? Was life really that of a stranger in a strange land, isolated and alone?

A spittle of rain rapped the glass door as she left the Arrivals Hall. Beside her, the woman who had been waiting, walked with her and indicated the van. The man was standing by the rear doors.

The hand struck her cheek and she bit her tongue, tasting blood. Shrill peels rang in her ears. Instinctively, the beast turned and glowered at the woman, deep inside she heard a growl. She knew that there was some part of her soul that belonged to the migrant beast, that would never be gone. She wanted to tear out the woman's throat.

"Do you really think we are that stupid? The number of times we have done this trip and there is always someone who thinks they are smarter." The woman pulled the Makarov from her pocket. "Did you not think we would find the gun? You scum think you are so clever. Why else would we leave that panel loose? The whole point of the hiding place is so that idiots like you will use it. Without it, you would have the gun. Now we have it." The woman grabbed at Satya's arm and steered her to the open doors. "Get in the back." Satya grabbed for the Makarov but caught only air, as the woman dropped it back into her overcoat pocket.

"I am in England now," she spat. "I have an English passport. Why do I need you?"

Suddenly her face stung again and her head hit the door frame.

"What you need is unimportant. We have a lot invested in you, so do what you are told. "

Feeling the fingers biting into her arms, Satya felt a sharp scratch and a coldness coursed up her neck. Then the world spun away to darkness.

***

Away across the car park, the binoculars watched as the girl fell into the back of the van and the man and the woman climbed in.

Earlier, he had watched as the van had appeared from the mouth of the ferry and driven round to the visitor's car park, as he had known it would. This was a routine that had happened many times before, in fact each time there was a trip to France. Today the ferry had been light. At this time of year many cars travelled to the Continent for Christmas markets, booze cruises to the hypermarkets, but few returned on Saturday, so the car decks had been practically empty. He had watched the man alight and lean against the vehicle scouring the steady stream of passengers leaving the arrivals hall. He watched as the girl and the woman had zigged and zagged through parked cars.

And he had watched the body tumble lifeless into the rear of the van.

Now it was clear.

The regular trips to the continent, the white van with its anonymous load space. The man who called himself Steven Franks and the woman who called herself Jill, and the body in the back unconsciously awaiting its fate.

As the van pulled out of its parking bay, the other car fired up and followed at a discrete distance.

***

As the van lurched, Satya startled from her dream, the black slurried molasses engulfing her mind began to drain. A dull red filled her vision and her neck ached. The van had slowed. Through the bulkhead, she heard conversation. Slowly her mind sifted the amorphous images of unconsciousness, dragging back memories of the docks, the boat trip, the scuffle at the van. She kept her eyes closed, feeling the van rock and bump beneath her, hearing the gravel beneath the wheels. As a wave of panic threatened to suffocate her, she could smell the acidic sweat of her own fear.

Gradually, the world below her slowed. Opening her eyes, she saw only greyness. A dull light shone though the tiny gaps in the door. How long had she been asleep? She strained to hear the voices above the idling engine.

"We need to get the girl sorted first." She heard the woman's voice. "She's trouble."

Satya heard the front doors open, footsteps on gravel. Immediately she flattened herself to the van floor and closed her eyes. She felt hands grab her ankles and she was dragged out through the mouth of the van, suspended in the air and placed, with thump, into a wheelchair.

Her body limp and lifeless, her heart was racing. Tentatively raising an eyelid, allowing in the briefest sliver of light, Satya took in what she could. To the left a large mansion house towered over her as the woman and the man wheeled her through a gate, down some steps and through a door into a dark corridor to another door. The man peered through the small round window. The darkness was punctuated only by the blinking lights from ranks of machines.

"Bed three." The man placed his back against the door and eased it open. Together they struggled, as Satya forced her body to remain limp, a dead weight. Taking her opportunity, she reached a hand into the woman's coat.

Suddenly the room exploded with light as neon strips along the ceiling clattered and flashed into life.

***

In the car park of the *Sir William Wordsworth*, the car had pulled in and watched the white van turn into the bowered driveway of Medway Hall. The roads were already busy and he had had trouble keeping up since leaving the docks. Leaving a discreet distance yet not far enough to lose sight. It was mid-morning on a Saturday and the pub car park was relatively empty but there was no chance of his car been spotted so he didn't bother to hide it.

Alighting and walking around to the boot, he retrieved a coat and zipped it up against the chill rain. Dashing through the traffic, he entered the drive, and trotted the fifty metres to the other end, checking himself as he saw the van parked by the Hall. In the front, the man and the woman were deep in heated debate.

He watched as the man left the van and disappeared into the Hall, returning moments later with a wheelchair, into which they manhandled their charge before passing through a gate at the side of the building.

The game was now complete, the circle joined. The figures were beginning to tally, the books to balance. Two had left the Hall and three returned.

Chapter 114

The man looked around the room, alarmed but not entirely surprised. The woman made to run but soon saw the futility of it, they were outnumbered. Daley and Whetstone moved together, blocking the exit. Daley pushed a button on his phone.

"Hello Nick, Caz. Or should I say Dominic and Carolina? You took your time. Sergeant Whetstone and I have missed breakfast. Looks like we'll miss lunch too."

"Inspector." The surprise yielded to a flash of annoyance before Snowdon smiled resignedly to himself. "Dominic. I haven't heard that name in a long while. I'd almost forgotten it was mine." But the eyes which rose to meet Daley's belonged to a different era. Sinister and cold and utterly deadly. Yet still he was looking for an escape, assessing the room, the dour sergeant at the door, the Inspector. Then he saw the others.

Marion, Steve and Connor stepped out from a side closet. Connor held Marion, visibly traumatised. Steve Franks eyes were ablaze.

"Well, look who it is, Varsa Ruparelia's *best friends forever.* Thank you for keeping the meat fresh all this time. I can honestly say, we couldn't have done it without you."

Franks started to move, but thought better of it, the dragon writhing and snarling.

"You knew?" Marion stared at Snowdon, astounded. "All this time, you knew?"

"What do you take me for? Of course I knew. You can't count the number of times I have sat outside the door listening to you reading to these...vegetables. You always have been a champion of lost causes, Marion. Do you really think they heard a single word?"

And for the first time, Whetstone heard Marion scream as she leapt across the room and began to beat Snowdon around the shoulders. Whetstone raced over and pulled the woman back, dragging her behind the desk, to the arms of a shocked Connor Smith. The nurse turned and sobbed into his chest.

"You bastard, Snowdon! Isn't enough that she had to look after these people? Isn't it enough that, when she learnt what you were doing, she kept it to herself?" Franks stepped forwards into the light. "Connor, Marion and me, trying to preserve their dignity as they came and went, all the time protecting your obscene perversions. Holding on to the belief that, despite all evidence to the contrary, it was us who had got things wrong."

"Well, more fool her. More fool all of you," sneered Snowdon. "I never asked for your help. I never wanted you to interfere with my project."

Franks paced forwards, finger raised and jabbing at air. "You just shut up! This is *my* turn. You shut up or I'll bloody well shut you up." Franks took another step and this time Daley intervened, grabbing hold of the man's arm. "Steve. He isn't worth it, honestly." Franks flailed and Daley bounced to the floor.

Franks continued, his eyes moistening. "And you Caz, all those months, leading me on, drawing me deeper and deeper into this...this mess. All the time, setting me up and like a fool, I really thought you felt something for me and now I find you're nothing but a cheap whore."

"Hardly cheap, darling, but come on. Do you really think there could ever be anything between you and me?"

"Franks. Get back in your box and stop behaving like an idiot." Snowdon was a matter of feet from Franks. It was a powder keg and the heat was cranking up. "It was going perfectly well before you got involved and would have continued on regardless. Do you not realise, it was your misguided beliefs, that somehow this was all above board, your reckless interventions, that enabled me to service so many more units? Without you three taking on their care, there would have been less than a quarter the amount. What's that? Nearly thirty bodies which would never have entered the farm, would never have ended up where they did, if I hadn't had you to care for them? How does it feel? Tell me. Each of you, the instruments of death."

Franks and Snowdon stood their ground, each facing the other, eyes locked. Daley picked himself up from the floor. He needed to stop this infantile posturing before someone, probably him, got hurt.

Chapter 115

2012

The face at the window made me start.

It was high above the courtyard, peering through a window which I knew led from the clinic across to the Hall. The eyes were small and laser sharp. I ducked behind the door of the van, hoping she would not have seen my face, even though I had seen hers.

The success or otherwise of a venture lies in the planning. There had been many benefactors who we had invited in, many we had rejected. That was the secret, as Lina later told me. One has to analyse the chances of success. One has to assess the risks and work out strategies to mitigate them. The ultimate pleasure, the spoils would come, not from the kill but from the anonymity that surrounded us. Our hosts had to be isolated, stripped gradually of their identity, of their being, of everything. Then they would simply cease to exist, as we had in 1990. The papers would carry the stories, fading with every passing day. Like us, there was no-one to miss them, no-one to grieve. No-one to care.

Varsa Ruparelia had become a risk which needed to be mitigated. Like every employee, the mitigation had been denial and dismissal.

When I saw her staring, I thought I had been mistaken, a trick of the light, but I knew something had to be done. I was sure that she had not seen the boxes, the heads, the limbs, the torsos which were destined for the sheds, and with her suspicions over Franks' activities rife, Lina was entertaining the degenerate in her own particular way. He was our mitigation. Varsa had already claimed to have seen him at the garages when he was away or at *Limewood* satisfying his needs. I arranged for Varsa to be dismissed. I hope it would blow over, but still she came to the clinic with her lies and half-truths, digging ever deeper into our affairs, threatening to uncover our secrets. Then she confronted Franks outside the garage, within yards of our playroom, and I knew there was only one outcome. The shed.

No-one comes between us. We are one.

Lina administered the dose. Small, barely half that we would normally use but Franks would sleep through. By the time I reached Varsa's house and parked up the van, she was inside and Varsa was offering tea. The dose she gave Varsa was much the same. Except for the ketamine. That was a necessary extra. By the early hours, we had placed her in the bath and she had woken, confused at her position, confused at her nakedness, confused as we removed her hands, her feet, her legs, her arms. The bath was not the perfect operating room but beggars can't be choosers and of all of them, she needed to see the most.

Varsa saw her own heart beating. Varsa saw her own heart stop.

Chapter 116

"You need to move away from the beds. It's over now. We'll take it from here." Daley glanced around, the tubes and wires, the flashing screens. He had a feeling it had just begun. Snowdon sighed and walked across to the edge of an empty bed, perching himself uncomfortably. Caz stood frozen to the spot, head slumped. Steve Franks held firm, his eyes tracking Snowdon every step of the way.

"We found the water tank. Our forensic guys are digging up the floor of the shed. They reckon there will be others. How many are they going to find?"

Snowdon shrugged, unconcerned. "To be honest, I have lost count. What? Two a week for perhaps two years? Then all the others before."

"Two hundred?" Incredulous, the ball started to form in Daley's stomach again. *All the others before.* How long had this been going on? How many had been taken before Varsa Ruparelia started to notice? Over his shoulder he could hear Marion Edmonds sobbing. Smith was whispering to her, comforting her. Franks was unmoved. "All those people? Did it not occur to you that someone was going to notice? That this grisly scheme was going to be found out eventually?"

"Of course it did. Why do you think we bought the place abroad? We have disappeared once, we could do so again. Your *Zone 6* kidnappings? They, Inspector, were the ones that noticed. They saw the van, or trespassed onto the Farm. They were expediency. They made up the numbers."

"Is that all these people are to you? Just numbers?" The eyes turned and stared at Whetstone as she spoke. They bore a malevolence that chilled her to the core. "How can you have such callous disregard for lives, for experiences, for their loved ones?"

"Easily, Sergeant. Just numbers." It was Caz Albin. She walked across to her brother and perched a hand on his shoulder. "Humans are a virus, starting from nothing and multiplying to epidemic proportions, contaminating the planet, poisoning the world, polluting the land and the seas, sucking the earth dry of its resources. If left unchecked, eventually the virus will burn itself out but until then, I am sure we can spare a few."

"But can't you see how wrong all this is? I can understand medical research; the use of human cadavers but this? Surely a human life has some value, deserves some respect?"

"Oh, grow up, Daley," spat Snowdon. "You know how the world works as much as I. What do these people contribute? They steal the food from your plate and the air from your lungs. They dip their hands into the pockets of the hard working and give nothing in return. I simply cut out the middleman and gave them a purpose. You can't tell me that you don't cut a few corners to achieve what you want?"

Daley resented the implication, a common ploy to diminish the severity of a crime by reminding others of their fallibilities. "I am nothing like you. Of course I cut corners. Of course I bend the rules, tell a few white lies but nothing like...this. This is inhuman. It's barbaric."

"Barbaric?" Snowdon stood and faced Daley. Whetstone tensed as she backed against the door. "I'll tell you what's barbaric. The Killing Fields of Cambodia. Piles of skulls as far as the eye can see. Iraq, Afghanistan, ISIS, Boko Haram, even the US, Britain. Humans are basically inhuman. They destroy anything that doesn't conform to their own personal view of the world. We kid ourselves that civilisation supports social and ethnic diversity but all we see are rival sects, opposing religions, tribal divisions and we are so blind we allow the free movement of people in the foolish notion that they will blend and homogenate and all will be well. We allow these warring factions to nestle cheek-by-jowl in crowded, stinking ghettos and we wonder why there is social unrest. Oil and water will never mix however hard you stir.

"And it falls on you to play God, to be the arbiter of what is right and what is wrong?"

"Don't be so bloody naïve. God? Tell me, what is God, or Allah, or Jehovah but a comfort blanket for the feeble-minded? Someone is taking care of them, validating the death and destruction that they perpetrate in His name. A higher power to vindicate every right or wrong decision they make. I don't give a shit about the people on this earth, just like they haven't given a shit about me and Lina for all these years. And I don't give a shit about a concept so basically flawed as right or wrong."

"So why?" Whetstone was fumbling in her pocket, knowing her phone was in her handbag on the desk.

Caz Albin looked up. "Must there be a reason? Maybe there are many reasons. Why don't you choose the one that makes you feel most comfortable? Money perhaps. Delta project has made us rich. Power, maybe. The control we exert over a life and the way it leaves the body. Enjoyment. I like the feel of blood on my fingers, the taste on my lips." The eyes that met Whetstone's were cold and malevolent.

"Or maybe," added Snowdon, "insanity? Maybe we are both off our trolley? The world is full of secrets. This one is ours. Taking people from right under everyone's noses. Right under your nose and you had no idea."

Caz Albin rose and removed her coat, the atmosphere now warm and cloying. "Have you ever wondered what life is? What specific ingredient of a human being constitutes life? Well, here we can separate that life from the body. All of these people. They are alive in every sense. Except they no longer have their lives. We can watch as the brain starts to decay, the last breath leaves a person." She sighed, a slow, steady, haunting outrush of air. "The merest hint of sound as the soul escapes. What goes through the mind in that final second? Do the eyes still see, the ears hear, the mind still feel even though the body is dead? The absolute realisation that all is lost. I have seen the light leave hundreds of eyes and I still don't know. Then to eviscerate and dismember, to damage and to maim. To smell the warm blood and the sweet metallic intestines. To feel the saw rasping at bones and ripping flesh. Can the brain feel the pain, sense the defilement? Does sensation persist long after the brain has ceased to register it? Maybe the person is inside screaming to get out?"

Daley felt a knot of nausea in his stomach and his head began to spin. Behind him, Smith vented into a cardboard dish. She was utterly depraved. Further debate would be pointless. Whatever had happened at Chatham Woods all those years ago, whatever warped sense of truth these two siblings sought to justify their killings, was for someone else to fathom. Seeing the ranks of beds, hearing the sounds of the machines, recalling the images of the tangled limbs and staring disconnected eyes heaped in the old water tank, he knew he would never comprehend the madness that had overtaken Dominic and Carolina Blanchard.

***

Along the corridor, he could see the shard of light, he could hear the voices inside. Measuring every footfall, he reached the door and edged his eyes to the window. The man and the woman were gathered around a bed, the girl lying on it. The others were further along around a desk. Except for one, tall, muscular, a dragon on his forearm, enraged, pacing. Through the small pane he could see the back of a head. He could hear them talking but the words were indistinct, far off.

Along the walls, ranks of beds. The machines and wires.

Should he race through the door, take them by surprise, overpowered the man, the woman? No, the odds of success were poor. He would wait for the right opportunity. A moment of confusion.

In his mind, a jumble of emotions threatened to overwhelm him, to cloud his thinking. He thought of the van and the girl, of the *Grepo* and the desperate steps to avoid capture, of the cold of the night and the warmth of her skin. He pushed them all away. This was a time for clarity. When the moment arose, it would be but a moment. Easing a foot between the doors, creating a gap, he listened to the conversation. The tall stooped man in the raincoat and the driver of the van, the one who had taken Satya away from him.

Chapter 117

"Tell me, Nick, Caz. Why all the others? What had they done that was so wrong?"

"Again, Inspector, the myth of right and wrong. Do this; don't do that. They had done nothing at all. This was about me and Lina, not them. We had done nothing wrong, all those years ago. We did not deserve to be treated how we were. But still it happened. When we disappeared. When we moved away from the farm. When we hid in the old ice house, no-one came looking. No-one cared if we lived or died. We made our own life and when we wanted some fun, we would go out and find it."

Daley recalled what Terri Somerville had told him. Dominic Blanchard had been fourteen and Lina eight when they had disappeared. Left alone, the children had made their own society. They had established their own rules. Their own separate sect away from world. He felt his phone buzz in his pocket. He would need a distraction if he were to use it.

"The average man or woman lives for, what, sixty-five, maybe eighty years and what do they achieve? They procreate a few more humans and they add to the misery of the world. How many are remembered, fifty, twenty, even five years after their deaths? They are born, they lead a pointless existence and then they are gone, barely an imprint on the universe. At least this way some good comes of their miserable anonymous existences."

"But every one of these, each body we are exhuming from Chatham Woods had a life, experiences, families, loves. Somewhere there is a heart that beats for each one of them." Whetstone pictured her mother in the armchair, *Saturday Kitchen* and an empty house, full of memories, and she yearned to be there.

"Aren't we the sentimental little flower." Caz Albin's tone was contemptuous. "Is there, Sergeant? Is there a heart beating for them? No-one missed us. When our parents died, when we went missing, no-one came looking. We were completely on our own."

"But we looked for you. Even now the case file is still open. A missing persons case is never closed until the person is found - alive or dead. When they discovered the farm, empty, that was all they had. There were no leads to follow. No way they could trace you. You made that difficult all by yourselves. You didn't want to be found."

***

Peering through slits in her eye lids, Satya too bided her time. Their attention was elsewhere, on the others. Slowly she moved her head to the side, saw the figure, it's chest rising and falling, it's heartbeat measured in short blips. Suddenly she realised. The yawing rafts of the Mediterranean, the heaving stinking transit camps of Germany and Romania, overflowing detention camps of Sangatte. She had been spared all of these, given a route and money. However hard she had imagined the trip, it had been easy compared to the overwhelming majority. As they walked the highways, she had ridden. As they had begged and stolen, she had bought food.

As they clung to inundated rafts, she had been chosen.

That was the only answer. For their age, their ethnicity, their status. They had been chosen and brought to this place, via *The Brotherhoods* route. Then she felt sick.

Had Alaam been chosen?

Beneath her back, the Makarov recovered from the woman's coat, cut into her flesh. She could almost smell the gun oil in the knurls of the handgrip, the faint cordite burn in the barrel. She had to hope that their attention was on the others. She had to hope that the beast was quick enough, powerful enough as it had been with Gregor Wolfe and the soldier.

Just then, Franks leapt at Snowdon, tendons rippling as he clawed at his neck. Suddenly, there was a flash of silver and his eyes widened before he dropped to his knees and then to the floor, the syringe still in his neck.

Caz Albin stood glaring down as Franks fought for breath. "Never try to come between us. You will always lose."

Daley dropped down and pulled out the syringe, casting it behind him.

Springing to her feet, back to the wall, Satya thrust the gun out in front of her, staring down the barrel, pointing at Snowdon. The other man in the raincoat turned towards her, his hand outstretched. She clicked the small oval catch.

"I am Satya Meheb and this time the safety is off. So stay away."

"Jeez." Daley turned his hand, beckoning, stared at the gun. "No, this isn't the way. It's finished now. We have stopped this." He heard the tracks fizzling, a pulsating diesel engine, heard the blaring horn saw the woman, cold eyes and dead smile. "Give me the gun."

Franks lay on his back, his rasping breath slowing, his back arching with the effort. The dragon bucked and railed as the muscles in his arms flexed.

"How can it be finished? For you it may be. You have the bad guys but for me, for all these people, how can it be finished?"

Daley raised his hands. A placatory gesture. "Look...Satya? This isn't the way. You need to put the gun down." He had no other words. Right now, she faced arrest, months in detention, deportation. There really was no other way.

Then the rasping stopped. The dragon lay still.

Whetstone slowly inched towards Satya. "Please, love. You don't need to do this. Too many people have died already. You have my word, this will never happen to anyone else."

But Satya's trust, diminished by the trials of her journey, had now completely deserted her. "I don't care about anyone else. This is happening to me. I leave Aleppo because they killed my family before my eyes. I watched as the flames came from the machine guns and the blood of my parents spat at my face and I prayed to Allah to take me as well. But he did not. He spared me and I have hated him every minute since. I have crawled through the mud and the snow to cross the border and again I watched as the last breath left a soldier and the water filled his lungs and that is not enough. I have been pawed by filthy men who have minds in their groins and still that is not enough. Allah sends me to Budapest, to the lecherous arms of Gregor Wolfe. Not content with taking my mother and father and the border guard, Allah needs to take Gregor Wolfe and leave the blood on my hands. Allah has made me a killer and spared my life. He has made me pay for robbing Gregor Wolfe's girlfriend of the love of her life by stealing away mine. And now I must regret it every passing day for the rest of my life."

Nick Snowdon slowly turned and grinned at Satya. "Ah, so the scum has a voice? Isn't it strange how, all of a sudden, it's about what you want? Streets once safe for our children to walk now teeming with immigrant rats, stealing our food, stealing our houses, raping our women. To scrounge, to exploit our benefit culture, leech off the sweat of our backs. And it's all down to Allah. His will inflicted these catastrophes upon you, He drove you to these things. See Inspector? Right and wrong are just perspectives."

Caz Albin put her hand on his arm. She saw the determination in Satya's eyes, the tendons in the fingers around the trigger guard. "Not now, Dom." He shrugged her away.

"No. Exactly now! Britain, once a great empire, now a squalid hotchpotch of mongrels. Science tells us that the mixing of genes should bring out the most dominant traits, the best traits of the mix. But what are those? Generosity, altruism, civility, respect? How many civilisations have thrived on those qualities? No, the human is an animal. It survives by aggression and dominance, violence and fear. What it wants it takes, what it can't take, it destroys. Immigration drags everything down to the lowest common denominator.

"And survival of the fittest? Again, the human animal corrupts the theory. Its brain enlarged, capable of rational thought, it chose safety in numbers, to protect the weakest, the sick in the tribe. And now, our hospitals, our streets, our asylums are full of the weak, the sick, the insane, those who are different. Darwinian philosophies mean nothing where humans contaminate the gene pool so thoughtlessly."

Satya stood firm. She could feel the beast steadying the gun, she could feel the sinews in her forearms tighten and she was content for the beast to grasp the handle. "You know nothing of me, nothing of my family yet you judge me from your white English *Middle Class* high ground? Great Britain conquered the world. It was built on immigrants from the Indies and the Americas yet you call us all *scum?"*

"Just put the gun down, love, please. I'm telling you. We can put all of this right." Whetstone saw the gun sway as it pointed first to Snowdon, then to Daley as each looked to their options. "We can't bring back your parents. Nobody can, but trust me. Though the pain never goes away, you can learn to live with it. The dark memories get replaced by the light. Your father's smile, your mother's voice. You will remember the good times. I promise you."

The tears were streaming down Satya's face. "It has been one week and already the sound of her voice has left me."

***

All around the darkness there are voices, shards of sound, like darts in the clinging, cloying black morass that holds me. As they hit my being, they explode and I sense colours, vivid and bright. The static shock of recognition sparks like lightning across the darkness. There are words and the words are familiar and the familiarity is a name. The face appears, distant and faded in the eye of the mind and I sense the monster rear on its hind legs, spitting and growling and the silt clears and the conduit opens. The tiny slit in the fabric of these worlds through which my spectre can pass. Around me the sludge thins and the air is alive as the sound connects with the picture and the word is in my head, the word is formed on my lips and the word echoes around the Hell that has imprisoned me for too long.

***

At first, it was muffled, tenuous and faint, barely a groan.

"S-Satya. Satya."

The room froze and Marion let out a small cry. Despite the tubes impeding the voice, the strangled words were plain.

"Satya. Satya."

With the gun still held high, Satya turned her head towards the faint voice, a mere croak between the machines and the bleeps and the rhythmic tides of air. Trusting her aim to the migrant beast, she edged her way around the beds to the source of the sound, wiping the tears as they ran down her cheeks.

"Satya."

Along the barrel of the gun, the two men became indistinct, almost immaterial in the moment. Lowering her left hand, she edged the mask from the face and felt her whole world crumble to dust on the floor in front of her.

"Alaam!"

She dropped to her knees and her brother's head was against her and she could smell his hair. In an instant, the last week became a memory and all she could see were Guensrin Garden and the climbing rocks, the king of the castle and the endless days. Al Jalloum and the shouting traders, their house, her bed and the safety and security of the old town.

Out of the corner of her eye, the beast sensed the movement, a flash of blue and the Makarov raised its head. Marion froze as she saw the black of the muzzle.

"Please. We have to help him. He's breathing on his own, we have to remove the tubes. He will be safe. I promise." Marion opened her arms and smiled. "Please. You can trust me. I am not like...them."

Satya fell back against the next bed, her mind reeling as Marion Edmonds tended to Alaam Meheb, as her mind processed the seismic shift. As monitors were adjusted, tubes removed, gag reflexes coughed and hacked.

Daley took the opportunity to edge closer to the melee. He needed to subdue Nick Snowdon but he needed to help Franks. He needed to punch Caz. "Deb. Call it in." We need to get medics out here, quickly."

***

Through the door, the man watched the activity unfold at the bedside, the scream from the girl, the nurses scurrying around, turning dials and removing tubes. The girl was kneeling now, her hands to her mouth, sobbing, the Makarov hung limply from her fingers. He started as he saw the tall man inch towards Satya. If they reached her, it would be over. As a hostage, she could afford them a way out. At least until they reached the door. He had that avenue well and truly blocked. Around the room, he could see cabinets and bottles, cardboard trays with syringes. He could see the faces of the man and the woman. There was no fear there, only hatred. A deep, soulless enmity he had seen before in the faces of those with nothing more to lose. To the right, the two police were creeping ever closer. Would they reach the man and the woman before they reached Satya?

Alaam?

He crouched against the opening conflicted, a bystander watching a scene unfold, blind to what was really happening, the true story behind all of this subterfuge, but ultimately, he was responsible for these people being here.

Pietr had transported Alaam to Sofia, as he had many before. He had played cards in the Skoda, he had left him at Sofia with forty euros and a few Bulgarian *lev*, shared a cigarette at Edirne and talked about their lives, their loves and their families. Then he had returned to Şarköy for the next paycheque. And as *The Brotherhood* had arranged the next payload, he had thought about the playful sister that Alaam had left behind, imagined her round face and almond eyes that sparkled with playfulness, the mischievous smile and he had fallen in love with the images he created. He imagined the streets of the old town, the Aleppo street rat charming all the traders and flirting with the boys. Then, as he had hauled a half-drowned wretch from the Sea of Marmara, the images had become real.

Now, the wisdom of Vasil's words rang clear through his mind. *Don't get involved.* The weight of responsibility was now his. He needed to make things right, whatever the consequences or nothing that he had done would mean anything again.

The tall, impassive man began to crouch, his arm slowly stretching, his hand forming a grip. It was clear he was eying the Makarov, first a pace forward, then two. Sizing up to make the move. To the left, Satya was consumed by the blinking eyes of Alaam, her brother, the gun hanging limply in her right hand. It would be an act of faith, Allah would need to smile upon him for a brief moment, perhaps only a second, to see his contrition and guide his hand. Pietr watched, his heart beating through his chest, as the man's arm extended towards the gun. The moment would need to be judged to perfection.

***

Slowly, Whetstone removed her phone from her bag. Saturday morning, who to call? Monaghan would be at Waitrose with Margaret, Mike would still be entwined under a duvet with his girlfriend. Taylor was probably on some computer forum. She searched for the one number that she had never needed to use before and pressed dial.

Daley whispered to Whetstone. "Look, I am going to try and

overpower him while he's distracted. You get Caz Albin...and make it hurt."

"Just take it easy, gov. She still has that gun."

Daley nodded, a subtle gesture, drenched with meaning. Lesson learnt. Inching ever closer, he could see Snowdon's outstretched hand. There was less than a yard and a half between them now. The girl was oblivious, consumed by the patient who was shaking his head from side to side, dazed and frantic as the nurse pulled at tubes and cannulas. With a gun, with hostages, perhaps his sheer pathological disregard for life, Snowdon would escape, Daley was sure.

And, as Snowdon had pointed out, if the pair had disappeared once, they would do it again.

There would be one chance. He needed to go for the knees, firm and quick, unbalance him, then grab as he fell. His mind saw Smith falling into the mud of Chatham Woods, felt the hardness of the concrete on his shoulder and he gritted his teeth. This was going to bloody hurt.

Suddenly, Whetstone grabbed the lamp from the table, tearing the flex from the floor and swinging it. Caz Albin wheeled around. Her eyes grew large and she screamed as the aluminium shade folded around her skull. As she fell, Daley seized the opportunity and leapt for Snowdon's knees, closing his eyes and linking his arms around the legs. The huge form toppled in slow motion against the empty bed and Daley felt the sinews in his shoulder groan and complain and he heard the thundering behemoth, it's horn blaring, as it thundered past and disappeared into the distance.

"Satya!" The doors burst open and Pietr Lazaro ran headlong into the room, leaping across the empty bed. Briefly alarmed, Snowdon regrouped and his hand reached out for Satya. Instinctively, she turned and saw the evil in his face as his hand grabbed at the Makarov. But the beast was too quick. With a snarl, it levelled the gun. There was a loud pop, closely followed by another as the pistol bump fired. A flash of crimson burst from Snowdon's shoulder then a round black hole appeared above his eyes and a halo of red surrounded his face.

"Safety off, bastard!" The migrant beast growled as the air left Snowdon's lungs, a slight knowing smile crossing his lips as he collapsed to the floor, still.

Behind, spattered in her brother's blood, her own blood intermingling as it ran down her face, Caz Albin stood rooted to the spot, her face unchanging, solid, expressionless. For two endless seconds as the echoes of the gun died out in the room, it froze in time, a pool of scarlet seeping across the linoleum.

Then the room filled with the sound, starting as a murmur, the sough of the wind in the trees, slow and plaintive, and it rose in pitch until the sobs became whimpers and the whimpers became a long, animal howl. The beast that was Caz Albin stared at the prone form of her brother, her mind now utterly gone.

Chapter 118

"Damn! Another bloody suit!" Daley reached up and grabbed a pillow from the bed, tearing away the pillowcase and forcing it onto the ragged gore which was once the back of Nick Snowdon's head. Soon, the red oozed through and with a sigh, he rammed the pillow down in its place.

"Out of the way." Marion Edmonds hand reached across his shoulder and pushed him back. Quickly, she flipped Snowdon onto his back and checked for vital signs. "He's still alive...just." Daley could see the open lids, the eyes rolling in their sockets and he wondered if he really cared any more. Behind him, Whetstone was strapping handcuffs onto Caz Albin, now on her knees, supplicant, defeated, lost to the demons of the night with their insidious probing hands, their hammers and the buzz of the saw on bone. She was moaning forlornly to herself, or perhaps to her brother, or maybe to the legion of dead.

Smith had reached Franks. "I think he's just sedated. I hope... His breathing is shallow but steady. He'll be OK."

Daley returned to Snowdon, as Edmonds barked orders, watching the life drain across the linoleum, slick with gore, reaching for bandages and wad after wad of absorbent material. Still the blood kept coming.

"Sir!" Whetstone was standing over Caz Albin. "They've gone!"

Daley wheeled around, bewildered. Surely it had only been a second? A minute at the most. Behind the desk, a crack of darkness in the wall betrayed a second door from the basement room. Unnoticed, Pietr and Connor had spirited Satya and Alaam away.

"Shit! Shit! Shit! We have to get after them." Daley hovered between the beds, momentarily conflicted. Should he head for the double doors or follow the other route under the Hall? Where did it lead? Would he be walking into a bullet? He dashed towards desk. Whetstone swung an arm and reached out for his coat, grabbing a handful, halting him.

"Let them go, gov. This is the real crime."

Daley railed and tried to yank himself free. They were but a few paces in front. He needed to stop them.

"Scott. What will it serve, really? It's over. With what they've been through, just let them go. If it is meant to be, we will pick them up later."

"We need to put out a call before they get too far." Frantically tugging at his sleeve, eventually Daley yielded and leaned on the corner of the desk, exhausted.

Chapter 119

The white Transit Connect, RN08 DVB, had been abandoned on the car park of the *Sir William Wordsworth*. A squad car had been called as the first licks of flame twisted the dashboard and popped the windscreen. Smith sat on the kerb, watching the soot blacken the white paintwork; a pall of smoke bubbling and frothing the sky above. There was no sign of the young woman, her brother and the other man who had broken the stalemate and made Daley's decisions for him. Nobody had seen the vehicle they left in.

It had been a full five minutes before black storm-troopers from SCO19 had virtually torn the double doors from their hinges and a further one before the blokes in the green paramedic overalls and *hi-viz* were allowed anywhere near the bloodied bedside. By that time, Daley and had screamed *Police!* and *Unarmed!* at the top of his voice three times and the life had all but left Nick Snowdon's body. Edmonds was still busying herself with chest compressions and Whetstone was frantically squeezing a bag valve mask over his face. Caz Albin had not moved a centimetre from where she had fallen to her knees. A small, insignificant puddle of blood had dripped from her chin and blended with the lake soaking into her trousers.

Climbing the steps from the basement, gulping in the sharp, fresh air, Daley saw the muzzle flash and he saw the diesel locomotive and smiled quietly to himself.

They had both missed.

The courtyard was now a hive of activity as ambulances flashed and radios cackled. A uniform placed his hand on the back of Caz Albin's head and eased her into a marked Focus. Smith had been locked behind the mesh interior of a Ford Transit. The irony was not lost on Daley. He and Whetstone watched as Snowdon was carried out on a stretcher, Edmonds still bagging his face and a box of electronics across his chest. Then, one by one, more ambulances arrived for Franks and the other inmates of the farm.

Daley patted his coat, found his phone and dialled a number.

It was the newest number in his contacts list.

"Somerville."

"Terri? It's Scott...Scott Daley."

"Erm. I know so many Scotts. Which one are you? Ah, yes. The train-spotter." Daley could hear the laughter in her voice and just for a moment, the pain and the blood and the cacophony faded away. "I was waiting for your call. I really enjoyed last night."

The previous evening, the easy conversation, the softness of her lips as he had kissed her goodnight. They seemed a century ago.

"Same again tonight? Maybe somewhere slightly cheaper? Pick you up at 7:00pm?"

"I can't believe you actually booked *Andros*. That was meant to be a joke."

"'Fraid I've lost my sense of humour a little lately. Oh, and I'm afraid I have wrecked another suit."

"Oh, please tell me it was that grey one."

"Yep."

"Made you look like Worzel Gummidge anyway."

Chapter 120

The small outer office was tired. Louvered windows, duck egg walls, a spider plant and a picture of a cottage. There were a few grubby stains around the door handle. But it was peaceful and Daley struggled not to doze off. Across the flecked grey carpet, the young girl sat typing into a computer, a steady tip-tapping which added to the somnolent air. She was around eighteen with an effulgence of brown hair sweeping forwards across her face. Daley was reminded of a red setter, trying to eat, matted ears dangling forwards. Then, he recalled Baxter, skin drawn back in a death grin, matted and wet in Chatham Woods. Sensing his eyes, the girl raised her head and smiled, Daley reciprocating, embarrassed to be caught staring, adjusting his tie self-consciously.

He was early, a novelty in itself but with a woman in his life, a good many things had changed. He had even read three caravanning magazines and wondered what it would be like to own a Range Rover and an Elddis Avante. Then there was the suit, it was green. Never a colour he would have chosen. Terri had suggested a shade of bottle green which he hoped the woman in the next room would understand.

"Those who love the colour green are often affectionate, loyal and frank. Green lovers are also aware of what others think of them and consider their reputation very important." Terri had smiled as she had thumbed along the rack in Harvey Nicks. "Don't want you looking like a *numpty* for the nice lady, now do we?" He had obligingly shelled out for the suit, along with slacks, shirts and sweaters, taking her word for it.

It had been three weeks since a 9mm bullet had removed half of Nick Snowdon's skull. In another of life's ironies, he was now wired to life support machines similar to those which had previously kept his victims' bodies working long after their minds had gone. Caz Albin was under twenty-four-hour suicide watch somewhere South of the river. She had not spoken, eaten nor drunk since the moment her brother had fallen. Her hands were tethered to the bed frame, so that she could not remove the drip which would ensure that she, at least would stand trial. If she ever would. The occupants of the remaining beds in the basement ward were not so lucky. With brain stem death confirmed they had been allowed to slip away. Tom Phillips young boy was born prematurely a week later with only images of his father to look upon.

Smith had been charged with leaving the scene and both he and Edmonds with obstruction. There was talk of other charges but no-one could figure out exactly what they would be, so the feeling was that the CPS would let the whole lot drop. Both had lost enough already.

For Franks, it was mixed blessings. He had made a full recovery and now had to answer to his wife.

As for Medway Klein, the Hall was still a crime scene, the clinic closed to patients and staff alike. The final tally of victims would never be fully known. A forensic team at an unknown location were busy piecing together as many parts as they could, searching for anything that might distinguish one femur from the next, one anonymous migrant, searching for a better life, from the next. So far, the femur count was up to four hundred and twenty.

Bulldozers were already circling like vultures around Chatham Woods Farm.

Looking up as his name was called, Daley saw the head through the part open door. A woman, around the same age as himself, beamed broadly and ushered him through, affording a limp handshake that felt like squeezing a soggy dishcloth. A large bay window filled the room with light and Daley immediately felt comfortable as he sat in the upright floral cottage armchair. The woman sat opposite and linked her fingers across her lap.

"So, how can I help you, Mr Daley?"

Scott Daley shuffled in the seat then leaned forwards, linking his fingers into a pyramid below his chin. He took a deep breath.

"I need help. I think I have become addicted to Tramadol."

Chapter 121

The torch scanned above Alikah Hakim as she pressed herself down into the litter strewn yard. She clamped her hand across Selim's mouth, as her son shook uncontrollably. Under her breath, she prayed and waited for the hand, the boot, the bullet. Over the wall, the engine of the truck screamed as the driver lay dead across the wheel. The night was filled with shouts and screams and the chatter of automatic weapons. She listened intently for Yusuf's voice, hoping that in the crash, when they ran, he had escaped, or at least been caught. Not killed.

The journey from Homs had taken five slow, dusty days. Food and water had been scarce and Selim was weak. They were to cross at Hemamê, that much they had worked out, but so had the authorities. They had run into an ambush.

Above her, Alikah, sensed a shadow but still she kept low, gripped with fear. Beside her, Selim was sobbing and the smell above the rotting food that served as a carpet told her the boy had defiled himself in his terror.

As her own tears came, she begged Allah to take them both.

Suddenly, she heard a sound behind. Bodies hauled over the wall, landing in the yard, footsteps in the dry scrub.

"You have to come with us - now!"

Easing an eye open, Alikah saw the rifle and feared the worst but the hand stretched out for her.

"We must be quick. There are many dead but you are not. We are 'akhuww, *The Brotherhood of the True Faith,*" said the man. "They will be here soon. Come on!" He unslung his rifle.

"Yusuf?" She watched the head cock to one side. "He is my husband. Glasses, brown waistcoat."

"We have him. Now come." The woman stretched out a hand.

Alikah drew back. Was this a trap? "Who are you?"

"I am Satya. This is Pietr, and tomorrow you will be someone else," whispered the dark-haired woman. "We have to go!"

EPILOGUE

Black, oh so black and I am blinking but there is nothing but the deepest bitumen black coating my eyes. I am floating and drifting on a sea of black. Around me there is nothing and I can't make sense of it. I am nothing. I stare down at my hands, my arms but there are none, no movement of my head, no twist of my neck nor limbs to raise.

Think, think! Where am I? How has this happened? The gun, the flash.

Hello!

I call but the words have no shape, no form, no meaning. This limitless void consumes the sounds before they can be uttered. It is behind, large and predatory, it smells my fear and awaits its opportunity.

Anyone?

Slowly, there are memories, flitting and fleet, vague essences of dreams, of fields and flowers, of farms.

Of death.

Outside the infinite blackness there are noises, worlds, realities but the opening to them is hidden, too far, this void is at once as empty as space and as thick as oil and I cannot sense the directions of the noises. I cannot swim through nothing to reach them.

I concentrate on the sounds. The sounds of birds in the trees, a morning chorus and the wind over the tulips. I see the fields and the windmill, the cottage in the trees, small rustles in the verdant branches. There are animals and insects. crickets chirping, scratching, and I am confused. Then I realise the scratching is a voice and I strain to hear the words from a distant mouth.

"...like this for over a month now. We have assessed the possibility of PVS..."

Behind me the animal still lurks. Its patience is as infinite as this universe.

I search the blackness for a sign, some fragment of what has gone before and I see the girl and the dolls, I see the farm and the shed. And I see the monster as it circles around, it's eyes are on me and the slavering tongue slips in and out of its mouth.

"...coming back negative, which indicates little chance of..."

And slowly, insidiously, the idle zephyrs of breeze become a wind. The regular inrush of air and the slap of the machine. The insects fly and the birds still, leaving the steady rhythmic beep and the ticking of clocks and the trolleys and the nurses. And the monster senses my panic and paces ever closer.

I am trapped, like all those that have gone before. All those that I sent on before me.

A spark lights the black. Then another and a third.

"...no stimulus to pain..."

And I scream that I am here, that I felt the sharp point, that I am alive. And I struggle with the thick oily vacuum. I strain to move a muscle, an eyelid, a single nerve but there is no connection. My efforts fall into the black abyss.

And the regular beats of the machine are the angry breaths of the monster, it's vigil nearly over. I struggle and writhe in the morass but the viscous nothing ebbs and swells and floes and I cannot get away. I hang like a fly in a web awaiting my fate.

"...lack of active stimuli, no next of kin, we have little option..."

And the monster's breath grates, drawing in and out, as the eyes bear down on me, biding its time.

And I am shouting and pleading but still they hear nothing. Why do they not hear my voice percolating through the void, echoing into their lives? Are they deaf? I am screaming for them to hear me, to give me time, to force my way from the darkness. How can there be no hope? I am here.

I hear the click and the monster turns, it's breathing slows and the eyes are large and greedy.

Lina! It's me. Dominic. Where are you?

And I see the tulips in the fields and the winds ripples the colours, creaking the sails of the ancient wooden mill. The door of the cabin is open and there is Lina. She is wearing the blue dress and she waves for me to hurry. I run but my leaden legs are treading air as the fields drift up and away. The beast bares its teeth and lets loose a mighty roar. I am screaming for them to hear me as the monster begins to circle and the winds howl louder and louder. Then at last everything stops and the jaws gape wide about me.

ABOUT THE AUTHOR

Austen Gower has spent his life working as a Business and Information Technology Consultant. He has been commissioned to write technical works on topics as diverse as programming, networking, communications, project management and anger management, for which he has a number of published articles.

After a hankering to write a novel, which stretches back around twenty years, Austen finally took creative writing seriously, with the avowed intention to quit the rat race and use some of the left side of his brain so repressed by his day job.

One day that may happen.

Writing as Ryan Stark, *The Farm* is Austen's second work of fiction.

Married, with two grown-up children, Austen lives in Redditch, Worcestershire.

Whilst he owns a number of Seiko watches, he has never travelled through Europe on a train nor owned a Makarov 9mm.